RESCUING STITCH

Guardian Hostage Rescue Specialists: Charlie Team
Book 2

ELLIE MASTERS   MASTER OF ROMANTIC SUSPENSE

USA TODAY BESTSELLING AUTHOR

JEM Publishing

Editor: Erin Toland

Proofreader: Roxane Leblanc

Published in the United States of America

JEM Publishing

ISBN: 978-1-952625-90-9

Dedication

This book is dedicated to my one and only—my amazing and wonderful husband.

Without your care and support, my writing would not have made it this far.

You pushed me when I needed to be pushed.

You supported me when I felt discouraged.

You believed in me when I didn't believe in myself.

If it weren't for you, this book never would have come to life.

Also by Ellie Masters

The LIGHTER SIDE

Ellie Masters is the lighter side of the Jet & Ellie Masters writing duo! You will find Contemporary Romance, Military Romance, Romantic Suspense, Billionaire Romance, and Rock Star Romance in Ellie's Works.

YOU CAN FIND ELLIE'S BOOKS HERE:

ELLIEMASTERS.COM/BOOKS

Military Romance

Guardian Hostage Rescue Specialists

Rescuing Melissa

(Get a FREE copy of Rescuing Melissa

when you join Ellie's Newsletter)

Alpha Team

Rescuing Zoe

Rescuing Moira

Rescuing Eve

Rescuing Lily

Rescuing Jinx

Rescuing Maria

Bravo Team

Rescuing Angie

Rescuing Isabelle

Rescuing Carmen

Rescuing Rosalie

Rescuing Kaye

To My Readers

This book is a work of fiction. It does not exist in the real world and should not be construed as reality. As in most romantic fiction, I've taken liberties. I've compressed the romance into a sliver of time. I've allowed these characters to develop strong bonds of trust over a matter of days.

This does not happen in real life where you, my amazing readers, live. Take more time in your romance and learn who you're giving a piece of your heart to. I urge you to move with caution. Always protect yourself.

ONE

Stitch

———

When I was a kid, I had a lot of dreams. Being at the top of the FBI's most wanted list for cybercrimes and terrorism was never one of them.

But isn't that how life works?

I got cocky, and that made me sloppy. Now, I'm doing the time. Twenty to life is what I expect to get slapped with at my sentencing later today. Wonder where they'll send me?

The harsh rap of knuckles on metal jars me rudely from my restless dozing. I jolt upright, blinking against the bright fluorescent lights burning my retinas.

What time is it?

"Rise and shine, princess. You've got a visitor." The guard's gravelly voice grates through the bars.

I unfold myself from the cramped cot, joints cracking, run a hand through my tangled black hair, and tug my fancy orange jumper into some kind of order—the stench of stale sweat and B.O. clings to me. I'd kill for a shower right about now.

A visitor?

"Who is it?" My voice comes out rough and unused. Raspy. Actually, it's kind of sexy in a sultry kind of way. Bet it would drive the boys crazy. Too bad I'll never find out, rotting away in this hellhole.

"You'll see soon enough." The guard cuffs my wrists, letting the metal bite my bony skin.

Happy joy-joy. He loves his job way too much. Like, I'm going to get the jump on him.

Asshole.

He shackles my ankles, too, chains clanking. Standard transport protocol, even for a scrawny twenty-one-year-old accused of cyber-crimes against the good ole U.S. of A. Just his way of constantly reminding me that I'm nothing but a number to him.

An animal in a cage.

My future gone.

I want to spit in his smug face, but that would earn me nothing but a backhand or worse. So I keep my head down, biding my time, as he leads me through a maze of featureless concrete halls. The debilitating stench of industrial cleaner burns my nose, barely masking the underlying funk of unwashed bodies packed too close together.

We reach the visitation room, empty save for a cold metal table and two chairs. The guards shove me down roughly onto one and retreat outside. I sit motionless, steeling myself for hours of mind-numbing boredom. It's not like I have any other pressing engage-ments to get to, but I hate when other people waste mine.

A minute later, in walks a woman with spiky rainbow hair, an assault of glittery psychedelics that makes my eyes ache after days of gray. She wears casual attire—jeans and a loose-fitting shirt, with chunky combat boots: weird combo and a strange choice for someone visiting a prison.

Speaking of, she's an unlikely visitor for a delinquent like me. Instant suspicion coils in my gut as I size her up, trying to figure out her angle. The woman smiles brightly, stopping just inside the doorway.

"I'm Mitzy. Been looking forward to meeting you." Her voice rings with sincerity, but I don't trust that for a second. No one's happy to visit this hellhole out of the goodness of their heart.

"Yeah? Who the hell are you?" I scowl and slump lower in my uncomfortable chair.

"Direct, I like that. Gets rid of all the nonsensical fluff." Her smile doesn't falter under my belligerent tone. If anything, it widens. Guess she likes a challenge. "I'm with an organization that requires your particular skills."

"Thanks, but hard pass. Kinda fucked six ways to Sunday here if you didn't notice." I rattle my cuffs pointedly and snort in derision.

"I did notice, and like I said, I'm with an organization that requires your particular skills."

"Oh yeah? And what skills are those? Card counting? Gambling fraud? Or maybe you need a computer whiz to hack into your ex's Facebook?" I tick the crimes off on my fingers mockingly. "No offense, but you've got the wrong girl. I'm just a petty thief trying to survive on the streets."

It's a blatant lie, and we both know it. No street thief could crack high-level government servers without leaving a trace like I did. But no way am I selling myself out before I know what this chick's endgame is.

The woman's eyes gleam with amusement, almost as if she enjoys our verbal sparring. "I think we both know hacking government intelligence systems takes certain expertise. You're no street thief."

I stare back stonily. Clearly, she knows more about me than she should, but two can play this game.

Mitzy leans forward. "I'm here to offer you a way out of this mess." She slides a slim folder across the table. "A contract for you to work with my team, effective immediately if you sign. How does freedom sound?"

I eye the documents with suspicion and a little more interest than I'm willing to admit, but I make no move to take them. Everything inside me screams this is a trap.

Too good to be true.

The government doesn't let computer criminals walk free out of the goodness of their hearts.

"And why exactly would you help me?" I challenge.

"I don't need a reason to help you." Mitzy leans back casually. "The question is, do you want to avoid prison or not? From what I hear, you're looking at twenty to life. Sucks for a kid."

Well damn.

Wasn't expecting such blunt honesty. This chick doesn't play around. I study her more closely, curiosity unwillingly piqued.

"Ain't no kid," I fire back, defensive and scared at my prospects for a dull future.

"Definitely won't be after rotting in a cell for decades." She pushes the folder closer. "Come on, could it hurt to look?"

"What's the offer?"

"I admire talent. What you did, hacking into NSA servers impressed me." Mitzy's eyes gleam. "How would you like a job putting those skills to use?"

"What's the catch?" I press her. "Somehow, I doubt you work for the forgiveness and redemption department."

She laughs sharply. "Smart girl. Let's say I have connections, people who are interested in utilizing your skills for more—productive ventures." Leaning back casually, she delivers the final blow. "Look, it's simple. Either you work for me on my terms or enjoy a very long prison sentence. I need to know if you have the skills or are nothing but a one-hit wonder."

The challenge sparks my pride. Who is she to question my abilities? But though it grates to admit it, she's backed me into a corner here.

"What? By work, you mean you become my warden?"

"Consider it a kind of parole. You play by my rules but get to walk free instead of enjoying prison life. You fuck up, run, or disappear, then you're right back here with an additional ten years added to your sentence."

"Sounds like prison wrapped up in a fancy bow."

"Probably right, but it is a really fancy bow."

"A gilded cage is still a cage."

"Compared to where you're going, I'd say it's a no-brainer."

She's right. Compared to the squalid hellhole I'm headed to, it's hardly a choice.

"Fine. If you can get me out of this dump," I shrug with feigned indifference, "I'll sign your contract or whatever."

"Excellent." Mitzy smiles like a cat with a juicy canary. "I think this will be the start of a very productive partnership." She holds out an elegant hand for me to shake, but I stare at it stonily until she lowers it with a quirk of her eyebrow. Wheels are already turning in my mind, looking for an angle to gain leverage in this arrangement she's forced on me.

This lady doesn't know it yet, but no one owns my loyalty. I'm a survivor above all else. I'll play her game—for now—but once I get the lay of the land, all bets are off.

I'll be damned if I let myself become some weapon for them to aim where they want. This Mitzy chick with her psychedelic hair and fizzy personality doesn't need to know that yet. Let her believe she has me under her thumb.

Instead of returning to my tiny cell of misery with its rickety cot, the guard takes me to prisoner out-processing. The barest hint of a smile tugs at my mouth. I might actually be getting out of here. As far as Mitzy goes, I'll bide my time and play the demure protégé, but soon enough, I'll be flying free.

No one owns me.

And this rainbow-haired chick is about to find that out the hard way.

After I'm processed out of jail or prison—there's some distinction there—I squint against the harsh sunlight as I'm led outside for the first time in weeks. After being processed out, the cuffs and shackles are finally removed. I'm free to go—as long as I report to my new "employer" immediately.

That's not hard to do, considering Mitzy waits by a sleek black car, looking impatient.

"Took you long enough." She gestures to the passenger door. "Get in. We've got a long drive ahead of us."

I slide silently into the passenger seat, nerves warring with my curiosity. Mitzy peels out of the parking lot, and the looming prison disappears from view.

"Where exactly are we going?" I finally ask as the city fades behind us.

"Guardian HQ. I'm taking you there to get started."

"Not wasting any time, I see."

"You got somewhere you need to be?"

"No."

"Then what do you care?"

"Whatever." I snub her, pretending indifference, which is a total lie. I'm a bundle of nerves buzzing with fear.

Mitzy glances at me sideways. "You'll love it, I promise. State-of-the-art facility along the northern California coast. Nothing like the hellhole you left."

I hum noncommittally, watching the scenery blur by. Sandy scrubland gives way gradually to rolling green hills and thick forests. The air blowing through the vents even smells different—clean and pine-scented compared to the city's smog and ozone.

After hours of driving, Mitzy takes an unmarked turnoff. We wind through rolling hills until the ocean comes into view, a deep blue expanse meeting the sky.

We round a curve, and sprawling modern buildings perched appear before us. People move briskly about the lush grounds surrounded by imposing security fencing.

So this is the infamous Guardian HQ? It looks more like a luxury resort than the secretive base I imagined. As we roll to a stop inside the gates, Mitzy turns to me with a smile.

"Welcome to your new home."

"You mean prison."

"Initially, you'll live on the grounds. It's just temporary housing until you find a place of your own. No guards. You really are free to go wherever you choose."

"As long as I report to work each day."

"As long as you report to work each day." She stops and gives me a long look. "I'm loving the rebel vibe, but you're not very different from me."

"We're nothing alike."

"As soon as you see where you'll be working, what you'll be doing, and the resources you have at your disposal, I won't be able to drag you away from your work."

"Those are some pretty big words, but I'm not exactly a go-to-work-each-day kind of gal. Punching timecards is…"

"You won't see a single timecard. As for how long you work, that's up to you. Get your job done, and the rest of the day is yours, but I have a feeling you're going to be like the rest of my team."

"What does that mean?"

"I pretty much have to drag them away from their work, too."

"Whatever." I give her the most flippant, exaggerated eye roll I can manage.

Apprehension and curiosity war within me as I take in the scene. This gleaming compound is a world away from the cold concrete cell I thought would be my home for the next twenty years.

Twenty to life.

That's what my lawyer said. Twenty if the judge felt sympathy. Life if I pissed him off.

I don't know what awaits me here, but it's got to beat prison food and hostile cellmates. As I follow Mitzy inside, determination wells up within me. I'll stay wary and keep playing things close to the chest—but maybe, just maybe, this will turn out to be the unexpected opportunity I never knew I needed.

Or, it'll be total crap, a meaningless desk job I'm trapped in for twenty to life.

Only one way to find out. Squaring my shoulders, I step through the doors to meet my unknown future. A future that begins with me standing uncomfortably in Mitzy's slick office, unsure what to think about this twist of events.

The drive was enlightening. I appreciated that. After weeks locked away, the vast expanse of rolling hills and blue sky felt like freedom. When I rolled the window down, much to Mitzy's displeasure, the cry of circling gulls melded with the faint crashing of waves. The tang of salt air still teases my nose.

I forgot how good freedom smelled like.

It's a far cry from the reeking confines of that cell. Or the fear of facing twenty to life.

One thing I will say is this. Whoever Mitzy works for, they're rolling in dough.

"Have a seat. We've got a lot to cover. Not that it'll take much time to get you up to speed but humor me." She gestures to a fancy leather chair sitting across from her glass-topped desk.

I sit gingerly, eyes roving the space. Multiple monitors cover the far wall, and I can't decipher the code scrolling by on a continuous feed. That says something when someone like me is stumped. I live and breathe code, but I've never seen what's on those screens. This lady means serious business.

Mitzy glances at the monitors, and her mouth turns up in a smirk.

"What?" I hate being played. Hate tests even more. "That some kind of test?"

"We'll get to the tests later." But she noticed my interest in the code. "Impressive, isn't it? I built these systems myself."

I force an indifferent shrug, not wanting to inflate her ego further. Truthfully, I'm stunned and a little jealous. She must be incredible to develop something so advanced.

Not that I'd ever admit it out loud.

Not that I'm ten times better.

"So, you gonna explain about this organization I sold my soul to?" I half-joke, but I wonder if that might not be the case. "Am I on house arrest or something? Gotta wear an ankle bracelet?"

She smiles indulgently. "No house arrest. No ankle bracelet. We offer non-Guardians the option of inserting a tracker, just in case, but it's optional."

"Just in case of what?"

"Abduction, kidnapping, stuff like that."

"What the fuck?" My mouth gapes as I spring to my feet. "Never signed up for that kind of shit. That's some majorly false advertising."

"Relax and take the chair. You're giving me a neck ache craning to look at you. Nice shirt, by the way."

"What? This ratty thing?" I glance down at my favorite shirt. I'm a mega fan of the band and wear Angel Fire's black T-shirts exclusively.

Mitzy laughs but doesn't say anything else about my shirt. Chick is probably into classical music or some such boring shit. She wouldn't be able to appreciate the genius behind Angel Fire's music.

Instead, she goes all corporate on me, explaining this and that. "I work for Guardian Hostage Rescue Specialists, Guardian HRS, or Guardians for short. We recover kidnap victims and take down the scum responsible for human trafficking. We're the good guys. You're a part of that team now."

"Of course, you're do-gooders." I roll my eyes at the spiel.

"You'll come around." She winks and stands. "Now, let me give you the tour."

The first stop on Mitzy's tour is the operations room filled with men and women monitoring a dizzying array of screens and controls. Phones ring, voices call out status updates, fingers fly over keyboards. It's a hive of frenetic activity.

Despite my attempt to look bored, I'm awed by the complex systems and top-notch gear. Mitzy notices me ogling the setup and smirks knowingly.

"This is home base for our technical team. They call us Techies."

"Techies?" I roll my eyes. "Who calls you that?"

And why do they allow it?

Scrap that.

Mitzy's fucking proud of the derogative term.

"We gather intel for the Guardians, run comms, coordinate missions, all that good stuff." She smiles at my wide eyes. "We're big into VR and robotics. Impressive, right?"

"Uh-huh, got it, very impressive." I try to appear blasé, but it's incredible, leagues beyond anything I could have imagined. "Better than a jail cell."

The setup is phenomenal. State-of-the-art and right up my alley. My fingers itch to start exploring the systems and programs. And by *exploring*, I mean doing things I shouldn't. I'm so going to hack the hell out of Guardian HRS.

"This is where you'll be working most of the time, but I want to give you the full tour before bringing you back for the boring *job* stuff."

Before I can so much as touch a keyboard, she whisks me back outside.

"Let's continue the tour before bringing you in here."

"Great." Like, I wasn't itching to dive in and explore this incredible setup.

Not at all.

TWO

Jeb

THE SCENT OF BACON AND THE SOUND OF CARTOON CHATTER GREET me as I shuffle into the kitchen. My son, Maverick, perches on a stool at the counter, still in his Spiderman pajamas as he gobbles up breakfast.

"Morning, buddy." I ruffle his sandy blond hair and grab a piece of bacon. At five years old, he's the spitting image of me at that age, all knobby knees and restless energy, but those vibrant green eyes came from his mother.

May God bless her soul.

"You leaving, Daddy?" Maverick asks around a mouthful of eggs, blinking up at me.

"Yeah, got training this morning with my team, but I'll be back to tuck you in tonight. I promise."

He nods and returns focus to the TV, his attention span short, like any kid his age. I kiss the top of his head and squeeze his skinny shoulder.

"Be good for Grandma and Papa today."

My parents chatter over coffee and the morning paper as I grab my gym bag. Though we had rocky moments when I was younger, I'm thankful they're here for Mav when duty calls me away.

"Jebediah," my mother glances up from her coffee, lips pursed, "you were out late again." Her tone holds a note of motherly disapproval.

That's the only downside of asking my parents to move in with me and help me raise my son. They can't help but parent me, in addition to my son.

"Just hanging with the team after work, Mom." I clear my throat, avoiding her gaze.

The evening started with my team, but I spent the rest of the night losing myself inside a woman. Can't remember her name. Don't know if we ever got *that* personal.

She frowns, seeing through the evasion.

"Don't you think it's time to start healing in healthier ways?"

Guilt pricks at me with her emphasis on the word *healthier*. She worries the nameless hookups and partying are my way of grieving and not moving on.

She's not wrong.

"I'm fine, Mom, really." I kiss her cheek and snag some bacon. "I better head out, or I'll be late."

Her *'we're talking later'* look follows me out the door. With a heavy sigh, I load up my truck, thoughts drifting to Sarah like they often do.

Maybe Mom has a point—maybe it's time I deal with the past in a better way? For Maverick's sake, if not my own.

Shaking off my melancholy, I point the truck toward Guardian HQ and look forward to the distraction of training, but my mother's words linger in my mind, an uncomfortable truth I can't ignore forever.

After losing Sarah, I tried to trade the danger of the SEALs for MIT, thinking that was the responsible path for a young dad raising a kid without his mother. I could be there for Maverick with a safe tech job, but that kind of life felt hollow, like I was going through the motions.

Mom thinks my endless string of one-night stands is unhealthy, but I never bring those women home. I won't disparage Sarah's memory in front of my son.

Maverick is untouched by my vices.

And when I tuck him in at night with tales of his mother, I hope he knows how deeply I still love her. My broken heart doesn't negate that truth.

Some days, this job is the only thing holding me together. As much as it worries Mom, being a Guardian makes me feel whole in a way nothing else can.

For now, it's enough to keep the demons at bay.

Six grueling years in the Navy and BUD/S training molded me into a SEAL, but joining the Guardians gave me a new purpose after—everything. Now, it's my job to save innocents from the worst of humanity. A duty as satisfying as it is grim at times. I pivoted from computers back to boots on the ground for a reason. The thought makes me drive faster, eager to be back among my brothers.

I find Charlie team's bullpen empty when I arrive. Cursing, I change in record time and sprint for the gym complex across the compound. Ethan's ruthless about handing out penalties when one of us is late.

A cavernous facility looms ahead of me. The size of a stadium, sparring mats stretch out before me. The guys are already at it, the smack of skin on skin and mocking jabs echo through the vast space.

"Sleeping Beauty finally made it," Ethan calls out when he spots me. "Late night entertaining the ladies again?" He makes a point of rolling his wrist to check his watch.

The others heckle and laugh as I jog over sheepishly. "Yeah, yeah, laugh it up," I shoot back, dropping my gear next to the mats. "Got stuck behind a never-ending convoy of semis, sue me."

"Excuses won't get you gains, brother," Hank ribs, tossing me a pair of gloves. "Maybe lay off the late nights chasing tail and get here on time."

I flip him off with a grin and start wrapping my hands. "What can I say? All you ugly mugs wore me out. Needed some eye candy to restore my sanity."

"Careful, Jeb, keep popping off, and I'll make you run suicides next," Ethan threatens, but his eyes glint with humor.

I hold up my hands in surrender. "Point taken. Now, are we gonna gossip like girls or get some work in?"

Ethan's expression sharpens. "Since you're so eager, drop and give me five hundred. A hundred for every minute you were late."

I groan but knock out the pushups as the others laugh. By three hundred, my abs and triceps are screaming, but I grit my teeth and power through.

When I finish, Ethan jerks his chin approvingly. "Maybe that'll teach you punctuality. Now, let's get to work."

The sharp smack of blows landing on pads and grunts of exertion fill the air as we pair off to spar. We razz and trash-talk each other, laughter punctuating groans when a good hit lands.

I pair off with Blake first, bouncing lightly on the balls of my feet as we circle each other. He feints left, then shoots a jab at my ribs, which I deflect. I counter with a leg kick he sidesteps before driving forward in a flurry of combos. He's got a steady hand and an eagle eye. The man's sniper skills are legendary, but his hits carry power and pack a punch. My ribs are going to be bruised.

We trade blows back and forth, going hard but controlled. I misjudge the timing on one exchange and catch a hook to the jaw that makes my teeth rattle. Shaking it off, I come back at Blake twice as fierce, using my size to my advantage to force him onto the defensive until he's pinned.

"Alright, alright, I submit," Blake laughs breathlessly, shoving me off.

I grin and offer a hand to help him up. Both our chests heave from exertion. The satisfying burn in my muscles primes me for more as we separate to find new opponents.

After fifteen minutes, Ethan calls out, "Rotate!" and we switch partners seamlessly. The outside world falls away as we lose ourselves in the visceral joy of combat drills with trusted brothers. Gabe and I touch fists. He's all raw strength and brilliance. He's our munitions expert and an all-around MacGyver when it comes to creativity and solving problems in the field. And he plays dirty when he fights, but I dig in, unwilling to cede defeat.

This is what I live for: the sweat and ache of muscles pushed to their limit alongside soldiers who'd die for you. Before Gabe wipes me on the mat, Ethan's shout pulls up short. Breath dragging in and out, I try to catch my breath.

"Alright, ladies, let's go two-on-one," Ethan orders, beckoning me over. "Jeb, you're with me and Walt."

Walt's our team medic. A certified paramedic, he's a former Para jumper; the Air Force's equivalent to the Navy SEALs, with the same brutal training I underwent in BUD/S. Adrenaline surges as we flow into the familiar dance of strikes, blocks, and grapples. All thoughts fade as instinct and training take over.

We're sparring hard when Mitzy enters the complex, joined by a stunning woman. Actually, stunning doesn't begin to describe the woman; she's a knockout dressed all in black and gave me whiplash when I took a second look. It's unusual for Mitzy to show up at the gym; the woman must be a new hire and is getting the official tour.

Porcelain skin, pouty ruby-red lips, and lithe curves hugged by dark jeans; from a distance, Mitzy's new techie radiates beauty. As they approach, her vivid blue eyes lock with mine. Sharp intelligence and simmering defiance blaze in her piercing gaze.

My pulse spikes as she takes in my sweat-slicked torso before she hastily looks away. In that split second, before she looks away, a flicker of interest flashes in her eyes, and a blush turns her pale cheeks pink. Something about her sharp gaze and proud posture exudes an intellect lacking from the brainless airheads I bed. My eyes greedily trace her alluring curves.

Although our wordless exchange lasts barely a heartbeat, I'm hooked.

I'm also distracted from my fight with Ethan and Walt. Ethan catches me hard in the ribs with a brutal uppercut, making me grunt in pain. Before I can recover, Walt sweeps my legs out from under me. Despite getting knocked to the mat, I find myself angling for another glimpse of the mysterious siren trailing Mitzy and pay no attention to Ethan or Walt.

"Eyes front, Romeo." Ethan kicks my feet and stretches out a hand. "No ogling the new recruits when we're working." He pulls me to my feet with a laugh.

I force myself to refocus but discreetly track the beauty's progress through the gym. The teasing curve of her lips and the defiant tilt of her chin linger in my mind long after she's gone.

Something tells me that alluring, raven-haired girl spells nothing but delicious trouble. My interest is most definitely piqued.

"Who's that with Mitzy?" I ask Ethan when we pause to hydrate.

"No clue, but clearly, she's got your attention." He ribs me with a knowing grin. "Though she looks a bit young, even for you."

"Just admiring the view, nothing more. I don't poach trainees." I shrug nonchalantly, though my pulse has quickened.

"Twenty bucks says Romeo seduces her within the month," Gabe challenges.

The others chuckle, fully aware of my habit of bedding anything willing.

"Nah, this one seems smarter than his usual type," Walt counters. "I say he strikes out."

I snort dismissively but can't deny a twinge of intrigue at their words. There's a fire to that girl despite her youth. Perhaps she'd be worth the chase?

Nope.

I cut that train of thought off before it forms. Just appreciating her beauty. No need to complicate things. At least, that's the lie I tell myself.

With renewed focus, I turn my mind back to the raven-haired siren and focus on honing my hand-to-hand combat skills.

A few hours later, my muscles are pleasantly fatigued. We cool down and towel off in Charlie team's bullpen. The ribbing and crude jokes start immediately.

"What kept you this morning?" Ethan's tone is light and teasing, but there's a message in his words. "Not like you to be late, and don't give me that bullshit about traffic. Another late night with the newest flavor of the week?"

"Week?" Walt scoffs. "Jeb's not interested after a single night. How the hell is he going to keep one for a whole week?"

I flip him off casually. "Some of us have important responsibilities like raising the next generation of elite operators."

"Is something wrong with Maverick?" Ethan's tone suddenly turns serious.

I'm the only guy on the team with a kid, and it sets me off a bit from the others. Not that I don't join them at the bar. We're all on the hunt for a woman to warm our bed.

"Mav's great. Just spent a few extra minutes with my kid this morning."

"Shit." Ethan runs his fingers through sweat-soaked hair. "Now I feel bad for making you do those pushups."

"Don't." I flex my arms, making my guns pop out. "Chicks love muscles."

"Speaking of chicks," Walt says. "Mitzy's new hire caught your eye. Be careful poaching one of hers."

"Like I said, I don't poach trainees." I lift a challenging eyebrow.

"But you noticed her," Hank joins in, gray eyes glinting. "Come on, that Goth chick is cute, but she's a few too many years younger than you."

"Can't blame Jeb for looking." Blake acts like he has my back, but I wait for the other shoe to drop. "Bet she's barely twenty-one, which makes you…"

"Legal is legal." I shake my head. "Even if she's eighteen."

"That would definitely be stealing the cradle. Ten years is…" Walt gives me the eye.

"It's eight, nine at most, and age is just a number."

They exchange knowing looks but let it drop as we all head to the showers. I shake my head at their antics but can't deny my pulse kicks up a notch when they mention Mitzy's new recruit.

I'd love to learn more.

Find out her name. Hell, maybe I can get a bit of one-on-one time. If the chick's new, she's going to need self-defense training. I file that fact away for later use. It wouldn't take much to make that happen.

That fiery and defiant gaze, along with those curves, definitely spiked my interest.

But I meant what I said—I don't mix business and pleasure. Much.

The conversation slowly shifts from my sex life and turns to our next op. My teammates mean well with the razzing. Losing my fiancée in childbirth left me commitment-shy. They poke fun at me but never judge.

We've all seen darkness.

Freshly cleaned up, I rejoin my brothers lounging in the bullpen. Our home away from home, filled with mismatched chairs, faded sports posters, and a sense of belonging.

I snag water from the battered fridge and sprawl on the couch next to Gabe. His sheer bulk takes up most of the space, but I don't mind the cramped quarters. After a childhood of rigid rules, this easy male camaraderie suits me fine.

"So—Romeo..." Gabe's meaty paw claps the back of my neck. "About Mitzy's newest recruit?"

"Clearly, you dogs have too much free time." I crumple my water bottle and aim it at the trash can. It goes in nice and clean. "Don't you have gear to prep instead of gossiping like schoolgirls?"

"Touchy." Gabe clutches his chest in mock affront, but he takes the hint and talk turns to weapons maintenance and tactics.

My overactive brain is pulled back where it belongs when I grab my weapon and set it on the countertop. I meticulously clean my weapon, thinking it'll distract me, but thoughts of Mitzy's newcomer creep in.

She's distracting in all the wrong ways.

Better to admire her from a distance.

But that's a load of crap.

THREE

Stitch

———

WE HEAD OUTSIDE FOR THE TOUR, AND MITZY LEADS ME TO THEIR training facilities. Upon entering, I stop short, intimidated by the enormous, muscle-bound men drilling inside. With their imposing frames, they look ready for the most perilous missions imaginable. Not an ounce of fat among these living weapons. It's just deep-cut muscle and the raw mastery of brute force.

I watch them grapple and spar, the smack of bodies on mats punctuated by occasional grunts of exertion. Their sheer physicality is daunting, but I can't deny a fascinating curiosity. Inspecting closer, a handful of women are training alongside the men. Lean and toned, but my eyes skim past them and catch on one man—a tall blond built like a titanium wall.

His piercing blue eyes meet mine briefly before he's pulled back into the fray. He takes a punch, rolls with it, and uses the momentum to put his opponent in a chokehold.

Impressive reflexes and stunning power.

Something in his commanding presence awakens a primal hunger deep within me. He glances my way again, brazen interest flashing in those icy blues. A charged tension crawls over my skin, raising goosebumps. My gaze locks with his.

Hard.

Unyielding.

Steel forged in fire.

The room spins. Time slows. It's just him and me, a predator and his prey. It's exhilarating. Terrifying.

Abruptly, I turn away, nerves buzzing—face heating. Heart pounding against my ribcage.

As much as I outwardly scoff at these muscle-bound Guardian brutes, some secret part of me is drawn to their raw masculine power. The men I've known were never dominant enough to ignite my passion.

Timid betas at best.

Insipid omegas at worse.

Most men are intimidated by my prickly nature. Walking on eggshells instead of sweeping me off my feet like I secretly crave.

Shaking away the dangerous musings, I force myself to focus on why I'm here.

"Who are they?" I point to the women, but Mitzy thinks I mean the group of men.

"Those are the Guardians," Mitzy explains. "Our tactical teams. They're our muscle—the boots on the ground."

"I don't work with meatheads." Despite my desire, I shake my head in disgust.

"You'll mainly work with my tech team. Working directly with the Guardians will be rare, but you should refrain from calling them meatheads."

"Why?"

"It's rude."

"And calling us Techies isn't?"

"Glad to see you thinking in terms of *us*. Good first step in the right direction. Now, come on." Mitzy smiles tolerantly. "They seem intimidating, but trust me, they're harmless, I promise."

Harmless isn't a word I'd use for those massive brutes, but I stay silent. As for the *us* comment, I know what Mitzy's offering. Next, she shows me the temporary living quarters where I'll be housed.

"It's temporary lodging. Simple but comfortable." She shows me the modest apartment. "It's got the basics: a full-sized bed, simple desk, chair, and computer provided. There's a modest living room and a functional kitchen. Much better than a cell."

"Still feels like one."

"Settle in and get some rest." She rolls her eyes in exasperation. "We'll start your orientation tomorrow. The cafeterias are come as you are. The food is free, a perk of working for Guardians HRS. Just grab what you want, eat where you will, but bus your tray. We clean up our messes around here." She clasps my shoulder and then hands me a phone. "My number is on the phone. Need anything, call me."

"How about a change of clothes? Toothbrush? Metal cup to drag along the window?"

The look Mitzy gives me says she's getting tired of my piss-poor attitude. Well, I'm tired of it too. It takes a lot of effort to pretend I've got my shit locked down tight when I'm shaking inside, terrified of the unknown.

"Done and done. You've got clothes in the dresser waiting for you. Toiletries in the bathroom. Anything you need, we'll get. You can grab whatever you want once you get your first paycheck."

"Wait? I'm getting paid? I thought…"

"Told you this was a job. You're not a prisoner. I value your skills, and you'll see how much when that first check hits your bank account. We do all the fun paperwork tomorrow. Be at my office no later than nine. I've got a full day planned for you."

With that, she leaves me alone.

Alone.

No guard.

No ankle bracelet.

There are fences.

Don't know if I'm allowed off Guardian HQ grounds, but I'll figure that out later.

I perch tentatively on the foot of the plain bed, hardly believing this sparsely decorated room is mine. No cellmates breathing, snoring, or coughing to keep me awake. No lumpy cot digging into my side. Just peace and quiet. And a door I can lock for privacy and unlock whenever I want.

Definitely an upgrade.

After the deafening chaos of cramped communal cells, this silence feels disorienting.

Lonely, almost.

I didn't realize how much background noise I'd grown used to during my time in jail.

Shaking off melancholy thoughts, I boot up the computer. To my delight, it grants access to Guardian's systems without restrictions. Mitzy trusts me more than she should, or she's testing me.

I crack my knuckles, grinning eagerly—time to show this fancy system what I can do. Curling up in the desk chair, I delicately probe the network. I start subtly, scoping out Guardian's network architecture, probing for weak points. But Mitzy's security is smooth as glass—not so much as a crack I can wedge open.

Several hours later, I've mapped substantial portions of the system architecture and located a few intriguing vulnerabilities. Nothing too critical, and I'm careful not to leave traces that would trigger alerts.

I learned a hell of a lot about Guardian's technical capabilities, though. Several projects still in development spark my curiosity. They're doing cutting-edge things with Robotics, Artificial Intelligence, and Virtual Reality.

Very impressive.

I can't hold back a grin. I may be trapped for now, but at least this place comes with some sweet new toys to play with. Who knows, maybe I'll stick around when my time is up.

But not because they own me.

I'm still my own woman. I'll stay only if this place is legit and Mitzy lets me do what I do best without too many damn rules.

Two hours later, I test firewalls. I write a slick little worm, my viral calling card, and set it loose to open backdoors for me.

"Jackpot!" Rolling up my sleeves, it's time to get to work.

I discover a weakness in one of their older servers used for HR data. Amateurs left a tiny backdoor wide enough for someone with my skills to slither through. The worm gets me access to a low-level employee portal. I poke around their files, hungry for a bigger score. A portal this sloppy means bigger gaps await somewhere.

In no time, I'm in and scrolling through employee records. Boring stuff, mostly. I'm about to start digging deeper when a chat window pops open on my screen.

Impressive. A little slower than I expected, but not bad. Meet me in the cafeteria for a midnight snack.

I scowl and slam the laptop shut. So the psychedelic glitter queen was watching the whole time? Should have known this was a damn test.

Down in the company cafeteria, Mitzy waves at me from a table heaped with juicy steaks, baked potatoes, and even chocolate cake. I ignore her peace offering and load a tray with my first decent meal in weeks. I make a point of sitting alone in a far corner.

A minute later, she appears across from me, undaunted by my standoffishness.

"Didn't take you to be one to pout. Making a point?" She steals a fry off my tray with a grin. She refers to me deliberately not sitting with her, but to my chagrin, I'm right where she wanted me to be.

I glare at her and shield my food. "You planted that to test me."

"Of course. Had to gauge your skills. I traded a lot of favors to free you and had to know if you were worth it."

I'm curious as to what favors she refers to, but there's no way I'm going to ask. Engaging in *more* conversation with my glittering psychedelic boss ranks number one on my list of top things I don't want to do, but then—I go and open my mouth.

"Well, don't think you've got me all figured out." I glare at her and shield my plate from further unauthorized french fry incursions. "I was just warming up. You won't be smirking when you see what I'm capable of."

"Bring it on. I love a challenge." Mitzy grins cryptically. Her left eyebrow lifts in a challenge. She snags another fry, slipping under my shield. "You think you're the next best big thing, but don't expect things to be easy around here. You're swimming with the big guys now. This isn't a game. The next *level* won't be such a cakewalk." She uses air quotes on "level" like we're playing some damn computer game.

That cocky wink of hers ignites my stubborn, competitive streak. Oh, it is so on now. She's enjoying this way too much.

"Don't expect me to hack you all night to prove myself." I cross my arms defiantly.

"You do you. It's all up to you." Mitzy rocks back on her heels casually. "I could be wrong about you. Time will tell."

"Wrong? About what?"

"Whether you're good enough to work for me." The glint in her eyes ignites my competitive streak. Does she want a hacking duel?

"Oh, I'm plenty good," I threaten, absolutely devouring the rest of my meal.

Mitzy's challenge rings in my ears after she leaves me alone and returns to her table. She shamelessly digs into her meal, never sparing me a second glance.

Does she doubt my skills?

No more Ms. Nice Hacker. It's time to show this colorful queen of the techies what I can do.

FOUR

Jeb

THE SHRILL BEEP OF MY ALARM JOLTS ME AWAKE FAR TOO EARLY. I stifle a groan, knowing it's a big day at school for my five-year-old son, Maverick, and he can't be late for show-and-tell.

As expected, he's still fast asleep when I peek into his room. I sit on the edge of his toddler bed, festooned with superhero sheets, and gently rouse him.

"Time to get up, little man. You don't want to be late for show-and-tell day."

Maverick rubs his eyes and gives me a sleepy smile that melts my heart. Slowly, he becomes more alert as we go through our morning routine.

In the bathroom, I lather up my shaving cream, and Maverick insists on joining in, smearing some on his smooth little face. He makes a game of mimicking my motions with his plastic safety razor. I can't help but chuckle at his exaggerated expressions in the mirror. The little boy is eager to grow into a man like his dad.

After I help Maverick brush his teeth, some of the fog of sleepiness lifts from his eyes. Nothing like some cold water and minty toothpaste to jumpstart the day. We chat and laugh as Maverick gets dressed, telling me about his "cool guy" outfit choices for the day.

"Don't forget to grab Rexy for show-and-tell," I provide a gentle reminder.

"Oh yeah!" His eyes widen as he grabs the toy T-rex off his dresser. He beams at me with his prized 'Rexy' in his arms.

The savory smells of sizzling bacon and eggs waft down the hall from the kitchen, rousing our appetites and drawing us to the table. The aroma reminds me of childhood, awakening each morning to those same smells as my mom cooked breakfast for me when I was a kid.

We stride to the kitchen together. Maverick scrunches his nose, inhaling the mouthwatering scents with delight.

"Grandma, your cooking makes my tummy so happy!" He pats his stomach for emphasis.

"Take a seat, love, and I'll bring your plate." Her voice overflows with a grandmother's absolute adoration. My mom works the stove like a seasoned warrior.

My dad snaps the newspaper closed now that Maverick's at the table. "Whatcha got there?" He points toward Maverick's toy dinosaur, smiling indulgently.

"Eat up." My mom winks as she sets a plate before Maverick. He eagerly dives in.

The nostalgic smell of her cooking never fails to bring me comfort before the harsh realities of the day intrude. Maverick digs in hungrily while I savor my black coffee, needing the caffeine jolt. We'll have to hustle to avoid being late, but a few minutes together over a hot meal is worth the rush.

"Daddy, look!" Maverick holds up a piece of bacon he shaped into a dinosaur. I laugh and ruffle his hair, pulled back into the moment.

I remember being Maverick's age, eagerly bounding into the kitchen each morning to see what delicious creations my mom had whipped up for breakfast. Things were simpler then. Now, it's me sitting at the head of the table while my parents serve and dote over their grandson.

Our dynamic has shifted in subtle ways.

"Be careful with your juice, love." My mom gently repositions Maverick's cup. I smile softly, lost in memories.

"His name is Rexy, and he's the coolest dinosaur ever." Maverick chatters about his toy with my father between bites.

My dad takes Rexy, making exaggerated dinosaur-growling noises that send Maverick into a fit of giggles. I'm grateful my son gets to form these sweet memories with his grandparents. Though part of me wishes Sarah was here instead.

"Rexy's gonna have so many friends at school today!" Maverick tells my dad excitedly.

My parents and I endured our rough patches when I was younger. They disapproved of my decision to join the Navy at seventeen, seeing it as youthful rebellion. My mother threw a fit when I trained to become a Navy SEAL.

She fretted each and every time I went on a mission, terrified I might never come back. It's taken years to get her to understand this is simply the way I'm wired. I'm a protector, a defender, a Guardian for those who can't save themselves.

"More milk, dear?" My mom reaches to refill Maverick's glass.

My parents were disappointed when I got Sarah pregnant. It's not that we weren't planning on getting married—we were—but constant deployments as a Navy SEAL made it difficult to find the right time.

While my mother fretted, Sarah graciously waited through long absences and uncertainty. We planned to finally make it official when I completed my last rotation overseas and returned home for good.

I had the ring ready and everything.

But fate had other plans, prematurely bringing Maverick into this world and taking his mother away before we got the chance to get married and make things official. My beautiful Sarah was gone in the blink of an eye.

Losing her left a jagged hole that can never truly heal. In my darkest moments, the guilt and grief threaten to drown me. My son will grow up never knowing his mother; I can do nothing to change that, but most days, love wins out over grief.

"All done, Grandma!" Maverick proudly presents his clean plate.

He's a piece of Sarah I still get to hold, our flesh and blood combined—the best parts of both of us.

My parents showed their support when it counted the most after Sarah's passing, despite any past objections over my choices in life. They had one request: that I leave the Navy and the dangerous life of a SEAL behind me for the sake of my son.

Out of respect for their wishes, I pursued my second love—technology and computer science. I earned my computer science degree from MIT and began a new career path, but the need to help others and save innocents in danger never truly left me. I grew restless, living a "normal" life. The domesticity felt stifling when others continued to suffer and struggle.

After long discussions, my parents could see how unfulfilled I felt. Though it pained them to see me risk my life again, they understood my call to service ran too deep.

They had one condition: that I not return to the SEALs. The Guardians' covert missions aligned closely with my desire to help, and their cutting-edge tech meant I could put my new skills to use.

As I reflect, the present scene unfolds around me—my parents chatting with Maverick, the clink of forks on plates, the aroma of freshly brewed coffee.

These little details ground me.

Their willingness to uproot their lives and move in to help care for Maverick showed me how lucky I am to have them.

Our dynamic has shifted.

They went from parenting me to spoiling their grandson. Fortunately, despite the challenges, we're navigating this new phase of life together—me as a single father and them as adoring grandparents.

They still parent me sometimes, and I go to them for guidance when I need help, but I would trade all of that to have Sarah back. Our arrangement is complicated, but I couldn't be more grateful. If I can be even half the parent to Maverick as mine are to me, I'll consider myself a success. For now, I enjoy these chaotic mornings, finding joy in simple breakfast rituals and days of show-and-tell.

I ruffle Maverick's hair affectionately. "I can't wait to hear about

Rexy during show-and-tell, but remember to share him nicely with the other kids."

"I will," Maverick promises solemnly. "Grandma, can I have bacon for the road?"

"For the road?" She grabs a napkin and places some bacon inside. "Eat up so you grow big and strong like your daddy."

Maverick flexes his little arms, making us both chuckle. My heart swells watching him. I treasure every minute, however long or short, of our time together each morning.

"Your bacon is the bestest ever!" He's a good-natured kid overall.

"How about after school today, we get some ice cream, just you and me?" I propose. "Celebrate Rexy's big day?"

Maverick's face lights up. "Yeah! Rocky Road, please?"

"You got it, buddy." I cherish these simple father-son moments, never more aware than now how precious his childhood is and how quickly it will pass.

My phone rings as Maverick races off to put on his sneakers. I glance at the caller ID—it's Ethan Blackwood, leader of Charlie team.

Meaning we have a mission.

"Yo, what's up?"

"We have a situation that requires immediate action," Ethan says briskly. "A thirteen-year-old girl was kidnapped last night from her family's Cancún vacation rental."

"Any leads on who took her?" I stiffen, instantly on high alert.

"A local cartel is suspected. The family hid a tracker on the girl before she was taken. She's still in the area, but intel indicates they may try to move her out soon. Wheels are already spinning up."

"I'm ready, be at HQ in twenty." I move toward the stairs as Ethan speaks.

"No time. I'm sending a car to get you now—we'll prep in transit." His tone brokers no argument.

"Understood." There's no hesitation on my part, and because of my parents, no worry about who will take care of Maverick.

When I end the call, Mom gives me a sympathetic look.

"Another mission?" At my nod, she pats my shoulder. "Don't worry, we'll pick Maverick up from school and take him for that ice cream. He'll understand, honey."

I scrub a hand down my face. "I hate breaking promises to him." Guilt sits like a stone in my gut at the thought of disappointing my son again.

"Maverick knows his daddy is a hero." My dad picks up his newspaper from the table and unfolds it. He gives me an understanding look. "Just do what you must, and we'll hold down the fort here."

I nod, buoyed by their support even as the guilt lingers. I'd be lost without them.

Maverick comes barreling back into the kitchen with his Velcro sneakers haphazardly secured and backpack dragging on the ground. Oblivious to the change in plan.

I paste on a smile as I help him get sorted. "Papa and Grandma will pick you up from school today, okay? I got called in to work."

"Aww, but ice cream?" Maverick's face falls.

I kneel and tickle his tummy. "Don't worry, Papa will take you. We'll go another time." I kiss his forehead, hating to disappoint him but unwilling to expose him to the harsh realities of my work.

"Okay." Maverick accepts this with a five-year-old's resilience, but the droop in his shoulders tugs at my heart.

Too soon, his school bus honks outside. Hugs and kisses are exchanged, and I watch wistfully as he trots to the bus with a little wave. My mom squeezes my shoulder.

"He'll be okay. It's good for children to learn flexibility and patience." Her tone holds a note of wryness. She knows that lesson never gets easier as a parent. "Be safe out there." She then turns back to the dishes, pretending she isn't sending *her* son into danger.

I pull her into a fierce hug. "Thank you, truly. For everything you and Dad do to help with Maverick. It takes a weight off me."

"Of course, dear. That's what family is for. Now get out there and make us proud." She pats my back affectionately.

I trot down the hall, grab my gear, and then return to my parents.

A second honk sounds. This one's for me.

After a swift goodbye, I hop in the waiting vehicle, mind wholly focused on the mission. Personal conflicts take a backseat when innocents need our help. As the car speeds toward the airfield, I pray we arrive in time.

A little girl's survival depends on it.

FIVE

Jeb

THE SUV ROLLS TO A STOP BESIDE THE WAITING JET. TIME IS critical on this mission to reach the kidnapped girl before she's moved. I hop out and stride across the tarmac toward the rumbling aircraft, my duffel bag slung over one shoulder.

The rest of the team is here, prepping weapons and equipment. Our fearless leader, Ethan Blackwood, looks up from cleaning his weapon and gives me a terse nod. His features are set in their usual mask of stoic pre-mission focus.

Walt has medical supplies spread out, taking inventory with a meticulous eye. The former Air Force PJ will be our lifeline if this op goes sideways. Gabe checks his host of explosives and sabotage charges from his munitions stash. The big man is an artist when it comes to constructing chaos.

"How's it going?" I nod to the others as I drop my gear.

"Same shit, different day, gearing up to raise some hell." Gabe grins as he tinkers with explosives.

"Ready to get going and bring that girl home." Walt looks up from his medical kit. "What do we know?"

"What's the deal?" I turn to Ethan, our stalwart leader.

"I'll go over the full sit-rep once we're airborne." Ethan finishes putting his weapon back together. "For now, check your gear and verify supplies."

He or one of the others packed my gear from my locker back at HQ. It's Ethan's way of telling me to make sure they got everything before we take off. Once airborne, there won't be any resupply.

"On it." I check my gear and ammo.

"How's Maverick doing?" Gabe asks. "The little man staying out of trouble?"

"For the most part." I chuckle. "His new thing is shaping bacon into dinosaurs in the morning."

The guys laugh.

"Cute kid," Walt remarks.

"That he is." I smile despite knowing I'll miss bedtime with my son tonight.

But it's for a worthy cause.

The atmosphere is relaxed yet focused as we make final preparations. Our banter holds undertones of dark humor common in those who regularly face danger.

"Damn, look at all those explosives," I whistle appreciatively as Gabe pieces together his customized charges. "Saving some baddies for the rest of us?"

"No promises once I start blowing shit up." Gabe grins. "But I'll try to leave a few skulls for you animals to crack."

"Appreciate that generosity, brother." Hank chuckles as he field strips his rifle.

Walt tests the sharpness of a combat knife, eyes glinting with good humor. "If you hog all the targets, drinks are on you when we return."

"A sacrifice I'm willing to make." Gabe laughs.

We chat casually as we work, savoring these moments. Soon, mission masks will slip into place, movements honed by endless drills. For now, we're just grabbing some camaraderie before duty calls.

The cabin door thumps closed, muffling the engines as we taxi toward the runway.

"Let's do this." Ethan meets my eyes and nods.

Once airborne, the casual talk dies. We review schematics and plans, faces grim, rehearsing tactical maneuvers. Laughter ceases, the mission our sole focus.

We review the rescue plan until the mission unfolds in our minds—the crumbling hacienda holding the target, the rugged terrain to cross, our entry points, and contingency plans. No detail is too small when a little girl's life is at stake.

When we land, we gear up, faces disappearing behind masks, movements economical from endless drills. The only sounds are Velcro ripping, magazines snapping into weapons, and calm, steadying breaths.

Walt triple-checks his medic kit, stocked with tourniquets, clotting agents, and IV fluids—the essentials to keep us alive if things go sideways. The former PJ endured the same brutal training as the rest of us in BUD/S. He's our lifeline out here.

Gabe loads up with a small arsenal—shotgun, hand cannon, tricked-out M4. Plus enough ammo to besiege a fortress. Our munitions expert doesn't mess around. He's our all-around MacGyver in solving problems in the field.

Ethan coordinates final details with Command while we lock and load. The mission focus and adrenaline kicks in as we prep to insert into the hot zone. This is what we train for, day after day, night after night.

Go-time.

We slip into the darkness like ghosts. Intel tags the location as lightly defended, but we take nothing for granted. Situations morph, and surveillance misses things.

We're ready for the worst.

I take point, hyper-alert for signs of early warning. A mile out, the dilapidated hacienda appears against the night sky. A few faint lights indicate life. Intel is accurate—minimal defenses. Their cockiness will cost them.

We've done this countless times, but the edge never dulls. My senses strain for any sign of the enemy.

At the rally point, Ethan signals a halt and drops to one knee.

We follow and slow our breaths while scanning ahead with optics and thermal imaging, identifying sentry positions.

"Five hostiles on patrol, two mobile, three static," I report tersely. "Thirty-second gap between sweeps." We ghost across the open ground at the next gap in patrols, reaching the crumbling perimeter wall. Silent as ghosts.

So far, so good.

Crouched motionless, we observe two lackadaisical kidnappers strolling past, barely paying attention. Cocky fools, certain they're untouchable out here.

It's a fatal mistake.

Once the patrol moves on and their footsteps fade, Walt takes out his lockpicks and goes to work as we watch his back. Twenty agonizing seconds pass before the stubborn lock surrenders. I slip inside the gloomy rooms, sweeping for threats.

There are none.

I wave the team in, and we flow deeper, senses hyper-alert. My nerves wind tighter the closer we get to the room where intel indicates the girl is being held. Voices sound ahead—two oblivious guards standing outside her door.

Ethan signals Gabe and Walt right, Hank and Blake left. I'm to take the door. At his command, we strike as one. Gabe and Hank slash the throats of the guards while Walt and Blake watch their six.

I kick in the door. Ethan surges in ahead of me, gun up, while I flow in behind him. My muffled shots drop the lone stunned guard inside. I keep watch while Ethan and Walt rush to the whimpering girl curled in the fetal position. She's chained to the wall and lies on a filthy mattress.

"You're safe now." Walt rushes in and soothes her. "We're getting you home." He checks her for injuries while Gabe snaps the lock holding the girl.

Banged up and bruised, by some miracle, she's relatively unharmed.

Walt wraps a thermal blanket around the dazed teen's bony shoulders while Ethan radios Command that our target's secured.

Walt hands me his weapon as he scoops the weak girl in his arms. We slip outside and steal into the night, retracing our steps.

Objective achieved.

The trek to exfil is tense but uneventful—anti-climactic after the tension of infiltration. Soon, the teen is bundled into an SUV to be reunited with her family.

All in all, it was an easy mission.

Not all go this smoothly.

Before we're wheels up, I call home, hoping to catch Maverick before bed.

"Hey, buddy, wanted to check in before bedtime," I say when he picks up.

"Daddy! I miss you," Maverick replies. "When are you coming home?"

My heart clenches. "Soon, kiddo, just got some work stuff to finish first, but I'll be home before you know it. How was show-and-tell? Did the kids like meeting Rexy?"

"Yeah! I told them he's a T-rex. He's the biggest and has sharp teeth," Maverick exclaims. "They all wanted to hold him. I shared nice and let them pass him around."

"That's awesome. Sounds like he was a big hit." I smile proudly. We chat a few more minutes about his day before saying good night. I hang up, wishing I were there to kiss him good night in person.

Back at base, after quick showers, we debrief and rehash details from the mission.

"Who's ready to get shitfaced and find some hot tail to celebrate with?" Gabe grins lecherously as we start packing up, waggling his eyebrows.

"Hell yeah, I could blow off some steam." Hank eagerly high-fives him. "Or get blown."

When the guys start talking about celebratory drinks, I stifle a yawn and beg off. I'm too wired to sleep and not in the mood for a meaningless hookup. A protein shake and some quiet time will do tonight.

"You animals have fun. I'm gonna call it a night."

"You sure?" Hank gives me a look like I'm crazy.

Most nights, I'm the ringleader when it comes to booze, chicks, and sex with strangers. It's my way to decompress, but I shake my head, touched by his concern.

"Appreciate the thought, but I'll stick with a mellow one tonight. You enjoy, though."

"Your loss." Gabe claps my shoulder.

"Not like you. Anything wrong?" Blake rubs his wet hair with a towel, drying off after his shower. His expression is kind but serious.

"I know," I concede with a small smile. Something's shifted within me. Something I can't put a finger on. The thought of another nameless hookup at a bar suddenly feels empty.

Lonely.

"Just not in the mood."

"We'll drink your share then." Gabe cocks his head, studying me. The intuitive one of the bunch, perhaps he senses something is off with me.

I'd love to ask him what it is because I can't figure out what's suddenly changed.

"I'll tag along to babysit you reprobates," Ethan chuckles, though his smile doesn't reach his tired eyes. "But designated driver only for me tonight."

I nod gratefully at Ethan, knowing our normally party-loving leader is only going to humor the guys. He's been keeping to himself more after things with Rebel ended badly.

After her rescue, things got hot and heavy between the two of them, but then Rebel vanished. No one's been able to find any hint of her, and that's saying something, considering the resources at Guardian HRS.

The rabble heads out, whooping and hollering. I wave them off with a chuckle, my mind already looking ahead to a quiet night.

After a late-night run, I'm drawn to the empty cafeteria, craving protein to refuel.

It's after midnight, but a few others are up snacking. Including Mitzy, brooding over a neglected meal, face bathed in the glow of her tablet. She absently picks at what looks like a meal made for two, but there's no one sitting with her.

I grab a protein shake when movement catches my eye. A lone figure sits in shadowy solitude, and I feel an irresistible pull…

It's Mitzy's intriguing recruit. The raven-haired beauty snaps her head up, and our gazes clash and collide. The air between us seems to charge as we study one another. Damn if my pulse doesn't quicken. Her eyes narrow when I pivot, intent on approach. Even in darkness, that piercing blue gaze simmers with defiance.

Her full lips part slightly, but then, as if catching herself, she's suddenly on her feet, body coiled with tension. She buses her tray and storms out without a glance back, leaving me standing there, stunned and craving answers. Who is this mysterious woman who's gotten under my skin?

Unsure what to make of the tense encounter, I drain my shake.

Before I can process what just happened, Mitzy sidles up, regarding me with a knowing look.

"Well, that was intense," she remarks with a knowing glint in her eye. "Seems like you and Stitch felt some sparks flying, hmm?"

"Stitch?" I turn the unique name over in my mind.

Mitzy smiles. "She's got skills and an attitude to match. Could use some guidance settling in." She assesses me shrewdly. "In fact, I need someone to cover her self-defense training. Want the assignment?"

"I'd be happy to show her the ropes." Pulse hammering away, I jump at the opportunity to get to know Mitzy's new recruit.

"Excellent." Mitzy's eyes dance with mirth. "Fair warning, she's a handful."

"That's okay. I'm up for a challenge."

She saunters off, laughing under her breath. I shake my head ruefully, knowing I've been played, but the prospect of getting to know Stitch overpowers any hesitation. This assignment is too intriguing to pass up.

SIX

Stitch

———————

I ANGRILY STAB AT THE REMAINS OF MY CELEBRATORY STEAK DINNER when the cafeteria doors swing open. One of Mitzy's precious "Guardians" saunters in. The moment I see him, it's as if all the air gets sucked out of my lungs.

This man…

Gorgeous.

The most breathtaking man on the planet—tall, broad-shouldered, with the physique of a god. He's the kind of man who doesn't just walk into a room.

He owns it.

His unshakable confidence and how he holds himself give him an undeniable presence.

A magnetism that pulls at me.

Sooooo not my type.

But damn if that chiseled jawline isn't sexy as hell.

I shamelessly ogle his assets when he suddenly turns toward me. Our gazes clash, and he has the most intense, piercing blue eyes I've ever seen. The light dusting of his five o'clock shadow makes my fingers twitch, yearning to feel the burn of it against my face—and other places.

Lower places.

The way his professional indifference transforms into something more primal is something I'll never forget. Wish I could say I'm surprised, but men like him see women as conquests rather than people. Still, that hunger in his eyes and the way they make me feel —as if he's undressing me—causes me to squirm.

It's an unusual experience, something I've only read about in books, but the intensity of his gaze brings images to mind of being claimed in the most primal, most basic way a man can claim a woman.

Something stirs within me, igniting raw, uncontrolled desire. The rational part of my mind dismisses him, saying he's nothing more than an arrogant alpha male, but my heart...

Oh, my rebellious heart.

It beats to a different tune. A melody that yearns to submit to the raw, untamed power of this alpha male standing before me.

His eyes flare with heated interest, devouring every inch of me. The raw hunger in that penetrating gaze makes me shrink back, a rabbit sensing the wolf, but I can't look away, frozen by the intensity of his gaze. Banked desire smolders in those azure depths.

Worse than that, the expression on his face says he's going to have me whether I want it or not. My pulse skitters wildly, acutely aware of his sheer physicality and the coiled power barely constrained beneath the surface.

This man holds the power to uproot everything I know about passion and power.

He could overpower me if he wished.

As if it were inevitable.

As if it already happened.

My lips part when the corner of his mouth edges up. My squirming turns to another emotion as the hairs on my arms stand and fear grips me from the inside.

The thought of him terrifies me—and exhilarates me.

When he grabs a protein shake, muscles flexing under his tight, black tee, he turns toward me, and I do the only thing I can think of.

I run.

I bus my tray in record time and race from the cafeteria, vowing never to return. Once out of there, the doors close behind me, and it feels as if I can breathe again. My shoulders slump, and my ragged breath settles.

Coward.

Equal parts rattled and intrigued by the animal magnetism Mr. Tall-Blond-and-Intimidating exudes, I chide myself for such a school-girl ditzy moment.

But I don't have time to dwell on smoldering Guardians.

I've got a score to settle with their glittery leader.

Shaking off the odd encounter, I hustle back to my room. Once there, it's time for round two and time to show Miss Know-It-All I'm not one to be trifled with.

Game on, Mitzy.

My fingers itch to pick up where I left off.

Her "level two" firewall is tougher, more sophisticated coding—but still mapped out in a relatively conventional way.

Boring and more than a little disappointing.

It takes a little over two hours to pinpoint another "unintentional" gap.

I'm extra careful slipping inside this time, erasing traces of my intrusion as I go. No alerts or chat boxes pop up. So far, so good. I do a silent victory lap through their main databanks, copying files I can peruse later.

This round goes to me.

Moving carefully to avoid detection, I push my luck and probe the edges of the system, seeking points of entry to other connected networks. Jackpot—there's something called the "RUFUS server." Must be important if it's this well fortified.

I manage to work open the tiniest of cracks, holding my breath. Sliding into view comes a stream of data beyond anything I've ever seen: complex engineering schematics, terabytes of code, and 3D models depicting advanced robotic systems. My fingers hover reverently over the keys as I soak it all in.

Another chat box opens, making me jump.

RUFUS is off-limits. Impressive you found it, though. Get some rest, and we'll debrief tomorrow.

Fingers trembling in frustration, I log off. I was so close to unlocking whatever cutting-edge program this RUFUS is. Mitzy shut me down with such maddening casualness, like scolding a child for staying up past their bedtime.

She won that round, but I'm just getting warmed up. There's more to this system, and I'm going to find it.

Over the next week, I spend every free minute probing Guardian's networks, hungry for another shot at RUFUS. But Mitzy's no fool. Her security is a moving target, protocols constantly shifting to close gaps I exploit.

I spend the first three days tirelessly hacking Guardian's systems, seeking chinks in Mitzy's armor. When I think I'm in, doors snap shut in my face. She guides me away from restricted areas with frustrating gentleness, complimenting my persistence and making it clear I only see what she allows.

I spend every free minute digging for intel on the mysterious RUFUS. But Mitzy stays one step ahead, shutting down my routes into classified systems with maddening subtleness.

By day four, I'm frustrated and sleep-deprived—time to get aggressive.

I stay up all night coding the most elegant virus of my career. Once inserted, it will grant me unrestricted access to the entire system. No way Mitzy's cronies can detect it in time. Fueled by spite and one too many energy drinks, I launch an all-out brute-force attack.

Mitzy wants to play hardball? I'll show her what a real hack looks like.

Just before dawn, I unleash my creation into Guardian's networks. Let's see her watchdog programs detect me now. Immediately, it starts copying terabytes of data back to me.

Yes!

Not so smug now, huh, Mitzy?

Victory is in sight. My eyes widen as specs and diagrams spill across the screen. It's an incredibly advanced AI system beyond anything I've heard of. I'm so engrossed I don't notice the lights flickering ominously. Suddenly, the power cuts completely, and my monitor goes black.

"What the..."

A hand grasps my shoulder firmly from behind. I yelp and spin around to see Mitzy's face eerily lit by a flashlight.

"Nice Trojan, but I control the juice in this place." She grins and flicks the flashlight off, leaving me in darkness again. That insufferable, infuriating woman. "Sleep tight, Stitch."

As she leaves me fuming in the dark, one thing is clear—It's time to up my game.

My chance comes a few days later when Mitzy is dragged into an emergency strategy meeting. This leaves me free to roam unsupervised. Forget digital tactics. It's time for an old-fashioned analog hack—the perfect window to act while she's distracted.

Locating the server room is easy with my stolen building schematics. It takes less than five minutes to hack the digital lock. Once alone, I patch into the network and set my plan in motion. The vault-like door hisses open. Row upon row of sleek servers housed in glass cases stand before me. Now, to find which server information on RUFUS lives.

No holds barred this time.

The frequency of mentions around RUFUS suggests whatever it is, it's important, but details are scarce.

I finally scent a lead.

Ten precious minutes later, I locate the right hardware cluster. After circumventing the failsafe, I have direct access to the mysterious RUFUS database. Holding my breath, I initiate a download of the entire thing to a portable drive.

The overhead lights flare on just as the progress bar hits 99%. I whirl around to see Mitzy in the doorway, regarding me with amusement.

"Well done," she concedes, strolling up to inspect my unauthorized little operation. "You managed to evade my digital defenses by going old-school analog. Props for creativity and a gold star for thinking outside the box."

I cross my arms smugly. "Told you I could crack this place."

"Mmhmm. And now that you've had your fun?" She holds out a hand expectantly for the drive. I hesitate, tempted to bolt, but one look at her expression wipes that thought away.

Reluctantly, I surrender the device, along with any leverage I gained. She pockets it with an infuriating wink.

"Let's grab some lunch, and I'll tell you all about RUFUS."

Despite being thwarted again, I grin on our way upstairs. Mitzy has bested me at every turn. She's good, and that says a lot coming from me.

A genuine grin tugs at my lips. As frustrating as this past week has been, I respect this woman's skills. And if I'm being honest, I can't remember the last time I had this much fun.

SEVEN

Stitch

—————

OVER PASTRAMI SANDWICHES, MITZY GIVES ME AN OVERVIEW OF THE RUFUS program—AI mobile robots assisting the Guardians. The technology is mind-blowing. Despite my earlier pouting, I'm able to compliment her innovations sincerely.

"Someday, you can help develop tactical features for them," Mitzy offers. "But you need to learn patience and respect organizational security. One step at a time. And we begin with proper onboarding to Guardian HRS."

Her tone reminds me so much of Foster Mother #37. The only foster mother I genuinely liked. I hate it when Mitzy speaks reasonably. The projects she describes are drool-worthy, and I want to start now—like her dragonfly drones and the newest addition of a swarm of bumblebee drones.

Maybe I can stomach a little discipline to get in on that action.

"Onboarding? What does that mean?"

"Oh, you're going to love it."

"From the tone of your voice, I know I'm not."

"Probably not, but it's for the best and in your best interests."

"You gonna tell me, or do I have to guess?"

"Self-defense training." Her grin leaves me waiting for the other shoe to drop. "With one of the meatheads, and it's mandatory."

"You're kidding." I lean back and roll my eyes. "Mandatory?"

"Six weeks."

"Six weeks!" I bolt upright in my chair. "That's cruel and unusual punishment."

"Maybe, but far better than a prison sentence."

"How long are you going to hold that over my head?" I dislike being reminded I owe Mitzy my life. Because of her, I've got a chance to turn my life around—not to mention *not* living behind bars.

"Everybody does it. It's an essential skill considering our line of work."

"But six weeks?"

"Mandatory. You begin next week. Until then, let me show you what all we do around here."

Grudgingly, I accept. It's not something worth wasting my breath arguing over.

From then on, Mitzy takes me under her wing more fully. I still poke and prod when I get away with it, but it's more like a game between us. She's not terrible company when she's not ruining my fun. Bit by bit, she feeds me more access and more trust.

It turns out this gig isn't a death sentence after all. The tech is sexy as hell, and even psychedelic-boss-lady is kinda growing on me. But I'm not about to tell Mitzy that. She's insufferable enough as it is.

After one afternoon filling out boring intake forms, an important thought strikes me.

"The work I'll be doing…" I begin.

"Yes?"

"It's only ever white hat stuff, right?"

"White hat?" Her brow furrows at the reference.

"You know? The Westerns?" When she continues to regard me with a puzzled expression, I elaborate. "All the heroes wear white hats. The villains wear black ones. I won't be involved in anything illegal or sketchy, right?" I ask point-blank. "Because I won't do that shit."

"You mean you don't do illegal things like break into the NSA's computer system?"

"I didn't do anything malicious. Just wanted to see if I could."

"Which is why I wanted you."

"Huh?"

"You're a rebel only on the surface. Deep down, you're one of the good guys, and before you roll your eyes at me, you know it's true. You got a good sense of what we do when you poked around my systems. There's nothing illegal or unethical going on here."

"I thought it was a test." I can't help but grump.

"The first of many." Mitzy stands, a sign I take to mean our little meet and greet is at an end. "And you have my word. We're the good guys. I'd never make you cross lines."

I exhale in relief. Maybe this gig will be okay after all. A true second chance I never saw coming.

"Do you mind if I ask you something?" She squeezes my shoulder, a physical touch I hate, but I don't flinch at the contact. Which is really weird for me. I loathe physical contact.

"Sure."

"I've been thinking about your arrest."

"What about it."

"Something doesn't add up."

I shift uncomfortably. "What do you mean?"

"Why target their HR and financial records? Seems odd for a hacker looking to joyride in government servers."

I choose my words carefully. "It was a dare by some of my online friends. I wanted to impress them, I guess."

Mitzy's gaze bores into me. "So, just a random dare, then?"

"Yeah, we always dared each other to hit bigger targets and gain notoriety in the hacking world." I shrug, aiming for casual. "NSA seemed like the ultimate challenge."

"Who dared you?" Mitzy presses. "These online friends have names?"

"Just usernames in chat rooms." I hesitate, unsure how much to reveal about my past connections. "They don't mean anything. We mostly kept things anonymous."

Mitzy isn't buying it. She drums her fingers on her desk, considering. The silence makes me squirm.

Finally, she sighs. "Well, your skills are going to much better use now, but my door is open if you want to share about your online contacts."

"Sure thing." I keep my voice light and breezy but plan to never take her up on that offer. She doesn't need to know about my mentor, Malfor. I need to keep that part of my life separate from this new start.

My nerves prick. Does Mitzy suspect Malfor's influence? I haven't heard from him since getting arrested, but if he ever contacts me again, I'll have to cut ties for good. I don't need him causing more trouble.

I'll keep my old life separate from this one. My new life starts here, which means it's time to hang up that dusty black hat. With any luck, Malfor's moved on to corrupting some other hapless kid.

"Okay, let's move on then." Mitzy studies me a moment longer before nodding. "We've got an encryption system I want you to evaluate…"

The conversation shifts to technical matters, but an uneasy knot forms in my stomach—Mitzy's no fool. I'll need to be careful if I want to bury certain parts of my past.

"What's involved with that?"

Mitzy explains the encryption setup as we walk down a hallway leading away from her office. Suddenly, raucous male laughter echoes from a nearby room. I jump, nerves jangling.

Mitzy squeezes my shoulder reassuringly. "Sounds like Charlie team is here. I should introduce you to your new instructor."

"No thanks."

"They're harmless, I promise."

"I highly doubt those hulking brutes are *harmless*." I bristle at the thought of having to learn to defend myself.

Before I can object, the door swings open, and a group of enormous, muscle-bound meatheads stride out. They're even more imposing up close; aggressive testosterone swirls in the air. They dwarf me in size, and I shrink back instinctively.

One lingers behind, saying something to another that elicits a boom of deep laughter. When he turns, our eyes lock. It's the blond titan who caught me staring in the gym…

And the cafeteria.

His piercing blue gaze smolders, devouring every inch of me. I feel it again.

That magnetic pull.

Tall, with tousled blond hair and sharp blue eyes, his broad shoulders strain the fabric of his shirt. Every line of his powerful frame exudes arrogance and strength. And his scent—a distinct combination of unscented soap and male pheromones—nearly has me sniffing the air like a bitch in heat.

Something sparks in the air between us, and something else burns between my legs—desire on an order of magnitude beyond anything I've ever experienced before. While I search for the nearest exit, Mitzy makes introductions.

"Stitch, meet Jeb," Mitzy says. "Stitch is my new recruit, and Jeb is your self-defense instructor."

Jeb strides closer, tilting his head with shameless appreciation. Up close, he's even taller and more imposing, pure power in human form. I crane my neck to meet his brooding azure eyes.

We're not going to talk about the way he looks at me. How that hungry, possessive vibe is back, thrumming in the space between us. As if he's once again undressing me in his mind. There's a feral male power rolling off of him that claims and dominates, and now my mouth is hanging open like a goddamn fool.

A prickle of obsession coils in a delicious knot of heat at my core—something new and ominous. Something I've never experienced before.

"A pleasure to meet you, Stitch." His rumbling voice sends tingles down my spine. One corner of his mouth ticks up lasciviously. The expression on his face says he sees right through me and knows exactly what I'm thinking. That he will have me, whether I want it or not. That the force drawing us together is inevitable.

As if it already happened.

I shake my head, trying to clear the cloud of pheromones enveloping me and dropping my IQ by a hundred points. I'm not a needy female driven by base instincts of lust, but damn if I don't want to be for him.

Frankly, it scares me to hell. The fine hairs on my arms stand on end, and a delicious tingle works its way down my spine. I do everything I can to suppress a shudder and fail spectacularly. A tight ball of desire knots my stomach, fueled by what little distance is between us.

"Um, h-hi..." I stammer, cheeks flaming.

Something about this man leaves me tongue-tied and wobbly-kneed. The way he says my name sparks irritation, but for some reason, my cheeks flush. His smile widens at my flustered response.

"I look forward to getting—better acquainted." The deepness of his voice, the way it rumbles, tightens that knot in my belly, not to mention what it does to my pulse, making it flutter wildly.

Before I can recover and respond with anything snarky, Mitzy continues the introduction. "Jeb is one of our top field operatives and one of our best self-defense instructors. You're in good hands."

Hands I want touching me everywhere all at once.

"Yeah, whatever." I force indifference and fail.

The sheer physicality of this man awakens a forbidden hunger deep within me. This man does things to me, making me feel anxious and excited and horny as hell. If I don't get myself under control, I'm going to develop an unhealthy fixation. I take a deep breath, hoping it releases that tight knot in my stomach.

It doesn't.

I turn to leave, acutely aware of Jeb's searing gaze on my body. When I glance back, our eyes lock, simmering with unspoken desire and something primal whispers that this man could be my undoing.

I'm in for an intense six weeks with this man.

But I won't go down without a fight.

The thought both terrifies and exhilarates me.

Game on, Jeb. Do your worst to me.

Please.

EIGHT

Stitch

A FEW DAYS LATER, I STOMP TOWARD THE OUTDOOR TRAINING complex, dreading this mandatory self-defense nonsense. As the building comes into view, I stop short, intimidated, and debate what might happen if I turned around and ran.

The massive stadium-turned-gymnasium looms before me, nearly the size of a football field, the vast interior visible through glass walls. Endless mats cover the structure's floor, and a rock-climbing wall expands to fill the length of the building on the far wall.

But what gives me pause are the occupants. Muscle-bound men drill inside, limbs glistening with sweat as they grapple and wail on punching bags. Their shouts echo through the open space.

Up close, their imposing size and palpable aggression are even more apparent. I watch two of them spar, power and violence barely contained with each strike.

Unease twists my stomach. Training with these brutes for six weeks suddenly seems like my worst nightmare come true, but I square my shoulders and stride toward the entrance before I lose my nerve.

Time to meet my tormentor, I mean, instructor—aka Jeb. The

dominant alpha male may intimidate me, but I refuse to show weakness in front of these meatheads.

"This is stupid." I shake my head at the mandatory self-defense requirement of all new hires. What kind of crap is this?

I'm a hacker, not a fighter.

All Guardian HRS employees are required to train in basic combat skills. It's baked into the contract Mitzy forced me to sign. Even computer geeks like me, who want nothing to do with the meathead crowd, are forced to attend six weeks of training.

I argued vehemently, but Mitzy refused to budge. She said it was *non-negotiable*. So here I am, grumbling, on my way to meet my instructor. I may or may not be ten minutes late on purpose. The session is scheduled for an hour. I figure, why not trim off ten minutes by dragging my feet?

I head to the designated training space, where Jeb waits for me. He straps on padded fighting gloves and turns at my approach.

"You're late."

It happens again. The deep rumble of his voice twists my insides into knots. It's not exactly unpleasant, but it is unwanted.

"So?"

"Accidental or purposeful?" He rakes his gaze over me in a way that sets my teeth on edge.

"Does it matter?"

"Depends. Are you ready for your first lesson?"

I cross my arms, lifting my chin. "I'm ready to be excused from this nonsense. I don't need self-defense training."

Jeb's grin widens.

"What kind of weird assed name is Jeb?"

"What kind of weird assed name is Stitch?" He fires right back, leaving me reeling.

"Whatever." No way am I answering him. "Can't we just say we did this and not do it?"

"It's non-negotiable, I'm afraid." He ignores my snarky question and beckons me forward with a flick of his fingers.

How can something so simple make my knees wobble and my insides quiver?

"Let's start with the basics. I'll go easy at first."

"Excuse me?" I bristle at his condescending tone and tug on my faded Angel Fire shirt. "I don't need you to go easy on me."

"That so?" Jeb looks me up and down pointedly. "You sure you don't want to grab some protective gear? That shirt doesn't offer much padding." He cocks his head, staring at my chest, then slowly drags his errant gaze back to my face. I'm just about ready to read him the riot act when he asks, "You a fan?"

"Fan?" My brows scrunch, trying to figure out what he— Glancing down, I realize he isn't staring at my tits but at my Angel Fire T-shirt. "Why does everyone keep asking me that?"

His eyes widen, and then his low chuckle vibrates the air. "You don't know?" He laughs under his breath.

"What's so funny?"

"Nothing." He shakes his head, then strides across the padded mat to a rack of protective equipment. "Let's get you geared up."

The mocking note in his voice makes my hands clench. I manage a tight smile. "I won't need padding to take you down."

Where the hell did that come from? There's no way in hell I'm ever going to knock him down. Might as well throw my hands in the air and admit defeat right now. Although the thought of what self-defense means, the grapples and holds that come with it make my skin burn and my pulse race.

His answering laugh grates on my nerves.

That's all it takes to ignite my competitive streak. The arrogant bastard doesn't think I can hold my own?

Fine, I'll prove him wrong.

Not that I know anything about fighting, but I'm pissed.

And that makes me do stupid things.

"Okay then, let's jump right in." Jeb slides easily into a fighting stance. "Today, we start with basic strikes and blocks from Krav Maga." When I stand there staring blankly, he sighs. "Here, I'll show you first. Pay attention."

He demonstrates a simple punch-block combination, then looks at me expectantly. "Got it? Your turn."

I mimic him half-heartedly, feeling ridiculous. But Jeb shakes his head.

"You need to rotate your wrist more on the punch. Like this."

He steps behind me, grasping my hand and guiding my arm through the motion. I stiffen, shockingly aware of his firm chest barely brushing my back. A burst of goosebumps prickles my skin, which has nothing to do with the cool air.

Jeb adjusts my stance, nudging my feet wider with his foot. "Keep your base solid. It gives more power." His breath feathers against my ear, and I shudder before wrenching away.

"I've got it, thanks." My attempt to sound bored fails miserably. Despite my best efforts, my pulse kicks up several notches, and a thrill travels down my spine.

"Show me." He lifts a brow, looking far too pleased with himself. "And put your back into it this time." The command in his voice, laced with authority and confidence, is so damn—hot.

Clenching my jaw, I throw myself into the maneuver with focused intensity. My form looks damn good this time.

"Not bad." Jeb nods approvingly, infuriating me further.

I don't need this condescending jerk's validation. Not to mention the rush of heat racing through me at the compliment.

I don't need fake praise either.

Mouth dry from all the gaping and heavy breathing, I lick my lips and nearly jump out of my skin at how he zeroes in on the motion.

He reacts to me.

Is it possible this virile man is attracted to me?

Whatever energy I imagine is between us may not be all in my head.

It's real.

And that makes him dangerous. Despite knowing I shouldn't press the issue, I lick my lips again. This time, I watch for a response, and I'm rewarded by a hitch in his breath and his pupils dilating.

He makes me go through the same move ten, twenty, thirty-plus times until my muscles ache and sweat beads on my forehead.

Punching air is far more work than it should be.

My irritation grows with each word of praise and every time he touches me to correct my form. Finally, he seems satisfied, which is timely as I'm about ready to march out of here.

"Are we done yet?" I take a step back and shake out my arms. "My shoulders are burning."

Mitzy didn't mention cruel and unusual punishment when she yanked me out of that cell.

"Let's move on to combinations. I'll show you first, then you'll perform the sequence." He demonstrates a punch-block-kick combo at half speed.

I'll punch-block-kick his ass. I quickly glance at my watch and blow out a breath of frustration.

I'm so over this.

"How long is this going to take?" I drop my arms and stretch my neck. My muscles are going to be screaming tomorrow when I wake up.

"Love, you're booked for an hour of training with me every day. It's been less than ten minutes."

Ten minutes?

"Can't we just call it a day?"

"No, love."

"Stop calling me *love*. I'm not your girl."

"Note to self: Goth chick gets grouchy when she doesn't get her way."

"And stop talking about me like that."

"Like what?"

"Like I'm not here. And for the record, *chick* is derogatory."

"Sweetie, I'm going to call you whatever I want. At least as long as you're standing there wasting both our time. You've got six weeks of training, an hour each day. Don't make this miserable."

"I'm already miserable."

"Only because you're making this miserable, young woman."

I place my hands on my hips and stare him down, which is ludicrous, considering he towers over me. "I just don't see why I need some meathead teaching me stuff I don't need."

"Meathead?" He gives me a long, appraising look as if measuring me up.

"I can call you jarhead if you prefer."

"I prefer neither."

"Well, you're acting like a grade-A prick, and don't call me a *young woman*. It's derogatory. I'm a grown-ass woman, not a kid."

"I've got a whole repository of things I can call you. Keep stalling, and I'll fish more of them out. I'm half again your age. Trust me, you're very much a kid."

I cross my arms and glare at him. I'm nearly ten years younger, but I don't want him calling me a kid. Not after the fantasies I had about him last night.

"For the record, calling me a prick is offensive."

"Geez, what bug crawled up your butt this morning?"

He takes a step back, clearly irritated, which I count as a win. The longer we talk, the easier it is for me to think and form coherent sentences. When he touches me to fix my form or demonstrate a move, my mind heads to the gutter, conjuring sexual fantasies that make me blush. As far as I'm concerned, the faster my hour of purgatory goes by, the better for us both.

"Look, I don't want to be here, and you obviously don't want me here." I attempt to reason with him. "How about we call it quits for the day?"

"Didn't figure you for a quitter."

"That's not..." Geez, this guy is annoying.

"I get you want to return to your desk and bad habits, but physical exercise is good for mind, body, and soul, but I'll make you a deal."

"Great, the grunt wants to make a deal." I blow out a puff of air, pushing a wayward strand of hair out of my eyes.

"If you can tell me what meathead, grunt, and jarhead mean, then we'll call it a day." Jeb pins me in place with the intensity of his stare. Once again, I'm incapable of rational thought.

"You're kidding?" I cross my arms, expecting a trap.

"Definition and origin. Do that, and you're free." The moment he breaks eye contact, I want it back. It doesn't make sense, but I want it back with a fierceness I can't explain.

"That's easy."

"Then, by all means…" He folds his arms over his chest, which only accentuates his broad, muscular chest and bulging biceps. The dude is built.

"They all refer to men."

"*Bzzz*. Wrong. Two more chances."

"That's not wrong."

"Darling, totally wrong. Try again."

"That's what they mean, although jarhead is specific to the military."

"*Bzzz*, wrong again."

"How is that wrong?"

"I said definition and origin. So far, you've given me nothing. Fail again, and we get to spend ninety minutes training."

"Wait a minute. You can't arbitrarily add time. I've got places to be." I swallow thickly because he can pretty much do anything he likes. No doubt, Mitzy will support him over me.

"Sweetie, you've got nowhere to be but with me. Last chance."

"I'm done playing this game." I gesture to the mats. "Let's just get through this."

"As you wish." He takes a step back and waits for me to follow him to the center of the mat.

We continue running through various striking patterns. Jeb watches critically and adjusts my technique with annoying frequency. I grit my teeth, determined not to complain. The sooner I prove I know this stupid stuff, the sooner we can be done.

"Wow, that was almost recognizable as Krav Maga." After one combo, Jeb claps slowly, an insufferable grin on his face. "At this rate, you might be ready for intermediate lessons by next year."

That's it. I'm done.

"You know what? This is bullshit." I whirl to jab a finger at his chest. "You're just on some macho power trip, getting off on bossing me around. You're bigger, stronger, and have spent the best years of your life in a gym. Bet you get your rocks off pushing women around, but I don't need to prove anything to you or take this crap from some meathead."

A storm of conflicting emotions rages within me. I'm attracted. I'm repulsed. But my rebellious heart sings a different tune. It yearns to surrender and submit to the raw, untamed power flowing off Jeb in waves.

"I'm just doing my job, teaching you to defend yourself." Jeb cocks his head as if trying to figure me out and peel back the layers to see inside of me. "Or is it that the sparks between us are flaring so bright, you're running scared?"

"Scared?" I give him a look. "There are no sparks, and I'm not running."

"You telegraph your emotions in your body language." He lifts his hands placatingly, but his eyes glimmer with humor. The man's too damn sexy. "It's mutual if that makes it easier."

"Easier?" Did he say what I think he said? I shake my head and choose anger over lust. "I don't need this, and I can handle myself just fine."

"That so?" Jeb looks pointedly at where I'm standing, nearly toe-to-toe with him, glaring up at his six-foot-plus frame. "Want to prove it?"

"Bring it on." My eyes narrow at the challenge in his smirk. He thinks I'll back down, but I won't. All I have to do is land a swift kick to his nuts to bring him down.

Piece of cake.

"You sure?" Jeb grins, cracking his neck from side to side. That cocky look is going to be his downfall.

I give him a shove, making him rock back a step.

His eyes flash with surprise, then with something far more dangerous. "All right, lesson's over. Let's see what you've got."

Before I can react, Jeb launches at me. I'm forced to duck as he hurtles past. Spinning to face him, I fall automatically into a defensive stance.

Jeb presses his advantage, raining down relentless blows that I barely block. There's nothing slow or careful about this onslaught. He's out for blood, a vicious grin on his face.

"Not so easy one-on-one, is it?" he taunts as I desperately evade another punishing strike.

Fury rises in me, hot and choking. I dart inside his swinging fist, aiming a sharp jab at his obliques that makes him huff out a breath.

If I can get my knee to his groin…

"See, not as weak as you thought." I dance on my toes, surprised I hit him at all.

We trade real blows now, all pretense of practice gone. I run purely on instinct, dodging and lashing out wildly. Jeb anticipates my every move until frustration burns in my muscles.

He knocks aside my strike and hits my shoulder hard enough to make me stumble. He sweeps my leg in a flash, sending me crashing to the mats.

The air leaves my lungs in a painful whoosh. Before I can suck in a breath, Jeb's weight settles over me, pinning me flat on my back. I struggle furiously, but it's useless.

"Get off of me." I buck and squirm but can't budge him.

"Imagine I'm not one of the good guys." He reaches between us, and I go berserk, bucking and thrashing as he slides a hand from my hip to my inner thigh. He doesn't push any boundaries, but holy hell, what a way to make a point. "If you're paying attention, you would note my arousal and the danger you would be in if this were real." He flashes a feral grin.

"Asshole."

"That's where you're wrong, sugar. I'm the good guy teaching you how to defend yourself from the asshole."

If he's the good guy teaching me how to defend myself, why is he as hard as a rock? Yeah, I can read that kind of body language. I'm also acutely aware of my body's response to him. How my sex clenches. How my brain turns to total mush. How simple self-preservation escapes me.

"Get off!" I squirm and shove and manage not to budge Jeb one damn inch.

He keeps his hand on my thigh the entire time, fingers curling inward. Not touching things he shouldn't, but he's making a point he could if he wanted to.

"With the proper training, you'll be able to stop me. Or any man who thinks he's got a right to take advantage of you because of his size. You're wasting all kinds of energy thrashing beneath me. Give me ten seconds, and I could strip you, violate you, and rut like a fucking pig."

"Get. Off. Of. Me!"

Jeb removes his hand, infuriating me further. "Then put in the work. Learn how to defend yourself. The next time a guy throws you to the ground with the intent to rape you, you'll have the skills and training to know exactly what to do. Do you give up yet? Want to admit you're wrong about needing training?"

"Go to hell!" I snarl at him, though we both know I'm beaten. He can do all of that and more to me if he chooses, and hell, if that's not exactly what I want.

"Don't be embarrassed, sweety. I feel the same. Although, you already know that." His face hovers inches above mine, blue eyes alight with victory. Full lips inches from mine. His hard length pressing against my leg. "What if I didn't stop? What if we weren't on the same side?"

Shit.

Being trapped beneath Jeb's muscular body kicks my pulse into overdrive. I'm hyper-aware of every hard plane of muscle pressed against me. My heart thunders deafeningly loud from exertion and something far more dangerous.

Carnal attraction.

Jeb's otherworldly hot. Like, stick a fork in me I'm done kind of hot. The kind of hot where the only thought in my head is surrendering to his raw, untamed power. Stroking his hard length. Sucking him off.

Being pinned beneath him, subject to his desire.

The thrill of the fight sings through my veins as our heaving chests press together. I become intensely conscious of how compromising our position is, with his hips slotted snugly between my thighs.

Jeb's grin falters, new heat brewing in his gaze as the sexual tension brewing between us intensifies. His Adam's apple bobs as he swallows, and his breath quickens against my lips.

He leans down as if to kiss me, but then he abruptly releases me and springs to his feet. He turns away, raking a hand through his hair. His other hand makes a quick adjustment of his pants.

I sit up slowly, still catching my breath.

"We're done here." He keeps his back to me. "Not bad for your first lesson, but you have much to learn." Jeb clears his throat, studiously not looking at me. "With regular practice, you might eventually get good enough to defend yourself."

I want to keep biting his head off, but the fight is drained out of me. He made his point. He's right, and I'm the one in the wrong.

"We're done?"

"Yes."

"I thought you said…"

"If we don't stop now, things won't end on the mat."

"What does that mean?"

"Don't play coy with me. It's beneath you. You know exactly what I mean."

"No, I don't." I stand and fold my arms over my chest in defiance.

"Don't lie to me."

"I'm not—"

The words die in my throat as his finger traces a slow, deliberate path along my jawline. His touch is featherlight, yet it sears my skin and ignites a fire within me that I've denied for too long.

I crave dominant men.

More than crave.

I want to deny it.

Push him away.

But there is no denying the truth resonating deep within me.

Jeb somehow reached past the strong independent woman I claim to be and found something else. Something that makes me feel alive. I hunger for something more than timid Betas and insipid Omegas.

I want the Alpha!

My body leans into him, betraying my turmoil.

"For today, we're done."

"But it hasn't been the full hour."

"I don't trust myself right now." He leans in and whispers, his lips brushing the gentle curve of my ear. "I'll see you tomorrow, same time."

Ridiculous giddiness explodes inside of me. Knowing he's at the edge of his control makes me feel wonderful. He wants me in the same way I want him.

"I should have a different instructor."

"No fucking way another man is going to touch you. You're stuck with me." He pins me with those eyes that make my stomach clench. "And Stitch?"

"Yes?"

"Don't be late. You'll earn a lap around the track for each minute you keep me waiting." He levels a stern look at me before leaving.

I sit brooding as his footsteps recede.

Sorry to see him go.

Guilty to cut short our practice.

How did a simple sparring match turn into—whatever the hell that was?

Turned-on doesn't begin to describe my current state. I've never been this sexually aroused by a man I just met. I'm not that kind of girl.

I'm so not that kind of girl in so many ways.

It's sad.

I don't date.

I don't have sex with strangers.

I've never been reduced to a bundle of need the way Jeb flipped all the switches in my head.

As I trudge to my quarters to shower off the grime and sweat from being pummeled and simultaneously aroused, my thoughts keep circling back to the fight. The thrill of matching my body against Jeb's raw strength was disturbingly addictive, even if he mopped the floor with me.

Okay, he's right about needing proper training.

I definitely can't let him know how turned on I was grappling and straining against him, our bodies tangled together. I'd never live down that shame.

Yet, doesn't he already know?

Shutting the door firmly on those dangerous thoughts, I turn the shower as cold as possible. Maybe I'll get lucky tomorrow, and Jeb will get hit by a truck before our lesson.

I can dream, at least.

Despite my irritation, a tiny flicker of anticipation burns in my core at the thought of clashing with him again. As much as I hate to admit it, I'm looking forward to round two.

Jeb's unexpected lesson has thrown me. Maybe I misjudged him? Beneath all the muscle and testosterone, a decent guy might be in there somewhere. There's no denying he wants me, but he also wants me to be able to protect myself. It seems to be important to him.

Shaking my head, I reserve judgment on that revelation, but as I drift off to sleep, a foreign emotion uncurls within me. A fragile tendril of needing something I don't have the words to express.

I crave something fierce. Something wild. Something... real.

And I have the sinking suspicion Jeb can give me all of that if I let him.

NINE

Stitch

—————

OVER THE NEXT SIX WEEKS, JEB RUNS ME THROUGH ENDLESS DRILLS, slowly expanding my repertoire of strikes, blocks, and dirty tricks that leverage physics and weak points over brute force. I can take him down—well, one time out of a hundred instead of never.

But hey, progress.

Where there's a distinct lack of progress is the steam heating the mats that first day. When I returned—on time—for day two, all the sexual energy between us went *poof!*

It's as if Jeb steeled himself against the chemistry bubbling between us and donned a professional mask. He locked it away while I struggled with whiplash, trying to figure out what happened and whether I imagined it.

As for sparring, I'm a quick study, but damn if his approval doesn't make me glow inside every time I execute a sequence flawlessly.

Our spats have lost their former viciousness of that first day on the mat, settling into friendly banter and good-natured ribbing instead. The change crept up gradually until, one day, I looked forward to my lessons with Jeb.

Today, at the end of my six weeks of required training, I watch the clock as our afternoon sparring practice approaches, eager to see what new skills he will teach me today.

Sadly, this will most likely be the last day I get to see him. Glancing at the clock, I count down the hours, minutes, and then seconds before I can leave.

"Someone's excited for training," Mitzy teases me as I run out of the room precisely as the clock hits five.

"It's not the worst way to spend an afternoon." I shrug, fighting to keep the smile off my face. But secretly, I relish matching wits and skills with Jeb. Trying to find some edge that will let me beat him.

It's never going to happen, of course. The man's a beast, hardened by years of specialized combat training. It still shocks me sometimes—the raw power contained in his muscular frame—but I'm learning to use my smaller size to my advantage, turning his momentum against him.

I'm also cheating and seeing someone on the side. It's my competitive streak getting the better of me. Not a guy. Not that kind of cheating. Not that Jeb and I are a couple where I could cheat on him.

I'm talking about another instructor, a female instructor.

I can't contain my excitement when I flip Jeb on his back. Damn, I'm getting good at this.

"Not bad." Jeb laughs breathlessly from the mats. "You're getting tricky."

His eyes shine with pride, and something warm uncurls inside me at his praise. Then I see it, the briefest flash of emotion in the stormy depths of his eyes.

Something that takes my breath away—desire and dominance.

My heart races and my legs turn to jelly, but before my knees buckle beneath me, he reclaims control and shuts me out. We share a charged moment of connection before Jeb clears his throat and gets to his feet, but his small smile lingers, making mine widen.

Today, the last day of Guardian HRS's mandatory self-defense training for new employees, I've progressed to blocking one strike in four and taking Jeb down once in ten tries on a good day. He says most recruits can't touch him for months, so I'm excelling beyond expectations.

Or maybe he's being nice?

I try not to let the praise go to my head, but a funny fluttery sensation arises whenever I impress him.

Almost like—a crush.

Do not go there. After that first day, he made it crystal clear nothing would ever happen between us, maintaining his professional distance like a champ. He's my instructor, nothing more, and I refuse to be that silly girl catching feelings for an unattainable man.

Been there, done that, no thanks.

Our last scheduled session falls on a Friday evening. Jeb runs me hard, pushing me to perfect a tricky throw-and-disarm combo. We're both drenched in sweat by the time he calls a stop, looking satisfied with my progress.

"Pizza on me tonight?" The way his voice comes out—a deep rumble of sound—makes my insides knot and twist.

A date? Is he asking me out?

"To celebrate completing your training?" He takes a step back.

Not a date.

Disappointment rushes through me, but I try to keep things light. If he's not interested in me, I'm not going to make things awkward with my little crush.

Crush?

As if.

Let's call it what it is—I have a full-on obsession with Jeb.

"You just want an excuse to stuff your face." I pretend to consider it. "But I could eat, I guess." That warm, fluttery feeling turns into a herd of butterflies dancing in my gut.

It's not a date. It's not a date. It's not a date.

But I wish it were.

We end up at Gino's, a cozy hole-in-the-wall pizzeria not far from Guardian headquarters. The scent of baking dough and melted cheese fills the air as we slide into a checkerboard booth by the window.

"Hope you're hungry. They load these pies with toppings here." Jeb picks up a menu.

"Please, I'm always hungry after you pin me to the mat over and over." The moment the words fly out of my mouth, heat burns my cheeks. I pray he doesn't read anything into it, but the way his pupils dilate and the low growl in the back of his throat say otherwise.

My heart plummets when he turns his attention back to the menu. I shouldn't be disappointed, but while my words inadvertently suggested something sexual, I wished for something more.

"Umm…" I scan the choices, my mouth watering. "I could probably devour a whole pizza myself."

"I'm sure you could." The warm rumble of his laughter makes me wonder if he's not thinking about something else—something I'm eager to try.

It's not like I haven't imagined what sex would be like with Jeb. I'm obsessed in an unhealthy kind of way, but he's made it clear things are to remain strictly professional between us.

I can respect that, even if I don't like it. Instead of sex, or devouring parts of his anatomy, I turn my attention to the menu, pretending to read while obsessing about giving him a blowjob.

Fuck.

He seems more at ease away from the training area, quick to smile and joke around. I find myself opening up between bites of hot, greasy pizza. Sharing things I've never told another soul.

"Tell me something about yourself." Jeb takes another bite of pizza, his eyes closing as he chews and swallows.

"What do you want to know?"

"Where did you grow up? Only child, or one of many?"

"My childhood was lonely, being shuffled between foster homes every few months. Never felt wanted anywhere."

"I'm sorry. I didn't know you were a foster kid." The look he gives is full of empathy. "That must've been hard."

"You have no idea. There was one family—the Jacobs. They seemed okay at first, but then Mr. Jacobs started drinking heavily and flying into violent rages." I shake my head at the memory. "He hit me one night when I broke a plate clearing dishes after dinner. I was removed from there quickly after that."

"I hate that you had to go through that." He reaches across the table to squeeze my hand.

And doesn't let go. His fingers linger on my skin, burning into my memory. For distraction, I bite a piece of pizza and chew.

"After that, I started acting out. Shoplifting, vandalism, joyriding in stolen cars. I was so desperate for attention, for someone to notice me."

"It makes sense, given what you were dealing with." He strokes his thumb over my knuckles soothingly.

"My only constants were my online friends," I say with a sad smile. "Other hackers and gamers like me. We understood each other. For once, I felt like I belonged, even if it was just online. And when I got shuffled from one foster home to the next, they came with me and were always there in our virtual world. It's hard to make friends as a foster kid, especially when you're dumped into one foster home after the next."

"Having that support must've meant everything growing up. I'm glad you had that refuge." Jeb relinquishes my hand, but not before giving a little squeeze.

I nod, tears pricking my eyes as I dredge up painful memories I've buried for so long. Sitting here with Jeb, it all comes flooding out in a healing rush.

"I got so good at pretending I belonged while feeling totally alone, you know? Invisible." I trace patterns in the condensation on my glass.

"Is that where you learned your impressive hacking abilities?" Jeb asks. "From your online friends?"

"Yeah, we all taught each other. We shared tips and challenged each other." A nostalgic smile fills my face. "I spent most of my teens at a group home. Which sounds bad, but saved me."

"How so?"

"They had computers. Not many of the foster homes I lived in did, and if they did, they wouldn't let me on them."

"Ah."

"Yeah, I'd stay up late on chat forums, working on coding together. The rush of breaking through a new security system or spoofing an IP address…" I trail off, lost in the memories.

It was such a thrill back then. The sense of rebellion and belonging, all mixed together, filled the void the foster system could never touch.

Jeb smiles. "Your skills are self-taught and come from mentoring each other?"

"Yeah."

"That's cool. No wonder you're so good at it."

I chuckle. "Well, I've picked up a few more tricks over the years, but yeah, that crew set me on this path early on. I owe them a lot, but enough about me." I wipe my eyes, surprised to find them damp with tears. "What made you join the Navy and push yourself through SEAL training? That couldn't have been easy."

Jeb takes a sip of beer, gathering his thoughts. "I joined up right after high school. I needed direction and purpose. The Navy gave me discipline, purpose, and commitment. And I liked the camaraderie plus the physical challenge."

"I've heard it's hard to become a SEAL."

He pauses, looking into the distance. "SEAL training was—is hell. Pure hell. They break you down to build you back up. The cold, the lack of sleep, the constant physical torment… I've never wanted to quit as hard as I did back then, but I promised myself I wouldn't quit."

"I can't even imagine." I shake my head in amazement.

"There was this one time," Jeb continues. "We were in the freezing surf for hours on end. I was hypothermic, swallowing salt water, sure I would pass out." He meets my eyes. "But I wouldn't quit. Couldn't quit. That's what being a SEAL is about—persevering past what you think is possible. It shaped me in important ways. Taught me how strong I am, deep down inside."

I shake my head in disbelief at some of the brutal training rituals he describes from his time as a SEAL. "Do they *really* make you swim for miles in freezing ocean waves, weighted down with gear?"

Jeb nods, grinning. "Part of earning your trident. The bonds you forge with the other guys getting through hellish stuff like that are unbreakable."

"But you're not in the Navy now. How did you join up with the Guardians?"

His entire expression darkens. It looks as if he's going to say something but changes his mind at the last moment. He takes a bite of pizza and leans back. When he does speak, I'm certain he decided not to tell me whatever first came across his mind.

"I wanted to keep saving innocents, making a difference, you know? But on my terms." He takes a swig of beer. "Guardian HRS lets me use my skills for good, not just country."

"So, now you get to train charity cases like me?" I consider his words as I nibble a crust. "Trying to save my soul or something?" I aim for a joking tone to hide my genuine curiosity.

"You were never a charity case in my eyes." Jeb looks surprised, then shakes his head firmly. His eyes crinkle at the corners when he smiles. "I meant what I said about recognizing your skills and potential."

I glance down, pleasure warming my chest at the sincerity in his voice.

"And getting to know you these past few weeks, seeing how dedicated you are to improving…" He ducks his head to meet my eyes. "You already have more heart and inner strength than most. You don't need anyone to *save* you." His words hit me square in the chest, kindling emotions better left alone. I fiddle with my crumpled napkin, throat tightening.

"Didn't take you for such a smooth talker," I finally manage to tease. "Might want to save lines like that for the ladies."

"It's nothing but the truth." Jeb chuckles, bumping my shoulder affectionately. "Face it, you're not as prickly and standoffish as you pretend to be." His eyes dance with mirth. "There's a marshmallow center in there somewhere."

I roll my eyes dramatically at the jab. But secretly, I bask in the warmth of his praise. That this man, whom I respect above most others, can see value in me means more than I'm willing to admit.

Not just in my skills—but in my character—it's a novelty I'm still struggling to accept.

"I do have a question for you," he says.

"Fire away."

"What possessed you to hack into the NSA's computer systems? I mean, there's rebellion, and then there's *rebellion*."

"Yeah, hacking the NSA was definitely stepping it up a notch." I laugh sheepishly at his question. "Even Mitzy thought I was nuts." I tilt my head, thinking back to that three A.M. adrenaline rush. "Honestly? I just wanted to see if I could do it. Kind of a personal challenge, I guess."

Malfor dared me. Challenged me in front of everyone in our group chat. I *had* to take the challenge. There was no refusal. Not if I didn't want to be shunned.

"You're telling me," Jeb raises an eyebrow, "you risked *federal prison* for the thrill of it?"

"Pretty much," I admit with a smirk. "I didn't do anything malicious like planting viruses or stealing data. I was just kind of—poking around. Testing my skills against their security protocols."

I lean back against the vinyl booth.

"Obviously, I got cocky and wasn't as careful as I should've been covering my tracks, but yeah, just a challenge to myself that I took too far." I leave out any mention of Malfor. The stuff he wanted was useless junk. It wasn't about the information. It was about the challenge of breaking the NSA's encryption.

"Well, you've got guts. I'll give you that." Jeb shakes his head, looking torn between amusement and concern. "And one hell of a rebellious streak." His expression turns serious. "But I hope you realize if you'd been caught, you could be in a very different place right now. Facing serious jail time, labeled a criminal."

"But I did get caught." I laugh sheepishly at Jeb's question. "I thought you knew?"

"I didn't. Just knew you were new to Guardian HRS, going through mandatory training." Jeb looks surprised. "So you got caught? What happened? There must have been a trial. Sentencing? How the hell did you wind up with the Guardians?"

"NSA cybersecurity eventually traced the intrusion back to me. I was arrested and charged with unauthorized access to a federal computer system. At twenty-one, I became a national security threat and was branded a terrorist. I faced twenty to life at my sentencing hearing."

"I bet. That's… Damn, Stitch, you've got balls doing that. What did you hack? Codes to nukes?"

"Nothing that bad."

"Then what?"

"I hacked into their accounting department."

"Accounting? You hack into the NSA and decide accounting is where you want to go poking around?" He gives me the eye, but I return a flat stare.

"It was a dare." All I can do is shrug.

At the time, I thought nothing of it. Malfor handed out the challenges. All I did was play the damn game, gaining prestige one hack at a time.

It sounds silly now, risking as much as I did to hack into such banal areas of the NSA, but it wasn't about terrorism. That's not what we were about.

It was a game to us.

"You risked prison for a dare?"

"What can I say."

"What happened when you were caught?"

"Other than watching all my friends disappear into the woodwork? I have to say, that was a sobering moment for me. Finding out all my so-called friends did nothing to help me was illuminating." I absently shred a napkin as I answer Jeb's question. "I was terrified. The day I was supposed to be sentenced, Mitzy showed up. She gave me a choice—prison or join Guardian HRS and use my skills to help people. It was a no-brainer."

"You were already in custody when she recruited you?" Jeb nods thoughtfully.

"Yep. I owe her big time." My comment is more honest than I'm comfortable admitting. "If it weren't for her, I'd be in an orange jumpsuit making license plates right now."

Jeb smiles. "Well, I'm glad she saw your potential and stepped in. And that you got a second chance to chart a new course."

"Me too." I return his smile gratefully. "I won't waste it, I promise."

After we finish eating, Jeb insists on paying despite my protests.

It's not a date.

But I wish it were.

"My treat," he says firmly. "Consider it a graduation dinner for getting through training."

We step outside into the cool night air. I zip my jacket against the chill, suddenly reluctant for our evening to end. I'm very well aware that Guardians and Techies rarely mingle outside of work.

This could be the last time I get to hang out with him.

During the drive back to Guardian HQ, I stare out the window, thinking of something to say to prolong our time together. My mind goes blank, and I'm hyper-aware of Jeb's presence beside me in the darkened cab. His clean, woodsy scent mingles with traces of pizza and beer to create a potent aphrodisiac.

I don't want this night to end.

Jeb pulls up outside my quarters at Guardian HQ and puts the truck in park. The radio plays softly in the background, and an awkward silence descends when neither of us makes a move to exit. He turns to me with a gentle smile.

"For what it's worth, I enjoyed these past few weeks." He chuckles. "You kept me on my toes, that's for sure."

"Yeah, it was—fun." I resist the urge to smack myself for the ineloquent response.

"I'll, uh…" He clears his throat. "I'll walk you to your door."

We climb out and amble across the parking lot. Out of the corner of my eye, I watch Jeb's profile and admire the strong line of his jaw. The way his T-shirt pulls across his muscular shoulders makes me curious about what he looks like under that poor shirt.

Too quickly, we reach the door to my barracks. We turn to face each other, both shifting on our feet uncertainly.

"So…" Jeb rubs the back of his neck, looking like he wants to say something but can't find the words.

"So…" I nibble my bottom lip, debating whether I should invite him in, but the nervous flutter in my stomach holds me back.

"Don't be a stranger around the office, okay?" Jeb's gaze holds mine, his expression suddenly difficult to read. He brushes a strand of hair from my face, and his fingers trail lightly down my cheek. Then, he steps closer, his eyes warm and longing.

My breath hitches at the contact. Before I lose my nerve, I lift on tiptoe and kiss his cheek softly.

"Thank you for everything," I whisper.

Jeb looks surprised, then smiles. "My pleasure. I meant what I said about you being a quick study." His thumb grazes my jaw tenderly. "Sweet dreams."

With obvious reluctance, he steps back. I watch wistfully as he walks away, broad shoulders disappearing into the night.

Alone in my room, I shake off the melancholy threatening to sink in.

This is good, I remind myself fiercely. Jeb was doing his job training me, not looking for a fuck-buddy. Now, things can go back to normal.

But as I drift off that night, I can't ignore the hollow ache settling into my chest. An ache that whispers I'll miss our time together more than I want to admit.

TEN

Jeb

THE NEXT DAY, AS SOON AS I ENTER THE CHARLIE TEAM BULLPEN, I'm greeted by a chorus of ribbing, laughter, and crude jokes. The guys are in rare form, gearing up for a joint training op with Mitzy's robot dogs we affectionately call Rufi. Banter and insults fly as they prep weapons and load packs.

All I can think about is Stitch. For the thousandth time, I kick myself for not pursuing her further. Six weeks of excruciating hell. That's what training felt like. Six long weeks of intense physical contact, countless hard-ons, and more cold showers than I've had in a lifetime sum up my frustration.

I should've made a move last night. Should've pulled her into my arms and kissed her the way she needs to be kissed. I should've held her the way she needs to be held.

I fucked up and missed my chance.

"Well, look who finally decided to show his ugly mug. How was your hot date with Stitch last night?" Gabe grins, waggling his eyebrows suggestively. "Did ya get lucky after your little celebration dinner that totally *wasn't* a date?"

"It wasn't a date, jackass." I flip him off good-naturedly, heading to my cage. "Just two co-workers wrapping up six weeks of intense training over pizza and beer. Nothing romantic about it."

"Riiight," drawls Walt, elbowing me in the ribs. "Intimate dinner alone with that sexy thing? I'm sure you were completely focused on work stuff. A bit young for you, though?"

"Give it a rest, animals." I grab my rifle to clean and inspect it. "I was just being nice since she doesn't know anyone here yet."

"So her being smokin' hot has nothing to do with it?" Blake smirks. "You need to ride that fine young thing before someone snatches her up and you regret all your professional bullshit."

The guys know all about how I cooled things down with Stitch. Officially obsessed, I had to do something, or I would've crossed too many lines.

"She's been through a lot and is just starting to find her footing." I snort, checking my scope settings. "A fling is the last thing she needs right now."

"Aww, leave him alone." Hank chuckles, elbowing Blake in the ribs. "Jeb's allowed to get a little action for his hard work babysitting the newbie." He twists a towel and snaps it at my ass.

I dodge out of the way—barely.

"Robbing the cradle with that one." Walt can't help but snicker.

"Get your mind out of the gutter." I toss a sock at his head, which he easily dodges. I shake my head, chuckling despite myself. I forgot how relentless these guys can be. "It's not like that. Stitch is…" I search for the word. "She's trying to get her life on track. She doesn't need me complicating things."

"But you like her," Walt states matter-of-factly. "I've seen how you look at her when you think no one's watching. And the fact you haven't fucked her says volumes."

"Volumes?" I give Walt a flat stare. "What the fuck does that mean?"

"You know exactly what I mean." Walt doesn't elaborate, but there's no need.

I know exactly what he means. Stitch is special.

I hesitate, grabbing a rag to wipe down my gear. Do I like Stitch as more than a trainee? The question kept me up most nights. She's definitely on my mind.

There's no denying I find her attractive. Intense blue eyes, jet-black hair framing a heart-shaped face, and curves that even over-sized workout clothes can't hide.

But it's more than her physical appeal. Her wit, her tenacity in training, and seeing glimpses of her vulnerability beneath her prickly facade stirs something within me I thought I lost when Sarah died.

"Earth to Jeb." Hank's voice shakes me from my thoughts. "Man's got it bad if he's zoning out this hard."

I flip him the bird. "Can we talk about something else? Preferably something useful, like this training op?"

The guys exchange knowing looks but let it drop. For now, we turn our focus to prepping gear and strategizing for the exercise.

Ethan appraises me thoughtfully, blue eyes piercing beneath his buzzed blond hair. "No judgment, brother, but you're sweet on her, whether you admit it or not."

His insights are tough to shrug off, even if he's newer to the Guardians. I consider his statement as I strap on my vest and holster my sidearm.

Gabe claps me on the back, handing me an energy bar. "Nothing wrong with catching some feels for a girl. She may be younger, but you're both consenting adults. Quit playing coy and ask her out before it's too late."

I mull over his advice. He's right that age shouldn't matter as long as we're both willing and unattached, but I'm nine years her senior, the grizzly veteran she sees as her instructor. Not a guy she wants to date.

"Saddle up, gentlemen. Kill the gossip." Ethan's gravelly baritone jars us into readiness. "Time to play with Mitzy's toys."

The training complex has been transformed into a mock urban site—concrete buildings, burnt-out cars, and debris strewn everywhere to mimic a war-torn cityscape. Derelict buildings loom, and rusting hulks of cars litter the streets. Our boots thud dully on the dirt. The only other sounds are the hum of the robots trailing us and occasional terse commands over comms.

We take up tactical positions at the edge of a building. One of Mitzy's Rufi awaits my command, its glossy black alloy body poised to strike. No fur or tail wagging for these ruthless beasts built for combat.

"Use them to flank and confuse the enemy. Let's see what these tin cans can do." Ethan directs our movements, putting his team and the Rufi to the test. "Hank, take point."

Hank moves up, his Rufi's scope cam feeding him intel. Mine tucks into a heel, moving beside me while feeding me imaging from its scope cam. I particularly like how they can peek around corners. Adrenaline surges as we approach the first concrete structure. I take a position at the door, ready to direct my Rufi into the breach.

The door buckles under Ethan's forceful kick, swinging open. We surge through the breach, our boots pounding against the floor. The Rufi move with us, silent as death.

Our weapons sweep right and left, up and down, as we clear room to room, shooting hostile decoy targets while avoiding civilian ones.

The Rufi's agile frames allow maneuvers no human can match. Their speed lets us eliminate targets brutally fast. I direct my Rufi, leveraging its sensors to boost my situational awareness tenfold. My technical skills rapidly process the visual data, weaponizing it into actionable intel.

I move to the front, peeking around a corner using my scope camera. "Multiple targets ahead," I report quietly. We advance, executing the bogeys flawlessly.

Blake and his Rufi climb to a sniper's perch, providing eagle-eyed overwatch. His shots snap out, guided by the Rufi's intel. Gabe and his Rufi flow through rooms in sync, his brute strength and its speed clearing threats with creative fury.

Two hours in, we're a seamless machine. Our instincts, fused with the Rufi's sensors, combine in violent harmony. We flow through the buildings, bodies low, weapons up, hyper-aware. The Rufi peel off, flanking hostiles, herding them into our lines of fire.

Sweat drips as I scan for our next threat. A Rufi's eyes flash red —enemy ahead. We press forward to clear the last room. Rounds snap from rifles, and empty shells clatter to the floor.

Finally, Ethan signals that the mission is complete.

As we exit the training ground, I glimpse Stitch observing intently from the observation deck far above. Our eyes briefly meet before she turns back to her screens. Her brow furrows, deep in concentration, as she monitors our op with the rest of Mitzy's tech team. Other than the briefest flicker of acknowledgment, she ignores me.

If it's not the age gap keeping us apart, the divide between Techie and Guardian will keep us separate. The mere glimpse of her makes my pulse inexplicably quicken.

As much as I want to pick up where we left off, pursuing a more intimate relationship could jeopardize the tentative footing she's gained. Right now, she needs friendships within her crew, not romantic complications with me.

Still, the urge to catch her eye again tugs at me. To offer an encouraging nod or gesture conveying I'm glad to see her settling in but wish we could spend more time together.

With effort, I wrench my focus back to the task at hand. Our time together, brief as it was, sparked something worth nurturing. If Stitch is willing, I'll stoke that fledgling flame between us into something real.

While we wait for the debrief, Walt sidles up next to me. "Seriously though, Stitch seems special. I haven't seen you light up talking about someone like you do about her in a long time." He bumps my shoulder. "Maybe it's time to put yourself out there again, brother. Not a one-night fling, but something more?"

I chew my lip thoughtfully, pondering his words. Something about that girl worked its way under my skin in the best possible way. The prospect of exploring it is equal parts exciting and scary.

Walt has a point. I've kept romantic prospects at a distance after losing Sarah. Focusing on my son, my career, and the team above anything else.

Above anyone else.

Something about Stitch's wit, her tenacity, and seeing glimpses of vulnerability beneath the prickly facade makes me feel alive in ways I've forgotten.

As we debrief, slapping each other on the back and comparing hit counts, my thoughts drift to Stitch. Is she settling in okay? Making friends? She seemed so lonely during our talk over dinner. Almost wistful when our time ended.

"Head still in the clouds over the new girl?" Gabe snaps his fingers in my face. "Bet you nerds had fun talking code and debating algorithms."

"Give it a rest already." I shove him.

"Don't tell me rolling around wrestling and grappling all day didn't get your motor running."

"It was strictly professional." I shoot him an exasperated look. "I trained her no differently than any other trainee."

His words plant an uneasy seed. The vultures in this place will be circling Stitch before long. She's brilliant, beautiful, and soon to play a vital role in our missions. Her smile and defiant blue eyes linger in my mind.

Maybe I should ask if she wants to grab dinner again.

No pressure, just friendly co-workers getting to know each other better.

I smile to myself as I stow my equipment. For now, I'll play it cool when the guys are around, but there's no denying a certain fiery recruit has gotten under my skin.

Weeks later, thoughts of her still creep in when I least expect it. During mission prep, waiting in line for coffee, driving home after a long day—her sly grin and defiant blue eyes appear in my mind's eye, making me smile.

I spend my nights lying awake, wondering if I should have been bolder. Picked up where our charged farewell left off and asked her out properly, but it's been a long time since I considered dating—anyone.

After Sarah's death, my priority is raising Maverick. My heart is too shattered to allow anyone else inside, but Stitch feels different from the random flings and one-night stands littering the dark days after Sarah's death.

But here's the real kicker.

If things progress into a real relationship, how will it impact Maverick? He's too young to understand Daddy moving on from Mommy if I bring a new woman home.

I can't risk hurting him and causing confusion unless I'm certain Stitch will be more than a one-night fling. While she feels special, the girl comes with major baggage. She's a felon. A convicted cyber-crimes terrorist.

What if I inflated our connection? Using my loneliness to manufacture something that was never there to begin with?

I may not have made a move since her training ended, but she hasn't sought me out either. She's probably happy to move on, eager to establish herself with the tech team.

But what if letting her go was a mistake? A missed chance at something meaningful?

The thought nags me late at night.

ELEVEN

Stitch
_____

THE NEXT FEW WEEKS PASS IN A BLUR. THE RETURN TO MY REGULAR technical work leaves little time to dwell on anything outside of staring at computer screens. If I burrow into coding complex algorithms until my eyes blur, it keeps my mind from straying where it shouldn't.

Namely to musings about a certain infuriating, arrogant, and altogether distracting Guardian who seems determined to occupy my thoughts no matter how hard I try to forget him.

But despite my best efforts, it's still a shock to the system the first time I run into Jeb after so long apart. Walking down a hallway, head buried in a tablet, I run into a solid wall of muscle.

I yelp, and my tablet clatters to the floor. Strong hands grasp my shoulders, steadying me before I topple over. My heartbeat skyrockets as the familiar woodsy scent of Jeb envelopes me.

"Whoa there." Jeb's amused voice rumbles close to my ear.

My head jerks up, my throat seizing when I realize it's him. His hands remain on me, a searing heat against my skin.

"Sorry. I didn't see you." My tongue feels clumsy and inarticulate.

"No harm done." Jeb smiles crookedly but makes no move to

step back. His striking blue eyes pin me in place. "Getting distracted walking these days? I seem to remember lectures about staying alert to your surroundings."

I roll my eyes, grateful for the familiar banter. "Yeah, yeah, lesson learned." I expect Jeb to laugh, to make some witty retort, but his expression remains serious, almost—wistful.

"It's good to see you. How've you been? Settling in?"

"Busy." I fidget under his probing look. "Coding new breaching programs for Mitzy. Working on swarm intelligence for her bumblebees. Riveting stuff."

Why does this feel so awkward? Get it together.

"That's great. You're incredible at what you do." Jeb seems to hesitate. "So listen, a group of us are going out tomorrow night. You should come." He rushes on before I can reply. "Low key, just food and drinks." When I don't immediately answer, uncertainty flashes across his face. "But no pressure if you'd rather not."

"No, that sounds nice." I offer him a small smile, hoping it conveys how much I miss our easy rapport. "I'd like that."

"Great." Jeb's answering grin is like sunlight bursting through the clouds. "I'll swing by and grab you at eight?"

He squeezes my shoulder, then continues down the hall, whistling off-key. I stare after him, emotions tangled in my throat. I miss that ridiculous man.

But he didn't ask me out on a date. It's a group thing. Inherently safe. What's wrong with me that he doesn't want to ask me out for real?

From the frantic pitter-patter of my heart, my plan to forget my inconvenient obsession with one particular and stunning Guardian is in shambles. I miss spending that hour a day in close, physical contact with him more than I should.

Later that evening, I fuss endlessly over my outfit before forcing myself to take a chill pill. It's just co-workers getting drinks.

Not a date.

At exactly eight o'clock, a knock on my door finds me taking one last steadying breath. When I open the door, Jeb looks unfairly attractive in dark jeans and a button-down. His face lights up when he sees me.

"Ready to go?" He offers his arm with an exaggerated flourish. "Milady."

I snort out a laugh, looping my hand through the crook of his elbow. "Such a gentleman." But secretly, the old-fashioned gesture makes me melt a little inside.

We chat casually on the way to the bar, but my nerves jangle loudly with every brush of his fingers over mine. *Get it together, Stitch. Just friends catching up after a long absence.*

When he glances down at me with that infectious grin, I can't deny how right it feels to be with him like this. How much I want this easy companionship between us to continue.

The bar is packed and noisy when we arrive. Co-workers, for him, mean very large, muscular Guardians milling around tables laden with drinks and food. It's a bit overwhelming.

"They don't bite." Jeb leans down to whisper in my ear.

The heat of his breath against my skin sends a riot of sensations shooting through my body—a prickle of heat that flushes my skin, followed by a swarm of tingling butterflies in my stomach.

I suppress a shiver at his closeness, acutely aware of the hard planes of muscle beneath his shirt as he guides me through the crowd with a gentle hand at my back. He smells of spice and sandalwood with an undertone of seduction.

The testosterone is palpable as we weave between packed tables of off-duty Guardians shouting greetings to Jeb over the din. I feel their assessing eyes rake over me—the outsider.

A fox in a den of hounds.

But Jeb's solid presence at my side is reassuring. His casual arm thrown across my shoulders stirs that now-familiar warmth in my core. I can't prevent a small smile at his protective gesture.

"Everyone, meet Stitch," Jeb announces loudly. "Stitch, meet everyone."

He gestures to each man in turn. "This unruly bunch is known as Charlie team."

I know every member of each Guardian team, but keep silent, realizing he's excited to introduce me to his teammates.

"That's our fearless leader, Ethan Blackwood. He's new to Guardian HRS." Jeb indicates a man who gives me a polite nod. "Next to him is Hank."

Hank raises his glass in greeting, gray eyes glinting with humor.

"Walt is our medic." The bearded man elbows Hank with a chuckle. They whisper something under their breaths, and from how they both look at me, whatever was said is about me. "That's Blake." A dark-haired man tips his hat to me with a roguish wink.

"Of course, there's me." Jeb thumps his chest. "Sexiest bastard on the team." His friends boo loudly as he laughs. "And bringing up the rear is Gabe, Charlie-Six." A muscular, tattooed man sketches me a mock salute.

"Nice to meet you, Stitch." Gabe's the only one to greet me by name, but all the others welcome me to the table, scooting closer to make room for me and Jeb.

The guys immediately start in with good-natured teasing after Jeb introduces me.

"You two sure looked cozy walking in just now," Hank jokes, elbowing Jeb in the ribs. "So when's the wedding?"

Jeb shakes his head, chuckling as he scoots closer to me, close enough that our thighs brush. The contact sends licks of heat shooting through me.

Is he just being friendly, or could he want something more? My skin tingles every time his arm grazes mine, reaching for his beer or grabbing a fistful of bar nuts. I'm hyperaware of his solid warmth beside me in the noisy din of the crowded bar. My nerves sing, desperately hoping this might be a date but fearing I'm inflating it in my mind.

A perky waitress appears, snapping her gum. "What can I get y'all?" Jeb orders two beers as she bats her eyelashes at him. "Excellent choice, hon."

She's there and gone before I have a chance to correct his order. As she sashays off, I shift uncomfortably. She seems a little too friendly with Jeb.

"Beer?" Once she's gone, I make a sound of disgust and glare at Jeb. "Are you trying to poison me?"

"Not a fan?" He places his hand on my thigh, sending delicious sparks shooting along my nervous system.

"I hate beer." Leaning back, I pretend not to notice his hand on my thigh.

"How can anyone hate beer?" Jeb looks offended. "It's the nectar of the gods."

"More like piss water. It's bitter and blech." I scrunch my nose in disgust.

"Blasphemy! A good pint is a thing of beauty." Jeb shakes his head in dismay.

"Or a thing that tastes like moldy bread soaked in dirty dishwater," I shoot back.

When the waitress returns with the beer, she leans close to place Jeb's on the table, giving him an eyeful of cleavage. "Here you go, sweetie. Enjoy."

I bristle as she blatantly flirts with him. Jeb smiles politely but does nothing to stop her. If anything, he eggs her on with a wink.

"It's an acquired taste," Jeb continues his argument with me.

"More like sewer water. I'd rather lick the floor than drink that swill." I eye the beer with revulsion, pushing it away like a petulant child.

Jeb and the waitress exchange surprised looks.

"Fine." Jeb glances at the waitress. "Can we get a cranberry vodka for my beer-hating friend?"

"Sure thing, hon." The waitress whisks away the rejected beer, giving me a curious side-eye.

His teammates watch the entire interaction with amusement.

I bristle every time the flirtatious waitress makes eyes at Jeb, leaning close to give him an eyeful of her ample cleavage whenever she comes by. She's shameless in her attempts to snag his attention, but he appears oblivious, caught up in our playful banter.

I want to stab her in the eye with a fork but restrain myself. The alcohol buzzing through me only amplifies my irritation, though.

Doesn't Jeb realize how inappropriate she's being? I'm still unsure if this is meant to be a real date between us or just friendly co-worker drinks. His tolerance for her behavior makes me question if he's truly interested in me.

My aggravation must show on my face because Hank calls out, "Uh oh, looks like Stitch wants to take out the waitress. She's getting feisty."

Jeb glances at me in surprise, taking in my evident annoyance. I avoid his eyes, sipping my drink sullenly.

"Everything okay?" Jeb asks, leaning in with concern etched on his handsome face. His woodsy scent envelops me, momentarily distracting me from my irritation.

"Just peachy." I shrug off his hand on my shoulder. His touch is like fire, sparking conflicting emotions.

Jeb frowns, picking up on the tension, but it's clear he doesn't understand why I might be upset. He opens his mouth to respond when the waitress reappears, derailing the moment.

"Need anything else, sugar?" She beams at Jeb, blatantly angling for his attention again.

Before I explode, Jeb intervenes. "I think we're all set for the moment." He glances around the table. "Anyone need a drink?"

The guys rattle off their orders while I continue to sip my drink, trying my best not to appear sullen.

The waitress huffs off with the drink orders, clearly irritated by Jeb's brush-off. Maybe she finally got the message? I relax slightly now that she's gone, but residual annoyance lingers within me.

This begs the question of why.

What do I care if he flirts with the waitress? We're not a couple, but if this night is going to amount to anything, we need to talk.

Gabe calls out across the table. "Make sure Jeb behaves himself tonight, Stitch. He may act like a gentleman, but he's got a wicked wild streak and loves the ladies. He's a heartbreaker."

At that, Jeb throws a wadded-up napkin at him. "Watch yourself, buddy. I know where you sleep." But he winks at me, letting me know it's all in fun.

Jeb takes a swig of beer and fires a murderous look toward

Gabe. Meanwhile, his hand finds my knee under the table, giving a playful squeeze that thrills and confuses me.

"I think I can handle him." I smirk at Blake's wink, but inside, my thoughts whirl.

As the drinks flow, the insults and comments fly.

Walt eyes me over the rim of his glass. "Jeb sure knows how to pick 'em. They keep getting younger and prettier." He tips his glass in a mock salute, leaving me flustered and struggling to come up with some witty comeback.

"Watch it." Jeb points a warning finger at him, but his thigh presses closer to mine under the table.

I'm lost, unable to interpret his mixed signals. Is this just friendly affection or something more? It's casual and friendly when he wraps an arm around my shoulders—more like a brotherly hug than something else.

The contact, innocent yet intimate, sends warmth spreading through me. I shouldn't read into it, but I crave his subtle caresses, even as I question their meaning.

Despite their ribbing, Jeb stays relaxed and good-humored, letting their jokes roll off his back, but with each of his subtle touches, he leaves me increasingly muddled. I don't know where we stand. Except, with him at my side, his friends' rowdy approval feels more welcoming than intimidating.

One thing's clear: this motley crew treats each other like family. At least a family that genuinely loves one another. As for me, I scold the flutter in my stomach when his hand brushes mine. Honestly, I'm as skittish as a schoolgirl with her first crush.

Pathetic.

As the night continues, the atmosphere is lighthearted, the exact unwinding I need. Next to me, Jeb joins the lively debates with enthusiasm. His leg presses cozily against mine beneath the table. Neither of us shifts away, letting our knees rest together as conversation swirls around us. The contact sends tingles up my leg that I try desperately to ignore.

When Jeb grins at me, blue eyes bright with laughter, I can't fight an answering smile. I know the hope shining through has to be obvious, but for once, I'm powerless to hide it.

Tonight has opened my eyes to what life could be if I can only gather the courage to act. A future where I never again have to feel like an outsider peering in, hungry for connection. For once, I'm no longer afraid to reach for more.

Jeb insists on driving me home from the bar. Back at the barracks, my temporary home, I step out of his truck into the cool night air. The breeze helps clear my buzzing head, and as we walk from the parking lot, the backs of our hands brush lightly, sending sparks up my arm.

He doesn't take my hand, but we walk close, shoulders bumping. Neither of us speaks as we approach my building.

At my door, we linger uncertainly. The energy between us charged with nervous anticipation. He moves closer, his tall frame crowding me against the door. His eyes drop to my lips, burning with undisguised hunger.

My heart stutters.

Is he going to kiss me?

TWELVE

Stitch

———

BEFORE IT HAPPENS—JUST LIKE LAST TIME—I ACT ON IMPULSE. Rising up on tiptoe, I press a featherlight kiss to his stubbled cheek. As I pull away, I scold myself for the silly peck.

He makes a rough sound low in his throat as I pull away, but then he snakes his arm around my waist, yanking me hard against his chest.

"Not so fast, girl." The way he says *girl,* in a voice dripping with sex, brings goosebumps to my skin. His mouth descends, claiming my lips in a blistering kiss that steals my breath.

At first, I freeze, stunned by the rawness of his passion, but as his mouth claims mine, his lips moving over mine, I melt into his embrace. My hands creep up to grip his muscular shoulders, nails digging in reflexively. A ridiculous giddiness fills me, making me want to run to my bestie and scream *Jeb kissed me!*

But I have no bestie.

I draw a sharp breath as his mouth moves from my lips to nibble at my earlobe. My head rolls to the side, exposing my neck to grant him more access. Access he takes and makes his own. He nips down my neck, making me shudder at the sensations flooding my body.

Ripples of desire rush through me, transforming the timid

butterflies in my stomach into a herd of hippos happily hopping up and down. Each bounce, a blissful beat that sends shivers of sheer joy shimmying through my veins.

I loop my arms around his neck to steady myself while he curls an arm around my waist, pulling me close and obliterating the space between us.

His nips and licks end when he takes my mouth again. Instantly, he claims me. There is no other way to describe what happens or the way I whimper in his arms.

He tastes of beer and spice. Our tongues tangle hotly, sending fire racing through my veins. I've never been kissed like this—forceful yet sensual, urgent yet unhurried, wild yet wonderfully tender.

The man is talented. I give him that. He slips his tongue where he wills, with skill, with possession, with dominance, coaxing me to come out of my shell and meet his passion with my desire for more.

I do my best, but I don't know how to kiss the way he does.

I'll say this. He kisses with the same confidence he displays in all things, demanding and taking charge. I melt into him, and he takes my reaction as encouragement and deepens the kiss, tongue sweeping along the seam of my lips in blatant demand. I gasp, and he takes advantage, his tongue surging in to mate with mine.

It's not just his tongue, either. His lips set a tempo, stealing my breath and sending sensations that buzz and surge down to lower parts of my anatomy. My lady parts tingle and are on fire simultaneously.

Oh. My. God. If this is the way he kisses, what will it feel like when he puts his lips and tongue to use *down there?*

The kiss turns carnal, his unyielding frame pinning me to the wall as our mouths tangle hotly. My head spins as he kisses me ravenously, like a starving man. And I'm just as desperate, intoxicated by his dominance after wanting him for so long.

My hands twine around his thick neck, trying to eliminate any space between us. I want to crawl inside him, fuse our bodies into one, and feel him everywhere.

His large hands grasp my hips, fingers digging into the curve of my backside as he effortlessly lifts me. My legs wrap around his waist instinctively. We both groan as my sex presses against the hard bulge in his jeans.

I need him inside of me. I arch my back and roll my hips against his, begging for more contact, feeling the long length of his arousal pressing back.

"Want you so damn bad," Jeb rasps against my swollen lips. His molten blue eyes burn with lust and raw need. The proof of his desire throbs insistently between my legs.

My body is liquid fire, pulsing and aching for his touch, but uncertainty wars with my raging hormones. This intensity is uncharted territory, and I'm unsure how to navigate these waters. When we finally break apart, panting, his smoldering eyes sear into me.

"Not sure I can stop at just a kiss, girl," he rasps, voice rough with need. "If you don't want this, you gotta tell me right now. Say *No*. Otherwise, I'm taking this inside. Right now."

My body aches for more, but uncertainty wars with my desire.

But damn if I don't want him.

"I'm not saying *No*." Reluctantly, I unwind my legs from his waist, lowering my feet to solid ground.

Jeb releases me slowly, chest heaving as we stare at each other. His lips are damp, and the skin around my mouth burns from his five o'clock shadow.

With a shaky laugh, I caress his stubbled jaw and lick my swollen lips, tasting him there.

The yearning in his gaze as I slip from his arms tempts me to throw caution aside.

Jeb closes his eyes with a tortured groan. His entire body goes taut before he drags a ragged breath.

"Dammit, Stitch—we have to slow down, or I won't be able to control myself." Raw and hoarse with desire, his words shake me to the core. "You undo me like no one else."

He closes his eyes, struggling visibly to regain control. When he looks at me again, the hunger remains, but now it's leashed. He drags a hand through his hair, blowing out a harsh breath.

"If I go in there with you right now," his eyes blaze with restrained hunger, "I'll have you naked and under me until neither of us can walk." His fingers flex on my hips. "As much as I want that, we should wait."

"But... Don't you want this?" His passion seemed unbridled moments before.

"Does this feel like I don't want you?" He grabs my hand and shamelessly presses it against the erection straining beneath his pants. He groans, dragging me closer until our foreheads touch. "Believe me, I want you more than my next breath."

His other hand strokes my hair tenderly even as his body remains taut with restraint. "But I don't want to fuck you like an animal. That's what will happen if we go inside right now. When I fuck you, I want to savor the experience. Not rush through it." He wraps a hand around my neck—the dominant grip makes me swoon—and presses his forehead against mine. "When I fuck you—when I take you, it will be where I can pleasure you properly and adore you the way you deserve."

My cheeks flame at his blunt words but hearing the tenderness beneath them soothes my bruised ego. I don't know what to say.

How to respond.

Am I disappointed?

Or in awe of what he implies?

"This feels special, and I want to take my time with you." His thumb caresses my cheek. "I want to get to know you before we take that next step. Not rush into something in the heat of the moment. I don't want to ruin what we can become."

"O-okay." I take a shaky breath and resist the urge to curl my fingers against the turgid length of his erection.

I'm no virgin, but my experience is limited. I've never felt or seen anything close to what he's packing beneath those jeans.

"Don't be disappointed." His piercing eyes burn into mine.

"I'm not."

"You forget that I can read you like a book, girl. I want to fuck you, but I don't want to *just* fuck you. I want to possess you. Claim you." His voice drops to a rough growl. "Dominate and ravage you with my mouth, my hands, my body. I want to hear you scream my name as you surrender to me. It's the way I'm wired." He shudders. "Once we start down that road, I won't stop until I've dominated every inch of you. Until you're flying on pure sensation, owned entirely by me and me alone. There's no stopping until you're mine."

His explicit words spark heat low in my belly, and my knees go weak at the raw sensuality in his voice. Knowing he wants more than just a quick romp in the sheets excites me.

My knees weaken, and my thighs clench instinctively at the erotic images his promises conjure. His raw words spark a riot of butterflies in my core.

"Wow, okay. That's, um—a lot to process." I let out a shaky laugh.

"Did I scare you away?"

"It's a lot to wrap my head around, but also kind of thrilling to imagine—something like that." I bite my lip, equal parts anxious and eager. I honestly can't imagine what he describes, but it sounds incredible.

To be wanted with such passion?

"Have you ever surrendered to a man before? And I'm not talking about the physical act of sex."

"No." I shake in his arms. I don't understand what it means— what he needs—but how he says it makes my blood run lava-hot.

"It's not something to be rushed." His husky laughter brings a smile to my face. "And I want you to be ready for all of it."

He kisses me softly, then breaks off as the heat kicks in between us.

"I don't want you to go." I yank on his belt and his low, sultry laughter fills the air.

"Yeah, better not kiss you anymore tonight. I'm barely hanging by a thread as it is." With a final lingering kiss, he pulls away, releasing me. "Get inside before I fuck you against that door and put on a show for everyone to watch."

"Honestly, I don't think I'd notice anyone but you."

"Well, I'm not willing to share that with anyone. Not even a voyeuristic thrill. I'm serious, Stitch, when this happens between us, there's no stopping it."

"Then, I should go inside."

But I don't want to!

Satisfied I'm onboard, Jeb brushes a tender kiss over my lips. We reluctantly separate, nerves still thrumming with anticipation of all that awaits down the road.

"You better do that before I change my mind, girl."

"What if I want you to change your mind?"

"Get! We fuck when I say. How I say. You don't control that." He spins me around, opens the door to the barracks, and pushes me inside with a swat on my ass.

With a squeak, I stumble inside. As much as my body screams for more of his delicious torment, plunging headlong into this fiery thing between us could ruin everything.

Reluctantly, I head down the hall toward my quarters, lips still burning from our explosive first kiss. My skin heats everywhere he touched and my legs shake so much I weave down the hall like a drunken sailor.

Well, one thing is certain. After tonight, nothing will ever be the same between us again.

"Good night, Jeb," I speak to the air because Jeb is gone.

I make it down the long hall and stumble inside my quarters. The next thing I do is press cool fingers to my burning cheeks and imagine surrendering to his passion.

To Jeb.

THIRTEEN

Stitch

I AWAKEN SLOWLY, SUNBEAMS WARMING MY FACE. FOR ONCE, MY thoughts aren't consumed with worries about the future. Instead, I relive every heated moment from last night with Jeb.

His explicit words whisper through my mind. How he wants to utterly possess, dominate, and ravish me with hands, mouth, and body until I'm screaming his name.

Claim.

He said claim.

And he growled—like an animal.

A man intent on something more than sex.

A delicious lick of heat sweeps through me and settles as a throbbing ache at my core.

Such raw sensuality is unfamiliar, even taboo, for me. Yet, his words, their promise, ignite needs I'm only beginning to comprehend.

I stretch lazily under the sheets, skin tingling with the memory of his touch. His raw sensuality ignited needs foreign to me, and I ache to explore them. To give myself to him. To explore what it means for him to claim every inch of me. It both thrills and intimidates me.

The desire rushing through me is both insistent and irresistible.

The vivid images make me squirm against the sheets. I've never felt this addictive allure of submitting to someone. I ache in places I never knew existed, craving his possession.

I want to surrender everything to him. To place my trust in his capable hands. His restraint shows me I have nothing to fear. I'll welcome the ensuing blaze when he finally unleashes the fire between us.

I should be terrified.

Surrendering?

Submitting?

Relinquishing control?

I'm not frightened. Instead, his words spark something primal in my core.

I want to give him everything… My mind. My body. And my unwavering trust. I welcome the sweet ravishment.

Just thinking about being pinned beneath his muscular frame, utterly overwhelmed by his raw masculinity, makes me tremble. Ah, I can't wait to relinquish myself to that exquisite domination when the time comes.

Until then, I'll luxuriate in these decadent imaginings. Stoke the flickering heat his bold promises ignited within me. Fan my secret yearnings until they blaze into a wildfire neither of us can tame.

Lost in steamy daydreams, I don't hear the first trill of my phone. By the second shrill ring, I scramble to answer, heart already pounding. I fumble for my phone on the nightstand.

"Stitch here." I try to steady my breathing after my heated fantasies.

"It's Mitzy. We have a situation that requires immediate action. I need you in Command pronto to run point on coordinating this op." Her no-nonsense voice snaps me into focused awareness.

"What's up?"

"A billionaire's daughter was abducted. We located her and have a narrow window to execute extraction. Wheels up in twenty on this one."

"I'll be there in five." I'm already out of bed, adrenaline flooding my system.

My lazy daydreaming fades away. Time to focus on the task at hand—my first real mission since completing training.

My adrenaline spikes as I throw on clothes after Mitzy's call.

This is happening—I get to coordinate a live operation. No more simulations or practice runs. In many ways, it's a rite of passage, proof that Mitzy sees me as ready for the responsibility. That my skills and training have equipped me for this.

I hurry to Command, heart racing. Yes, I'm anxious about the stakes, but the sense of pride that swells in my chest is even stronger. After months of feeling like an outsider, I'm finally welcomed as a valued member of Mitzy's team.

Today, my chance to prove I deserve the opportunity she gave me and that her faith isn't misplaced has finally come. The hacker girl with a troubled past can rise to the occasion when lives are on the line.

My steps quicken. Am I ready for this? Doubt wars with excitement churning inside me, but I don't have time to overthink it. It's time to show Mitzy I belong here. Most of all, I'm ready to prove it to myself.

There will be time to explore Jeb's heated promises later.

For now, duty calls.

The door to Command hisses open to reveal controlled chaos. Techies hunch over glowing monitors, voices clipped as they relay information. At the center, Mitzy stands rigid, radiating authority. Her sharp gaze pins me when I enter.

"There you are." She gestures me over to the main console. "A billionaire's daughter was abducted. We're prepping a rescue op. I'm putting you in charge of running point from Command."

"Me? In charge of coordinating a live mission?" My mouth goes dry.

"Sink or swim." Mitzy's eyes bore into mine. "Today's the day. Time to see if you can handle running an op without choking or falling apart."

I swallow hard and sit, hands slick with sweat as I access the mission data. So much depends on me getting this right. Mitzy briefs me on the abduction of Ally Collins, the nineteen-year-old daughter of a billionaire tech mogul. She's been missing for five days.

My heart drops when I see Charlie team being dispatched for the dangerous on-site rescue. Jeb will be out there, walking straight into danger. I school my features to hide my anxiety, but inside I'm reeling.

Can I direct the man I've developed intense feelings for into a hostile situation? What if I panic and freeze up, unable to make critical decisions under pressure? His and his team's lives, not to mention poor Ally Collins, rest in my hands now.

I take a deep, steadying breath and force myself to focus. Their survival depends on me keeping a cool head no matter what goes down.

You've got this!

Nothing like a little pep-talk and pick-me-up.

Time blurs as I issue orders, hands flying over keyboards (*yes, multiple keyboards*) with newfound confidence. I coordinate transport and armaments for the team, my heart rate elevating as the countdown ticks lower.

Satellite imaging confirms the hostage's location—a seedy motel off a remote highway. I scan the layout, memorizing details that could mean life or death once boots hit the ground.

The jet touches down, and Charlie team drives to the motel, stopping a half mile out. I monitor vitals and comms as the team stealthily covers the distance on foot. My eyes keep returning to Jeb's strong heartbeat tracing across the screen.

We don't know what awaits them inside. There could be armed hostiles, improvised explosives, booby traps. I shove my worries down, hyper-focused on mission success.

"Approaching target," Jeb reports tersely.

I visualize Charlie team stacking up, prepping to breach. Jeb's steady voice calms my racing heart. He's done this countless times before.

"You have the green light," I respond firmly over comms. I mean it as encouragement, but it comes out like a command.

"Roger that. Breaching in 3...2...1..."

Even expecting it, the sudden cacophony of splintering wood and breaking glass makes me jump. Muffled shouts sound through Jeb's comms alongside the all too familiar rip of gunfire. I clench my fists so tightly my nails bite into my palms.

Come on, where are you?

My eyes flit from screen to screen, willing his vitals to reappear. An eternity later, a scrambled signal pops up—they have her.

One by one, the team reports in. Ethan, Blake, Walt, Gabe, Hank... And finally, Jeb. My lungs empty in a rush of relief when his voice comes through. The tightness in my chest loosens, and I shake off my lingering anxiety. The rest of my muscles unlock, my whole body easing as I exhale in relief. I didn't realize how tightly wound I was, waiting anxiously for him to report in.

"Target secure. One hostile down, one in custody. Beginning extraction." Relief crashes over me at his words. But I can't celebrate yet. Not when they still have a prisoner in their custody, elevating the risk.

I coordinate transport to their location, hands shaking now that the immediate crisis has passed. It's too soon to lower my guard, but we're close.

Within minutes, I confirm all friendlies plus the hostage are airborne and en route to safety. Only once they touch down at HQ can I finally loosen my white-knuckled grip on the console.

Now that it's over, I glance at the organized chaos around me. I'm in a daze, and then it hits me. This is just another day in the office for everyone else. They live and breathe rescue missions like they're common everyday events.

Supporting the Guardians.

Boots on the ground.

The pointy tip of the spear.

Will I ever feel as calm as those around me?

But I did it.

I ran point on my first real-world op without falling apart or freezing up. Turns out Mitzy was right to trust me after all.

Maybe, just maybe, I belong here.

But my worry for Jeb still lingers. I won't catch my breath until I see him safe with my own eyes. The thought of losing him out in the field leaves an icy pit in my gut. This begs the question: Can I handle the constant danger and stress of this job, especially where he's concerned?

It feels like forever before Charlie team returns. They march a handcuffed prisoner into Command for processing. The man looks surly but unharmed. I scan the faces of the others—Walt favors his left leg slightly, and Gabe sports bruised knuckles, but no critical injuries. Jeb enters last, moving with a confident stride. His gaze finds mine across the room. The barely perceptible smile he offers soothes my frayed nerves.

He's okay.

They all made it back.

"Nice work, Stitch." Ethan claps me on the shoulder as he passes. "Kept a cool head your first time. Couldn't have done it without you."

I nod shakily, warmed by his praise. Maybe in time, I'll earn the trust of these battle-hardened men and prove I can watch their six, no matter the chaos unfolding on screen.

But I know Jeb trusts me. His subtle smile says it all, and I won't betray that faith, no matter how terrified I might get seeing him put himself in danger to save the lives of others.

As the adrenaline rush fades, bone-deep weariness sets in. It's a good tired—the kind of tiredness that comes after a job well done. I catch Jeb's eye across the celebratory crowd and tilt my head meaningfully toward the hall. Wordlessly, he follows me out.

As soon as we're alone in the empty corridor, I dive into his arms, embracing him fiercely.

Surprised, he staggers back a step, but then his strong arms wrap around me.

"Hey, what's going on?" he asks, concern in his voice.

"I was so scared for you," I confess in a tremulous voice.

Now that it's over, my nerves are shot. I wrap my arms around his solid frame, needing reassurance.

"You don't need to worry about me." Jeb rubs my back gently. "I know how to handle myself out there."

I cling tighter to his muscular frame. "But so much could've gone wrong. You could've…" I swallow hard, unable to finish the thought.

Jeb pulls back and stoops to meet my eyes. His gaze is filled with tenderness. He brushes a strand of hair from my face. "No matter what happens out there, I'll always come home to you."

Tears well up in my eyes as I take in his solemn vow. I bite my lip and nod, wanting desperately to believe it's true.

"You have to promise me." I cling tighter, comforted by the steady beat of his heart. His strong arms make me feel safe.

"I promise." Jeb cups my face in both hands. "Wild horses couldn't keep me away." His thumb strokes my cheek with exquisite tenderness, then he presses a kiss to the top of my head. "You were amazing today. Handled support like a pro. I'm so proud of you." His voice resonates with quiet strength.

His praise soothes my frayed nerves. I nuzzle into his chest, memorizing his woodsy scent. With him here, solid and real, the chaos fades away. Reassured by his words, I bury my face in his chest again, breathing him in.

Maybe one day, I'll stop feeling like an imposter. Maybe there will come a day when I feel I truly belong. Lost in my thoughts, I don't hear Mitzy's clipped stride approaching until she speaks.

"Well, isn't this cozy? If you're done groping the Guardian, I need my Techie."

I spring apart from Jeb, cheeks flaming as Mitzy surveys us with an arched brow.

"What can I say?" Jeb grins unabashedly. "Your new recruit is irresistible."

Mitzy ignores the quip. "Well, I need Stitch." She shifts her attention to me. "Griff got intel out of the kidnapper, but all he gave up was one word—Haven."

"Haven?" Jeb asks with a furrowed brow.

"It's some shadow organization connected to the abduction." Mitzy shrugs. "Won't know more until we dig. I need Stitch on a deep dive into the dark web immediately to find whatever we can on them."

Flustered but snapping to attention, I smooth my rumpled shirt and try to pull away, but Jeb reels me back in. Before I can react, he dips me into a dramatic toe-curling kiss right in front of Mitzy.

I surface, dizzy and breathless.

Mitzy rolls her eyes.

"Keep the tonsil hockey to your own time, Jeb. Stitch, I need your brain unscrambled." She pivots on her heels, calling over her shoulder, "Honestly, Guardians and their women…"

"I'd better get to work." Cheeks flaming, I try to twist out of Jeb's arms.

But he tightens his hold, flashing a roguish grin. "What, no goodbye kiss?"

Before I can react, he dips his head and captures my mouth in a blistering kiss that leaves me dizzy. I'm powerless to resist the heat of his lips slanting over mine.

Mitzy spins on her heels, calling back to me. "Keep the petting sessions with the meatheads to your own time." She snaps her fingers. "Come."

"Go get 'em, trouble." Jeb steals one last kiss.

"Maybe we can go out tonight?" I bite my lip, avoiding his amused gaze.

"No." Jeb moves in close, backing me against the wall. He traces a finger slowly along my bottom lip.

"No?" My brows pinch in confusion.

"I'm not taking you out."

"Oh, okay." Deflated, my shoulders slump, but then his low, rumbling chuckle has me looking back up at him.

"You are trouble." He leans in close, pressing me back against the wall. "I'm not taking you out because we're staying in."

"In?" I'm thoroughly confused now.

"I've been fantasizing about these pretty lips wrapped around my cock since last night." His eyes smolder with unrestrained hunger. "Tonight, I'm taking everything I want from you."

"But—I thought... What happened to waiting?" My eyes widen, and I flush hotly, shocked by his explicit words.

"I don't have the patience to wait." He braces one forearm above my head, caging me in. "I need to be inside you, feel you, and claim every inch of your sweet body until you're screaming my name." His voice is rough with primal urgency. "Tonight, you become mine."

His searing promise leaves me breathless and aching. With a last heated look, he strides off down the hall.

I sag back against the wall, pulse racing. I thought we were waiting, but Jeb's restraint has reached its limit. His raw sensuality awakens an unfamiliar yet undeniable need in me.

Squaring my shoulders, I return to my workstation to research Haven, skin already tingling in anticipation of what tonight will bring.

FOURTEEN

Stitch

_____

THE SOFT HUM OF MY COMPUTER IS THE ONLY SOUND IN MY SMALL, sparsely furnished dormitory at Guardian HQ. As I sit there, the anticipation for Jeb's arrival later tonight swirls within me—a tempest of anxiety and excitement.

I'm not one for grand gestures or elaborate preparations.

No candles.

No scattered rose petals.

No sexy music.

That's not me.

But nervous energy propels me to tidy up and create a space that feels welcoming yet unmistakably mine. My hands move almost of their own accord, straightening the few personal items on my desk, fluffing the pillows on my bed, and ensuring everything is just so.

The simplicity of my actions is soothing, a small balm to the tumultuous emotions raging inside me. I take a deep breath, trying to calm the butterflies determined to take permanent residence in my stomach. My mind flashes back to Jeb's words, his promises of possession, of claiming me. The thoughts send shivers racing down my spine, a blend of fear and longing that feeds my anxiety.

I change my clothes several times, unable to decide what's appropriate for an occasion like this. It's silly. It's Jeb, the same Jeb I've known and—well, more than liked for some time now.

But tonight?

Tonight is different. We're crossing a threshold that we can never uncross.

Finally, I settle on something simple and comfortable yet undeniably me. A pair of soft leggings and a loose-fitting Angel Fire concert T-shirt. This isn't about impressing with appearance; it's about being authentic, being me.

The knock on the door comes sooner than I expect. The deep thud on the door echoes through the compact space of my dormitory, resonating like a drumbeat. My heart leaps into my throat, pounding so loudly I'm sure he can hear it from the other side of the door. For a moment, I freeze, my hand hovering over the doorknob.

This is it.

There's no turning back now.

I open the door, and there he is.

Jeb.

Just as rugged and captivating as ever, but tonight, there's a softness in his eyes I haven't seen before. It's disarming, sending a new wave of jitters through me.

"Hey." His voice is a low rumble that vibrates the air and sets up a resonance inside of me.

"Hi." I manage barely a whisper. My voice flutters like a butterfly.

We stand there for a moment, the space between us charged with unspoken words and unfulfilled desires.

"You going to let me in?" He cocks his head to the side, and the corners of his mouth lift into a smile.

"Sorry." I step aside, letting him in.

Our eyes lock as he crosses the threshold, and the world disappears. It's just me and him, and the promise of a night where we discover each other in ways we haven't before.

He doesn't say much but looks around, a small nod of approval at the tidy, unpretentious space. I wonder what he's thinking. Is he as nervous as I am? Is his heart threatening to beat itself out of his chest like mine?

No way.

A man like Jeb is never nervous when it comes to sex.

We gravitate toward the couch, an island in the small sea of my living space. Sitting down, the air between us is thick with unspoken anticipation, charged with the electricity of our unexplored connection.

"How did it feel leading your first mission?" His voice is a mix of pride and genuine curiosity.

"It was intense." I draw in a deep breath, feeling a flicker of pride. "Like, I knew everything was riding on my decisions, but when it was happening, it felt good."

"You were incredible." Jeb nods, his eyes reflecting his understanding. "Took charge like you've been doing it for years."

"Thanks." A blush warms my cheeks at his praise. "It means a lot coming from you." I pause, collecting my thoughts. "But this thing with Haven…"

"What about it?"

"It's been consuming me all day. Griff extracted that one word. Usually, after an hour or two of digging, I'd have something to show for my efforts."

"Did you find anything?"

"Nothing."

"Sounds like you've got a real mystery on your hands." He leans back, his brow furrowing.

"I'll figure it out. I never met a puzzle I couldn't figure out." I sigh and lean back as well. "No one is that good at hiding."

"If anyone can get to the bottom of it, it's you." Jeb reaches over, squeezing my hand reassuringly. "You've got a knack for making sense of chaos."

"An interesting way to put it." His confidence in me stirs a warmth in my chest. "I hope you're right. It's just… There's so much at stake. I can't afford to miss anything."

"You won't," Jeb says firmly. "You're too thorough and too stubborn."

"Stubborn, huh?" I chuckle, the tension easing slightly. "I'll take that as a compliment."

"It is." A smile plays on his lips. "It's one of the things I admire most about you. Not that I won't paddle your ass when you turn that stubborn streak toward me."

Our eyes meet, and there's a depth of emotion that's both exhilarating and frightening. It's a look that speaks of mutual respect and something deeper, something neither of us has fully explored yet. I should say something, comment about what he just said, but for some reason, I don't.

As if what he said is perfectly normal. It's not. Not at all. And while I should be insulted and enraged, I find myself strangely turned on by the casual way he dropped that into the conversation.

Our conversation shifts naturally, flowing between the details of our day, the challenges we face, and the undercurrent of something more personal, more intimate.

It's in the way Jeb looks at me, a smoldering intensity in his gaze. It's in how our hands brush together, sending jolts of electricity shooting through me.

The tension builds, a crescendo of unspoken needs and desires. It's exhilarating and terrifying all at once. I want him more than I've ever wanted anything, but the fear of the unknown, of this new aspect of our relationship, holds me back.

Our eyes meet, and there's a flicker of something that sends a thrill of excitement mixed with anxiety through me. Jeb takes my hand. His grip is firm, reassuring. The room feels warmer, the space between us charged with sexual tension.

He leans in, and his lips meet mine in a gentle yet insistent kiss. It's a kiss that says everything that words can't. In that kiss, all my fears and anxieties melt away. I'm no longer worried about what might happen or what it means for us. All that matters is this moment, here and now, with Jeb.

He doesn't rush. There's no need.

I will say this…

Jeb's kisses leave me breathless, awakening nerves I never knew existed. My body comes alive under his confident touch. I ache for more, to give myself over completely to the desires I've kept locked away for so long.

As his hands and lips explore me, my mind clouds over, lost in the heady sensations. I whisper his name like a fervent prayer, my fingers tangled in his hair. With our bodies entwined, I know I'm ready to take this leap with him.

FIFTEEN

Jeb

THE WAY STITCH RESPONDS TO MY TOUCH FANS THE FLAMES INSIDE me. Her soft moans and the arch of her back communicate her readiness.

Every caress, every grazing of my lips over her skin is calculated. With infinite patience, I will unwrap the layers of her, one by one, until she lies bare and trembling before me.

With each passing second, the intensity between us grows. My kisses become more demanding, my hunger for her evident in every brush of my lips against her. I want to give in to the raw desire that courses through my veins, but for our first time, I want it to be all about her.

That begins with her pleasure over mine, and I know exactly where to begin. Slowly, I slip my fingers beneath the fabric of her jeans.

Her breath hitches as she arches her back, craving more of my touch. The anticipation in the air is palpable, thick with desire and yearning.

I slide my fingertips further down, feeling the heat radiating from her core. Her hips instinctively move toward my hand, silently pleading for me to delve deeper into the depths of her pleasure.

With a mischievous smile, I grant her wish, slipping my hand past the barrier of fabric and sliding a finger through her slick folds.

A low moan escapes her lips as I explore her delicate, sensitive nub. Her eyes flutter closed, and she rolls her lower lip inward, biting down gently with her front teeth.

"You're beautiful, sinfully so." I can't help but comment on how she reacts to my touch. "But there's too much clothing between you and me." My other hand cups her breast, teasing and pinching her hardened nipple, amplifying her pleasure.

"Take them off," she cries out.

"Take what off?" I can't help but tease.

"My clothes." She squirms in my hands. "Take them off."

"And here, I thought my little hacker would resist my advances."

"Jeb..." The warning in her tone says much. "If you don't..."

"If I don't, what?" I give her a look. "I don't take commands when it comes to sex. I give them."

She suddenly stills beneath my touch.

"Does that scare you?"

"Y-y-yes?"

"Is that a question or an answer?"

"I don't know." She squirms beneath me. "Can't we just..."

"Just what?" Although I know what she's going to say. I want to hear her say it.

"Just...."

"Yes?"

"You're messing with me." She puts her hands on my shoulders and pushes me back.

"Love, my fingers are two seconds from plunging deep inside your pussy and driving you toward the most intense orgasm of your life. I assure you... I am most definitely not messing with you. I very much want to fuck you."

She hesitates for a moment, her eyes filled with desire and uncertainty. A battle rages within her, the need to relinquish control, fighting against her innate resistance.

"Then fuck me."

"Ah, all in good time. First, I want a taste of you."

I lean forward and capture her lips in a fierce kiss. Sweet and intoxicating, her taste consumes me entirely as our tongues dance in a sensual tango. Our bodies press flush against each other, the heat between us growing more intense with every passing second.

My hands travel down her body, tracing every curve until they reach the waistband of her jeans. Slowly, torturously, I hook my fingers into the fabric and gently tug them down, revealing lacy black panties.

"You're so fucking hot." My voice thickens with desire.

The sight of her exposed and vulnerable fuels the fire within me, igniting a primal instinct I can no longer suppress.

I break the kiss, my breath ragged as I forge a trail of hot, wet kisses along her jawline, down her neck. My teeth graze her pulse point, eliciting a gasp from her lips. The taste of her skin on my tongue only intensifies the ache between my legs.

I lift her from the couch and carry her to the bed. Her chest rises and falls with anticipation, her eyes locked onto mine as I crawl over her body. The electricity in the air is palpable as I explain the kind of lover I am.

"Someday soon, I will ask you to trust me," I whisper, my voice laced with a seductive promise. "I want to show you pleasure beyond your wildest dreams."

Her breath hitches at my words, curiosity mingling with desire in her eyes.

"I will bind you, blindfold you, and treat you to the intensity that comes with surrender, but for tonight, I plan on exploring every inch of your exquisite body."

Lowering myself over her, I brace myself on one arm and pepper soft kisses along her collarbone. My free hand traces circles on her quivering thighs. My touch teases and taunts.

Each time she arches toward my touch, yearning for more contact, I pull away ever so slightly.

"First lesson, you can beg for whatever you want, but I decide what you get." I slip off the silky lace, baring her completely. Then I remove the tired Angel Fire concert T-shirt and relieve her of her bra, freeing her tits.

Her body is a masterpiece of desire; every inch of her skin beckons me closer.

Without warning, I dip my head down and capture one of her hardened nipples in my mouth. A guttural moan escapes her lips as I suckle and tease the sensitive bud with my tongue. Her hands instinctively find their way into my hair.

Which I allow.

It suits my purposes. Driven by an overwhelming desire to give her more, I shift my position, moving down her body until my mouth is just inches away from her pulsating center. Her fingers dig into my scalp as she squirms beneath me.

My hot breath fans over her sensitive flesh, making her tremble with anticipation. Slowly, I lower my head and let my tongue flicker against her clit.

Stitch's body convulses beneath me.

"So damn responsive." I can't help but admire her.

Her grip on my hair tightens as she chases pleasure. Her moans grow louder with every passing second, and she trembles on the edge of something incredible.

I continue my assault, alternating between gentle licks and firm strokes, completely focused on driving her to the brink of madness. Her hips buck against my mouth, desperate for more contact, as I delve deeper into her velvety folds.

Her moans fill the room, fueling the fire within me. I taste her desire, the sweet tang of her arousal mixing with my hunger. Her body tenses with each flick of my tongue, and her muscles coil like tightly wound springs.

Sensing her imminent release, I change tactics, adding a hint of teeth to my ministrations. She arches her back, surrendering herself completely to my touch. Her nails dig into my shoulders, leaving crescent-shaped marks that will serve as a reminder of our carnal encounter.

The heady scent of sex permeates the air, driving us both further into this abyss of erotic pleasure. There are no inhibitions here, only unbridled passion and a hunger that demands to be sated.

As she reaches the precipice, I increase the pressure, thrusting two fingers inside her while my mouth continues its torment. Her body tenses and shudders beneath me as her orgasm crashes over her like a tidal wave. She cries out in sheer bliss, her voice reverberating off the walls.

But our exploration doesn't end there. As the waves of pleasure recede, leaving her trembling in their wake, I rise from between her thighs. Our eyes lock, an unspoken understanding passing between us. The intense desire still lingers in the air as our bodies collide in a frenzy of need and longing. As she catches her breath, I crawl up to meet her gaze, a smug smile on my lips.

"Enjoy yourself?"

She nods, a flush spreading across her cheeks. "More than I could have ever imagined."

I lean down and capture her lips in a searing kiss. "That was just the beginning," I whisper against her mouth, my voice filled with promise. "There's so much more pleasure in store for you tonight."

Her eyes widen with anticipation, mirroring my desire. With a swift motion, I remove my clothes, open a foil pouch, sheathe myself, and position myself above her.

Our bodies align perfectly as if made for each other.

I enter her slowly, savoring the delicious sensation of being enveloped by her warmth. She gasps at the feeling, gripping tightly onto my shoulders as I sink into her silken heat.

The desire between us intensifies as I slowly enter her, inch by agonizing inch. Her breath hitches, her hands clutch at the sheets, her nails digging into the fabric. Being so intimately connected fills us with raw vulnerability and overwhelming desire.

I start moving, a steady rhythm pushing us closer to the edge. The room is filled with our mingled moans and the rhythmic slapping of our bodies coming together. Time seems to stand still as we lose ourselves in this dance of ecstasy, each thrust bringing us closer to that ultimate release.

Her legs wrap around my waist, pulling me deeper, urging me to go faster. I oblige, my own need driving me to match her intensity. Our bodies move in perfect synchrony, a symphony of pleasure that threatens to consume us entirely.

As I feel her walls tighten around me, signaling her impending climax, I lean down and capture one of her hardened nipples between my lips. I suck and nibble on it, teasing her further and pushing her over the edge. She cries out my name in a mixture of pleasure and desperation, her body convulsing beneath me.

But I'm not done yet.

With relentless determination, I continue thrusting into her, prolonging our pleasure. My release builds within me, a primal urge that demands satisfaction. Her body trembles beneath mine, aching for that final release.

And then it happens.

We reach our climax together. Our bodies lock in that moment of pure bliss as we ride out simultaneous waves of pleasure.

Yet, I'm still not done.

As we slowly come down from the heights of passion, I collapse beside her, both of us panting heavily as our bodies writhe and tremble with aftershocks.

After we come down from our mutual high, she turns to her side and draws lazy circles over the skin of my chest.

"What did you mean?"

"About what?"

"About not taking commands…"

I pause, my fingers finding solace in the soft strands of her hair. The room is still heavy with the lingering scent of desire, and I find myself lost in her gaze once more. I take a deep breath, searching for the right words to explain what I meant.

"I'm dominant when it comes to sex."

"How dominant?"

I smile at her playful curiosity, enjoying how her fingertips trace patterns on my chest. The room is bathed in a warm afterglow, and my desire for her grows stronger with each passing moment.

"Very dominant," I say, my voice low and seductive. "I demand complete control and lead the way, exploring the depths of pleasure with my partner."

Her eyes widen in anticipation, her lips parting slightly as she waits for me to continue. Desire flickers in her gaze, matching the fire burning within me.

"I don't believe in holding back," I confess, my voice a mere whisper. "I want to see you surrender to your desires, to feel your every quiver and tremble under my touch. But," I add with a hint of vulnerability, "it's not just about physical dominance for me."

She tilts her head, her expression a mix of curiosity and intrigue. I take a moment to gather my thoughts before continuing.

"When I say I don't take commands, I mean I want us to explore our desires together," I explain. "To create a space where we trust each other completely, let go of our inhibitions, and give in to the raw intensity of our connection."

A soft smile graces her lips as she leans closer, her body radiating warmth against mine. "That sounds—incredible," she murmurs, her voice filled with desire.

"It is," I reply, my words laced with anticipation. "But it requires trust and communication between us. It's something we'll build over time."

As our bodies intertwine again, I take her face in my hands, gently caressing her cheeks with my thumbs. I lean in, capturing her lips with a hunger from our shared understanding.

Our kiss is intense yet tender, a fusion of passion and vulnerability. Our bodies merge once again, each touch eliciting moans of pleasure.

I take my time, exploring every inch of her body as if it were a sacred temple. My touch ignites a fire within her, stoking the flames of desire until she is an inferno of need. With each gentle stroke of my fingers, I push her further to the edge of ecstasy.

Becoming more attuned to her needs and desires, I listen to her body's language, the subtle cues that will guide me. I adjust my touch accordingly with every gasp and sigh that escapes her lips.

My little hacker is a world of wonders I can't wait to explore.

SIXTEEN

Stitch

THIS PAST MONTH HAS BEEN THE GREATEST CHALLENGE OF MY hacking career. I've been tirelessly scouring the dark web, diving into its deepest, most obscure corners in search of any trace of an organization called Haven. It's been a grueling journey, navigating a labyrinth of misdirection, where each scrap of information felt like a hard-won victory against a faceless adversary.

In the scarce moments I have to myself, Jeb is there. What started as stolen moments shifted to something deeper between us.

An awakening.

A hunger that drives us to find any opportunity, no matter how brief, to be alone together. He's shown me new heights of pleasure I never knew could exist. His confident touch—exploring and possessing every inch of me—lets me lower my defenses and embrace a new sensuality.

I've opened up in ways I never imagined possible with a man, emotionally and physically. It terrifies me even as it exhilarates me. No one has ever affected me like he has. The rest of the world fades away when I'm in his arms. There are only his lips, his hands, and his breath. I drown in him, losing myself in the blissful oblivion he creates with a single caress.

As much as I yearn to remain lost in Jeb's embrace, the demands of my job refuse to be ignored. This daunting search for Haven consumes me, forcing me to compartmentalize the demands of my job with my desire to be with Jeb.

I shake out my fingers and straighten my spine, mentally preparing for the demands of my work.

Because last night, my tenacity yielded results.

Amidst the cryptic layers of the dark web, I found tangible evidence of Haven, a breakthrough that set my heart racing with both triumph and anticipation.

Their digital fortress seems impenetrable—security seamless, encryption sophisticated. Traps and decoys guard every layer.

Hunched over my computer, I wage digital war against Haven's fortifications. The glow of the screen casts a pale light in the dim room, reflecting off my tired eyes that haven't seen sleep in over thirty-six hours. My back aches from the constant tension, a physical manifestation of the mental strain I endure. Fingers sore and slightly trembling, they dance across the keyboard with a rhythm born of desperation and determination.

The desk around me is a testament to the battle I fight. The clutter speaks of long hours spent in this very chair. Crumpled snack wrappers peek out under a tangle of cables, remnants of quick, unsatisfying meals consumed without leaving my computer. The only thing keeping me awake is the caffeine content of the empty energy drink cans that litter the floor.

The grime of exertion coats my skin. My clothes, unchanged since I first sat down to dive into this task, cling uncomfortably to my body. The room is heavy with stale air mingling with the faint, acrid scent of unwashed hair and spent energy.

Every so often, a sharp stab of pain shoots through my wrist, a cruel reminder of the physical toll this is taking. I ignore it, focusing instead on the lines of code scrolling across my screen, each a potential key to unlocking Haven's secrets.

In this small, cluttered space, time loses meaning.

The outside world fades to a distant memory. My entire existence narrows to this mission, to the flickering cursor on the screen.

My determination to breach Haven's defenses consumes me, a singular obsession that pushes everything else to the background.

Their digital fortress is a masterclass in security and paranoia—a complex web of advanced firewalls and sophisticated encryption, each layer more daunting than the last.

I'm drawn into an intricate dance of cunning and skill with every firewall I encounter, pitting my abilities against their meticulously crafted defenses. It's a relentless battle of wits, where each step forward is a testament to my resolve and tenacity.

But this is where I thrive.

And I rise to the challenge.

Daily video conferences with Mitzy and the rest of the team are a ritual of frustration. We're all working to crack Haven's defenses and share our disappointment at continued failure.

As days bleed into nights, the pressure mounts. The weight of knowing innocents are at the mercy of Haven's elusive secrets gnaws at me, but amidst this relentless pursuit, a breakthrough shimmers on the horizon.

I feel it in my gut, almost within grasp. Some people may find that odd.

There is no intuition in coding, except when there is.

From my perspective, coding is a world ruled by flawless logic and analysis, an intricate dance of numbers and commands that thrive in the absence of emotion. It's a language of pure rationality, where every input has a predictable output, and every problem has a solution buried in lines of code.

This digital realm is methodical, almost sterile in its precision. It's a stark contrast from the tumultuous world of human emotion, where I struggle the most.

Yet, despite its seeming detachment, I find a deeper connection within this web of algorithms and functions. There's an intuition, that gut feeling, which guides me, whispering through the rhythm of keystrokes and the flow of data. It's a sense that lives beneath the surface of logic, an almost primal understanding that comes not from the mind but from somewhere deeper.

As I sit here, entrenched in my battle to infiltrate Haven's network, that feeling is more pronounced than ever. It's a subtle shift in the air—a change in the cadence of my heartbeat. Despite the emotional neutrality of my work, I sense I'm on the verge of something significant.

It's like standing on the precipice; anticipation hums through my veins. It's in the way my fingers hesitate for a fraction of a second over the keyboard, the way my breath catches when a new pathway in the code reveals itself.

Right now, that feeling is undeniable.

It's an electric charge, a pulsating rhythm. I feel the pieces falling into place.

Victory inching closer.

The line between the analytical and the instinctual blurs. The cold logic of the code intertwines with the visceral sense of nearing my goal. It's a paradoxical harmony, reason and intuition fused into one.

Suddenly, there it is—a flaw so minute it's almost imperceptible, but to a trained eye like mine, it's a beacon. I dive in, exploiting the opportunity. It's not a full victory, but it's a start.

Fingers shaking, I call Mitzy.

"It's three in the morning." Her sleep-blurred voice sounds muffled through the phone.

"There's a vulnerability in Haven's network." I blurt out my discovery as my fingers keep one step ahead of Haven's defenses.

"Details. What did you find?"

"An anomaly in the SSL encryption pattern." My words tumble out with urgency. "It's not a full system breach, but it's something. A foothold we can use."

"That's incredible." A spark of excitement ignites in Mitzy's voice. "Meet me at HQ. We need to strategize fast and exploit this opening before they patch it up."

"Let me finish one thing, then I'll be on my way." I end the call, my heart pounding with adrenaline and anticipation.

Haven will discover the breach. It's only a matter of time. Minutes at most, but I can do a lot of damage in those few minutes. After inserting a hidden backdoor in their systems, I take one sniff of my pits and scrunch my nose at the offending smell. After a quick shower, I head to HQ.

I'm ready to delve into the nitty-gritty when I arrive, but Mitzy stops me just outside the briefing room.

"Give us a minute," Mitzy says. "We'll call you in soon."

I nod, my frustration barely contained. I'm the one who cracked Haven's network, yet here I am, sidelined. Through the door, I hear the muffled tones of the briefing—Ethan's deep voice, Jeb's familiar timbre, and others discussing Haven.

I lean closer, trying to catch snippets of the conversation. It's infuriating. I deserve to be in there.

"Mitzy, brief Ethan on where we are." I don't know that voice, but it exudes confidence.

"Their deepest layers of encryption prevent outside access." Mitzy's voice shifts to lecture mode. "But we found a way in."

We?

She means me. I'm not an attention hog by any means, but I deserve recognition for the work I do. I take a deep breath and tell myself to chill. Mitzy continues her lecture.

"I can spoof an origin point from inside, make it look like there's a mole." The rapid-fire tapping of the keys continues as she explains. "I built out backgrounds for each team member. Their aliases have thorough digital footprints as security professionals specializing in networks and encryption. Your team is now positioned as cutting-edge IT and security experts. All that's left is to make some noise and let Haven come calling."

There's a pause before Ethan responds. "That will get us in the front door, but gaining full facility access will require a more finessed approach."

"Mitzy had a thought about that." The voice I don't recognize responds.

More tapping keys, then Mitzy again. "In addition to the system breach, I'm inserting strategically placed breadcrumbs. Hints and whispers there's a mole inside Haven passing information to outsiders."

"You think that will convince them to give us more access?" Ethan asks.

"It should provide leverage. They'll want someone searching for the mole if they suspect information is leaking out."

Their conversation continues, going over the plan while my frustration rises at being excluded.

Mitzy continues explaining how she's setting Haven up, thinking they have a security breach and a mole inside their organization. The first part of that plan is all Mitzy's, but I suggested the mole. She continues to explain our plan of attack.

"That should justify bringing in outside security specialists like yourselves to investigate for a breach." She continues, explaining how creating that breach leads to inserting Charlie team directly into Haven itself. "There's one problem."

"What's that?" Ethan asks.

"Charlie team can't pull off being IT experts. Not with this level of encryption. No offense to your team, but this is complicated stuff."

She's not wrong about that. There's no way Jeb and his team can pull something like that off. Not in person. It would require someone like me, someone with the skills to run rampant through their security protocols.

"What about Jeb?" Ethan asks. "He's our team geek."

Jeb?

A geek?

My brows scrunch in confusion. He's never said a word about being a tech guy. Although, they're probably talking about simple tech work. Nothing like the programming skills I bring to the table.

"This is beyond him," Mitzy explains how knowledge about dark web encryption isn't something that can be faked.

"Can you prep him on what he needs?" Ethan asks.

"Already on it." She explains how she's already asked Jeb to shadow her team, then drops a bombshell. "That's why I'm sending one of my best with you."

I about choke when I hear those words. Mitzy didn't specifically *ask* me to go on an op with Charlie team, but I'm no idiot. There's a reason she asked me to come in person.

Ethan coughs. "No offense, but a spindly, acne-faced geek barely out of high school is a liability."

How dare he? I sniff in indignation.

"Stereotyping much?" Mitzy chuckles, and I realize she baited Ethan into making that comment. She might be old, in her thirties, but she's a cool boss. Even her psychedelic hair is beginning to grow on me. "Stitch is not your average pimply-faced nerd."

Stitch.

Yup, she's talking about me.

Holy shit! I jump when it sinks in. She's talking about me going on the mission. Like boots on the ground.

Mitzy goes on to explain who I am, although Ethan already knows. She talks about my exploits hacking into the NSA and how I was facing serious jail time.

Unable to take it anymore, I shove the door open and stride in, combat boots thudding on the floor. All eyes turn to me. Jeb meets my gaze, a tiny smile playing on his lips. The heat between us is a rolling boil.

I snap my eyes away, focusing on Ethan, who regards me with a frown.

"NSA security was pathetic," I state mockingly, just to get under their skin. It is time for Ethan and the others to see me for who I am and what I can do.

I catch Jeb stifling a laugh. We share a subtle look of amusement before he returns to the discussion, leaving me to state my case. I'm ready to prove myself to these people—especially Jeb, who already believes in me. I won't let him down.

Ethan's frown deepens. "If you're taking Jeb for additional training, I want Stitch to join Charlie team. I'm not taking along a young twenty-something female without basic self-defense skills."

"Who says I can't take care of myself?" I bristle at his words. "Please. I think I can handle babysitting a few grunts."

"This is non-negotiable." Ethan's tone brokers no argument. "You train with my team, or you're off the mission."

I seethe but bite back a sharp retort. As much as I hate the mandated training, jeopardizing my role in this op isn't worth it. "There's no mission without me, dumbass." I want to say more but catch Mitzy's stern gaze. "Ugh, fine. Whatever. I'll train with the grunts."

SEVENTEEN

Jeb

Over the next six weeks, life is a blur of training and prep. While I deepen my computer expertise under Mitzy's watchful eye, Stitch sharpens her combat skills with Charlie team.

Our paths barely cross, and it's a frustrating kind of separation. Today, however, we train together with the team.

I like to think her newfound prowess in self-defense stems from those initial lessons I gave her, but I get the distinct impression she's been a bit of a rogue. We're on the mats today, geared up for sparring. I watch her, a mix of pride and amusement swirling inside me with how far she's come.

The air crackles with a blend of competition and an unspoken, simmering attraction. Her sharp and focused gaze never leaves mine, and I can't help but be drawn to the intensity in her eyes.

At one point, as we circle each other, I seize the moment, lunging in with a quick jab, but she's ready. She catches my arm and uses my momentum to send me crashing onto my back. The impact forces a gasp from my lungs as I find myself staring up at the ceiling, dazed.

"Gotta be quicker than that, old man." She looms over me, a victorious smirk playing on her lips.

"Old man?" I retort with hearty laughter, scrambling to my feet. "Alright, now you've asked for it…"

Our sparring session shifts gears, transforming into a charged dance of attack and defense. Each move we make pushes the other to their limits. I'm struck by how effortlessly Stitch has grown and adapted, her fighting spirit and unorthodox techniques making her a formidable opponent. The way she breaks the rules, the unexpectedness of her tactics—it's more than just impressive.

It's downright captivating.

We reset, and I go on the attack again. This time, I get her in a hold, our bodies pressed close in the struggle. There's a palpable tension between us, a mixture of combat and something deeper.

"Mmm, this feels familiar," she says. "If this is the kind of training I've been missing, sign me up for more."

"Careful what you wish for, trouble." I chuckle, my pulse quickening.

"Nice try, brainiac. But I've got some new moves," she counters with a smirk.

I try to flip her, but in a nimble display of agility, she slips from my grasp.

"Brainiac?" I look at her in surprise.

"Mitzy told me about your CompSci degree from MIT. You never mentioned it." Her tone is a mixture of surprise and admiration.

"Didn't think it mattered." I shrug off the compliment modestly.

"Well, I'm impressed." She winks playfully. "Brains and brawn are a potent combination. Sexy."

"I'm happy to teach you some new tricks." I grin, enjoying her praise. "How do you feel about restraints?"

"Restraints?" She chokes at my words and glances around to see who might have heard.

We reset once more, the energy between us electric. Stitch keeps me sharp in more ways than one. Her competitive spirit is infectious.

"Bring it on." I give a little flick of my fingers. "Show me what you've got."

Without warning, Stitch launches into a barrage of lightning-quick strikes, her movements fluid and precise. I'm barely able to block her assaults in time. She's better than I expected, and her martial arts skills are impressive and effective.

"When did you get this good?" She's giving me a run for my money. "You've gotten significantly better since we started these sessions. Been holding out on me?"

Stitch continues her assault, raining down blows from all angles. I defend myself, countering her attacks when I can. We trade strikes back and forth relentlessly, neither of us giving ground.

"Yeah, well, I had a little help." She grins, a spark of mischief in her eyes.

"Oh?" I raise an eyebrow, circling her. "Care to elaborate?"

She ducks under a feigned strike, quick on her feet. "Let's just say I might have asked Jinx and Lily for a few lessons in jiujitsu." She dances back with a playful smirk.

Jinx and Lily are somewhat new to Guardian HRS. Lily is a former DEA operative. Jinx is a former DEA cryptologist who happens to be a master of Brazilian jiujitsu.

"You mean you've been practicing behind my back?" I stop, feigning shock.

"Guilty as charged." Stitch nods, a whirlwind of kicks and spins as she advances. "I need every advantage I can get, including turning my size into an asset rather than a liability."

"My crafty girl, always full of surprises." I can't help but laugh, even as I defend against her agile movements. She catches me off guard again in another swift move, and I find myself on my back for the second time.

Our banter continues as we spar, both impressing and challenging each other. There's much more to learn about Stitch. This remarkable woman keeps surprising me at every turn.

She mixes up her moves—jabs, hooks, roundhouse kicks—keeping me on my toes as I try to anticipate her next move. I counter each combination she throws at me but find myself concentrating to keep up. Stitch has come a long way, no doubt about it.

I throw a punch aimed at her shoulder, but she deftly sidesteps, using my momentum against me. As my fist sails past, she grabs my wrist with lightning speed and tries to twist my arm behind my back.

Sensing her intention, I rotate my body to relieve the pressure before she can lock in the hold. Her grip breaks as I slip free. We reset, circling each other warily.

I bounce lightly on my feet, ready for her next attack. Stitch looks focused. Her chest rises and falls rapidly, hints of perspiration gleaming on her skin. Then, she's in motion again, continuing her assault, raining strikes on me from all angles.

I defend and counter, but she matches me blow for blow. She's giving me a serious run for my money now.

Her technical skill is undoubtedly top-notch, but I worry her new prowess might make her overly cocky. She may think her skills can compensate for her slender build against a larger, trained opponent, but in the field, brawn and decades of training often win out over book smarts when things get ugly.

I'll need to keep an eye on her if things go sideways and ensure that intellectual arrogance doesn't blind her to real dangers. She's come so far, and I'd hate to see her compromise her safety to prove something.

Suddenly, she feints left, then aims a spinning back kick at my midsection with blinding speed. I absorb the blow against my forearm, wincing slightly at the force of impact. She packs a mean kick, that's for sure.

Before Stitch can regain her balance from the missed strike, I grab her from behind, wrapping my arms around her petite frame and trapping her in a bear hug. She struggles furiously, but my superior strength keeps her immobilized.

My arms lock firmly around her torso, which presses the firm globes of her ass against my crotch. A wave of heat washes through me. A distracting ache that throbs below my belt.

Get it together, man. This is just sparring.

I shake my head, trying to clear my mind, but my hands slacken around her waist.

Big mistake.

Sensing the subtle shift, she slams her head back, catching my chin in a perfectly timed strike. Pain explodes in my jaw, and stars burst behind my eyelids.

"Fuck!" I grunt in shock, grip loosening just enough for her to twist free. Note to self—never underestimate this woman.

She fights dirty.

We reset several feet apart, both breathing hard. I work my jaw gingerly from side to side, assessing for damage. Thankfully, nothing feels broken.

Stitch tightens her long ponytail and flips it back over her shoulder, hiding a satisfied little smirk. My pain amuses her.

"Tricky move," I say, working my jaw to relieve the residual ache. "I won't underestimate you again."

"See that you don't." Her eyes glint with mischief and something far more dangerous.

We explode into motion again, Stitch flowing smoothly from one strike to the next. I counter each attack, our moves turning into a heated dance. Each grapple builds the tension higher as we strain against each other. I can no longer ignore the sensual energy simmering between us.

At one point, I trap Stitch against the wall, our lower bodies pressed tight. My thigh slips between her legs, and I stifle a groan at the contact. She takes advantage of my distraction to reverse our positions again.

We go back and forth, battling for dominance. With each touch, my blood heats further. I grab at her hips, seeking out her curves. Her nails rake down my back possessively. Our evasive footwork deteriorates as I focus on the feel of her body under my hands. Her supple thighs grip my hips, straining against me.

I'm lost, drunk on her nearness, my tactical mind drowned out by sheer wanting. We clutch and grasp desperately, both seeking the upper hand through unconventional means.

Finally, exhausted and drenched in sweat, we collapse onto the mats, our chests heaving. My entire body thrums pleasantly, every nerve alive and tingling.

I turn my head to look at Stitch splayed beside me. Her cheeks are deliciously flushed, and her ponytail comes undone. She meets my gaze, something dangerous sparking between us.

I sit reluctantly, willing my body under control. "I think that's enough for today." My voice comes out rough, still affected by our close grappling.

Stitch sits up languidly. "If you say so."

I stand and offer her a hand up. When her fingers slide into mine, a jolt races up my arm. Our eyes catch and hold for a moment. With effort, I gently pull her to her feet. The smell of her shampoo surrounds me, something light and floral.

"Good match," I manage to say. My voice sounds gravelly to my ears. I clear my throat and take a subtle step back before I do something stupid like crush her against me and kiss her senseless.

Down boy. Let's not complicate things.

"Yeah, you weren't completely terrible." Stitch smirks, tucking a loose strand of hair behind her ear.

"Thanks, I think?" I chuckle at her backhanded compliment. This woman sure knows how to stroke a man's ego.

I enjoy these glimpses of the raw courage and resilience within her. She won't back down or break, no matter how grueling the training gets.

Stitch is shaping up to be a formidable ally, someone I'd be glad to have at my side watching my back. With skills like hers on the team, our odds of taking down Haven increase significantly.

We both seem unsure what to do next. I rub the back of my neck, grasping for something neutral to say. I settle for something dumb.

"You want to grab some food? I'm starving after that workout."

"Definitely. I could eat a horse right now." Stitch perks up at the mention of food.

I laugh, leading the way toward the locker room. "I don't know about a whole horse, but let's grab showers and figure out dinner."

"Alone or together?" Stitch asks boldly, eyebrow raised.

Her challenge hangs between us, her eyebrow arched in a bold, unspoken dare. I'm momentarily speechless, her forwardness catching me completely off guard.

"As tempting as that offer is…" I finally manage, my voice slightly rough. "Fooling around in the locker room showers seems unwise. You don't want to give the guys that kind of ammo. They'd never let you live it down."

Her eyes gleam with playful defiance. "I was thinking more about my place, not the communal showers in your bullpen. But hey, if you'd rather shower with the guys…" Her voice trails off, the tease in her tone unmistakable.

The tension between us, always simmering just below the surface, now crackles with a newfound intensity.

"Now that's an offer I can't refuse." The words are barely out before I act on the impulse.

I scoop her up in one swift, fluid motion, lifting her effortlessly off her feet. Stitch lets out a surprised squeak, a sound that sends a thrill straight through me. I hoist her over my shoulder in a classic fireman's carry, her body light yet substantial against mine.

Her initial shock gives way to laughter, her body vibrating with it against my shoulder. Her hands pound playfully against my back as I stride confidently toward her quarters. Heads turn as we pass, but I don't care.

It's just Stitch and me—the rest of the world fades into insignificance.

The hallway to her quarters stretches before us, my steps purposeful and unwavering. I sense Stitch's excitement, her energy infectious. I'm a man on a mission, driven by the magnetic pull of our mutual attraction and the unspoken promise of what's to come.

As we reach her quarters, I gently set her down, our eyes locking in a moment charged with anticipation. The door closes behind us, enveloping us in the privacy of her space. The room is a stark contrast to the chaos of the training grounds, a quiet sanctuary away from prying eyes and relentless routines.

Stitch stands before me, her breathing quickened, a flush spreading across her cheeks. The air between us is thick with unspoken words, a tension that's been building since the day we met. Since that first night together, we've been perfecting this dance, a slow burn of desire broken by the hunger we share for each other.

She steps closer, closing the gap between us. Heat radiates from her body, the subtle scent of her skin filling my senses. There's a moment of hesitation, a fleeting second where everything hangs in the balance, and then the space between us disappears.

Our lips meet in a kiss that's urgent yet somehow tender, a perfect contrast of emotions. My hands find their way to her waist, pulling her closer as she wraps her arms around my neck to deepen the kiss. The connection is electric, a current that runs through us, igniting every nerve.

We break apart momentarily, breathless. Stitch's eyes are bright, alive with a fire that mirrors mine.

Our lips meet again, this time with a newfound intensity. The world outside her quarters fades away, leaving only the two of us lost in the moment, giving in to desire.

EIGHTEEN

Jeb

—————

It takes seconds for my restraint to shatter. I ball a fist in Stitch's hair, controlling her, and release the carnal beast within me. My mouth grinds against hers with maddening pressure.

I take.

I claim.

I possess and dominate.

She surrenders to my hunger, flipping my dominance into overdrive. I take her mouth deeply, then pull away. With firm pressure on her shoulders, I force her to her knees.

Her fingers grab at my waistband buckle, frantic in her need. Together, we fight to free me from the confines of my clothes. Somehow, we manage in our haste.

My pulse accelerates, sending hot blood rushing to my groin, where I swell and harden.

Where I throb with need.

For her.

I need her touching me everywhere and all at once.

This desire isn't something I control.

It's raw.

Visceral.

Incredible.

Over the past few weeks, I've been testing her boundaries, seeing how far I can push her, and I've been pleasantly surprised. At first, she was reserved and somewhat shy, but it quickly became clear she craved more than a firm hand.

A glimmer of her submissive side is a magical awakening and tells me everything I need to know to drown her in sensation and lavish her with unadulterated pleasure.

On her knees, she opens her mouth for me. I shouldn't, but it's too hard to restrain myself. I shove my cock straight to the back of her mouth.

Sweet, holy… Fuuuuck. That feels so damn good.

She takes me deep. Wrapping her soft lips around my girth. Her hot tongue licks along my turgid length. I love the way she sucks me to the back of her throat.

I groan as pleasure spikes, and that's when I take over. I plunge mercilessly, loving the sensations sweeping through my body.

Initially, I never took pleasure first, always focused on her needs above my own, but we've found our rhythm. One thing she loves is switching things around, serving before receiving.

She does that now.

My insides tighten as she licks and sucks my cock. The woman's oral skills are devastating: applying a precise amount of pressure, teasing with tantalizing licks at the tip, and using the suction of her mouth to stimulate and drive me insane.

She explores my body, caressing my thighs, digging her nails into my ass. By the time her hands move back around to my balls, I'm panting and fighting the demands of my body.

Holy shit, I'm going to come.

Might even black out.

I never want this to end.

Stitch gets creative, sucking the sensitive tip while using her tongue to stimulate the underside of my glans.

Holy hell.

It feels so damn good.

Then, she hums. The low vibration of her mouth makes my balls draw up.

Tighten.

I can no longer stop the jerking of my hips. Once again, my hands fist the hair at the back of her head. I crush my groin against her sweet mouth, drilling as deep as I can go.

Mindless need envelops me. I have to have her. Fuck her. Consume her. Shit, I need to bury myself deep within her.

I fuck her mouth. Her throat. Ravage her. And she takes every inch.

Sucking harder.

Drawing me deeper…

My cock swells. My head tilts back, and my breaths career out of control as pleasure rockets through me. My toes curl, and my hips slam forward as I bury myself as deep as I can.

Stitch slows the tempo of her tongue, lapping me through the powerful release. My body shakes, and feral sounds fill the room as I ride the powerful waves of pleasure.

I pull out and look down at Stitch, so damn sexy on her knees, her eyes bedazzled with the pleasure of giving.

But she's not the only one to give.

I want to drown her in pleasure until she loses control of her body, surrendering to my desire. Tonight, I aim to torment her and utterly destroy her.

She deserves it with the way she makes me come undone.

I grab Stitch by the hair and pull her up to her feet, a wicked smile playing on my lips. She looks at me with desire filling her eyes, anticipation and a hint of mischief in her gaze. Her hunger builds, matching my own.

I push her against the nearest wall, my body pressed against hers.

The heat of her body warms my chest. Our breaths mingle, hot and heavy, as I trail kisses along her jawline, nipping lightly at her earlobe. Goosebumps rise on her skin, a delightful shiver courses through her body.

My lips crash into hers, hungry and demanding. I want to

devour her, consume every ounce of her being. Her moans fill the room, a song of pleasure that fuels my desire. I break the kiss, trailing hot kisses along her jawline and down her neck. Nipping and sucking on her sensitive skin, I leave behind marks that will fade in a few days, but until then, they'll serve as a reminder of this night.

My hands roam her curves, exploring every inch of her. The rapid beat of her heart against my chest matches the rhythm of my racing pulse.

"Please," she whimpers, her voice dripping with need.

"I love it when you beg."

"Do you?"

"Don't you know it, and tonight, I'm going to make you beg for it."

With a swift motion, I tear off her clothes, revealing flawless skin that begs for my touch. She gasps as the cool air hits her nakedness but leans into me, craving more. I oblige, my hands gliding over her breasts, teasing her hardened nipples.

I take one between my thumb and forefinger, pinching and twisting it gently as she moans in pleasure. My other hand moves lower, slipping between her thighs to discover just how wet she is for me.

She drips with anticipation—aching for release—and I'm more than willing to give it to her. Pressing two fingers inside her tightness, I curl them upward to find that sweet spot that makes her scream my name.

Her legs tremble, and she clings to me for support as I thrust into her with an irresistible rhythm.

With one swift motion, I lift her up, wrapping her legs around my waist. Her damp core rubs against my hardened length, causing us both to groan in delicious agony.

It's been weeks since we traded condoms for medical tests and birth control. No longer is there any barrier between us.

I carry her to the bed, laying her down with a possessive hunger in my eyes. I crawl over her as if I'm stalking my prey.

My mouth finds its way back to hers while my hand dips

between her thighs, feeling the wetness that has pooled there. With precise movements, I tease her entrance before finally plunging two fingers deep inside.

"So damn responsive," I growl the words against her neck as my fingers go to work.

Stitch arches off the bed, wordlessly begging for more. Her nails dig into my back as waves of pleasure crash through her body.

"You're mine," I growl against her lips. "Say it."

"I'm yours."

"Who do you belong to?"

"You…"

"I want to feel you surrender completely to me," I growl, my voice rough with need.

Stitch's breath hitches, and she nods, a fire burning in her eyes. She craves the same intensity that I do. The ache between her thighs matches the throbbing in my veins. Slowly, I trail kisses down the column of her neck, nipping at her sensitive skin before moving lower.

My lips find the swell of her breasts, teasing her nipples with gentle flicks of my tongue. Her body arches toward me, craving more. With each passing second, her control slips as pleasure consumes her senses.

I lower myself to my knees, tracing a path with my mouth along the soft expanse of her abdomen, feeling the tremors ripple through her body. Her fingers clutch at the fabric of my shirt, desperate for something to hold onto as I continue my descent.

When I reach the apex of her thighs, I part them with a firm grip, exposing the glistening folds that ache for attention. My tongue dips between them, savoring her taste as I tease against her entrance. Stitch gasps, a melody of pleasure escaping from between her lips.

"Please," she moans, her voice filled with need. "Don't make me wait." Her legs tremble, and she clings to me for support as I thrust my tongue into her with an irresistible rhythm.

Her moans grow louder, resonating through the room as I delve deeper into her velvety depths. With each flick of my tongue and each stroke of my fingers, I push her closer to the edge of ecstasy. Her hips buck against my mouth, seeking more friction, more release.

But I'm not finished with her yet.

I withdraw momentarily, leaving Stitch panting and desperate for more. I reach into the drawer beside the bed and retrieve a silk scarf—a symbol of both our trust and our insatiable desires.

"To surrender means to trust implicitly." Gently, yet firmly, I show her the scarf. "Do you trust me?"

Stitch's chest rises and falls rapidly as she locks her gaze with mine. Her eyes flicker with desire as she gazes at the silk scarf in my hand.

"Yes." Her voice is laced with anticipation, husky with longing, but is barely more than a whisper that sends shivers down my spine.

A surge of primal excitement courses through my veins as I trail the silk scarf lightly across her skin. I bind her wrists, securing them gently yet firmly, ensuring her comfort and safety amidst the intoxicating haze of pleasure that surrounds us.

"The scarf binds you to my will." I secure the silk around her wrists, tying it in a delicate knot. "Do you accept my power over you?"

As I trail my fingertips along the length of her arm, I'm acutely aware of the power I hold over her, the responsibility to both fulfill her deepest longings and push her beyond her limits.

"Yes."

"Surrender is not weakness." Leaning in close, my lips brush against her earlobe, sending a tremor through her restrained body. "It's a sacred gift," I whisper, my breath hot against her skin. "An act of bravery, of giving yourself fully to pleasure."

Stitch nods, her eyes shining with a mix of excitement and vulnerability. She craves the intensity that this new level of surrender brings.

The dominant part of me relishes control, but it's underscored by an overwhelming tenderness for this woman who has willingly placed herself in my hands.

With her arms restrained above her head, Stitch lies there

vulnerable and exposed, her body a canvas awaiting my touch. The sight sends an electric current surging through me, heightening my senses with each passing second.

Her body thrums with desire as I trail kisses along her neck and down the curves of her breasts. Her nipples harden beneath my touch as I cup them gently, eliciting soft moans from deep within her throat.

I capture her lips in a searing kiss, my tongue tangling with hers as our passion ignites anew. My cock hardens once again.

Hungry.

Eager.

Voracious for her.

Our bodies press against each other with an urgency that borders on desperation. The scent of our desire fills the air, mingling with the sounds of our shared moans.

As I break away from our kiss, I drink in the sight of her before me—flushed cheeks, heavy-lidded eyes, and swollen lips. Aching to please her further, my hands trail a path down her trembling body, exploring every curve and dip along the way.

A soft growl escapes my throat as I reach the apex of her thighs once again. With each stroke of my fingers against her soaked core, I am met with a symphony of gasps.

"I'm going to devour you." My words send an intoxicating shiver down her spine. "Every ounce of your pleasure will be mine to give."

Her eyes flutter with a potent mix of desire and surrender as I lower myself back between her legs. Taking my time, I press gentle kisses against the inside of her thighs, savoring the muffled gasps that escape her parted lips. My tongue traces a wicked path along the silky contours of her sex, teasingly avoiding the places she craves.

She will beg for it.

A surge of lust courses through me as her hips press against my mouth, a silent plea for release. But I won't give in just yet. Not until she's reached the pinnacle of her desire.

Not until every nerve in her body quivers with anticipation.

With deliberate slowness, I run my tongue along the length of her, tasting her essence on my lips. She bucks against me, her need becoming more urgent with each passing second. But I maintain my pace, teasing her, denying her that final release she desperately craves.

Her breath comes in ragged gasps as I flick my tongue over her swollen clit, the sensation sending shockwaves of pleasure coursing through her body. A low moan escapes her throat, and I know she can't take much more.

But I'm not done with her yet.

I slide a finger inside of her, savoring the slick heat that surrounds me. She clenches around me, her walls pulsating with need. The sound of her pleasure fills the room as she bears witness to the depths of my control over her.

"Please," she whispers hoarsely, her voice heavy with desire and desperation. "Please, don't make me wait any longer. Fuck me."

Her plea ignites a fire within me, urging me to give in to our shared craving. With a wicked grin, I increase the speed and pressure of my movements, driving her closer to the edge.

Her moans crescendo into a cry of ecstasy as I bring her to the brink. Her body convulses beneath me as waves of pleasure wash over her, shattering the last remnants of control she had left.

I watch with satisfaction as she comes undone, and then, it's my turn to dominate and claim.

I revel in the aftermath of her release, her body still trembling beneath me. The room is filled with a haze of desire and satisfaction, the air heavy with the sweet scent of our shared passion. But my hunger is far from sated.

Moving up, I capture her lips with mine. Our tongues tangle and dance in a fervent battle of desire and need. As I deepen the kiss, her need mirrors mine.

My fingers trail along the curves of her body, tracing invisible patterns along her heated skin. Every touch elicits a gasp or shiver, heightening our desire for each other. I revel in the power she has bestowed upon me, allowing me to push her boundaries further than ever before.

With a predatory growl, I pin her beneath me. Her eyes meet mine, dark with lust and a hint of defiance. A challenge that only fuels the fire burning within me.

I lower myself onto her, notching the flare of my cock against her center, my own need throbbing and demanding attention.

Her body arches up to meet mine, the slick warmth between her thighs beckoning me closer. The anticipation in her eyes feeds my hunger, fueling my desire to consume her completely.

With a slow, deliberate pace, I sink into her depths, savoring the sensation of every inch, claiming her as mine.

A gasp escapes her lips as I fill her completely, our bodies molding together in perfect harmony. My hips rock, thrusting in and out until the rhythm of our bodies becomes a symphony of pleasure and release, each thrust pushing us closer to the edge of oblivion.

Her nails dig into my back, and I revel in the sting, cherishing the marks that will fade but bear testament to our unbridled passion. With each thrust, I devour her gasps and cries, lost in the hedonistic realm we've created for ourselves.

Time loses all meaning as we surrender to the primal dance; male and female united as one. We become lost in the sensations, drowning in the depths of our insatiable lust. Her body tightens around me like a vise, signaling that she's teetering on the precipice once again.

But this time, I'm consumed by a different kind of hunger—a hunger for total surrender. With a predatory glint in my eyes, I flip her onto her stomach and continue my assault, claiming her from a new angle.

The change in position ignites a primal instinct within both of us, intensifying the raw passion that courses through our veins.

Her moans become more urgent as I grip her hips, guiding her movements to match my own. The sound of our bodies colliding fills the room, mingling with our ragged breaths and fervent whispers. Time stretches thin as we lose ourselves to the moment.

Her body tenses beneath me, signaling that she's reaching her peak. I take her to the edge, pushing her until she succumbs to the overwhelming pleasure crashing through her.

As her trembling subsides, I pull back slightly, my length still buried deep inside her. A wicked grin plays on my lips as I lean down to whisper in her ear.

"You're not done yet," I murmur, my voice low and filled with a dark promise. Her eyes widen with anticipation, a mixture of desire and curiosity sparkling within them. I know her so well, every inch of her body and every secret desire that lies hidden beneath the surface.

With a swift movement, I pull out of her, leaving her empty and gasping for more. The ache in her eyes matches the fire burning within my own. I reach down and grab a handful of her hair, pulling her head back to expose the delicate line of her throat.

"Turn around," I command, my voice laced with authority and desire. She obeys without hesitation, eagerly flipping onto her back to face me. Her chest heaves with anticipation, her nipples puckered and begging for attention. I let go of her hair and trail my fingertips down the curve of her body, relishing the delicious shivers that follow my touch.

"No touching," I growl, knowing how much it will drive her crazy.

She nods frantically, understanding the rules of this new game we're about to play. Slowly, I release the bindings on her hands and lift the silk.

"Your hands are free, but if you touch without permission, I'll smack your ass and leave you wanting. For now, I take away your sight."

Blindfolded, she lies there, vulnerable and eager, her senses heightened by the darkness. Anticipation hangs heavy in the air as I move around her, tracing my fingers lightly over her exposed skin. Her body arches toward me with each gentle caress, silently begging for more.

I lean in close, letting my breath tease the delicate shell of her ear. "Do you trust me?" I whisper. My voice a seductive murmur that sends shivers down her spine.

She nods in affirmation, her body trembling with anticipation. The weight of my dominance hanging over her like a veil of desire.

With a swift motion, I grab her wrists and secure them to the headboard.

I never told her I wouldn't bind her a second time.

"Now," I say, my voice filled with command. "You are mine to pleasure as I see fit. Or to take pleasure from as I desire."

Her breath catches in her throat at my words, melding with the sound of silk sliding against silk as I tighten the blindfold around her eyes. In this darkness, she surrenders herself entirely to me, giving up control and basking in the intoxicating unknown.

I step back to admire my creation—bound and blindfolded before me. The fire within me burns brighter as I imagine all the ways I will bring her pleasure tonight. Every touch and sensation carefully calculated and designed to push her further into ecstasy.

I slowly trail my fingertips across her body once again, savoring the way she arches into my touch, yearning for more contact. With each whispered promise that escapes my lips, she trembles beneath me.

"Patience."

The fire burning within me grows hotter with each breath. Her body, bound and blindfolded before me, is an intoxicating sight. I can almost taste her desire in the air as I trail my fingertips across her skin, savoring the way she arches into my touch.

With a primal growl, I climb over her once again and fuck her like a man possessed, the intensity building with every thrust.

Our bodies move together in perfect rhythm, fueled by our shared hunger and desire for one another. Her moans and whimpers are music to my ears as I take her higher and higher, pushing us closer to our peak.

With one last thrust, we reach climax together, crying out in a symphony of pleasure that echoes throughout the room.

But even after she's fully spent, I continue to tease and pleasure her with my hands and mouth until the sun starts to rise on a new day.

With gentle kisses and whispered promises of more nights like this to come, I release her from her bindings and remove the blindfold from her eyes. As she blinks against the sudden light, a satisfied smile spreads across her face.

"I never knew submission could be so exhilarating," she says breathlessly.

"Submission?" I chuckle. "No darling, you did not submit to me. You surrendered."

And it is glorious.

NINETEEN

Stitch

ANOTHER COUPLE OF WEEKS PASS IN A BLUR OF PLANNING AND training. Mornings are spent with Mitzy's tech team, developing infiltration tactics to take down Haven. Afternoons are reserved for honing my combat skills with the men of Charlie team. They teach me everything from sparring to shooting to infiltration and assault tactics.

It's overwhelming, but I absorb every detail.

Frankly, I'm scared.

Sitting behind a computer screen is the safest place to be, but on this op, the Guardians need a technical operative with my skills. Which means I'll be with them on the ground.

As such, they immerse me in a crash course of everything it means to be a Guardian.

Jeb and I steal what few private moments we can between mission preps. But it's not enough. I ache for more of his consuming touch, his confident possession of my body.

Our trysts leave me trembling, desperate for his lips and hands, but all too soon, duty calls, ripping me from his arms.

After a long day of training with his team, we break and head to the local pizza joint to unwind over drinks and food.

The bar is packed when we arrive, but the moment the men of Charlie team enter, there's a tangible transformation in the room's energy, like a ripple of masculinity spreading out from their presence. Their towering statures and chiseled physiques scream of raw power and fierce discipline, remnants of their Navy SEAL days compounded by their roles now as Guardians.

"First round's on Ethan, but we'll cover the pizza." Gabe slaps Ethan's back.

Ethan laughs. "Deal."

"Man, I could kill for a slice of pizza." Hank rubs his hands together in anticipation.

"Looks like tonight's prospects are looking good." Blake nudges Walt, pointing out a group of women at the bar.

"Not two feet in the door, and Blake's already chasing tail." Walt clamps a hand on Blake's shoulder.

Jeb gently guides me through the crowd with a protective hand at the small of my back. As we move, whispers follow us. Every step the Guardians take resonates with authority, and every gesture exudes undeniable confidence. They're a powerful force on the battlefield, but here?

Here, they're unstoppable.

"Table in the back okay?" Jeb whispers close to my ear, making sure I'm comfortable.

"Perfect," I reply, my voice softer than I'd like, feeling dwarfed by the overwhelming aura of the team.

They're like a gravitational force, drawing all the attention, making everything—and everyone—seem inconsequential. Beside them, I feel small and overshadowed. Each step they take vibrates with visible power, while my strengths remain hidden and intangible.

Jeb leans close, murmuring in my ear. "In your world," Jeb senses my unease, "you're the giant." His uncanny ability to sense what I'm thinking never ceases to amaze me.

He's not wrong. In the vast world of codes, hacking, and the dark web, I overshadow them by miles, my fingers dancing on a keyboard as I infiltrate the most secure systems, but here, in this physical world of muscle and might, I'm dwarfed by their power.

It's an unsettling feeling and a quiet reminder that while my skills are formidable, they don't command attention like the physical prowess of the Guardians.

I retreat into myself, wishing for a moment that my technical skills could be as outwardly evident as their physical prowess.

The din of clinking glasses, laughter, and chatter engulfs me. Overhead, strings of light cast a warm, welcoming glow, making the atmosphere feel cozy and familiar. Neon signs flicker and buzz, advertising different beer brands, and the delicious scent of hot pizza and yeasty dough fills the air.

We grab a table in the back, and the worn wooden benches creak as we slide in. Settling in, the table's surface is a tactile map of carved names, initials, and dates, slightly sticky from past spills.

Jeb flags down a busty, bleach-blonde waitress.

She sashays over to our table, her hip cocked and a pencil poised behind her ear. "What can I get y'all tonight?"

Her eyes linger on Jeb, her lashes fluttering heavy with flirtation as she twirls a strand of her hair and pops her gum. Her name tag reads "Candy."

With a confident smirk, Jeb responds, "I'll take a meat lover's pizza and a veggie for our resident health nut over here." He tilts his head in my direction, winking mischievously.

Excitement stirs around the table as the guys add their orders.

Ethan, eyes shining with anticipation, grins wide. "Meat lover's for me, but make mine extra cheese." He rubs his hands in anticipation.

"Pepperoni for me," Hank adds, licking his lips.

"I'll take supreme," Walt chimes in, his fingers drumming rhythmically on the tabletop.

Not missing a beat, Jeb adds, "And let's get some pitchers of beer to wash it all down."

I can't contain my reaction, my nose scrunching, or the sound of pure disgust escaping me. The very thought of that yucky, yeasty, hoppy intoxicant makes me shiver in revulsion.

"Come on, you know you want to try it." Jeb nudges me playfully, eyes dancing with mischief.

"You know damn well I hate that piss water." Returning his gaze, my lips curl in disgust. "That stuff is liquid trash. Tastes like moldy bread soaked in rancid rainwater."

"Such cruel words. A crisp, cold beer is a thing of beauty." Jeb's laughter is infectious. He places a dramatic hand over his heart, looking genuinely wounded.

"Yeah, if by beauty you mean something that'll make you hurl. Hard pass from me." I roll my eyes, unable to stop the teasing lilt in my voice.

"Not a beer gal, huh, sweetie?" Candy looks between us, clearly sensing Jeb is ribbing me. "What can I get for you instead?"

"I'll just take a Diet Coke, thanks. Unlike these heathens, I possess a refined palate." As an added taunt, I stick my tongue out at Jeb, the childish gesture making him chuckle.

"You're missing out." Jeb points a finger at me. "There's nothing about a Diet Coke that says refined palate. Someday, I'll get you to change your mind."

"Yeah, good luck with that." I snort inelegantly. "Like I'll ever drink nasty, skunky beer." Secretly, I love these lighthearted moments. Our playful debates are quickly becoming a cherished ritual.

Except for my goth vibe, I fit right in with the laid-back attire of the regulars. Most patrons look like they've come straight from a long day at work, with smudged uniforms and windswept hair.

Ethan's gaze lingers on me, particularly on my shirt. His eyebrow arches in mild amusement. "Considering what Guardian HRS pays you, you could refresh that wardrobe. Especially that shirt. It looks like it's been through war and is barely hanging on by a thread."

I glance down, fingers brushing the faded print of my cherished Angel Fire concert T-shirt. "Angel Fire hasn't been on tour in ages. No new swag to snag." I sigh wistfully, fiddling with its thin, tattered edges that whisper of countless washes and wear. "The memories attached to this shirt make it irreplaceable."

Hank, ever the joker, snickers, "Why not ask Forest? He'll give you a whole box of their T-shirts."

Confusion knits my brows, "Why would Forest do that? Is he a fan?"

A hush falls over the table, followed by suppressed laughter. Feeling like I'm missing the punchline of a joke, I turn to Jeb, searching his face for clarity, but he bites his lip, struggling to hold back his laughter.

"Umm…" Hank looks around the table. His gaze lands on Jeb. "She doesn't know?"

"Know, what?" I turn to Jeb, suddenly suspicious he's been holding out on me.

"Let's just say that Angel Fire and the Guardians…" Ethan leans in and lowers his voice to a whisper. "We're more connected than you think. I'm surprised you don't know."

"Again… What don't I know?" Frustration rises within me. I hate being left out. I like it even less when I'm the butt of a joke.

"Forest isn't just a die-hard fan or your regular guy who loves Angel Fire." Hank continues, "He's their manager."

"Their, what?" My eyes have got to be bugging out of my head. "No way."

"Next time we're roasting marshmallows on *Insanity's* rocky shores, you can ask the band for a private concert." Blake rubs his hands and winks at me.

"Wait, you guys *actually* know Angel Fire?" My jaw drops, the pieces falling into place. "And when you say *Insanity*, are you talking about the song or the place?" I glance around the table, looking for signs they're pulling my leg.

The team exchanges amused glances, clearly enjoying themselves.

Ever the mischievous one, Gabe chuckles, "Well, you could say we've had a couple of cookouts together, and we might've shared a few stories about our new hacker."

Their laughter is infectious, even though they're making fun of me. It means they're slowly drawing me into their close-knit circle. I've never had that in the real world.

Sure, I had it with Malfor and the others. We were tight, but that was all online. After my arrest, they scurried like cockroaches, slipping out of sight. If they were ever my friends, they were fair-weather friends at best.

Jeb wraps an arm around my shoulder and smirks, "You're in for a lot of surprises, sweetie. Welcome to the family."

"Just wait 'til we introduce you to the band." Walt wipes frothy beer from his chin. "Maybe you can get them to sign your shirt?"

Ethan leans forward and props his elbows on the table. "Especially if you show up in one of their shirts that's barely holding on."

Hank raises an eyebrow, "Or maybe they'll think she's their number one fan?"

"I *am* their number one fan." I thump Jeb in the arm. "Why didn't you mention you knew the band?"

Gabe's words finally percolate through my brain, and my heart practically leaps out of my chest. My eyes widen with shock and elation.

"Hold on... You spoke to Angel Fire about me? Like, *mentioned* me?" I sputter, barely containing the torrent of emotions threatening to spill over.

The table vibrates from the intensity of my excitement. My face grows hot, and nervous energy courses through me. My hands clasp together, almost as if praying, fingers twitching.

Blake smirks, leaning back in his seat, his eyes dancing with mirth. "More than a few times. They're curious about Guardian HRS's infamous baby hacker Mitzy took under her wing."

Hank takes a swig of his drink and grins. "Didn't Ash mention something about dedicating a song to a certain 'genius hacker?' "

"Ash, as in Blaze? Lead singer Blaze?" The shocks keep coming.

"Well, we call him Ash." Gabe's nonchalant comment has my eyes widening. He adds fuel to the fire with a wink. "You really didn't know Forest is their band manager? He claims *he* is their number one fan. You might have some competition."

Jeb nudges me playfully. "Maybe you should challenge him for the title of Number One fan."

"Hell, yes." Blake sucks down the last of his beer. "Now that's a fight I wouldn't miss. Stitch vs. Forest in a battle of the Angel Fire superfans. I'd pay to watch that showdown."

"Wait a second." My brows knit in confusion. "Forest? As in—Forest Summers? Head of Guardian HRS? That Forest?"

Blake nods, laughing at my bewildered expression. "The very same. Always going on about being Angel Fire's number one fan. It's a riot watching him and the band banter about it."

Still in shock, I mutter, "The things you guys keep from me."

"Not Bash." Ethan chuckles, "Mitzy's married to Noodles."

"Noodles? Their keyboardist? You're shitting me?" I gasp, nearly spitting out my drink. "Mitzy? And Noodles? Married? Forest Summers is their manager? How did I not know this?" My head spins with this influx of information. The room is suddenly brighter and more alive.

Gabe nods, the wicked gleam never leaving his eyes. "Absolutely. You might want to prepare yourself for some mega-fangirl moments sooner than you think. And challenge Forest for that 'number one fan' title. It'll be fun to watch the two of you duke it out."

"No." I shake my head. "You're just messing with me. Trying to get your little goth girl to fall for your lies."

Ethan pats my hand reassuringly. "We're serious. Angel Fire and the Guardians have more connections than you could ever imagine. In addition to Forest and Mitzy, Skye's married to Ash."

"Skye?"

"Forest's sister. Head of Medical." Ethan adds. "How are you their number one fan and not know this?"

"In my defense, I'm a fan of their music, not a crazy stalker who digs into their personal lives. I'm too busy for that kind of trivial shit." Boy, do I regret that now. "Honestly, Mitzy keeps me buried in work. I don't get out much."

In the middle of our conversation, Candy strides over with a tray full of pizzas, the delicious aroma preceding her. She sets them down with a flourish, ensuring each one lands with a soft thud that teases our hungry stomachs.

"Here you go, hot and fresh, just like y'all like it." Candy's eyes fix on Jeb for a moment longer than necessary.

Jeb grins, taking a moment to admire the perfectly crisped crust and the colorful toppings. "Looks fantastic, Candy. You always know how to deliver."

Candy leans over the table, allowing her cleavage to be more evident, casting a sultry look in Jeb's direction. "Oh, I aim to please," she says with a flirtatious lilt, her fingers brushing Jeb's hand as she hands him an extra napkin. "Anything else you'd like, love?"

Jeb, ever the charmer, smirks and leans back in his chair, giving her a once-over. "Well, you've already brightened the table, but maybe another round of drinks for the group?"

"Anything for you." She giggles, playing with a strand of her hair. Her gaze remains fixated on him, her intentions clear, before turning on her heel, leaving a trail of lingering perfume in the air.

I lean in, whispering to Hank, "She's laying it on thick, isn't she?"

Hank chuckles, "Yeah, but can you blame her? Jeb's got that effect on people."

Gabe snorts, diving into a slice of pizza, "I'll say. If I had a nickel for every time someone flirted with Jeb…"

Jeb shrugs, playing it cool. "What can I say? The ladies love my tips."

"Pretty sure Candy's hoping for more than *just the tip* from you, buddy," Hank ribs him crudely.

Jeb casually drapes his arm over my shoulders. "Too bad. Poor Candy. I've already got everything I need right here." He brushes a light kiss over my hair, subtle but intimate. Under the table, his hand gives my thigh a gentle squeeze. "But you can have her."

"Might take you up on that." Hank leans back, eyes on Candy serving her customers.

I smile softly, leaning against Jeb.

His message is loud and clear—I'm his girl.

I've never been a guy's girl before.

Jeb's thumb strokes my shoulder as he steals heated glances my way. I take a long drink of soda to temper the rising flush the glances provoke. He sure knows how to stake his claim.

I glance around the table, taking in the animated faces, shared laughter, and team camaraderie. A pang of insecurity hits me. Do I belong here? Among these giants, these heroes? Or are they only being kind to me because they have no other choice?

TWENTY

Stitch

OUR TABLE BECOMES A MEDLEY OF EMPTY GLASSES AND HALF-EATEN pizza as the conversation flows with rapid-fire banter, jokes, boasts, and crass comments. The hoppy aroma of the pitchers mingles with the seductive scent of baked dough, spicy pepperoni, and melted cheese.

Jeb's subtle touches and affectionate glances continue as the night goes on. Under the table, his hand rests on my thigh, thumb idly stroking. It's a small, innocent contact, but each brush sends sparks skittering through me.

When I shiver, Jeb notices immediately.

"You cold?"

Before I respond, he slips off his jacket and settles it around my shoulders. The residual heat from his body envelops me, along with the woodsy scent I've come to crave.

"Better?" he asks. His eyes crinkle at the corners when he smiles.

"Much. Thank you." I snuggle into the oversized jacket, warmed inside and out.

Our faces are close.

Gazes locked.

The background noise fades.

Jeb's attention flicks to my lips.

My breaths turn shallow, and my heart pounds in anticipation…

He leans in…

A raucous cheer from his teammates breaks the spell. We jerk back, both flushed.

"Get a room, lovebirds." Gabe cackles. He wads up a napkin and tosses it at Jeb's face.

Jeb snatches the napkin out of the air and flips Gabe off good-naturedly, but Jeb's heated look promises we'll continue this later. I cross and uncross my legs, suddenly restless to be alone with this man—my man—his knee presses against mine, stoking the spark between us.

Tonight promises to end far more intimately than drinks with friends…

"Where the hell is our waitress?" Hank swirls the last drops of his beer and complains. "Who's up for a refill? My throat's as dry as a desert."

Blake gives an exaggerated sigh, "I'll go with you."

"I gotta take a piss." Jeb stretches, making a show of it.

"Ewww. Must you announce it so graphically?" Rolling my eyes, I grimace.

"Sounds better than saying I have to pee." He grins cheekily. "How about drain the lizard instead?"

"No. That's worse." I shove him playfully.

Jeb tilts his head slightly, mischief twinkling in his eyes. He clears his throat dramatically, then, in a deep, cinematic voice that reverberates past the booth and through the room, he loudly proclaims, *"I Must Unleash the Kraken!"*

Several patrons turn their heads, some chuckling and others rolling their eyes. Seeing my exaggerated eyeroll, he chuckles and continues, still in the theatrical tone.

"How about tapping the keg?"

"That's *more* worse." I groan. "And that just proves my point that beer smells like piss."

"Watering the plants, or maybe—" His eyebrows wiggle suggestively, "—paying the water bill?" He leans in, his voice a playful whisper.

"Okay, okay. Just do your thing and spare me any more colorful descriptions." My face contorts in a mixture of amusement and exasperation.

Jeb, with a playful salute, slides out of the booth. Almost in unison, the rest of the team shuffles out. Hank and Blake head to the bar while Gabe and Walt move toward the arcade games at the far end. Ethan stays with me.

The moment the guys leave the privacy of our booth, heads turn through the crowded bar. A gaggle of women eye Jeb like a piece of meat as soon as he's on his feet. More women stare at the others. Not that I blame them. The men of Charlie team are not only a formidable fighting force, they're sinfully hot. The ladies can look at all of them except Jeb.

He belongs to me.

I'm left sitting opposite Ethan. The dimmed lighting casts deep shadows over his face, making his piercing gaze seem more intense. I watch Jeb navigate through the packed bar, women pausing to steal glances, some blatantly ogling, and a surge of jealousy flows through me.

Several brazen hussies sidle up to Jeb, fluttering their lashes and touching his arms. Their bony-assed fingers playfully walk up his biceps. He smiles politely but seems focused on hitting the head rather than flirting.

"Ugh, those skanks need to keep their paws off what's mine." I bristle, seeing them fawn all over him.

"Jeb's just being polite." Ethan chuckles at my jealous streak.

"He could be a little *less* polite and tell those bitches to back the fuck up."

"Don't worry about Jeb. He's not a player." Ethan leans forward, his voice gentle yet firm.

"It's not that. It's just…" I force a smile, my fingers fidgeting. After weeks of training with the guys, I'm accustomed to their crass language. I don't even blink at Ethan's comment.

Under his tough exterior, the man is a gentleman. He waits, giving me space.

"This is all new for me." I take a deep breath. "I grew up in the foster system and bounced from home to home. I've never been a part of anything."

I'm not used to having people look out for me. I guess it doesn't feel real, like any moment I'm going to wake up, and it'll all be gone. Whatever is brewing between Jeb and me feels too good to be true. It's not jealousy.

"Then what's wrong?" He's intuitive enough to see my insecurities.

"Fear." There's no other way to explain it. "I'm afraid of losing him."

"That's fair." He nods solemnly. "Fear is a natural reaction. It's a lot to take in, but Jeb's one of the good ones. Honestly, I'm glad he's finally putting himself out there. It's been too long."

"Too long?"

"Well, you know? After... Uh," His face pales slightly, and he stammers briefly, eyes darting as if searching for a way out. It's clear he's mentioned something he shouldn't have.

"After what?" I press, curious about what he's hinting at.

"Not for me to say." Coughing to clear his throat, Ethan quickly sidesteps and changes the conversation. "Since we're alone, how do you feel about your training? Feeling good? You showed impressive skills today."

I'm momentarily caught off guard by the sudden topic shift, but I appreciate his interest in my training. "You're the expert. You tell me. There's a lot to learn."

"You're doing great."

"All five-foot-three of me?" I lean back, appreciating his praises while doubting his sincerity. "I'm glad I'm learning self-defense, but in a real fight, I'm practically useless."

"Remember, you're here for a reason. You're skilled, and the team sees that. I hear you've been sparring with Jinx. How's that been going?"

"I'm getting better and holding my own. She says with more time and practice, I might be able to take down one of you for real."

"You've taken us down to the mat plenty of times." His voice is steady and reassuring. "That says something right there."

"I think you guys let me do that."

"Trust me, none of us are *letting* you do anything. Those tosses and wins are all yours."

"But the size thing?"

"I'm certain Jinx has explained size doesn't always matter. If you know how to use momentum and speed to your advantage, a smaller person can take down someone much larger. Close quarters is where you'll struggle. So keep your distance as much as you can."

"But I'm a total newbie to this."

"It comes with time, but I've watched how you fight. You hold your own, but you'll never be alone out there. We've got your back the whole way."

"Thanks."

"What about weapons training? How are you feeling there?"

"My aim's pretty solid." A slight hesitation slips through my voice. "But the rifles? They're just—heavy. I struggle to hold them for any length of time."

Ethan nods thoughtfully, his thumb rubbing a slow circle on the table. "Handguns offer mobility. They're effective in close quarters, especially for someone your size and with your agility. What about blades? Have you worked on knife combat?"

"No." I shake my head, the admission making me feel a tad vulnerable.

"Then we'll focus on that." He leans forward slightly, a glimmer of determination in his eyes. "A knife, in the right hands, is deadly. It's light, quick, and can be an extension of your body when used properly."

"Do you think I have enough time to learn?" A mixture of anticipation and nerves rush through me. Any day now, Haven should be desperate and reach out to the dark web for help.

"There's enough time." Ethan's smile is confident. "It's all about leveraging your strengths, and we'll ensure you're ready."

"Thanks. I appreciate that. Hopefully, I'll just be sitting at the keyboard doing my thing while you and the others do your thing."

"Hopefully, but this world isn't perfect. I want you ready for anything." His unwavering belief in me is both humbling and empowering.

Needing to shift the conversation, I lower my voice and point at the crowded bar. Hank, Walt, Gabe, and Blake are making the rounds with the ladies, singling out their conquests for the night.

"Why aren't you out there joining the fun? You don't hook up at these things? Are you gay?" I play with the straw in my glass, unsure if my words are too personal.

"Is that a problem? I'm not, but it shouldn't matter."

"Nah. I know you're not."

"Then why did you ask?"

"I dunno." All the other guys are pairing off for the night. Several ladies are wiping drool from their mouths, staring you down, begging for a chance at you, but you're not biting. Why not?"

"Just not interested." Ethan flinches almost imperceptibly. His jaw tightens, and a shadow passes through his eyes. His fingers tap a steady rhythm on the table, a telltale sign of discomfort.

"It's Rebel, isn't it?" Remembering suddenly, my eyes widen in realization, "Oh god, Ethan—I didn't…" A flash of memory tugs at the edges of my mind as I realize my mistake. How could I have been so stupid?

I don't know her, but Rebel is one of the women Charlie team pulled from the grimy depths of a human trafficking operation in Nicaragua. Those few stolen weeks she spent entwined with Ethan, their souls connected in ways I can only guess? Then, just as suddenly as she entered his world, she vanished—leaving a trail of chaos and a hollowed-out Ethan in her wake.

Mitzy handed me that assignment. It was one of my first, a way to get used to Guardian HRS protocols and technology. I was supposed to uncover any trace of Rebel and track her down. Despite tireless deep dives into every lead, Rebel remains elusive. Like a ghost, she slipped through the fingers of Guardian HRS without a trace.

Once we discovered the existence of Haven, any search for Rebel and her whereabouts was put on the back burner. We turned all our attention to unearthing Haven's secrets.

And poor Ethan...

The raw hurt in his expression tells the tale of betrayal, a heart shattered by the weight of Rebel's deceit. To think, she wormed her way into the very fabric of Guardian HRS, extracting its secrets through him. The wounds left by Rebel aren't those of a fleeting romance. She devastated Ethan, and the sting of betrayal from someone he opened his heart to remains open and raw.

"It's fine." He waves me off, trying to brush it aside. "I'm just not interested."

But it's not, and we both know it. I bite my lower lip, cursing myself for treading on painful territory.

"I just meant... Rebel's a ghost. No reason for you to sit on the sidelines." I try to find the words, but how do you make up for something like that? Evidently, if you're me, you dig a deeper pit and jump right in. *A ghost?* Why the hell did I say that?

"What if I like the sidelines?" Despite my words, he smiles at me.

"You're a horrible liar but suit yourself."

"You're right." He meets my gaze, pain evident but also understanding. "Rebel is—" he pauses, looking for the right word, "—history."

"I'm sorry. I shouldn't have..."

He interrupts with a shrug. "It's in the past. And besides," he adds, forcing a smile and changing the subject, "You should be more concerned about *your* game plan for the evening." He gestures toward the crowd, where Jeb returns from *"Unleashing the Kraken!"*

Jeb strides back, easily navigating through the bustling crowd. There's an unspoken command in his posture that has people stepping aside, granting him a clear path. His eyes immediately find mine, and there's an unreadable intensity to his gaze.

"Ready to go?" he asks, extending a hand to help me from the booth.

"That's my cue. See you in the morning." I say goodbye to

Ethan, leaving him to his thoughts, and turn my attention to Jeb. I place my hand in his, loving how his fingers close around mine.

Solid.

Reassuring.

As we make our way toward the exit, I can't help but glance back at Ethan. His gaze is on us, thoughtful, but he offers a nod and a subtle wink, signaling his approval.

Once outside, the cool night air washes over us, a stark contrast to the stifling heat of the crowded bar. The distant sounds of laughter and music fade behind us, replaced by the muted hum of the night.

Jeb's fingers entwine with mine as we walk side by side, and I find my thoughts drifting back to Ethan's cryptic words. The weight of unsaid history hangs between Jeb and me.

"Hey," I begin hesitantly, "back in there… Ethan said something."

"Yeah? What?"

"He was talking about you…"

"Me?"

"Yeah."

"What did he say?"

"Something about it's been too long since you put yourself out there. What did he mean?"

Jeb's steps falter for a split second, a brief hesitation before he resumes his pace. He exhales deeply, raking a hand through his hair. "I'll tell you, but not here. Let's find somewhere quiet."

The promise of a looming revelation sends a shiver down my spine, and a torrent of questions swirls in my mind. Whatever Jeb has to say—it sounds ominous. Suddenly fearful, I'm afraid I won't like whatever he has to say.

TWENTY-ONE

Stitch

———

MINUTES LATER, WE'RE DRIVING DOWN THE PACIFIC COAST Highway in his truck. The bright city lights fade as the untouched coastline takes over, casting everything into shadows. The sea to our left, gleaming under the moonlight, stretches as far as the eye can see. Its rhythmic crashing sounds are both calming and tumultuous, mirroring the storm of emotions brewing between us.

Without a word, Jeb steers the truck into a scenic overlook, parking near the cliff's edge. The panoramic view of the ocean and starry sky above feels infinite, making my worries seem minuscule.

Jeb reaches for my hand, fingers twining with mine. With a gentle tug, he guides me to the low rock wall separating us from the sheer drop to the raging waters below. Though cold and hard, the wall offers a contrasting comfort as we settle against it. His fingers, still laced with mine, pull me a fraction closer until our shoulders touch, adding another layer of warmth.

Jeb's free arm wraps around my waist, anchoring me against the sudden gusts of wind that attempt to disturb our solitude. With him, I feel both vulnerable and shielded, an odd combination. The ocean's roar, coupled with the salty breeze that tangles my hair, heightens the raw intensity of the moment.

"It's beautiful here." My voice is almost lost in the symphony of crashing waves, trying to fill the silence and ease whatever Jeb is going to tell me.

He nods, his gaze fixed on the horizon, where the last remnants of sunset give way to the creeping darkness of night. "It's one of my favorite spots. A place to think. A place to remember."

The depth in his voice suggests layers of memories, some perhaps too painful to revisit. But tonight, with me, he seems ready to share.

I tilt my head to look at him, studying his face, bathed in the moonlight. His strong jaw is set, eyes shadowed, haunted even.

"What did Ethan mean?" I shouldn't push, but I can't help myself. I like Jeb, and the thought there's something bad in his past makes me question our future.

"It's not an easy story to tell, especially not one I share often." A sigh escapes his lips as he turns to face me.

"I'm sorry. I shouldn't push. You can tell me, but only when you're ready." I give his hand a reassuring squeeze, trying to convey my support.

He smiles weakly, appreciating the gesture, before taking a deep breath. "It's about my fiancée and our son, Maverick."

The world stops spinning.

It halts in its tracks.

Fiancée?

Son?

A bitter, cold sensation spreads through my chest, like icy tendrils gripping my heart. Every word after *fiancée* sounds distant, muffled as if I'm underwater. For a split second, the rock wall under me feels unsteady, and the ocean's vastness seems to swallow me whole.

Memories of the countless foster homes, the rejections, and the feeling of never being enough rush back in a suffocating flood of inadequacy.

Is history repeating itself?

Panic grips me, and I fight the urge to run.

But I can't.

I can't let Jeb see how much his words affect me.

I have to stay, to listen, to understand. There could be more to the story. Maybe I'm jumping to conclusions too soon?

God, I hope so.

Taking a shaky breath, I force my features into a neutral expression, a mask I've perfected over years of hiding my true feelings. But my fingers unconsciously clench the hem of my shirt, the fabric wrinkling under the pressure, betraying my turmoil.

"Go on," I whisper, my voice surprisingly steady despite the maelstrom raging inside.

"Five years ago, while I was deployed, Sarah, my fiancée, went into labor. She had complications, and—she didn't make it. I was on the other side of the world, powerless, unable to be there for her, and absent during the premature birth of our son."

My heart shatters, pieces tumbling into the abyss below. Tears well up, but I force them back, focusing on being here for him.

The night grows still, the waves crashing below, almost in sync with the rhythmic beating of my heart. Jeb's voice, heavy with pain, breaks the silence, revealing an agony that goes far beyond words.

"That mission… God, it was supposed to be straightforward, but things can change in the blink of an eye in this line of work. We were deep in enemy territory, moving quietly under the cover of night, but they knew we were coming. We were ambushed. Bullets came from all directions. It was chaos. And then Mike screamed." Jeb's voice shudders, the rawness evident.

"Mike?"

"My teammate." Jet takes in a steadying breath. "I turned to see him clutching his leg, blood pouring out. Without thinking, I crawled over to him. Yanked my belt free and fashioned a makeshift tourniquet, praying it would stem the flow."

The memories seem to wrap around him like chains, dragging him back to that harrowing moment. "We had to move. Had to get out of that hellhole, but Mike couldn't walk. Couldn't swim. He was losing strength fast."

"Swim?"

"Our exfil was through the ocean, a two-mile swim. We killed the men who ambushed us, then carried Mike to the water, trading his weight between us, and then we towed him out to sea. With each stroke, his breathing turned labored as he fought to stay conscious. I begged him to hang on the whole time I pulled him through the water."

His eyes reflect the moonlight and carry the shadows of that night. "When we finally reached our extraction point, the distant chop of the helo blades felt impossibly far away. With every ounce of strength I had left, I pushed Mike into the basket, watching him dangle, swaying, as the helicopter's powerful downwash churned the water around us. I remember the coldness, the weight of wet gear clinging to my skin, and the sharp sting of salt in my wounds as I waited for my turn."

"I can't… I can't even imagine."

Tears form in his eyes but don't fall, a testament to the strength he showed that day and every day after.

"The moment we were back on board, the ship's medics were all over Mike. I was still catching my breath." His grip on my hand tightens, and he swallows hard, his eyes glistening in the dim light. "My CO approached. His face… God, I'll never forget the look on his face. Before I could get my gear off or check on Mike, they had me on another helo, racing back to base. I didn't know why."

His voice finally cracks. "From the helo, I was forced onto a plane, still in my dirty uniform, still bleeding, heading home. No one would tell me anything the entire flight, but the pit in my stomach grew. I thought maybe something happened to my mom or my dad. But when we refueled, a senior officer boarded and sat beside me. He broke the news. Sarah was in labor, but there were complications. She was fighting, clinging to life, and they didn't know if she would make it."

I can almost see him in that plane, helplessness consuming him as the engines roared.

"Because we weren't married, getting permission to evac me home was hell. I fought through red tape and raced through airports, praying to reach her in time. I remember staring out the airplane window, begging any god who would listen—to let me make it. Let me hold her one more time."

Tears slide down his face, but he continues despite the painful memories. "But the universe didn't listen. Sarah fought hard…" He chokes up for a moment, then continues, his voice broken. "She passed away an hour before I got there."

"Oh, Jeb, I'm so sorry."

"The world I knew shattered." His voice is barely audible, choked with emotion. "I walked into the sterile hospital room, the smell of antiseptic thick in the air, to find a nurse holding a tiny bundle. My son, Maverick. Born into a world without his mother."

The rawness of his memories is palpable. His pain is as fresh as if it had happened yesterday. Holding onto him, I feel his heartbreak, the cruel twist of fate that ripped away his love and handed him a tiny life to care for without her.

"I'm so sorry. I… I can't comprehend what that must've been like."

He continues, his voice raw and gravelly. "After Sarah's death, I separated from the Navy. I was drowning in guilt and grief. I enrolled at MIT. Got my degree in three years rather than four. I was determined to build a safe life for Maverick, but a 9-to-5 job wasn't in my DNA. I needed action and purpose. So, I talked to my parents. They moved in to help me raise him, and I joined the Guardians."

A tear slips down his cheek, but he brushes it away impatiently. "I was torn between my responsibilities as a dad and my need to make a difference in this messed-up world."

We sit silently for a moment, the gravity of his words weighing heavily in the silence between us. I slide closer, our thighs touching, offering silent support.

"I had no idea." My voice is barely audible over the crashing waves.

His shoulders slump, an uncharacteristic sign of vulnerability. "The thing is, dating… It's not simple for me. Maverick, he's seen too much loss for someone his age. Bringing a woman into his life, it's not just about me. It's about him. I can't risk confusing him, or worse, having him get attached to someone who might not stick around."

Swallowing hard, he continues, the pain evident in his voice. "That first year after Sarah… God, it was a blur. I was so consumed by grief, anger, and guilt. But I couldn't show it. Not with a newborn relying on me. So I found—other ways to cope." He hesitates for a beat, then adds with a bitter chuckle, "I became someone I hardly recognized, seeking solace in strangers' arms, using women to numb the agony tearing me apart. Nameless faces, no strings attached, just a desperate attempt to feel something other than crushing grief."

The honesty in his voice cuts deep, and I feel the weight of his regrets. He's baring his soul, revealing the darkest parts of himself.

"But then, things began to change. I started to heal, bit by bit. My folks stepped in, and together, we built a new life for Maverick. With that came a promise. A promise to protect him from any more pain. Which meant keeping my personal life separate and not letting anyone get too close."

Looking down at our intertwined fingers, he adds softly, "I didn't mention any of this because… It's complicated. It's messy. And I wasn't sure if I was ready to bring someone into that chaos."

"I can understand that." I swallow the lump in my throat, realizing there are strings attached to whatever is growing between us. Not the strings I thought, but strings, nonetheless. I lean against him. "You don't have to worry about me. We can keep things casual. I would never want to come between the two of you."

"But that's the thing." He suddenly turns, facing me. He grasps my hands. "Ethan's right. I've shut out the world for a very long time. It's been too long since I let anyone in. With you, it feels different. I want to be open and honest. If there's a chance for something real between us, I don't want to hide any part of me."

He meets my gaze, his eyes searching mine. "I want you to know the real me. The wounds, the scars, the guilt I carry. If we're doing this, I want it to be real. But I come with emotional baggage, a precocious five-year-old, and parents who live with me. It's messy. I didn't say anything at the beginning because I… Well, things between us continued, got better, and we grew closer. By then, I didn't know how to bring up my son."

"I don't mind messy." I swallow hard, emotions swirling. "It's real for me too. What are your parents going to think when you bring home a convicted felon?"

"They'll be eager to meet you."

"And when they find out I'm ten years younger than you?"

"Nine." He huffs a soft laugh. "We'll make it work."

"When they say you're robbing the cradle and I'm not fit to parent a five-year-old, what will you do?"

"I'll tell them age is just a number." He grins like a fool. "And you're not scared to parent a five-year-old?"

"I'm terrified."

"You know…" He squeezes my hands. "You technically have to be married to me before you can be Maverick's stepmom."

"Oh shit…"

"Yeah."

"I didn't mean…" I try to pull out of his grip, but Jeb holds me firmly. "I didn't mean…"

He draws me close, our foreheads touching, our breaths mingling. "Usually, the guy does the proposing. You seem to be doing things backward, but I don't mind." His chuckle vibrates through the air between us, teasing yet gentle.

My cheeks flush. "I just meant… I care about you."

"Oh, I get it. You're trying to put a ring on it before you meet my son. Ambitious." He quirks an eyebrow, playfully tapping my nose with his finger.

I groan, playfully shoving him. "Stop making fun of me. It's just… I can see our future."

"I see that future, too." His eyes soften, the playful glint replaced by sincere emotion. "But maybe we should take things one step at a time. Meeting Maverick would be a good start."

"Is it too late to take back what I said?" I laugh at my forwardness.

"Way too late, but how about we take Maverick to the beach below *Insanity?* We can play in the tidepools and hang out with

Angel Fire around the bonfire." With a teasing smirk, he adds, "And for the record, I love that you're thinking about our future. Just let me get on one knee first, okay?"

My heart skips several beats. "Wait… What? Angel Fire? Like…" I stammer, my voice rising in pitch with each word. "You mean… I'd be—hanging out with them? Around a bonfire?"

"Yeah." Jeb chuckles, clearly amused by my fan-girl reaction.

My mind races. Hanging out with the biggest rock band in the world? That's every fan's dream. And now, here it is, offered to me on a silver platter.

"Should I be worried you're more excited to meet Angel Fire than me going down on one knee?"

"Shit. No. It's just…"

"Try not to freak out too much when you meet them. They're just regular people." Jeb leans in, whispering conspiratorially.

I snort, rolling my eyes. "Easy for you to say. I've had their posters plastered on my walls for years."

"Consider this your all-access backstage pass," he teases, tapping my nose.

"My head is spinning." I shake my head, still in disbelief. This night has been a whirlwind of emotions. From his story. To Maverick. And now this?

"Still nothing about the knee thing?"

"I'm pretending that didn't happen."

"But it did."

"Still, pretending it didn't."

Jeb wraps an arm around my shoulders, pulling me close. "Well, just hold on tight. Because life is about to get a whole lot crazier."

TWENTY-TWO

Jeb

THE SCENT OF MAPLE SYRUP FILLS THE AIR, ITS SWEETNESS accentuated by the savory aroma of sizzling bacon. Warm sunlight filters through the kitchen window, casting a soft glow on the wooden table laden with breakfast delights.

There, in the midst of it all, sits Maverick. His blond hair tousled, cheeks smeared with butter and syrup. He takes another large bite of his pancake stack. Each blueberry he encounters is met with a delighted grin, their juices staining his lips a purplish hue.

Beside him, my parents, each with their plates, exchange amused glances and chuckle at Maverick's fervent eating pace. Mom takes sips of coffee between bites of toast, while Dad seems content with his eggs and bacon.

The atmosphere is light, punctuated by the occasional clink of cutlery and Maverick's muffled giggles. I'm captivated by the scene —these simple moments mean a lot.

With a satisfied sigh, Maverick pushes away his nearly empty plate, his little belly protruding slightly. "I'm *soooo* full," he announces, his voice high and playful, dragging out the "so" for emphasis.

I lean toward him, tapping my finger conspiratorially against my lips.

"Hey, champ," I whisper, drawing him in close. "What do you say we burn off some of that pancake energy at the beach? Maybe look for crabs in the tidepools?"

"Really? Can we?" His vibrant green eyes, so much like his mother's, sparkle with anticipation.

I chuckle at his excitement. "Of course we can, but you've got syrup all over your face. Why don't you go wash up and get ready?"

Maverick's nod is vigorous, his enthusiasm barely contained. "Okay! I'll go fast!" He hops down from his chair, making a beeline for the bathroom, his small footsteps echoing down the hallway.

With Maverick momentarily out of the room, the atmosphere shifts. I share a silent look with my parents, a mix of gratitude for our time together and the slight unease that comes with what I'm about to share.

Together, the three of us clear the table, clinking dishes and the splash of water from the sink fills the silence. Mom gathers the plates, her movements graceful and practiced, while Dad scrapes leftover bits into the trash. I take the lead with the washing, letting the warm water run over my hands as I scrub away the remnants of our meal.

The familiar routine of cleaning up offers a momentary distraction, but as the dishes dwindle, the weight of my forthcoming revelation grows heavier.

"I've found someone," I finally say, breaking the silence. The weight of those words presses heavily on my chest, but I need them to understand. This isn't just another fling.

"What does that mean?" Mom wrings her hands, clearly agitated.

"You've 'found someone' more times than I can count." Dad meets my gaze with those familiar piercing blue eyes.

The reminder stings. Yes, I've been with women. Lots of them. But this is different."

"It's not like that. She's different. I want Maverick to meet her."

"What do you mean?" Mom stops her pacing, her worried eyes fixed on mine.

"I'm introducing them today."

"Today?" Mom shares a look with my dad. "Shouldn't you wait? Make sure she's special?"

"She is special." I grip the dish sponge a little tighter. "Her name is Stitch."

"Stitch?" Dad's eyebrows furrow. "That's an unusual name."

"She's had an unusual life," I reply.

Mom's voice trembles. "Maverick's already been through so much. He doesn't need someone coming and going from his life."

Her words cut deep, but I get it. They're afraid. Maverick's the center of our world, and they've seen me broken before.

"I know, Mom. Trust me, I know." I want to reassure them, but I'm not asking for their permission. This is where lines get blurred. Where parenting roles intersect and clash. "I've been reckless before, but Stitch isn't just another fling. I feel a connection with her. We understand each other."

Dad puts a hand on my shoulder, giving it a gentle squeeze. "It's just—Maverick's still so young. We don't want him getting attached to someone who might disappear."

"I get it. I do." I lean against the counter, running a hand through my hair. "But I have a gut feeling about this. About her."

"Alright, tell me about her." Mom's lips press into a thin line, her eyes narrowing slightly.

"What do you want to know?" Caught off guard, I pause, water dripping from the plate I'm holding.

This is the sticky part. I'm no longer fifteen, asking if I can go on a date. I'm a grown man capable of making my own mistakes. Not that Stitch is a mistake.

Far from it.

"Details. If she's as special as you say, more than a fling, you should know her." My mom continues throwing out question after question. "What's her favorite color? What scares her? What makes her laugh? Does she even like the beach? What are her likes, dislikes, and dreams?"

I take a deep breath, my heart beating faster.

Mom's barrage of questions throws me off for a second, but then a soft smile creeps onto my face as I think of Stitch.

"Her favorite color is black. I intentionally skip mentioning her goth persona, not wanting to give them any reason to criticize Stitch. "She's passionate about Angel Fire. Can you believe that? She's not someone I picked up at a bar."

"Well, how old is she? Where did she go to college? Do you know her parents?"

I hesitate for a split second, deciding to sidestep the age issue. "She's brilliant with computers and recently landed a job at Guardian HRS. As for college, I haven't delved deep into that yet. About her parents… She grew up in foster care."

Dad places the last fork on the drying rack. Mom's eyes widen at the mention of foster care, her hands instinctively clutching the counter's edge.

"Foster care?" she repeats, her voice laced with both surprise and concern.

"Yes, she had a tough childhood." I brace myself for her reaction. "She's strong because of it, not despite it."

"But, Jeb, someone from such an unstable background… Is she fit to be around Maverick?" Mom's gaze is filled with genuine worry, not criticism. "I mean, he's had enough instability in his life. He needs a steady influence." She takes a deep breath. "I don't know. This feels too soon. Too fast." She punctuates her last comment with her index finger, pointing at me.

I clench my jaw, fighting back the frustration bubbling within. "Stitch isn't her past, Mom. She's overcome so much and built a life for herself. She's resilient, understanding, and compassionate. That's what Maverick needs—someone who gets the idea of facing adversity and not being defined by it."

Dad intervenes, resting a hand on Mom's shoulder. "Honey, we can't judge someone solely based on their past. Everyone deserves a chance."

Mom sighs, her gaze drifting to the floor. "I just want what's best for Maverick. I don't want him to get his hopes up only to have his little heart crushed."

"I wouldn't do anything that would hurt Maverick." It's tough, but I keep my voice soft but determined. "And I believe Stitch could be a positive presence in his life. Just give her a chance, okay?"

Mom sighs, her defensive demeanor softening just a bit. "If she's the one, then date her. Have fun with it but wait to introduce her to Maverick. There's no harm in waiting."

"How long do you want me to wait?"

"A year?"

"A year?" The thought of waiting that long to integrate Stitch into our lives frustrates me, but I understand where they're coming from. "A year is a long time. I'm not making a mistake. Let's see how things go, okay? As far as Maverick's concerned, she's just a special friend. We'll keep the PDA to a minimum around him."

"Please think of Maverick." Mom's voice holds an edge of desperation, a hint of the years when she'd step in to guide me as a young father. She's battling her motherly instincts.

"I always think about Maverick," I counter, frustration evident in my tone. "I appreciate everything you and Dad have done, helping me raise him. But he's my son. I have to make decisions for him."

"It's hard, Jeb." Mom's face contorts, torn between her role as a grandmother and as my mother. "Watching you make choices, hoping they're the right ones for our grandchild. We've been through so much together." She takes a deep breath, the lines on her face softening as she gives in. "It's hard. We worry. It's what parents do."

Dad interjects, his voice calm, trying to bridge the gap, "It's not about doubting your choices, Son. It's just—old habits die hard."

"I'm sorry." Mom's gaze softens, but there's a weight in her eyes, a silent plea for understanding. "It's impossible not to be overprotective when it comes to Maverick."

I exhale, feeling the weight of their concern. "I know, Mom, and I promise, Maverick is, and always will be, my top priority."

Maverick zooms into the kitchen, his small feet padding against the floor, eyes wide with excitement. "Daddy! Daddy! Beach time! Can we look for starfish and crabs?"

Crouching to meet his height, I can't help but grin at his boundless energy. "Yes, bud. We're gonna have so much fun. And I have a surprise for you."

Maverick tilts his head, curls bouncing. His tiny hands clutch at the hem of his shirt in anticipation. "What?" His green eyes go wide with anticipation.

I glance up briefly, meeting my parents' watchful eyes before looking back at Maverick. "I want you to meet someone today. Someone very special to me."

"Like a new friend?" His eyebrows furrow, a mix of curiosity and innocence.

"Yeah, bud, like a new friend. She's cool. I think you'll like her."

His gaze shifts between me and my parents, trying to grasp the situation. "Is she nice? Will Grandma and Papa meet her too?"

Before I can answer, Mom gently smiles, "Maybe another time, sweetie. Today is special for you, Daddy, and his new friend."

Maverick's face breaks into a bright smile. "Is she coming to the tidepools? Can she help find sea creatures?"

I nod, ruffling his hair. "Yes, she's coming. And I bet she'd love to help you spot all those little critters."

"Are we having ice cream later? Beach days are always ice cream days." Maverick claps his hands, the idea already solidifying in his young mind.

I chuckle, ruffling his curly hair. "If you're good and listen to Daddy, maybe we'll get a treat later. How's that sound?"

He claps his hands together in glee, enthusiasm evident in his every move. "Okay. I'll be super good. Let's go. I can't wait."

His excitement is infectious, and despite the heavy conversation moments before, I can't help but grin. This is a new chapter for us, and I'm hopeful it'll be good.

We make it out of the house on the third try. Maverick snuggles into his car seat with Rexy in hand. That was the first trip back to the house. Since Rexy made such a splash at show-and-tell, he wants to show my *new friend* his favorite toy. The second time is my fault. I forgot the snacks my mother made for the three of us. Attempt number three requires one last potty break, but we eventually make it into the car and out of the driveway. My parents stand at the door like they've done a thousand times, waving goodbye with both eagerness and trepidation.

The winding coastal road demands my attention, but focusing on the beauty of Northern California's coastline is hard when my thoughts settle on Stitch. On my left, the vast Pacific Ocean stretches out, its angry waves smashing against the jagged cliffs, filling the air with a rhythmic rumble. To my right, the golden hills march off toward the mountains far away.

In the back, Maverick's giggles and a stream of questions pull me back. "Daddy, are we gonna see starfish? Can I find a big one?" His excitement is palpable, and it lights up the whole car.

"We sure can. We'll see who can find the biggest one."

What few trees cling to the rocky coast have been shaped by years of coastal winds. They stand as haggard sentinels, watching over the land like ancient guardians. Every so often, fog rolls in, wrapping around the trees, making the journey feel almost other-worldly.

As the towering silhouette of Guardian HQ comes into view, my heart rate picks up. The excitement isn't just about the beach or the bonfire later. It's about Stitch.

How will Maverick react to her? How will she react to him?

TWENTY-THREE

Jeb

———

THE TEMPORARY QUARTERS WHERE STITCH STAYS LOOK MORE LIKE posh condos than any barracks I've ever lived in.

Parking the car, I take a moment, inhaling deeply. There's a crispness to the air, a mixture of salt and sea combined with the earthy scent of distant forests.

"Are we there, Daddy?" Maverick's voice, filled with curiosity, breaks my chain of thoughts.

"Yes, buddy. We're here." I smile at him, my voice betraying a hint of anxiety. "And you're about to meet someone special."

As if my words conjure her out of thin air, Stitch appears, stepping out of the barracks. Black jeans hug her legs, paired with another of her faded black Angel Fire concert shirts. Her raven-black hair dances wildly, an untamed tempest spurred by the coastal breeze. She struggles to control the flowing strands, but her attempts to tame her mane only add to her allure.

But it's her smile that hits me the hardest.

The moment her eyes lock onto mine, her lips curl into a genuine, radiant smile that not only reaches her eyes but fills her entire being. The kind of smile that makes my insides twist with happiness and tells me I'm exactly where I'm meant to be.

My heart thuds loudly in my chest, a reckless drumbeat matching the racing thoughts in my head. Seeing her like this, so relaxed yet vibrant, only solidifies what I've been feeling—my growing attraction and deepening fondness are real. With Maverick eagerly peering out of the car window, I realize how much I want to integrate these two worlds.

My son and this enigmatic, beautiful woman.

Stitch trots to the car before I can climb out. Her pace quickens as she closes the distance. Playfully knocking on my window, I roll it down and am completely blown away when she leans in and gives me a fleeting but tender peck on the cheek. The sensation lingers, and warmth spreads across my skin.

She opens the back door and slides in next to Maverick.

"Hey there," she says, hand outstretched to him. "I'm Stitch."

Maverick's wide eyes dart between her raven-black hair, striking blue eyes, and all-black ensemble. "Are you—a superhero? My dad only works with superheroes." His voice fills with both wonder and uncertainty.

"I tell him I work with heroes." I shake my head at how Maverick takes my words, innocently twisting them with the imagination of a five-year-old.

Stitch's lips curl into a playful grin, delighted by the question. "Hmm," she muses, tapping a finger against her chin. "Maybe not the kind that flies or shoots lasers from their eyes, but I have some pretty awesome computer superpowers. What do you think? Does that count?"

Maverick contemplates this momentarily, his gaze flitting between her and Rexy. "I think… That's cool. Super cool!" he declares, eyes brightening with newfound admiration.

Stitch chuckles softly, her attention diverting to the toy Maverick clutches tightly. "And who's this?" she inquires, pointing at the toy T-rex.

"That's Rexy," Maverick proclaims proudly.

"Well, hello, Rexy." Stitch playfully waggles her fingers at the dinosaur. "Mind if I join you on this adventure? I hear we're hunting starfish."

I can't help but smile at the scene unfolding in the rearview mirror. It's not the typical greeting, but it's perfect. It's them. It's real.

Switching gears, I pull away from the curb, directing us to our next destination. It doesn't take long before we're at the iron gates of *Insanity*, Angel Fire's iconic group home. As we approach, I sense Stitch's mounting excitement. This is the epicenter of her fandom, the place she's only ever dreamed about seeing, and I'm about to drive her through the gates and directly into the inner sanctum of her rock idols.

"Oh my god," Stitch whispers, her voice shaky with emotion as we drive through the gates. The sprawling estate reveals itself, every detail magnified by her awe. "I can't believe I'm here."

"We come all the time." Maverick is chatty with Stitch. "Every month for the bonfire. Are you staying for the fire? If you do, we can roast marshmallows."

"I would love to roast marshmallows with you." Her expression brightens when she sees *Insanity* in all its glory. Unfortunately, that's not where we're headed. Maybe another time.

The ocean's vastness stretches before us as we approach the cliff's edge. Far below, the waves bang against the rocky shore with determined force. The tang of salt fills the air, accompanied by the distant cries of seagulls.

Up ahead, a gondola gleams in the sunlight. Its glass walls and roof offer an unhindered panoramic view of the surroundings. The sight might be daunting to anyone unfamiliar with it—a tiny glass cage suspended over a vast, untamed abyss.

But for Maverick, this is just another adventure.

Without hesitating, Maverick grasps Stitch's hand and rushes to the gondola. "It's all glass, but super safe. Just be brave, alright?"

I chuckle, recognizing my own words in his enthusiastic reassurances. It's amusing and heartwarming to see him stepping into the unexpected role of the *guide*. I'm not sure what I expected, but it wasn't this level of acceptance.

For her part, Stitch plays along, her eyes wide in exaggerated wonder. "Oh, wow. It looks scary. Can you show me? I've never been in something like this before." She fakes a shiver of apprehension, earning an excited giggle from Maverick.

He eagerly presses a button on the side, and the gondola's doors slide open. We step inside, and Maverick makes a show of pointing out the various buttons and levers, his explanations a blend of accuracy and imaginative embellishment.

As we begin our descent, the world outside the gondola shifts. The cliffside seems to rise above us, its rugged face dotted with colorful wildflowers swaying in the breeze. The crashing waves—the coast's rhythmic and powerful heartbeat—grow louder.

Sunlight reflects off the water, creating shimmering patterns on the gondola's glass walls.

"There!" Maverick's finger jabs at a cluster on the cliffside. "Bird nests! The seabirds live there. Momma birds, daddy birds, and baby birds."

Stitch leans in, genuinely intrigued. "Wow, you really know this place."

Maverick nods proudly and then points dramatically out to the sea. "And that's where Old Joe lives."

Stitch's eyebrows shoot up. "Old Joe?"

"Noodles' pet shark! A great white," Maverick announces.

Stitch gives a playful scoff. "Oh, come on. Sharks can't be pets."

Before she can say more, I wrap an arm around her waist, pulling her to me.

"He's not kidding," I murmur into her ear, my lips brushing against her skin. "Old Joe's real. Noodles has a knack for the—unconventional."

Oblivious to our closeness, Maverick continues his role as the ever-enthusiastic tour guide, pointing out features on the cliffs and speculating about the mysteries of the deep.

"See? Easy-peasy!" Maverick declares with pride as we reach the bottom, the gondola settling onto the rocky beach with a soft thud.

Stitch bends down to his level, her eyes filled with gratitude. "Thanks for keeping me safe. You're a brave guide."

Maverick beams, puffing out his chest. "Anytime! Now come on, I wanna show you the tidepools."

I pause, practicing a moment of mindfulness. This is a perfect moment, a blend of adventure, bonding, and the simple joy of being together in such a magnificent setting.

I'm almost afraid to enjoy it, thinking this is too good to be true.

We head to where the tidepools have been exposed by low tide. Pebbles crunch under our shoes, echoing the rhythmic beating of the waves against the jagged, rocky shore. Every step is a symphony of sounds: the distant cries of seabirds, the clatter of stones shifting beneath our weight, and the ever-present roar of the ocean. Sharp rocks jut out from the ground, sculpted by eons of salt water and wind, bearing testament to the relentless power of nature.

To our left, the vast expanse of the ocean meets the horizon, its depths holding stories of old shipwrecks and mythical sea creatures. Glimmers of sunlight dance across the water's surface, creating a mesmerizing play of light and shadows.

Clusters of tidepools emerge ahead, trapped pockets of seawater teaming with marine life. They're nature's little aquariums, holding mysteries within their shallow confines.

With all the excitement a child can muster, Maverick dashes ahead, pointing out starfish and anemones. Occasionally, he crouches down, beckoning us to share his discoveries.

I glance at Stitch and smile when I see her face light up with wonder and amusement.

"Look, Daddy!" Maverick exclaims, pulling me toward a particularly vibrant tidepool, its colors seemingly painted by an artist's hand.

The tidepool is a microcosm of marine life, an intimate glimpse into the hidden world beneath the waves. The clear water lets us see straight to the bottom, where small fish dart about, their silvery bodies reflecting the sunlight. Starfish cling to the rocks, their arms sprawled out in a display of vibrant oranges and blues.

Neon green anemones, their tentacles swaying gently in the water, look like underwater flowers. Occasionally, a curious shrimp or tiny crab wanders too close, getting momentarily caught in the anemone's sticky grasp before breaking free.

Maverick's fingers hover just above the water's surface, his excitement palpable. "Look, Daddy! A sea urchin!" He points to a spiky purple ball nestled between two rocks. Its delicate spines move almost imperceptibly, sensing the world around it.

Stitch crouches beside him, her gaze following a hermit crab as it maneuvers its borrowed shell across the pebbly floor, its tiny legs skittering with purpose. "And over there..." she says, pointing to a rock covered in bright pink coralline algae. "Do you see the little sea snails?"

Maverick nods eagerly, his eyes wide with wonder. "It's like a treasure hunt, but underwater."

I kneel beside them, my fingers gently skimming the cool water. A small octopus, camouflaged against a rock, suddenly changes color, revealing its presence. Its tentacles flow gracefully as it moves to a new hiding spot.

Every inch of the tidepool tells a story, from the barnacles that cling tenaciously to rocks, filtering food from the water to the colorful nudibranchs that glide along the bottom, their delicate gills fluttering.

We spend the rest of the afternoon exploring the tidepools, drawn into this world of wonders until the afternoon sun casts long shadows across the rocky beach. The tidepools continue to enchant us, but slowly, the lure of the setting sun becomes too strong to ignore.

The sky transforms into curtains of crimson and gold flowing across the sky. They blend and deepen into purples and deep blues, setting the vast horizon aflame. Gulls cry overhead, their silhouettes stark against the fiery backdrop as they head to their evening roosts.

Maverick draws patterns on the wet pebbles with a stick, the last rays of sunlight catching the droplets on his lashes. The tide starts its inevitable return, the advancing waves nibbling at the edges of our world, heralding the close of our adventure.

Drawing a deep breath, I pull Stitch toward me and wrap an arm around her waist. Together, we stand at the edge of the tide-pools, lost in the breathtaking beauty of nature's canvas. The rhythmic crash of waves and the distant call of seabirds are the only sounds punctuating the silence.

The setting sun casts a golden hue on Stitch's face, highlighting the wonder in her eyes. We stand in shared silence, two souls intertwined, absorbing the sheer magic of the moment.

Finally, as the first stars twinkle in the rapidly darkening sky, I lean in, whispering, "We should head back before the tide claims the beach."

"One last look?" Stitch nods, her gaze still fixed on the horizon.

"One last look." I squeeze her tighter.

Stitch turns toward me, her eyes shimmering with emotion. The dying light from the sun reflects on them, revealing layers of gratitude and wonder.

"Thank you for sharing this day with me, for letting me into this intimate part of your life." She glances toward where Maverick hops from rock to rock, lost in his world of imagination. "Your son... He's incredible. I've never met a child with such unbridled joy and rambunctious energy. It's infectious."

Her fingers play absently with my shirt, and I sense her trying to find the right words. "Being around Maverick today, witnessing your bond with him... It's been—overwhelming in the best possible way."

Drawing her closer, the warmth of her breath against my skin makes me shudder. "I wanted you to see that side of me, of us," I confess. "I'm glad you were here with us today."

"So am I." She rests her head against my shoulder, her voice barely above a whisper. "So am I."

"And if you want overwhelming..." Jeb points to the gondola as it makes its way up the cliff. "We're going to have company."

The gondola begins its first descent, casting a shadow against the fiery backdrop. As it settles on the rocky shore, the door opens, revealing Ash and Skye, hand in hand, along with their son, Zach. Ash's brown hair catches the last golden rays of sunlight, and Skye's graceful presence draws immediate attention.

Stitch's face lights up in delight, her eyes darting from one member to the next. "I can't believe I'm here with them," she whispers, starstruck.

"Let me introduce you."

"I—just need a minute, okay." She grabs my arm and hangs back.

While she finds her courage, the gondola makes another trip up to the top. A minute later, it heads down. Bash, Angel Fire's drummer, emerges with Holly. They're joined by Bent and his wife, Piper. He bends down and whispers something in her ear that makes her laugh.

A third trip of the gondola brings Spike, his black hair contrasting sharply against the dusk, with Angel holding onto his arm. There's also Noodles, who shares a glance with Mitzy, both beaming with happiness.

"I can't believe I'm seeing them," Stitch murmurs, her eyes darting from one rock legend to the next.

With her unmistakable grace, Skye walks over, her arm linked with Ash's. "Stitch?" She extends her hand in greeting. "Welcome to our little beach soirée. Let me introduce you to the chick brigade."

"Chick brigade?"

"It's what we girls call ourselves. The women who've fallen for rock legends. We keep their heads from getting too big with all the fans fawning over them."

Stitch chuckles nervously, pushing a strand of hair behind her ear. Her eyes flit from Skye to Ash and back again, momentarily lost for words. She takes a deep breath, trying to contain the fluttering excitement in her chest. Her next words are for Ash.

"I've followed Angel Fire for years," she confesses, her cheeks tinting with a soft blush. "Seeing all of you here, like this… It's surreal. I can't even begin to tell you what your music means to me."

Ash studies Stitch for a moment, the playful glint in his green eyes revealing the rockstar persona he's known for. Then, with a lopsided grin, he replies, "Hearing that never gets old. It's why we do what we do. Music connects us, and fans like you keep the fire burning. It's an honor to meet someone touched by our sound." He offers a hand, pulling Stitch into a friendly, albeit brief, embrace. "We've heard a lot about you."

"Me?" Stitch's eyebrows rise in surprise. "What have you heard?"

Ash laughs, his gaze drifting to Mitzy, who's currently deep in conversation with Noodles. "Well, when someone impresses Mitzy *and* Forest, word gets around. Especially in our close-knit circle." He winks. "Heard you're quite the genius in your field and a bit of a rebel."

Stitch's cheeks flush again, and she chuckles, tucking a strand of hair behind her ear. "I do my best, but genius might be a stretch."

"And speaking of not being just anyone…" Ash leans in, voice teasingly low, "I hear you have a bit of a wild side. Something about hacking into the NSA? Takes a lot of guts."

Stitch lets out a nervous laugh, her face a deeper shade of red. "Yeah, I guess if you can't be famous, infamous will do, but I'm done with that. And for the record, I was trying to expose a vulnerability, not exploit it."

Ash smirks, holding up his hands in mock surrender. "Hey, no judgment here. I've always had a soft spot for rebels with a cause. It takes grit to challenge the system. And grit is something we value around here."

She nods, and a glint of mischief sparks in her eyes. "Well, then, I guess I'll fit right in. Thanks for the welcome."

"Ash, give Stitch a moment to recover." Skye leans in conspiratorially. "Let me introduce you to the chick brigade, and then I'll introduce you to the rest of the band." Skye's lips curl into a knowing smile. "Welcome to the family."

Skye steals Stitch and makes a round of introductions while I check in with Maverick. Never one to miss out on fun, he buddies with Zach, who's also five. With a shared spirit for adventure, they move away from the adults to plot their adventures.

As the atmosphere grows more festive, the bonfire roars to life, casting dancing shadows across the beach, and the last gondola descends. From it, Forest Summers steps out, a formidable presence. Paul and Sarah accompany him, their bond evident in their shared smiles and intertwined hands.

As the bonfire crackles to life, its flames reflect in every eye. The beach becomes a haven of music, laughter, and camaraderie. Members of Angel Fire, along with their loved ones, pull Stitch into their conversations, making her feel not just like a fan but part of the family.

Things couldn't be more perfect.

TWENTY-FOUR

Stitch

THE WARMTH OF THE BONFIRE KISSES MY SKIN, ITS HEAT MINGLING with the cool breeze blowing off the ocean. It's a night of juxtapositions—the bonfire's fiery brilliance against the sky's deepening black—the aroma of burning wood mingling with the ocean's briny scent—the contrasts ground me in this magical moment.

Never in my wildest dreams could I have imagined being here, on this beach, with the legends of Angel Fire and their families. The surrealism hits me in waves, much like the rolling surf.

There's Ash, the voice I've listened to for years, teasing me about my past transgressions. There's Bent, deep in conversation with Piper, and Bash, laughing heartily with Holly. With his raven-black hair and piercings, Spike gently holds Angel in his arms, and Noodles, the man behind the keyboards, animatedly talks to his wife, my boss, Mitzy.

I feel the wonder of every gaze, every introduction, every handshake and hug. The recognition, the camaraderie—it's overwhelming and heartwarming at once. The night contains stories, shared experiences, and family bonds formed by choice and intention.

It's as if I've been initiated into a sacred circle, accepted without reservation.

It feels too good to be true.

As the fire crackles and sends embers spiraling into the night, a thought dawns on me; this might be the best night of my life. The sense of belonging and being a part of something bigger than myself is intoxicating. I want to remember every second and fully immerse myself in the pure, unadulterated joy of the moment.

Children's laughter cuts through the air, drawing my attention from the fire's hypnotic dance. With mischief evident in their eyes, Maverick and Zach rush back toward the adults, sticks in hand. At their tips, marshmallows precariously dangle, ready for roasting.

To my surprise, instead of heading to Jeb, Maverick veers my way, plopping down into my lap with the ease and confidence of a child who's found his new favorite person. He offers me a bright grin, his face illuminated by the firelight.

"Stitch, look! We're gonna make S'mores."

I laugh, wrapping an arm around his waist to keep him steady. "I see that. And it looks like you got the best marshmallows, too." Zach, taking his position next to Maverick, grins.

As Maverick carefully inches his marshmallow toward the flames, I can't help but feel a swelling warmth in my chest, entirely unrelated to the fire before us. This child's trust, his open affection, is a gift.

For someone like me, who's lived life always on the outside, Maverick's simple act anchors me to this moment—to the family gathering around the flames.

Maverick's joy, unbridled, youthful, and infectious, only adds to the enchantment of the evening, reminding everyone present of life's simple yet profound pleasures.

Suddenly, a hush falls over the group. Ash stands, his voice breaking the stillness. "We've been working on something new, and this feels like the perfect moment to share."

With a deep breath, Ash sings, his voice rich and emotive, carrying the rawness of the lyrics. The band harmonizes, their voices melding together in a hauntingly beautiful acapella rendition.

Each note resonates, echoing the song's soulful depth. The melody wraps around us, uniting everyone in a shared experience of music and emotion.

Beside me, Jeb's presence is a comforting warmth, a steady anchor amidst the whirlwind of emotions. His arm, casually draped around my shoulders, pulls me closer, grounding me to this moment. Our fingers weave together, and the gentle pressure of his hand conveys sentiments too deep for words.

Drawn irresistibly to the intensity of his gaze, I meet his eyes, finding an ocean of emotions swirling within their depths. The world seems to fade as we share a moment of profound connection.

But as Ash's soulful tune ends, a reverent hush replaces the haunting notes. The silence is interrupted by the simultaneous chimes of Jeb's, Mitzy's, Forest's, and Skye's phones, and the mood shifts palpably.

Jeb glances down, the screen's glow casting a brief, eerie light on his features. As he meets Mitzy's eyes, she gives a subtle nod.

"What's going on?" I ask, a knot of unease forming in my stomach.

Jeb glances down at our intertwined fingers, his thumb tracing gentle circles over the back of my hand. "We have to head out," he says, his voice carrying the weight of the mission ahead. "We're spinning up for Haven tomorrow morning."

Maverick, nestled between us, rubs his eyes sleepily. "Do we have to go now?" he whines, his voice thick with fatigue.

"Yeah, buddy, it's time. Big day tomorrow." Jeb chuckles softly, ruffling Maverick's hair.

"But I'm not tired," Maverick protests, even as a wide yawn stretches across his face.

"Really? Could've fooled me." Jeb raises an eyebrow, the hint of a smile playing on his lips.

Maverick, his energy spent, struggles to keep his eyes open. His yawning is more adorable than convincing.

We rise and say our goodbyes. Mitzy joins us for the ride on the gondola, her silhouette stark against the backdrop of the ascending cliffs. Forest and Skye wait for the gondola to return.

As the gondola slowly ascends, the soft glow from its interior lights casts a gentle illumination on our faces. The distant murmur of crashing waves fades behind the hum of the machinery, creating a surreal sense of detachment.

I turn to Mitzy, a playful smirk forming on my lips. "You conveniently left out the part you're married to Noodles."

"I did." Mitzy chuckles, a hint of mischief in her eyes.

"But you knew I was a fan."

"Everyone knows you're a fan," Mitzy teases me. "We had a little pool going. We took bets on how long before you'd make the connection. Frankly, you took way longer than anyone expected."

"Wait, my Angel Fire obsession is office gossip? Is that why everyone gave me those smug smiles every time I walked into HQ wearing one of their shirts?"

"Your wardrobe screams 'fangirl.' Do you own any shirts that aren't Angel Fire?"

"No." But then, I don't own much. I keep things to a minimum, something left over from my days as a foster kid.

Our playful banter lightens the mood, serving as a brief respite from the gravity of the mission awaiting us.

Mitzy's gaze intensifies as it lingers on Jeb. "Can I hitch a ride to HQ? There are a few things I want to hash out with both of you before you leave."

Jeb shakes his head, glancing down at Maverick, who's now snuggled up against his side, his young features soft with encroaching sleep. "I need to get this one to bed. Once he's out, I'll likely crash, too. Ethan set muster for the team to brief in the morning, but if you need to chat with me—I can come back."

"Take care of Maverick. Stitch can brief you on the way." Mitzy nods, conceding.

It doesn't take long for the short ride to HQ. Jeb lets Mitzy and me out. Maverick's zonked out in the back seat, so I don't get to say goodbye. With a wave goodbye, Mitzy and I head up to her office.

Once there, she pulls up a holographic screen, and the intricate network of Haven's security system dances before us.

"You're first task is to hack their mainframe, which we've already set up for you. Don't be too cavalier about getting in."

"Cavalier?"

"Cocky." Mitzy gives me a look. "Get in fast, but not too fast. We don't want to raise red flags."

"Got it. Be a computer genius without being a genius." I agree with her only because I'm too tired to argue. She's wrong. I need to make a splash when I get to Haven. Knowing what role women play there, nothing but things to be bought and sold, I have to establish my worth from the beginning.

"Somehow, I get the feeling you're not listening." Mitzy chuckles.

"I'm listening to everything you're saying."

"Once inside, your mission is to create a backdoor, granting me unrestricted access." She points to several nodes on the display. "I'll launch a series of decoy attacks. They'll be loud. Chaotic. And they'll give you exactly what you need."

"What's that?"

"A reason to be there and a smokescreen for what we're really doing."

"What if they realize what I'm up to?" My voice betrays the unease building within me. This is suddenly all too real.

"They won't. I've seen what you can do with computers. You can dance circles around Haven's technical team. While everyone focuses on the attacks, you'll be in the shadows, making magic happen. Plus, the ruckus will reinforce the reason Charlie team brought you in."

"The mole?"

"Exactly." Mitzy leans in, her voice dropping to a conspiratorial whisper. "The only way to get Charlie team access to the entirety of Haven is to get them to believe they have a mole on the inside. You hack their interior security grid and show the hardware is a problem. That gives Ethan a reason to explore Haven and map out the movements of their men."

"I can do that."

"As long as you stick to the plan, they won't suspect a thing. Remember, you're their solution, not the problem."

I try to summon the confidence I need, but as the reality of the upcoming mission settles in, the ever-looming shadow of doubt creeps over me.

My fingers trace the holographic interface, the cool light pulsing against my skin. In cyberspace, I'm a force to be reckoned with, but I won't be able to hide behind a computer screen at Haven.

I'm headed into enemy territory where a woman's worth isn't determined by what she can do but rather what price she can fetch at auction. I force a smile, though a part of me screams how out of my depth I am. I shake out my hands and blow out a nervous breath.

"You've got this." Mitzy's hand briefly touches my shoulder, a gesture of reassurance.

She gives me a few last-minute pointers, then we wrap things up, and I leave to grab some shuteye. The door shuts behind me at my quarters with an almost inaudible click, leaving me suddenly alone with my thoughts.

I sink onto the bed, my mind racing. The sheets are cool and crisp, the room dimly lit. The contrast between this sterile environment and the warmth of the bonfire couldn't be starker.

Wrapping myself in the blanket, I close my eyes, trying to bring back comforting memories from the beach—the laughter, the salty sea air, the crackling of the fire—but it's Jeb's face that stands out, the way his eyes pierce through my defenses to see into my soul.

Sleep evades me. Each minute feels like hours, amplifying the looming danger of the mission.

The idea of infiltrating Haven is more terrifying to me than my darkest days in prison. At least in prison, I had some agency—some control over my life.

In Haven, I'll be surrounded by men who see me as nothing more than meat. The thought of being leered at, prodded, and auctioned off makes my skin crawl. One wrong move and I could be exposed.

All it will take is one misstep to blow my cover and put my life at risk.

Compared to the relative safety of prison walls, walking freely into Haven feels wrong.

As dawn approaches, I hope to find the courage to confront it.

TWENTY-FIVE

Stitch

THE FIRST HINT OF DAWN IS JUST A WHISPER OF LIGHT AS I HUDDLE together with the men of Charlie team for one final briefing. The coolness of the crisp morning air isn't enough to explain the shiver that travels down my spine, nor the faint tremor of my hands—it's raw fear, undiluted and sharp.

Our final briefing concludes with weighted silence, and as we move to the airfield, each step is heavy with unspoken thoughts. The silence stretches, a tangible presence inside the jet bound for Montana. This is my first mission—hopefully my first and last—but even I feel something's off. This tense quiet is out of the ordinary, starkly contrasting with the team's typical boisterous ribbing.

"Are you okay?" Jeb's voice, a gentle rumble, breaks the stillness. "Nervous?"

I keep my voice low. "As okay as anyone can be, heading into—this." I pause and take a breath. "Is it always so quiet before a mission?"

"No." He looks away for a moment, his jaw tight. "Usually, we're gearing up for a fight—busting in, taking down the bad guys, pulling out the innocents. But Haven..." He trails off, the weight of unsaid truths hanging between us. "We're going in as cyber security, working *for* these assholes rather than *against* them. It goes against the grain. We have to pretend what they're doing doesn't bother us. That we accept it. That we're like them, and the worst part…"

"Yes?"

"The worst part is knowing there will be women there—women we can't save." He reaches for my hand, his grip firm. "That's not something we're used to. I think we're all trying to get in the right headspace. The real mission is on your shoulders."

"Gee, thanks." I don't need to be reminded how critical my role is during this mission.

"Don't worry. I'm right here with you. Every step. Every breath."

"I'm not going to lie." I curl in my lower lip, biting it. "I'm terrified."

Jeb turns back to me, his eyes locking onto mine with a steadiness that belies the turmoil I know is churning inside him. "You need to remember who you are and who you were when Mitzy found you. That arrogance, that cockiness you wielded like armor in prison—you bring that girl. You dig deep and find the strength to stand in the lion's den and not flinch."

"The lion's den?" I nod, a tight bob that I hope looks more confident than I feel. "That sounds scary."

He squeezes my hand, his thumb tracing circles on the back of it. "You've got to be the one who looks these monsters in the eye and shows no fear. Pretend their twisted world doesn't faze you. You're playing a part, and I know you can do it because I've seen what you're made of."

"I'll try."

"Remember, it's just a role. It's not you." The corner of his mouth lifts in a half-smile that's all encouragement. "Underneath, you keep that fire burning, that relentless drive to do right, to bring them down from the inside. That's who you are—the real you. You're the key to this whole operation, and not just because of your skills. It's your spirit, your fire. Don't let them see anything but your arrogant façade, but never forget who you truly are."

In Jeb's pep talk, there's a blueprint for survival, a lifeline thrown to me as we edge closer to adopting our undercover roles.

We board the plane and settle in for the few hours it takes to fly to Montana. Once we land, the quiet lifts, and the mood shifts. The guys stretch and loosen up as Ethan's handed the keys to a rugged SUV by a man on the ground.

"Stitch, you're in front with Jeb and me. The rest of you…" Ethan glances at the two rows of bench seats in the back. "Stow your shit and find your seats."

The guys unload their gear from the jet and transfer it to the SUV. I wedge myself between Jeb and Ethan, my feet fighting for space against the hump in the middle and their military-grade boots.

I watch the world unfold through the windshield as Ethan takes the wheel. The plains of Montana stretch out like an ocean of rolling hills that make me feel small. It's endless in a way that both humbles and haunts me.

And where the earth meets the sky, the Rockies stand as sentinels on the horizon, the first light of day casting them in silhouettes of rugged beauty. Their peaks, part of the vast spine of the Continental Divide, reach toward the heavens, touching the clouds.

These peaks don't discriminate; they shield the good, the bad, the untamed, and the unspeakable all the same. They offer refuge to enclaves like Haven. It's a harsh reminder that beauty and danger often live side by side.

We drive for hours, and I doze fitfully, curled against Jeb's warm embrace. By late afternoon, we climb out of the plains, trading the highway for less well-maintained roads. The SUV lurches like a wild thing, bucking as Ethan navigates us along a treacherous stretch of road.

Each twist and turn wrings my stomach into knots, the rising bile a thick presence in the back of my throat. I press my lips tightly together, swallowing back nausea, my skin taking on a sickly shade that rivals the verdant green of the leaves flickering past the window. Sweat beads at my temples, and I fix my gaze on a distant point, willing myself not to get sick in the car.

I brace myself, hands clutching at the seat, while Jeb wraps an arm around my shoulder. The vehicle groans in protest as we turn onto a gravel road.

Or maybe that's me?

The groaning, that is…

"Looking a bit green, Stitch." Ethan gives me a look.

"Feeling a bit green." I'm a mess of nerves. Each jolt of the vehicle sends a fresh surge of adrenaline racing through my bloodstream. "Are we there yet?"

"Not yet, but getting there." Ethan exchanges a look with Jeb. "You need a break?"

"No. I've got this."

"You sure? Because if you hurl…"

"I'm not going to hurl." I swallow back the rising bile and convince myself I'm going to be okay.

Just then, we come to a place in the road covered by an old rockslide. Ethan's grip on the wheel tightens as the SUV staggers across the scarred ground. We lurch sideways, a seesawing motion that tosses me about the cabin. Beneath us, the tires grind against a carpet of scree—gravel skitters away from the tires, and the SUV veers perilously close to the edge.

I avert my eyes, focusing intently on the safety of the interior. The steep drop just beyond the glass is a blur I refuse to bring into focus. We make it past the rockslide and find ourselves surrounded by trees again.

A dense congregation of pine and spruce, their branches loom over us. We ascend the spine of the mountain, each switchback bringing us closer to the underbelly of a cloudbank that obscures the road in front of us. The mists swirl around us and swallow us whole.

Dense and all-consuming, the cloud thickens until we can barely see the end of the hood. Our world reduces to the immediate—the engine's growl, the jarring dance over uneven ground, and the cool dampness of the air seeping into the SUV.

My imagination runs wild. Haven isn't a destination. It's a

specter rising to meet us, shrouded in mist as if the mountain's desperately trying to keep it a secret.

Or it's warning us to stay away.

We suddenly break through the cloud bank, and the sky transforms into the most brilliant shade of blue I've ever seen.

And that's not all.

Haven's revealed.

It rises from the Montana wilderness like a sentinel. Its cold, imposing walls clash against nature's beauty. The concrete titan is as much a fortress as a scar upon the landscape, with sharp towers reaching up and windows shining like predatory eyes.

It's surrounded by high fences, topped with barbed wire. The "keep out" signs are as redundant as they are explicit.

Haven is no longer a mystery.

No longer a specter.

It's a chilling reality.

My heart kicks against my ribs, a frantic rhythm telling me to turn around. Turn around before there's no way out. The knot in my stomach tightens—a premonition of evil to come.

But it's too late to turn back now.

The SUV jostles violently as we drive along the profoundly rutted access road to Haven's sprawling mountain complex. I brace against the bouncing and swerving. Beside me, Jeb's hand finds mine, giving it a brief, comforting squeeze.

"You good?" His voice is a low rumble meant only for me.

I nod, not trusting my voice. My palms grow clammy with apprehension. I've never been on an infiltration before.

Hell, I've never been on any mission.

I belong behind a computer screen, running comms and tech, but this time, I'm going in.

Too late to question my choices; there's nothing to do but move forward.

Head down. Don't attract attention. Do my job. Get out of this hellish place alive.

Easy-peasy, right?

The SUV lurches to a stop at the gate. Two guards emerge, looking bored. As they check the forged credentials Jeb created, the bearded one pauses on mine. His gaze roams my body crudely before scoffing.

"We don't allow—her kind here."

By kind, he means female. But he's wrong. They do allow *my kind* here. They just don't let them walk around unchained.

Rage flashes hotly through me, but I keep my face blank. My fingers curl into fists. Beside me, Jeb bristles, leaning forward, but Ethan handles it smoothly with quiet authority.

"Stitch is one of my most valuable assets. I was assured having a female on my team wouldn't be an issue. I expect my entire team to have unrestricted access, regardless of gender. If that's a problem, we'll take our business elsewhere."

The guard's eyes flick uncertainly between me and Ethan's stony expression. After an interminable pause, he recovers and hands back the IDs with a smirk.

"Of course, sir. My apologies. Right this way."

As the gate screeches open, I shiver. First obstacle down. Too many more to go.

"I've got you." As we drive into the compound, Jeb's hand finds mine.

The guard waves us in, allowing us entry.

My heart swells. No matter what happens inside, Jeb will protect me.

The moment I feel like I've recovered and have my shit locked down tight, we're greeted by a cold-eyed man—Kaufman.

Kaufman's calculating gaze sweeps over the team. When it pauses on me, his mouth tightens ever so slightly. Jeb closes the distance, standing protectively beside me. Ethan and Kaufman exchange words.

Words about me. Finally, Ethan puts his foot down.

"The women inside might be your playthings, but mine is off-limits. Are we clear?" Ethan steps until he's nearly toe-to-toe with Kaufman, voice low and threatening.

"You have my word. Your people will remain untouched." Kaufman leads us into Haven.

Inside, the air carries a stillness that chills the soul, the quiet broken by the distant echo of footsteps in cavernous halls and the low hum of surveillance cameras that track every movement. The walls are thick and impenetrable, leaving no doubt that Haven's secrets are meant to remain hidden. Every corridor speaks of surveillance and control; every locked door hints at mysteries or worse.

Atrocities veiled in shadow.

Kaufman leads us to the computer control room. Or rather *a* computer control room. With one look, it's clear his entire operation is decentralized. And right on cue, frantic men try in vain to fight off a cyberattack Mitzy staged to hit the moment we arrived.

It's one I created, a variant of the Trojan horse I sent against Mitzy, what seems like ages ago. I hip-check one of Kaufman's men from his chair and get to work.

"You won't be able to access our systems without the passcode," Kaufman says smugly.

The monitor blinks to life before me, data streams cascading like a digital waterfall.

"No need. I'm already in." I announce my accomplishment with a swagger that's as much a part of my armor as the data I manipulate. A smirk pulls at my lips, my eyes daring them to challenge me. "Your system was easy to hack. Someone installed a back door, but they weren't very creative. Juvenile at best. Looks like you've got someone working from the inside to sell Haven's secrets. I've got my work cut out for me to fix this shit." I crack my knuckles and swivel away from Kaufman, tuning out everything but the code.

Kaufman's voice slices through the hum of electronics. "What does that mean?" He ignores me completely as if I don't exist, but then I suppose acknowledging a female as anything other than merchandise is beyond him. He confines his conversation to Ethan.

Despite showing him how easily I cracked his system, the asshole questions my skill? Doubts what I can do? What an arrogant fool.

Without turning around, I toss the answer over my shoulder, launching it like a grenade. "I've got to install basic security protocols. Your system is woefully outdated and inept. It's going to require a whole systems upgrade."

I sense Kaufman's glare boring into me. "I don't know if I like a…" His voice trails into suspicion.

"A *what?*" I whirl around, my eyelashes fluttering in mock innocence. "A computer expert? Is it my age that concerns you, or the fact I'm female? Because your system is shit, ripe for anyone with the right skills to waltz right in under your nose."

His IT squad frantically pecks at their keyboards, trying to trace my entry point.

Ethan steps in smoothly. "Your people are running into dead ends because they're working with limited data. To connect the dots, my team needs unrestricted access. The full picture, as it were."

Kaufman's face is a mask of controlled anger, eyes darting, mind racing. "And what guarantees do I have you won't abuse this access for your own purposes?"

Ethan holds his gaze, the unspoken power play as taut as a highwire. "Our reputation is built on discretion. Short story: you have no assurances. Longer answer: You decide whether finding the source is worth the risk of giving my people the access they need to do the job you're hiring us to do."

The silence hangs heavy, electric with the clash of wills—finally, Kaufman's head dips, a reluctant surrender.

"Very well. But know that we will be monitoring closely. Any suspicious actions will be dealt with accordingly."

Ethan acknowledges the threat with a subtle nod.

Hurdle one, cleared.

"We need space to work," Ethan declares, voice edged with authority. The armed guards exchange uneasy looks but back out, sealing us inside.

Once alone, Jeb and I work on setting up the equivalent of a disruption field—a bubble of tech-induced privacy courtesy of Mitzy's technical genius.

"All good?" Ethan asks, and we give the thumbs up. "I'm going to make a quick circuit of the halls. See what I can find."

"Want company?" Walt offers, but Ethan declines.

"No. I want to get a quick lay of the land and see what we're up against. Also, I want to see how closely Kaufman's men are watching us. Best you stay here."

As the door clicks shut behind Ethan, I turn back to the screens, my fingers dancing over the keys. This is where I thrive—my heartbeat syncs with the rapid-fire tap of keystrokes, and I enter a nearly trancelike state.

TWENTY-SIX

Jeb

THE WALLS OF HAVEN ENGULF US, COLD AND UNYIELDING. IT'S A fortress designed not to keep people out but to foster the darkness within those who enter.

I can't shake a deep-seated revulsion for this place, and I hate that we brought Stitch into this brutal world of criminals and madmen. It goes counter to every instinct to shelter and protect the woman I'm falling in love with.

Until we leave, she's in danger, and that threat to Stitch isn't just physical; it's a corrosive force that degrades her worth.

I proudly watch her, standing toe-to-toe with Kaufman and holding her own. I can't help but be impressed. There's steel in her spine and ice in her voice as she calls out his inadequacies, all without a flicker of fear in her eyes.

She's got guts—I'll give her that.

After Ethan leaves, his sudden absence cuts through the tension.

"How are you doing?" I keep my voice low, a soft counterpoint to the harshness of our surroundings.

She offers a shadow of a smile, almost convincing, but a tightness around her eyes says otherwise. "I'm fine," she says, but it's a brittle *fine*, like ice ready to crack.

"You sure?" Fine never means *fine.*

It's women's code for everything's wrong.

The air in the control room is thick with tension, a living entity that buzzes with the silent hum of electronics and unspoken thoughts. Stitch's hands move over the keyboard with a confident rhythm, her focus a sharp blade slicing through the digital maze. I lean against the wall, my eyes not leaving her for a moment.

"How are you really doing?" I ask again, pushing off the wall to stand closer to her. The proximity feels like a shared secret, a silent promise of solidarity in this den of vipers.

Her fingers pause, hovering over the keys. "Honestly?" She doesn't look at me, her voice a whisper lost in the sea of data streams. "I'm pissed. That guy, Kaufman, he didn't even see me. I might as well have been a piece of furniture." Her laugh is hollow, the sound of it more a shield than amusement. "Not that I should be surprised."

"You're anything but invisible." My hand hovers over her shoulder, itching to offer comfort. "You're brilliant, and he's a fool not to see it. But frankly, I like the idea of you not being in his scope. You're safer that way."

She finally turns, her gaze meeting mine. There's a storm in her eyes, a fierce determination that sets my heart racing. "I don't need him to see me. I just need to do my job and get out of this hellhole."

I nod, understanding her need to prove herself, not to Kaufman, but to her relentless standards. "You will. And I'll be right here, watching your back."

A small, genuine smile tugs at her lips, and for a fleeting moment, the harshness of Haven fades, replaced by something softer, something that feels dangerously close to hope.

"Thanks. It means a lot, having you here." Leaning back, Stitch cracks her knuckles and turns her attention to the computers. "Come on, make yourself useful." She pats the seat next to her in invitation. "Help me crack this system wide open."

I move to her side, my lesser skills ready to complement hers. Together, we're a force to be reckoned with, a blend of brains and brawn that Haven isn't prepared for. And as we dive into the fray, I realize this isn't just about the mission anymore. It's about protecting what's growing between us, no matter the cost.

Over the next few minutes, I find myself consumed by the brilliance of the woman sitting next to me. I know computers or at least the tech behind them. My major at MIT was in computer science. Lots of theoretical work. Very little practical knowledge. Sitting beside Stitch, watching how her mind works, blows me away.

I struggle to keep pace.

Stitch's fingers dance over the keyboard, a blur of motion that's both mesmerizing and intimidating. I watch her, trying to anticipate her next move and find a way to fit my skills into her rhythm.

"What's the plan?" I ask, my voice a low hum in the charged air of the control room.

She doesn't look away from the screen, her focus absolute. "We need to give Mitzy outside access, but it can't be obvious. If Haven's tech team spots an external entry point, they'll shut us down in seconds."

"Can we mask it?" My mind races for solutions. "Make it look like internal traffic?"

"Exactly." A smirk plays on her lips. "I'm going to create a series of virtual machines within their network. They'll act as decoys, drawing attention while Mitzy does her work."

"Can I help set them up?" I lean in closer, eyes scanning the code spilling across the screen.

"Definitely." She slides over, making room for me at the console. "Start by configuring the VMs. I'll work on the tunnel for Mitzy's access."

Working side by side, we fall into a rhythm. Her commands are crisp and efficient, and I find myself rising to the challenge, my fingers flying over the keys as I set up the virtual machines. Each is a carefully crafted illusion, a ghost in the machine designed to mislead and confuse.

As I work, I can't help but steal glances at Stitch. The way she bites her lip when she concentrates, the small frown that creases her brow—it's all I can do not to reach out and smooth it away. But this isn't the time or the place. We have a job to do.

After what feels like hours but is only minutes, Stitch leans back with a satisfied sigh. "The tunnel's ready. Mitzy should be able to access the system without raising any alarms."

"Nice work." I finish the last VM configurations and sit back, a sense of accomplishment washing over me.

"We make a good team." Stitch turns to me, her eyes shining with something that looks like pride.

The moment stretches between us, a fragile thread of connection in this place of shadows and secrets. But then the reality of our situation crashes back in, the weight of what we're doing settling heavily on my shoulders.

We sit side by side, and for a moment, I let myself imagine what it would be like to be on her side, not just in this mission but in everything. To fight alongside her. To protect her. To be the one she turns to when the world gets too heavy.

As Stitch and I focus on the computer screens, the rest of Charlie team lounges around the cramped space of the control room, their restlessness palpable. The lack of weaponry among us is a sore point, a thorn in the side of men used to being armed to the teeth.

Gabe, his muscular frame sprawled across a chair, breaks the silence. "Can't believe they got all our gear. Not even a pocketknife left."

Hank chuckles, his gray eyes twinkling with mischief. "Should've seen it coming. Maybe I can swipe a steak knife at dinner. You know, just in case."

Walt, always the practical one, chimes in from his corner. "Steak knife? Please, I'm eyeing that toolbox in the corner. You'd be amazed what you can do with a screwdriver and some duct tape."

Blake scans the room with a critical eye. "I prefer my rifle, but I suppose I can make do with a pair of pliers if I have to."

Their banter is a welcome distraction from the tension hanging in the air, a reminder of the camaraderie that binds us together. I smile despite the situation, grateful for these moments of lightness in the midst of darkness.

The laughter and jokes still ripple through the air when the door suddenly slams open with a force that sends a shiver down my spine. Ethan storms in, his steps heavy, each one echoing like a gunshot in the tense silence that descends. The humor dies instantly, suffocated by the palpable fury rolling off him in waves.

He stands there, a dark silhouette framed by the doorway, his chest heaving. The lines of his face are drawn tight, a mask of barely restrained rage. For a moment, he says nothing, his gaze sweeping over us like a blade, sharp and cutting. The air feels charged, heavy with unspoken questions and rising apprehension.

Gabe straightens, his usual light-hearted demeanor vanishing. "What's going on?" His voice is a low rumble, cautious, as if afraid to ignite a fuse.

Ethan's hands clench and unclench at his sides, a physical manifestation of his struggle for control. When he finally speaks, his voice is a low growl, each word laced with venom. "I just ran into Rebel." He spits out the name like it's poison.

That name hits the room like a grenade, sending shockwaves through us.

Hank's eyes widen in disbelief, Walt's expression turns grave, and Gabe shifts, his body tensing as if ready for a fight.

"Rebel?" Hank's disbelief echoes around the room. "From Nicaragua? Your Rebel?"

Ethan's jaw works silently for a moment before he nods, a single, curt movement that speaks volumes. "Yes," he confirms, his voice strained.

A stunned silence follows, each of us processing the implications. The name 'Rebel' carries a weight, a history that ties directly into Ethan's past and, by extension, ours. Her unexpected presence here at Haven changes everything.

The room feels smaller suddenly, the walls closing in as the reality of our situation hits home. This mission, already fraught with danger, has taken an unforeseen and potentially explosive turn. Ethan's stormy presence, a harbinger of the turmoil to come, leaves us all grappling with the uncertainty and risks that now lie ahead.

"Red hair, green eyes? That Rebel?" I can't help but interject, the shock clear in my voice. I heard what he said, but I don't believe him.

Hank and I exchange a look, an entire conversation passing between us in a single glance. *No-fucking-way* doesn't begin to cover it.

The tension in the room is thick, almost tangible, as Ethan grabs one of our gear bags, the fabric rustling loudly in the strained silence. He retrieves the computer inside, its matte surface cold and unyielding under his fingertips.

We all watch, holding our breath, as he types in the encryption code, the keys clicking in a staccato rhythm that echoes the pounding of our hearts. This code, reserved for emergencies, signifies the gravity of our current situation.

Stitch shifts uneasily beside me, her unease palpable. I move closer to her, an instinctive gesture, my body a silent vow of protection. The light from the computer screen casts ghostly shadows across her face, highlighting the worry etched in her delicate features.

The screen flickers to life, revealing CJ's rugged face. His image is grainy, distorted slightly by the connection, but his concern is clear as day. "Status update?" he asks, his voice a rough bark through the speakers.

"Rebel is here." Ethan's reply slices through the room, each word a bullet. The simplicity of the statement belies its enormity.

"Come again?" CJ leans closer to the camera as if proximity could bring clarity.

His response plays out like a slow-motion film. First, confusion, then disbelief, followed by the dawning realization that Ethan is dead serious. He exhales sharply, a sound of frustration and disbelief.

Ethan repeats himself, his voice a controlled rumble. "Rebel. She's here." The air in the room seems to grow colder, heavier, as he speaks.

Ethan clears his throat, a harsh, gravelly sound that seems to echo in the tense silence of the room. His eyes, usually so full of command and certainty, now flicker with a storm of emotions he's struggling to control.

"I was making my way through the east wing," he begins, his voice low and steady despite the turmoil behind his eyes. "I was checking the basics in their internal security systems when I heard it. A voice I never thought I'd hear again. It stopped me dead in my tracks." His eyes darken, reflecting a storm of memories.

The tension is palpable in the dimly lit control room as Ethan stands before us. His posture is rigid, a testament to the turmoil raging within him. The rest of us gather around, our expressions a mixture of anticipation and apprehension. The flickering light from the monitors cast eerie shadows, amplifying the gravity of the moment.

"It was Rebel," he continues, the name hanging heavy in the air. "She is here, in the flesh. Not as a captive, but... She's one of them." His words are laced with disbelief and a pain so raw it echoes in the silence that follows.

"We're not prepped for a hostage rescue." CJ leans closer to the screen.

"She's not a captive."

The rest of us exchange glances, shock registering on every face. Ethan's connection to Rebel is no secret: a tumultuous love affair ending abruptly when she disappeared. But to find her here, in Haven, is something none of us are prepared for.

"What? Impossible. Why would she... Explain everything." CJ's tone is terse and demanding.

"She was in a room," Ethan's voice grows tighter, "moving among the captives like she belonged there. Assessing them. So cold and detached." He visibly shivers, then swallows hard as if the memory is a bitter pill.

"There was this—this one girl, a blonde. Rebel was... She was cruel." His fists clench at his sides, the knuckles white.

The room feels colder now, the air thick with the horror of his words. Stitch shifts beside me, her face pale, a silent testament to the monstrous reality we've infiltrated.

Ethan's gaze is distant, haunted. "The woman I rescued; the

woman I-I thought I knew. She's not the same person. This Rebel, she's a monster."

This discovery is a raw wound, exposed and bleeding. The man before us is not just a team leader; he's grappling with a betrayal so deep it cuts to the bone.

"If she saw you... She's the single greatest risk to your safety. One word from her and this whole op gets shot to hell. She didn't expose you to the guards? I want to know why."

It's a thought that weighs heavily on all of us. If Rebel is indeed working for the enemy and she's spotted Ethan, then our entire operation is compromised. The danger we face has escalated exponentially.

But Ethan shakes his head, a flicker of something complex in his eyes.

His revelation offers a sliver of hope amidst the fear, but not enough to breathe easy. I close the distance between me and Stitch, placing a protective hand on her shoulder and shielding her from the door. If Kaufman's men barrel in, I'll protect her with my life.

"When I confronted her," Ethan continues, "she was—evasive but clear on one thing. She said it's not safe, that I needed to leave. She claims she's in too deep to be saved."

"That you need to leave?" Hank scratches his head. "Doesn't sound like turning you in."

"I know." Ethan slowly shakes his head, still processing the shock of his encounter with Rebel.

The room falls silent as we process his words. The fact that Rebel didn't expose Ethan to Haven's security suggests layers of complexity we haven't yet uncovered. Her warning to Ethan, her insistence that he leave for his safety, implies a conflict within her, a struggle between her apparent role in Haven and her past with Ethan.

"It's your call." CJ's voice is rock steady and calm. "We're limited in what we can do right now." CJ remains blunt and to the point.

Guardian HRS isn't prepped for a rescue mission. Not after we just arrived. Our organization works miracles every day, but there's a limit to what we can do.

Ethan's jaw sets with determination. "I need more intel, understand her role, why she's warning me off, yet playing a part in this place." His words resonate with purpose and a renewed focus on the mission.

"She's the single greatest risk to your safety…" CJ's voice trails off, his mind visibly racing through scenarios. He tugs at his chin, his expression contemplative. "She didn't expose you, and I want to know why."

The Rebel we thought we knew may be gone, but in her place is a key to unlocking the mysteries of Haven. Her actions are a puzzle we need to solve.

"We stay on mission," Ethan declares, his voice firm. "Keep a low profile until we know what we're dealing with."

They talk for a bit more, debating why Rebel might be there.

The screen fades to black as CJ signs off. Ethan's encounter with Rebel shifts the dynamics of our mission, introducing a new level of complexity and danger.

Her cryptic warning and the unresolved past she shares with Ethan are critical elements in the unfolding drama of Haven. The mission has taken a dangerous turn, and at its center lies a woman who was once an ally.

Now, she's a mystery we must unravel.

With the call to CJ ended, Hank's whistle cuts through the tension like a knife. "Daaayumn, didn't see that coming."

Suddenly, the door crashes open. We all instinctively reach for our weapons, weapons Kaufman's men relieved us of when we entered Haven.

TWENTY-SEVEN

Jeb

REBEL'S ENTRANCE IS LIKE A STORM BREAKING ON THE SHORES. Stitch practically jumps out of her seat as Rebel marches toward Ethan. We're all on high alert, ready to jump in if this goes sideways.

"What the hell are you doing here?" Rebel's voice cuts through the tension.

The exchange between Rebel and Ethan can only be described as electric. They go at it, flinging comments, threats, and pain; the hurt palpable in the air.

Ethan wields his words like a weapon, but Rebel's retort is just as sharp. Then, their anger suddenly turns to passion as Ethan grabs Rebel and kisses her on the lips.

What should be a heated kiss turns into a grunt of pain. Ethan pulls back, blood on his lower lip. He springs away from Rebel, covering his lip with his hand.

The guys and I advance on Rebel, but Ethan holds out a hand, telling us to hold position.

"Get out now." Rebel slowly backs toward the door. For a second, her steely façade cracks. Fear and desperation flash in her eyes. "You have to trust me. It's not what it looks like." She swallows hard. Her mask slips for a fleeting moment, revealing a torrent of emotions, but it's back in place.

"Trust you the way you trusted me?" Ethan doesn't give her an inch.

They go at it for a bit longer, frustration building on both sides, but Rebel doesn't reveal anything. No reason for why she's here. No reason why she's the only female, other than Stitch, walking about freely.

"You expose me, and I won't hesitate to tell Kaufman about the Guardians." Her voice trembles with fear. "I'm sure he'll be pleased as piss that a bunch of hostage rescuers are digging around inside Haven." Without another word, she turns and is gone, leaving even more questions swirling in her wake.

The team relaxes fractionally as the confrontation ends.

"You alright, boss?" I ask, eyeing Ethan.

"I'm good." He wipes the blood off his lip.

But this isn't over. It's not over by a long shot. I place my hands on Stitch's shoulder, gripping firmly, letting her know I'm here for her.

Truthfully, I'm never leaving her side.

Ethan, still reeling from the confrontation with Rebel, turns to us with a look that means business. The air in the control room is electric, charged with the aftermath of what just transpired. His gaze sweeps over the team, each of us ready for his command.

"Listen up." Ethan's voice cuts through the tension. "Our cover as security specialists isn't blown."

"Not yet," Walt scoffs.

Ethan ignores Walt's comment, but we all think the same thing.

"Rebel's here for a reason. Until we figure that out, we continue as planned. Our cover is our lifeline. Jeb, you and Stitch are on tech. Work whatever magic you need. The rest of us are splitting up. Canvas the grounds. Inventory their security systems. Make it look good."

His orders are clear, leaving no room for doubt. The team nods in agreement, each man aware of the stakes.

With that, Ethan gestures to the rest of the team, and they file out of the room, leaving Stitch and me alone. The door closes with a click, and suddenly, the room feels much larger, the silence between us a vast expanse.

Stitch looks shaken, her eyes wide and filled with fear for her safety.

This is why we don't bring Techies on missions.

They don't have the extensive experience the rest of us have in the field. It's not something you can fast-track over weeks to months. It takes years of harsh conditioning and brutal training.

Stitch has none of that.

I step closer to her, my hand reaching out almost of its own accord.

"Hey," I say softly, my fingers gently grasping hers. "You okay?"

"It's just—him seeing Rebel like that. It's a lot to process." She nods, but her hand trembles in mine.

I gently hug her, offering comfort in the only way I know how. Her body is tense at first, but then she relaxes into my embrace, her head resting against my chest. Her slow and steady breathing tells me everything I need to know. Stitch is a fighter. She's terrified but willing to continue and push through.

After a moment, she pulls back slightly, looking up at me. Her eyes search mine. They're filled with fear, uncertainty, and a flicker of something else—trust. My thumb brushes her cheek, a tender caress that says more than words ever could.

And then, in a moment as fleeting as it is profound, our lips meet in the lightest, faintest of kisses. It's a kiss that speaks of promise and hope amidst the chaos surrounding us. A kiss that says, despite everything, we're in this together.

We break apart, the moment lingering between us like a shared secret.

"Come," I say gently, guiding her back to the console. "We should probably get to work."

We sit side by side, our hands occasionally brushing as we dive into the intricate web of Haven's security systems. We're a team now, in every sense of the word. As we work, I can't help but feel a sense of admiration for her. Despite the fear and uncertainty,

Stitch is strong, her mind sharp as she navigates through the digital maze.

Our conversation is a mix of technical jargon and quiet reassurances, our bond strengthening with each passing moment. We're not just colleagues; we're partners, united by a common goal and a growing connection that neither can deny.

As we work, I find myself glancing at her, memorizing how she bites her lip in concentration, how her brow furrows in frustration, and how her eyes light up when she solves a particularly challenging problem. She's remarkable, and I find myself drawn to her in a way that goes beyond the mission.

Hours pass, and our work continues, the steady hum of the computers a backdrop to our shared determination. We're making progress, slowly but surely, unraveling the secrets of Haven piece by piece.

The tension in the control room dissolves as Ethan returns, his expression a mixture of seriousness and something unreadable.

"Kaufman invited us for dinner." He looks as if he's bitten something sour.

A flicker of apprehension runs through me not the thought of sharing dinner with the man behind Haven, but rather at exposing Stitch to his depravities.

Stitch looks up, her eyes wide with fear and determination. "Glad I brought a dress. Thought Mitzy was crazy when she told me to pack it, but—I guess we'd better look the part." Her voice remains steady despite an undercurrent of nerves.

We retreat to our assigned guest rooms to change for the occasion. The weight of what's to come hangs heavily between us. In my room, I quickly change into something more suitable for dinner with a criminal mastermind.

The irony isn't lost on me.

As I regroup with my team, my mouth gapes when Stitch finally arrives.

As Stitch emerges, ready for the dinner, I'm struck by her transformation. The demands of this mission do not compromise her gothic aesthetic but rather blend seamlessly into her preferred style.

A sleek black number, the dress clings to her slim frame in a way that accentuates her lithe figure and skims over her body with a tantalizing promise of what lies beneath. The fabric drinks in the light, giving her an ethereal, almost otherworldly presence.

Her long dark hair falls in gentle waves around her shoulders, framing her face in soft shadows and spilling down to the small of her back. It's a stark contrast to the sharpness of her makeup; her eyes are rimmed with kohl, adding a mysterious depth to her gaze, while her lips are painted a deep, dark blood-red that's both bold and unapologetic.

She carries an understated elegance, a quiet confidence in her posture and the tilt of her chin. She's not just dressing the part; she's embodying it, becoming a creature of the night that can stand toe-to-toe with the monsters we're facing.

Walking together, I'm acutely aware of her presence beside me. Part of me is fiercely attracted to her, not just to her physical beauty but to her strength and resilience. She's a beacon of defiance in a world drenched in evil.

Her attire feels like an expression of her inner self—a warrior dressed in the armor of shadows, ready to face the enemy. My woman is fierce and unapologetic.

The depths and complexities of her character are as captivating as they are inscrutable, and my admiration for her deepens, solidifying the bond that has formed between us since the day we met.

Despite the magnificence of her dress and the strength of her composure, the subtle tension in her shoulders and the slight tightening around her eyes belies her apprehension.

We make our way to the grand ballroom, a place of twisted beauty, its opulence starkly contrasting with the evil that permeates every corner of Haven.

Candlelight dances across crystal glasses and polished silverware, casting an eerie, golden glow. The stark contrast between the room's beauty and the underlying evil of this place raises the hairs on the back of my neck.

Kaufman is already here, his presence dominating the space. As we make our entrance, his gaze lingers on Stitch, cold and assessing, before moving on with disinterest. My instinct to protect her intensifies, and I subtly position myself beside her, offering a silent shield from Kaufman's unsettling scrutiny.

Rebel stands by his side as he introduces us to her while we take our seats.

At the table, the tension is tangible. Kaufman's oily voice drips with false charm as he greets each of us, but his eyes never stray far from Rebel seated beside him. His manner toward her shows a possessiveness, a stark contrast to his indifference toward Stitch.

His hand rests possessively on Rebel's arm, declaring ownership. It's unsettling to witness, knowing the history she shares with Ethan.

"What progress have you made tracing the breach?" Kaufman wastes no time, immediately laying into Ethan, demanding a status update.

"We're investigating several potentials." Ethan meets Kaufman's gaze coolly, unfazed by Kaufman's bravado.

Kaufman's interrogation of Ethan about the security breach is pointed, his words dripping with underlying threats. The atmosphere tightens as Kaufman continues to probe Ethan about the security breach. Ethan's responses are measured and calm, but the underlying threat in Kaufman's words is unmistakable. The danger of our situation is palpable; each word spoken is a potential trigger in this high-stakes game.

Leaning closer to Stitch, I keep my voice low, a whisper lost in the ambient noise of the grand ballroom. "How are you holding up?" I ask, my gaze flickering briefly toward Kaufman before returning to her.

She leans in, her response barely audible over the clinking of silverware. "This place… It's a gilded cage. Beautiful but suffocating." Her eyes scan the room, taking in the lavish decor and the opulent setting. "I keep expecting Kaufman to unveil his true nature, make a spectacle of his control."

I understand her unease.

Our attention shifts back to the conversation at the head of the table, where Ethan and Kaufman are deep in discussion. Ethan's voice is calm and controlled as he addresses Kaufman's concerns about the security breach.

"We're investigating several leads. It's a tedious process, but I expect results soon" Ethan says, his tone even. "The complexity of the breach suggests it could be an inside job."

Kaufman's eyes narrow, a predator sensing a threat. "Inside?" he asks, his voice deceptively calm. "You think one of my people betrayed me?"

"The breach is sophisticated, indicating a deep knowledge of your systems." Ethan meets his gaze unflinchingly. "It's a possibility we can't ignore."

"Find them. I don't tolerate betrayal." Kaufman leans back, his expression darkening.

"We need full access to your systems to track the digital trail. It's the only way to pinpoint the source." Ethan's expression is unreadable.

"Granted. Do what you must. But do it quickly." Kaufman's gaze lingers on Ethan, suspicion and calculation warring in his eyes. Finally, he nods. It's a slow, deliberate movement.

As the conversation drifts back to what passes for small talk in Kaufman's twisted world, I can't help but notice how he uses Rebel as a tool in his game of domination. It's a subtle yet unmistakable display of power and possession.

Kaufman leans back in his chair, his arm draped casually over Rebel's shoulder. The gesture might seem benign in a different setting, but it asserts ownership. He pulls her slightly closer, an almost tender move if not for the hard glint in his eyes.

"Rebel has been an invaluable asset to Haven," Kaufman says, his voice loud enough for the whole table to hear. His fingers play idly with a strand of her hair, a possessive touch that makes my skin crawl. "Isn't that right, dear?"

"Of course. I serve your interests." Her response is practiced, her smile carefully controlled.

Her words are like a performance, each one delivered with precision. But her eyes, when they fleetingly meet mine, betray a hint of something else—fear, perhaps, or desperation. It's a fleeting glimpse behind the mask she wears.

"Loyalty is a valuable commodity. One Rebel understands very well." Kaufman's laugh is a low rumble filled with unspoken threats. "If someone in my ranks is betraying me, they will meet with consequences most—unfortunate." His eyes, cold and calculating, sweep across the room. "Loyalty above all else is rewarded here. Betrayal, on the other hand, is punished in the most exemplary manner." His grip on Rebel tightens momentarily, a silent but potent demonstration of his ruthless control. It's almost as if his words are as much for Rebel as they are for our team.

Rebel maintains her composed façade, but the slight tension in her jaw betrays her discomfort. The threat hangs heavy in the air, a dark cloud over the glittering setting of the dinner.

Around the table, the reactions are varied, but a common thread of wariness is evident. Ethan's expression remains impassive, but his eyes are sharp, missing nothing.

In this world, loyalty is a weapon as much as a virtue, and Kaufman wields it with a tyrant's precision. The dinner, a macabre display of power and intimidation, reminds us of the danger we face, a danger that lurks beneath the surface of Haven's deceptive opulence.

Stitch shifts uncomfortably beside me, her eyes downcast. I place my hand discreetly under the table, giving her a reassuring squeeze.

We sit through the rest of the dinner, the atmosphere thick with tension and unspoken words. Kaufman continues to hold court, using Rebel as a prop in his display of power. Each gesture and touch is a calculated move in his display of dominance.

"Enough with business. Let's enjoy some entertainment before dessert is served." His thin lips peel back to reveal teeth in a predatory approximation of a smile. "A preview of my latest business venture."

At his signal, the ornate double doors sweep open. Ethereal visions of beauty glide into the candlelit hall. Stitch couldn't have predicted it better.

The room fills with the haunting melody of a lute, its minor chords wrapping around the dancers like an embrace. Their bare feet glide over the cool marble floor, each step a whisper of sensuality, a tender caress against the stone.

The dancers move with an almost otherworldly grace, the flowing fabric of their gowns rippling around them like the surface of a pond stirred by a gentle breeze. The way the material adheres to their curves, revealing and concealing in equal measure, feels like a carefully choreographed dance of shadows and light.

As they sway and twirl, flashes of bare skin are revealed in a tantalizing display—the curve of a hip, the valley between breasts, the dark mystery between their legs. It's an artful blend of grace and seduction designed to captivate and entice.

But to me, the air feels thick with the stench of objectification. This display, meant to allure, repulses me. I struggle to maintain indifference, but the taste of disgust is palpable in my mouth.

Around me, the team's discomfort is evident. Hank's grip tightens on his armrest, his knuckles whitening. Gabe shifts uneasily, his large frame radiating tension. Walt's lips press into a thin line, and Blake's face is an unreadable mask.

Beside me, Stitch recoils from the display. She crosses her arms and grits her teeth, pointedly looking away from the dancers, her posture a clear rejection of the spectacle unfolding before us.

This performance, meant to showcase Kaufman's power and wealth, highlights the depravity and exploitation at the heart of Haven. It's a stark reminder of the true nature of our mission and the darkness we're fighting against.

TWENTY-EIGHT

Stitch

I CAN'T EXPLAIN THE DREAD THAT FILLS ME WHEN KAUFMAN SIGNALS for the entertainment to begin. Jeb places his hand on my knee and gives me a little squeeze for support.

The ornate doors swing open, and ethereal dancers glide into the room. The haunting melody of the lute fills the air, but it's nothing more than music masking misery. As the dancers glide toward the table, my heart breaks, and a tidal wave of revulsion rushes through me. The room, a gilded cage of luxury and deceit, transforms into a grotesque stage for Kaufman's display of power.

The dancers move with a practiced elegance, their faces masks of serene beauty, but their eyes tell a different story. Their gazes are hollow and empty, resigned to the roles they've been forced to play. They move with beauty that's too painful to watch, and their diaphanous gowns flow around them, revealing and concealing in a dance as old as time.

But there's no beauty in this.

It showcases Kaufman's ability to bend wills, break spirits, and ruin lives.

The melody of the music, meant to be enchanting, feels more like a lament, a mournful soundtrack to the tragedy they endure.

Anger surges within me, not just at Kaufman for orchestrating this depravity but at a world that allows such injustices to exist.

Jeb's touch is a small comfort, a reminder that not everyone in this room is blind to the perversion of Kaufman's spectacle.

"Are you okay?" Jeb whispers in my ear so softly it's almost lost in the music.

"This is sick." I shake my head, unable to tear my eyes away from the tragic ballet unfolding before us.

The dancers move closer to our table, their routine designed to titillate and entice. Around us, the team's discomfort is evident. Hank's knuckles turn white as he grips the table. Gabe's massive frame tenses, ready to spring into action. Walt's jaw is set in a hard line. Blake's eyes are cold, detached.

Part of me wants to stand, shout, do something anything—to challenge the depravity here, but I remain seated, my hand clenched in Jeb's, my mind racing with the grim reminder of the mission we're here to accomplish.

"A magnificent display." Kaufman's lecherous smile sends shivers down my spine. His gaze sweeps over the room, lingering on each of us with a smug sense of triumph.

The dancers retreat as gracefully as they appeared, their departure a signal that the main event of the evening is over. Around the table, the rest of us exchange subtle glances, a silent consensus forming.

Kaufman is going down—one way or another.

Seemingly pleased with the impact of his entertainment, Kaufman turns his attention back to his guests.

"I trust you enjoyed the evening." His tone suggests it's more a statement than a question. "Feel free to retire at your leisure. We'll resume discussions tomorrow."

"Let's go." Jeb stands abruptly, offering me his hand.

As we make our way out of the ballroom, I lean on him. His strength is a shield against the darkness of Haven. The hallway seems to stretch forever, but Jeb's presence promises safety amidst the evil tainting the air.

When we finally reach my room, the door closes behind us with a click that sounds like a gunshot in the silence. The mask I've been holding crumbles.

"How can there be so much cruelty in one place?" My voice breaks as tears overcome me.

Within the safety of my room, the outside world fades away, leaving me scarred by what I witnessed. I know what the Guardians do, but I didn't really understand the plight of those they rescue.

It's worse than anything my imagination could conjure. I've only been involved in a handful of missions.

This mission…

I didn't understand how it would be different. I didn't comprehend how helpless I would feel. I don't know how Jeb and the others are containing themselves.

"What will we do about those women?" I sniff back more tears.

"I'm not sure." Jeb pulls me into his arms.

"We can't leave them."

"Agreed, but rescuing that many women isn't a part of our mission," Jeb speaks the truth, but I hate that truth.

"There must be something…"

"We came for intel. We have nothing but our hands to fight with. His men disarmed us. And we have no way to get that many women out. Not without great risk."

He won't say it, but I hear what's unspoken. He means we can't rescue that many women without great loss of life, both for the women and his team.

"I hate this. I hate being this powerless."

I bury my face against Jeb's chest, letting my tears seep into the fabric of his shirt. His powerful arms wrap around me, cocooning me in his strength.

I've always prided myself on my intellect and ability to think my way out of problems, but here in Haven? My gender is a vulnerability.

I'm fragile.

Weak.

Helpless.

"We can't just leave them," I whisper into Jeb's shirt. "We have to do something. There has to be a way."

Jeb's hold tightens, a silent vow that he's with me in this, but the daunting reality of our mission is clear. We're here to gather intelligence, not mount a rescue in enemy territory. Yet the moral imperative to act, to do something for those women, gnaws at me. Some battles are worth fighting, regardless of the odds.

"Promise me…" I lean back to look at him. "Promise we won't leave them."

"We'll do everything we can to save them." He reaches out, his hand gently cradling the side of my face. His fingers trace the contour of my jawline, a touch so featherlight it sends a cascade of butterflies through my stomach.

I tilt my head, leaning into his hand, my eyes fluttering shut for a brief moment. His touch soothes the raw edges of my nerves. When I open my eyes, his face is mere inches from mine, close enough that the flecks of gold in his blue eyes blaze like tiny suns. The concern in his gaze is tangible, a silent promise of protection.

My breath catches in my throat as I instinctively move closer. Heat radiates from his body, taking away the chill Haven induces. A different kind of tension builds between us, a magnetic pull that's terrifyingly intimate.

His hands frame my face, his palms rough. A duality defines him: strength wrapped in tenderness.

"We'll find a way." Touching our foreheads together, he makes a solemn pledge.

He leans in, and our lips meet in a gentle kiss. It's a kiss that speaks of shared struggles, the comfort we find in each other, and our growing affection that goes beyond physical attraction. Our embrace deepens, an exploration that's both new and achingly familiar.

In Jeb's arms, the horrors of Haven feel miles away.

"This is harder than I thought it would be." I hold him tight, terrified of letting go.

"I know."

"In the morning, I'm going to do everything possible to ensure Haven falls."

"If anyone can do it, it's you." Jeb kisses the crown of my head. "But let's save the heroics for tomorrow. Tonight, you need to rest."

I want to do far more than rest, but indulging in sex feels wrong in this place. I opt instead for curling up against Jeb and letting sleep overcome me.

TWENTY-NINE

Jeb

I LINGER IN THE DOORWAY, EYES FIXED ON STITCH. HER FINGERS blur across the keyboard, a maestro conducting a silent orchestra. She's been at it for hours, her focus never wavering from the monitors, combing through Haven's intricate networks. It's a hunt for anything—any thread that might bring Haven down.

Did I say hours?

Honestly, I don't think she's slept in days.

Her dedication is admirable, but she pushes herself to exhaustion. Her gaze lifts, frustration fading as she smiles at me.

"Hey." She breathes out a tired sigh.

"Hey, yourself. How long have you been working?"

We're here for a purpose greater than ourselves but discovering what secrets Kaufman wishes to hide could be key to dismantling their operation.

She looks up at me with dark circles under her eyes. "Honestly, it feels like we've been trapped in this place for years."

Approaching her, I place a gentle hand on her shoulder. "You need to rest," I say softly, my concern for her well-being outweighing the urgency of our mission. "Pushing yourself won't help."

"I'll sleep when I'm dead." She leans back. "How'd it go for today? Find anything interesting?" A brief smile cuts through her fatigue. Her eyes meet mine, flickering with that familiar spark of defiance.

The things Stitch is doing with Haven's systems are beyond me: heuristic algorithms to map out their security patrols, probing for weaknesses while looking as though she's shoring up their defenses. Her mind is phenomenal.

A few days ago, we discovered areas Kaufman tried to hide from us. I've been working with Gabe and Blake to get down there.

I shake my head, frustration lining my words.

"Another dead end. Kaufman's guards denied entry." My hand rubs over my face, the day's failures clinging to me like a second skin.

"Still not letting you into the deeper levels?" Her brow furrows.

"No."

"We have to find out what Kaufman's hiding." Her gaze is steely resolve. "What reason did they give?"

"Excuses about sensitive documents, but none of us buy it." I scrub a hand over my face in frustration.

"Sensitive documents? I've looked at every file on every server. If they're hiding something, it's not digital."

"What if that's the point?"

"What do you mean?"

"Only that, digital is a convenient way to store data, but if you want to hide something, there's nothing like good old paper. It's not discoverable electronically. Not searchable. Are we missing something?"

"Shit." She blows out a breath. "You're brilliant."

"Not brilliant, just thinking out loud."

What did I say?

"We have to get down there. If you're right…"

"If I'm right, it's still a shitshow. It's not like we can export paper files."

"No. But it's worth a look."

"No matter how we phrase our requests, his guards feed us the same tired story. The restricted areas contain confidential documents, and our access could compromise Haven's security." I cross my arms, bitterness seeping into my tone.

"Isn't that why we're here? Something important must be hidden down there if he keeps stonewalling." Her eyebrows furrow. "If asking nicely doesn't work, we'll have to take a more aggressive approach." Her eyes flash with determination. A devious smile plays on her lips.

"I'm not disagreeing with you. I think it's brilliant, but let's follow the chain of command. Ethan is in charge of this op. We read him in on this first, then see what he thinks." I can't help grinning back; her rebelliousness is infectious.

"Read me in on what?" Just then, Ethan strides in, his posture rigid, expression full of frustration.

Haven is wearing us all down, and Ethan has it harder than the rest of us, considering he's also dealing with Rebel's betrayal.

"Stitch wants to push for access to the levels Kaufman's stonewalling." I rub the back of my neck, knowing Ethan's going to need more than that to make a decision.

"Push?" He glances at her, then levels his steady gaze on me. "Exactly what is she suggesting?"

"Finding a way down there." My answer comes quickly, and I already know Ethan's answer.

"We've been trying to find our way *down* there for the past few days. Kaufman's grace extends only so far."

"But he hired us to…"

"Not saying it doesn't make sense." Ethan holds up a hand. "I'm only saying men like him operate along certain lines. He hired us to plug the leak in his business and find his mole. That doesn't mean he wants to grant us full access to his entire operation. There are secrets buried under secrets. The bastard is one hundred percent hiding things from us. All I'm saying is I'm not willing to jeopardize this mission by asking for something that sets off red flags."

"But…" Stitch isn't one to take no for an answer. "Isn't that exactly why we should find a way down there?

"It's too risky and out of the question. It could blow our cover if we're caught sneaking around prohibited zones. I won't allow it."

Ethan crosses his arms, face set in hard lines as he stares down Stitch's request. "Need I remind you, we're Kaufman's guests?"

"Need I remind *you* we're the security specialists he hired?" Stitch fires back. "We're not his guests. You need to talk to him. Tell him we can't do our job without access to those levels."

"This isn't up for discussion." Ethan remains firm. "You're a member of my team, under my leadership. You have ideas. I get that. But I know how things can turn on a dime. This isn't the place to push."

"But…" She desperately tries to be heard.

I place my hand on her shoulder, gripping hard. My gut says Stitch is right to suspect Kaufman. We all suspect him. She's not going to like what I'm about to say.

"Something is being hidden from us, but you have to trust Ethan."

Her instincts are sharp, but one misstep can spell disaster for the team.

"Kaufman could be hiding anything down there." Eyes blazing, she meets Ethan's stony glare without flinching. "Human trafficking is just the surface. What if there's worse going on? Don't we have a duty to find out?"

I find myself nodding along to her impassioned words. Stitch may present a tough exterior, but she cares deeply.

Ethan works his jaw, conflicted.

I read the calculations running through his mind. The intel could prove invaluable if Stitch manages to tap into off-limits surveillance. He thinks about it a moment, then finally concedes with a nod.

"Look." Ethan holds out a hand. "I don't disagree with you, but we do this my way. I'll speak to him. Describe how this is something a mole would take advantage of."

"We have to get down there." Stitch is persistent. I give her that, but Ethan's under a lot of stress, and pushing him isn't the best way to handle him.

"I'll work it, but you need to trust me. Until I say otherwise, we keep going the way we have been."

"It's not that I don't trust you, and I know it's a big ask, but thank you." Stitch tries to hide a smile of satisfaction, but I catch the gleam of triumph in her eyes.

Her determination is a force unto itself.

Eventually, Ethan excuses himself to speak with Kaufman.

Stitch and I spend the next several hours combing through Haven's systems.

Just before dinner, Ethan calls the entire team to the communications room. Once we're all gathered, he clears his throat and begins.

"Kaufman granted access, but under strict conditions."

"Yes!" Stitch jumps up and down.

"What conditions?"

"Tomorrow." Ethan blows out a breath.

"Shit." I rub the back of my neck and shake my head.

"This is a good thing." She glances between me and Ethan looking confused. "What am I missing?"

"He has from now until then to hide whatever he doesn't want us to see," Ethan explains, then glances toward the door. "In the meantime, we're invited to dinner."

"Count me out." Stitch is quick to respond. "I'm tired of his *dinners.*" She uses finger quotes for emphasis. "Perverse displays."

"Not arguing with that." Ethan shakes his head. "But I can't decline his invitation."

"Well, I can." She crosses her arms. "He shouldn't have a problem, considering I'm female and beneath his notice."

"You're probably right." From Ethan's tone, it's clear he wishes for the same excuse. "Sorry, I didn't mean to be so glib."

"It's okay. I didn't take it like that. I know you value me."

"We couldn't do this without you, and thanks for understanding." Ethan visibly relaxes.

"I'll stay with Stitch."

Kaufman's yet to try anything with her, but I think it's exactly as she says. He doesn't recognize her as human.

Such a tool. The guy deserves everything we throw at him.

"Sure, that's fine." Ethan releases a calming breath. "In the morning, Hank and Walt will come with me. Jeb, you stay with Stitch. The two of you will monitor from here. Gabe and Blake, you're topside. Keep wandering around. Focus on mapping the guards' routines and rotation schedules. Look for alternate exits and how heavily guarded they may be. Look like you're busy and working hard."

"On it." Gabe thumps Blake on the shoulder.

From the way his shoulders slump, I wonder if Ethan had another run-in with Rebel. This mission is taking a toll on him in ways it shouldn't. I can't imagine the betrayal he feels or the confusion Rebel's involvement brings.

He departs with the others for dinner with Kaufman. In the morning, with Hank and Walt, Ethan heads down to the restricted areas.

THIRTY

Jeb

THE NEXT DAY, THE TEAM RECONVENES TO DEBRIEF ETHAN, WALT, and Hank's foray into the restricted areas. Flanked by Walt and Hank, Ethan exchanges a solemn look, an acknowledgment of the gravity of their findings.

"Settle in, everyone." Ethan's voice holds a grave tone, and the team gathers around, anticipation flickering in their eyes. Stitch and I exchange a knowing look.

"Stitch was right about there being more," Ethan confesses, his words heavy and weighted with a somber tone.

"More? Like what?" Gabe shifts on his feet.

"More than simple holding cells," Ethan continues, the room growing colder with each revelation.

"What are we dealing with here?" Blake's eyes widen with interest.

"Operating rooms, organ harvesting, and…" Ethan sighs deeply, the burden of truth etched on his features.

"And, what?" Gabe asks.

"Identity erasure." Ethan's words hang in the air, engulfing the room in a tense silence.

Gabe and Blake exchanged troubled glances, their expressions reflecting the horror of the discoveries.

"What do you mean by identity erasure?" Stitch furrows her brow, breaking the silence.

"Folders with pictures of full facial reconstruction," Walt speaks up. "It's as if they're wiping away any trace of who these women were."

"A fucking nightmare." Blake's voice is barely above a whisper.

"Folders? You mean computer files?" Stitch shoots a puzzled look at Walt.

"No," Hank interjects. "Paper files."

Stitch exchanges a knowing look with me.

"Stitch and I talked about this yesterday," I speak up. "Paper leaves no digital trail. It's the perfect way to hide something." I clench my fists, my jaw tight with anger.

"It's not just about auctions or specialty kidnappings like Ally's anymore." Stitch's eyes widen as the realization sets in. "Facial reconstruction? Organ harvesting? We can't leave these women here. We have to rescue them."

"Without weapons or backup, it's too risky." Ethan looks torn, the lines on his face deepening.

"But we have to do something." Stitch isn't backing down.

"Our mission is intel, not combat. We're not equipped for a rescue." Ethan's voice betrays the conflict within him.

Hell, it's in all of us. We rescue those who can't save themselves. Walking away feels like the worst betrayal.

"Well, I can't stand by and do nothing." Stitch is unyielding. "With a careful plan, we might save some of them. I can use my skills to help."

"She's right." I feel a surge of admiration for her bravery.

"What are we going to do? Fight with cutlery?" Ethan points toward the door. "There are dozens of armed men patrolling out there. We're outnumbered six to one."

"We've been in situations worse than this." Blake, standing in the corner, chimes in. "We can make it work." His nod is one of agreement, a silent pact formed between us.

Walt, always the voice of reason, adds cautiously, "If we can somehow even the odds?" He turns pointedly to Stitch. "None of us want to get caught. That's a risk no one is willing to take." He turns to me for that last part.

The rest of us are extensively trained in surviving interrogation. Stitch is not. A feral growl builds in the back of my throat. If anything happens to her, I'll never forgive myself.

Ethan weighs options. Finally, he concedes, "We'll scout for escape routes, but proceed with caution. If we find anything, we'll bring it to Command. The way I see it right now, it doesn't look good."

"Nothing's impossible." Stitch is already at her laptop, her fingers a blur. "I'll look for other ways out of Haven. There has to be a way."

The room grows quiet as we grapple with the implications. She's right. None of us will be able to leave those women in this place.

"Might as well talk this through." Ethan gestures around the room. "Better get comfortable."

We exchange glances, a collective understanding of the sudden shift in our mission.

"The facial reconstruction is weird. Why would they do that?" Stitch shudders and looks at me. "Is that common?"

"First we've ever heard of it, but it makes sense." I can only shrug.

"How?"

"They're wiping away any trace of who these victims are. Erasing their identities makes it nearly impossible to find them again."

"But why go to such lengths? What's the endgame?" Stitch's disbelief deepens.

"Money, power, control." Hank, the stoic and seasoned member of the team, leans back in his chair, crossing his arms. "The more anonymous the operation, the harder it is to trace back to those pulling the strings. Honestly, Jeb hit it on the nose. It makes it impossible to trace the victim after the fact. As grotesque as it is, it's rather brilliant."

"And the folders you found?" Stitch nods, putting it all together. "It leaves no trail. The perfect cover for something this evil."

The gravity of the situation sinks in.

"This is beyond anything we've faced before." Ethan pinches the bridge of his nose.

"But why would Kaufman be involved in something like this?" Stitch asks the questions flowing through my mind.

"That's what we need to find out." I squeeze her shoulder. "The depth of his involvement, the reasons behind it. It's not just about hostage rescue; it's about dismantling an entire network. There's no way Haven's the only operation involved.

"Agreed." Blake runs a hand through his hair. "Stitch, have you seen any evidence of other partners with Haven?"

"None," she says. "But the women who are here now... What are we going to do about them?"

"We find a way to get them out." Ethan, flanked by Walt and Hank, locks eyes with Stitch.

"I hate this place." Stitch recoils in disgust and anger. "It's a grotesque smorgasbord of human suffering."

"Colorful description." I place a hand on her shoulder, letting her feel the weight of my hand.

She's right. This is no longer a reconnaissance job. It's a crusade to end the vilest form of human depravity.

"We can't let them get away with this." Gabe, normally the voice of reason, struggles to contain his anger.

"I'm with Gabe." Blake, his fists still clenched, spoke with a simmering intensity.

"We will, but we need to be smart about it. Not that it needs to be said, but we're outmanned and outgunned." Ethan nods in agreement, a steely resolve in his eyes.

"I've gathered as much documentation as possible from those files." Walt, a meticulous investigator, chimes in. "Took photos. Names, dates, locations. It's a start, but we'll need more."

"We also need to find out who the players are. Who's pulling Kaufman's strings." Hank, the strategist, leans forward. "Kaufman might be just a cog in a much bigger wheel."

When I glance at Stitch, a silent communication passes between us. "We'll dig deeper into Kaufman's connections and his finances."

Ethan leans forward, a determined glint in his eyes. "This mission just escalated. Fortunately, we're the best team for the job."

The room falls into a contemplative silence as each team member absorbs the magnitude of the mission ahead. The walls of the briefing room seemed to close in, creating an atmosphere charged with both dread and determination.

"We need weapons." Blake leans against the wall and stares at his cuticles.

"We need outside help." Hank tugs at his earlobe, then glances at Stitch. "I say bring it up to CJ and Mitzy. See what they can do."

"Agreed." Walt nods assent.

"Stitch, call Command. See what they say and what they can offer." Ethan claps his hands. "Looks like we're turning this into a hostage rescue after all."

The room buzzes with renewed energy. A testament to the power of Guardian HRS, less than twenty-four hours later, we have the beginnings of a plan.

THIRTY-ONE

Jeb

AFTER MAKING AN ENCRYPTED CALL, WE BRIEF COMMAND ABOUT what we found.

As if reading our minds about what we need, Mitzy's response is quick and comes through, clear and decisive.

"We'll send the Rufi. They're perfect for a stealthy delivery. They'll parachute in with weapons and gear."

"Weapons and gear may not be enough." Ethan grits his teeth. "It's going to be a shitshow. There're six of us against scores of guards."

"Then we'll send support." CJ's solid voice rings through the connection.

"What kind of support?" Stitch asks.

There's a pause on the other end of the line, then CJ answers.

"The Rufi will supply you, but they'll drop in with Alpha and Bravo."

"Excuse me?" Ethan glances up, arching a brow when our gazes connect.

"They'll coordinate an attack on Haven's external defenses. Draw out the guards and create enough chaos to allow your team to operate inside and rescue the hostages."

Ethan and I exchange a look.

"It's not a bad plan," I say.

"We need forty-eight hours to get everything in place." CJ's voice is clipped, as if he's multitasking.

No doubt, he's sending messages to Max and Brady, leaders of Alpha and Bravo teams.

"Forty-eight hours?" Ethan confirms.

"Correct," Mitzy says. "Stitch, we need you and Jeb in the control room. You'll be our eyes and ears on the ground, feeding live intel and surveillance data back to Alpha and Bravo. Use the system to sabotage and blind Haven's defenses in real time. That should make Alpha and Bravo's job much easier."

"On it." Stitch hunches over her terminal, fingers already flying across the keyboard. "I won't let you down, and I've got some great ideas for creating chaos."

"Sounds good," CJ says. "Just coordinate with us first. We don't want to be working at cross purposes."

"Will do." Stitch grins like a fool.

I can practically see her mind working to create chaos and confusion in the enemy.

"Stay sharp and keep in touch." CJ gets ready to wrap up the call. "Mitzy will stay in communication with Stitch, fine-tuning details. Ethan, we'll supply you with comms along with the weapons drop. We'll get Alpha and Bravo in position, but you'll call it."

"Understood."

"Good luck." With that, CJ and Mitzy sign off.

"We have marching orders." Ethan polls the team. "Any questions?" There are none.

"Great." Ethan claps his hands. "We've got two days to prep."

Over the next forty-eight hours, every moment is consumed by preparation and coordination. Sleep becomes a distant memory as Stitch and I take a deep dive into Haven's security setup, plotting the best disruption points for Alpha and Bravo's assault.

The tangle of firewalls and encrypted channels feels like a massive puzzle impossible to unravel, but Stitch isn't fazed.

This is where she shines the brightest.

As she delves deep into the base code, my mind races with scenarios and contingencies the team might encounter. There's no room for error.

And as the hours tick down, Stitch finds exactly what she needs. A master coder, she plants snippets of code throughout the labyrinthine of Haven's security network, then leaves it there until it's time to activate it.

"That's it." She leans back, brimming with pride. "The moment Ethan's ready, we are going to have so much fun."

The flickering light of multiple screens casts eerie shadows across the room as I lean back in my chair, rubbing my eyes. It's been a long forty-eight hours, and I'm exhausted.

Stitch, however, is bright and alert despite only brief naps over the past two days.

All we can do now is wait. The next step is crucial: getting Charlie team armed.

Tonight, the Rufi are dropping in with Alpha and Bravo. While I stay with Stitch, the rest of my team heads down to the deepest levels of Haven where Stitch discovered an old, unused drainage tunnel.

That's our exit point and where the Rufi will deliver our weapons and gear.

Once again, Ethan calls the team for a briefing.

He paces before us, his movements sharp and precise. The air in the room feels electric, charged with the imminence of what's to come. My shoulders tighten, not from strain but readiness, a physical echo of the mental alertness coursing through me.

Our team leader's gaze sweeps over us. "The moment Alpha and Bravo engage, we move. Walt, Blake, Hank, and Gabe head to the tunnels. Kit up and get the Rufi ready. One of you needs to bring Jeb and Stitch their gear. I need mine as well." He taps his ear, where a tiny earpiece is barely visible. "I'll be able to hear but will be limited in what I can say without rousing suspicion."

Stitch and I exchange a glance. Her eyes are sharp, mirroring my resolve. Our silent communication speaks volumes in this tense atmosphere.

"You two," Ethan points to us, "are key to pulling this off. Once Alpha and Bravo attack, your job is to create as much confusion as possible. I want Kaufman's men running around like chickens with their heads cut off."

"Ewww…" Stitch grimaces and glances at me.

Ethan cracks a smile.

"Not going to get that visual out of my head anytime soon, but I'm on it. I'll scramble their comms, trigger random alarms, and more. They won't know what hit them." Stitch's hands hover over the keyboard, a predator ready to pounce.

"Jeb, protect this room." Ethan's eyes lock onto mine. He doesn't have to say how important Stitch's safety is to pulling this off.

"Will do." I take one step closer to Stitch. I'm prepared to defend her with my life.

"Protect Stitch. Back her up as needed." Ethan takes note of my subtle repositioning.

My hand instinctively reaches for the reassuring grip of my weapon, but I grasp at the air, finding nothing there. My options are limited without a weapon, but one of the guys will bring us what we need.

Ethan pauses at the door, turning for one last look at Stitch and me. "Stitch, your skills here are critical. You're the key to this operation's success. I've seen how you handle yourself. You're a force of nature, with or without that keyboard, but in there," he nods at the array of screens, "you're unstoppable. We're all counting on you." His tone is firm, acknowledging her vital role in this mission.

Stitch's response is a swift nod, her eyes already on the monitors, her mind racing with strategies.

"And, Jeb," Ethan adds, "she may be the brains, but she needs your instincts. Stay sharp. Get her out of here. You'll know when to move." His words are a command, an order I'm ready to fulfill. As he strides out to play his part as Kaufman's honored guest at the banquet and auction, the rest of the team follows him out.

"Stay sharp, Jeb." Hank gives me a solid thump on the shoulder, a wordless message of trust and camaraderie.

Walt passes by, offering a brief nod. "So others may live." He echoes his PJ motto, a reminder of our shared purpose.

Blake, always the silent type, gives me a knowing look, his eyes speaking volumes of the respect he holds for this mission. He ruffles Stitch's hair in a brotherly gesture as he passes.

"Keep the home fires burning." Ever the giant with a heart to match, Gabe flashes a cheeky grin. His tone may be light, but his eyes are deathly serious.

The door shuts, sealing Stitch and me in our digital fortress. She wastes no time, diving into the sea of data, her fingers flying over the keyboard with mesmerizing speed and precision.

I take my position by the door, my senses on high alert. The room is alive with the buzz of machines, a stark contrast to the quiet determination that fills the air. Her focus is unbreakable, her mind orchestrating a digital ballet of chaos and disruption.

I watch her, not just as a Guardian but as an ally, impressed by her skill and acutely aware of the danger we're about to face.

"I'm going to start with their comms. Introduce a bit of static and noise," she announces, her focus absolute.

"Good." I split my attention between her and the door. "Let me know if you need anything."

"We'll mix it up after Alpha and Bravo attack. Fire alarms in some areas, sprinklers in others. Keep them disoriented."

"Perfect," I respond, my eyes scanning the room, every sense heightened. "Keep them on their toes."

As she orchestrates our digital assault, I'm reminded of her additional training and how she's formidable in her own right. Yet here, surrounded by servers and screens, she truly shines, a maestro conducting a symphony of disruption.

The room itself seems to pulse with the energy of our mission. I stand watch, a sentinel not just for Stitch but for the hope of all those we're here to save. The glow of the screens illuminate her face. Damn, if she isn't a fierce warrior, a picture of intense concentration and determination. At this moment, I'm not just her protector; I'm her partner in a battle where keystrokes are as deadly as bullets.

The soft glow of the monitors bathes us in a bubble of calm before the chaos. There's only the soft whir of machines and the clacking of keys as Stitch gets to work. Mitzy calls on a secure line, and the two dive right in, beauty and brains with fierce intellect.

Stitch speaks in hushed tones with her mentor, her gaze occasionally meeting mine. In those glances, she shares her nervousness and anticipation. There's also a profound understanding of the risks at hand.

Our future is not set.

It's not guaranteed.

There are so many ways things can go south. I move closer, about to speak, my thoughts heavy with the weight of what's unspoken between us.

"We're all set." Stitch ends the call. She turns to me, her expression a mixture of determination and a hint of something softer.

Something vulnerable and afraid.

For a moment, it's just us in the room. Silence envelops us as the rest of the world fades away. It's a rare pause, the calm before the storm. She looks at me with a complex storm of emotions—resolve, fear, and something deeper, something that resonates within my heart.

I'm drawn to her by an invisible force. My hand finds hers, a connection that speaks louder than words. The contact sends a jolt of electrical current racing up my arm.

"Stitch…" My voice cracks with what I need to say. "When this is over…"

"Don't say it." Her voice shakes, and her gaze holds mine. It's filled with hope that feels both fragile and unbreakable. "Tell me when this is over." Her fingers tighten around mine, her grip tight. "I can't think about the future right now."

She's right, of course. Now is not the time for promises or plans. I need to focus on the mission and the job at hand.

We have two goals: succeed in getting Kaufman's Angels out of this hellhole, and then survive ourselves.

Nothing else matters.

Our connection lingers, a brief respite before the storm that's about to break all around us. There's a future waiting for us. It's out there, but on the other side of what we're about to face. We share a look, a moment of connection that acknowledges what we both feel, but first, we have a job to do.

THIRTY-TWO

Jeb

IN THE CONTROL ROOM, THE AIR IS THICK WITH ANTICIPATION, A silent undercurrent of unspoken fears and unyielding resolve. Stitch and I stand side by side, our gazes locked on the array of screens before us, each a window into the chaos about to unfold.

For now, we wait in the calm before the storm—a storm we've been meticulously planning but still can't fully predict.

Our roles are clear, yet the weight of what's at stake hangs heavy in the air. We wait for Ethan's signal.

I glance at Stitch, her profile etched with determination and focus. Our mission demands our full attention, our skills honed to razor-sharp precision. We are Guardians, warriors standing on the precipice of a battle that could bring Haven down and rescue dozens of innocents.

And then, it begins—the distant rumble of explosions.

Those set off a low vibration that sends a shiver down my spine.

The battle for Haven has begun, and we're right in the middle of it.

Stitch's hand withdraws from mine, and we both snap back to reality.

"Time to focus." She turns to the array of screens, her posture of a warrior ready to go into battle.

The Guardian in me takes over, but the man who loves her never fades. In that brief exchange, we fortify each other for the fight ahead and the future we dare to dream of together.

I position myself by the door, my senses heightened, ready to protect this room and the woman who's become more than just a partner in this fight.

Sealed inside our technological stronghold, the reality of our isolation hits. It's just Stitch and me against the might of Haven. She's already at work, her fingers a blur.

"First order of business, disrupting their internal communications." Stitch returns to her console, her eyes scanning the screens. She types rapidly, and the screens flicker in response to her commands. "This will sow the first seeds of confusion," she mutters, more to herself than to me.

My gaze is fixed on the door, ears straining for any sound of approach. Every sense is heightened, every nerve on edge. What she does is crucial, but my role is just as important—ensuring nothing interrupts her.

"Fire alarms in the east wing will drive them in the wrong direction. Or rather, right into where Alpha team is waiting." She presses a few more keys. The sound of distant alarms filters through the surveillance feed, an incessant wail that signals our plan is in motion.

She doesn't stop there. "Now for the sprinklers in the storage areas. That'll hinder their access to additional gear. Not to mention making it more difficult to see."

The screens reveal the chaos unfolding in real time. Alarms blare. Sprinklers activate. Haven's personnel scramble in confusion. It's a testament to Stitch's skill, turning the fortress's defenses against itself.

"Nice work. Keep it up."

"I'm just getting started." Her focus doesn't waver. "Next, I'm going to loop surveillance footage in critical areas. They'll be blind to our movements while chasing ghosts that aren't there."

As she works her magic, I can't help but marvel at her ability to wage war from her keyboard. Her fingers are her weapons, the computer her battlefield. And in this fight, she's a general leading the charge.

I stand guard, ready to defend her against any threat while she turns Haven into a weapon of her own design.

The quiet is gone. The room thrums with tension. Stitch fully engages with her bank of monitors while I wait, every muscle tensed, ready for any sign of trouble. At some point, we will abandon this room, but not yet.

My eyes flicker between Stitch and the monitors, tracking our team's progress. Ethan stands alone in the banquet hall, chasing after Kaufman's Angels after the attack.

Suddenly, a series of soft raps at the door pulls my attention. It's a pattern I recognize immediately—Walt's signal.

"Brought you gifts." A ghost of a smile fills his face as he hands me a compact arsenal of my gear—weapons, extra magazines, and body armor.

"Thanks."

"How's it going?" Hank is with Walt, and he peers inside, his gaze landing on Stitch.

"She's creating complete mayhem."

Hank's expression is all business as he hands me additional gear. "Ethan's at the banquet alone. We're heading there now." His voice is muffled slightly by his HUD helmet. "Stay alive."

"You too." I equip myself with the gear.

Walt and Hank return to the fray, leaving me armed and even more prepared. I secure the door and feel better now that I'm reunited with my gear and armed to the teeth. A soldier in full readiness, I can't help but picture the scene in the banquet hall through Ethan's eyes.

The doors crashing open.

Hank and Walt making a formidable entrance in full tactical gear, rifles at the ready. Chaos swirling around them like a storm.

Amid the turmoil, their focus would be singular—locate Ethan and provide the support he desperately needs.

Stitch glances at me. "Hank and Walt are with him now." Her hands pause for a fraction of a second before resuming their dance over the keyboard.

From my vantage point in the communications room, the screens offer fleeting glimpses of Charlie team in action. They move like phantoms, each member a master of his craft. Their movements are precise and coordinated—the embodiment of skill honed through relentless training.

But what truly sets this scene apart, what adds an edge of awe to the deadly ballet unfolding on the screens, are the Rufi.

These autonomous, AI-driven robotic dogs are a sight to behold. They maneuver alongside my teammates, their movements fluid yet unmistakably mechanical. Technological wonders, they enhance my team's capabilities in ways that seem almost surreal.

We're a force to be reckoned with—on our own—each of us a weapon tempered by experience and resolve, but combined with the Rufi, we transform into something more.

We become an unstoppable force, a fusion of flesh and steel, instinct and algorithm.

Stitch catches my gaze, her eyes momentarily leaving the screens. "They're incredible, aren't they?" A hint of pride fills her voice. After all, the Rufi are a testament to the technological prowess of the Guardian HRS technical team, a part of her world.

"They're more than that," I reply, my eyes fixed on a screen where a Rufi skillfully maneuvers to flank Gabe and Blake, its sensors and cameras providing them an edge. "They're game-changers."

Stitch and I might be removed from the physical battlefield, but we witness the extraordinary synergy of man and machine through these screens. It's a partnership that redefines the dynamics of combat, blending the irreplaceable value of human judgment with the precision of advanced technology.

In Haven, amidst the chaos and the fight for justice, we're not just witnessing a battle. We're witnessing the dawn of a new era in tactical operations, where the likes of Charlie team and the Rufi set a new standard for efficiency and lethality.

"Ethan's got the women." Stitch draws my attention to a different monitor.

Ethan leads a group of frightened women, his movements protective, his focus unwavering. Hank and Walt are with him. They move as one, a unit bound by a singular goal—to save those who can't save themselves.

"Once they get the women to the tunnels, that's our signal to leave."

We need to stay in place as long as possible to protect our men and the women they're rescuing.

"I'm just getting started." Stitch doesn't look up from her monitor, but her response is firm.

We talked at length about her plans to spread chaos, but much of what she's doing now is unplanned and unscripted. She thrives in the moment, coming up with new things to throw at Kaufman's men on the fly. She's an unseen force in this battle, a mastermind turning the tide in our favor.

The shockwave of an explosion abruptly shakes the air. It's not just sound; it's a physical force that rattles the very air around us. Stitch's fingers freeze over the keyboard, her body tensing. Her eyes, wide with alarm, meet mine.

"That wasn't one of the outer walls." Her voice is edged with a sudden sharpness of fear. "That came from inside Haven."

A surge of adrenaline tightens my chest and sets my nerves on edge. My hand instinctively goes to my weapon as I step closer to the monitors, trying to pinpoint the source of the blast.

The screens flicker with the aftermath of the explosion. The corridors of Haven, usually so controlled and sterile, are now scenes of chaos—debris scattered, lights flickering.

The blast was close, dangerously close.

My heart pounds, echoing the lingering reverberations of the explosion. This wasn't part of the plan. Unplanned means uncontrolled, and that's the worst kind of danger in our line of work.

"I'm checking the internal sensors." Stitch returns to her keyboard, her movements more frantic as she tries to assess the new threat.

I move to the barricaded door, listening intently. The explosion might have been internal, but its consequences could bring external threats to our doorstep.

The quiet that follows the explosion is almost worse than the blast itself. It's the quiet of uncertainty, of not knowing what's coming next. Our position might not be safe much longer.

"Prepare to evacuate. We need to make exfil."

"I will, but the women aren't out yet." Stitch's focus sharpens, and adrenaline edges her voice. Her hands move deftly, flipping switches and typing commands.

On one of the screens, I watch as chaos unfolds. Alpha and Bravo teams, mere blips on the monitor, execute their part with precision. They aim to draw Haven's guards outside the walls, leaving Ethan and the rest of the team room to rescue the Angels without having to engage with Kaufman's guards.

Explosions light up the feed in brief, bright flashes. Haven's defenses are being tested like never before.

Stitch activates another group of Haven's internal alarms. The sound is jarring, a cacophony that echoes through the surveillance feeds.

Kaufman's security response is absolute chaos. I can almost feel the confusion of his men as they scramble, disoriented by the sudden blare of alarms.

She doesn't stop there. She activates the fire suppression systems in key areas with a few more keystrokes. On the screens, sprays of water rain down, adding to the pandemonium.

"Nicely done," I say, my voice low, my eyes never leaving the door. "Keep them guessing."

"I'm looping the surveillance footage now. They'll be blind to our movements. Ethan and the others should be relatively free to move." Her concentration is a thing of beauty.

The room shudders around us, a grim reminder that Haven's once-impenetrable walls are succumbing to the relentless assault. Screens flicker erratically, casting eerie shadows in the chaos. Stitch is still at her console, her fingers a blur, but the urgency is palpable.

"We need to go." The building groans under the strain. The

sound of crumbling concrete and twisted metal filters through the air, a death knell to the fortress that was once Haven.

"Just a minute," she insists, her voice tight. "Ethan's not with his team. He's still inside."

Her words hit me like a physical blow.

"Ethan's unaccounted for? How did he get separated?"

"I don't know. Hank and Walt have the women. The others are with them. They just exited the tunnels. I wasn't watching Ethan, but he turned back."

Why would Ethan turn back?

I understand her hesitation and the need to ensure everyone's safety, but every second we remain is a second closer to being buried under the rubble.

The building lurches again, a violent shudder that sends a cascade of debris from the ceiling.

"Stitch, now!" I grab her arm, yanking her to her feet.

The situation is escalating beyond our control, and our window for escape is rapidly closing.

Reluctantly, she abandons her post, her face etched with worry for Ethan. We both know the cost of leaving him behind, but our immediate survival is critical.

As we dash into the corridor, Haven transforms into an unrecognizable landscape of chaos and ruin. A cataclysmic aftermath now replaces the pristine orderliness it once boasted. Ceilings cave in, sending showers of debris cascading down. The floors are strewn with rubble, remnants of a fortress crumbling under its weight.

Our sprint is frantic, almost animalistic, as we dodge and weave through the destruction. We breathe in a choking cocktail of dust, smoke, and the sharp tang of scorched electronics. Incessant alarms create a dissonant symphony, punctuating our desperate bid for survival.

Suddenly, as we round a corner, two of Kaufman's men emerge, equally surprised to see us as we are to see them. Time seems to slow as we lock eyes. Instinct takes over. I shove Stitch behind me, shielding her with my body.

The first shots ring out, echoing through the shattered hallways.

Adrenaline surges through me, honing my senses and sharpening my reactions. I return fire, my training taking over.

Bullets fly in a deadly dance.

One of Kaufman's men goes down. The other ducks for cover, firing wildly. Debris kicks up around us, the air now filled with the deadly whine of bullets.

Stitch presses close behind me, her presence a reminder of what's at stake. I can't falter, not now. With calculated precision, I aim and fire. The second man falls, his threat extinguished.

The firefight, though brief, leaves my heart pounding, a drumbeat echoing in the turmoil around us. I glance back at Stitch, ensuring she's unharmed. Her eyes meet mine, a flash of fear quickly masked by determination.

"Come on," I urge, grabbing her hand.

We resume our frenzied escape. Gunfire echoes all around us. The corridor ahead is a gauntlet, but we navigate it with a singular focus—to reach the tunnels and escape this crumbling tomb.

Stitch runs beside me, keeping pace despite the chaos. Her resilience in the face of such danger only deepens my resolve to get us out safely.

We round a corner, only to be met with a collapsed section of the hallway. Without hesitation, we backtrack, finding an alternate route; our every move driven by instinct and the will to survive.

My heart pounds in my chest, a relentless drum echoing the chaos around us. The structure of Haven groans ominously, a beast in its death throes.

Time is running out.

Another explosion, closer this time, sends a shockwave through the corridor. We're thrown off our feet and hit the ground hard.

I'm up in an instant, pulling Stitch to her feet.

"Keep moving!" I shout over the din.

We navigate the treacherous terrain, our movements a blend of desperation and determination. The goal is clear—reach the drainage tunnels, our lifeline out of this crumbling hell.

As we run, my mind races with possibilities. Where is Ethan? Can he still make it out?

The uncertainty is a heavy weight, but I push it aside to focus on our escape.

Stitch, right beside me, stumbles over a chunk of concrete, but I quickly steady her. Her recovery is swift, driven by the same survival instinct that fuels my every move.

Suddenly, as we turn a corner, a new threat emerges. Another group of Kaufman's men, more than before, confront us in the hallway.

In an instant, the corridor turns into a battlefield.

Gunfire erupts, a deafening chorus in the already chaotic symphony of destruction. I return fire, my movements precise and calculated.

But this fight is different—it's more desperate.

More ferocious.

Stitch, no longer just a companion in escape but a partner in combat, pulls out her sidearm. She stands her ground beside me, her shots ringing out with mine. Her presence and firepower add to our defense, turning us into a formidable force against the onslaught.

We move in tandem, covering each other and firing at the advancing men—just like we practiced in the kill house simulations what seems ages ago—Stitch and I act as one.

The air is thick with the smell of gunfire, the hallway echoing with the shouts of our attackers and the relentless barrage of bullets.

Each shot we fire is more than defense; it's a fight for every breath we take, for every step we've fought to advance.

Stitch's aim is steady, her resolve unshakable. She's more than a tech genius; she's a warrior in her own right.

The firefight feels endless, a desperate struggle against overwhelming odds, but we push back with everything we have.

The same determination that burns within me blazes in Stitch's eyes.

Finally, the last of Kaufman's men falls. The corridor echoes in the sudden silence, save for the distant groans of Haven's destruction and our heavy breathing.

"Don't stop." My voice is rough with exertion and dust.

Stitch nods, her eyes scanning the corridor for more threats. Limping and battered but not broken, we press forward, seeking another escape route, our spirits fueled by the adrenaline of the firefight and the unspoken promise to each other that we will not give up.

Not here.

Not now.

Not ever.

The corridors of Haven, once a symbol of strength, now betray us at every turn. Our path is a relentless obstacle course; the terrain shifts underfoot, unstable and treacherous. Each step is a gamble, each breath filled with dust and the fear of the unknown. Lights show the way, and then they flicker and go out, plunging us into darkness.

We keep going until we reach the tunnel's entrance, but when we're about to step into the relative safety of the tunnel, a violent tremor shakes Haven's foundations. The ceiling above us groans, an ominous prelude to catastrophe.

With no time to think, I act.

"Back!" I push Stitch away from the collapsing entrance.

Debris cascades down where we stood moments ago, sealing the tunnel with an unforgiving finality.

Coughing, we retreat, our hopes dashed in an instant, but surrender isn't an option. We pivot, seeking another way out, driven by sheer willpower.

We attempt a second escape route, our movements frantic yet futile against the onslaught of falling rubble. Again, our path is blocked, the way forward snatched away by the merciless crumbling of Haven all around us.

Stitch's face, smeared with dust and streaked with sweat, mirrors my own determination. We share a look, unspoken but understood.

We're not giving up.

Not yet.

Our third escape attempt is driven by pure desperation. We push our battered bodies through unstable corridors, the promise of escape tantalizingly close. The outside world is just a few steps away, yet fate has other plans.

Without warning, the ceiling above us gives way with a deafening roar, a monstrous expression of destruction. The corridor convulses, and the walls cave inward. We run, fueled by adrenaline and sheer terror, but the collapse is relentless.

And now, the ceiling caves in.

In those frantic moments, my only thought is Stitch's safety. I act on instinct, throwing myself over her in a protective embrace. The world around us is a terrifying rumble of concrete and splintering steel crashing down.

A large chunk of debris strikes me with brutal force. Pain explodes through my body, a white-hot intensity that blinds me to everything else. I grunt in pain, but the chaos muffles the sound.

The impact pins me to the ground, trapping my leg under its oppressive weight. The pain is immense, a searing agony that threatens to overwhelm my senses. I fight to stay conscious, to maintain my protective hold over Stitch.

Darkness closes in, a suffocating shroud that muffles the sounds of destruction. Dust chokes the air, making each breath a painful struggle. I'm dimly aware of Stitch's efforts to move. Her determination undimmed, even in the face of our dire situation.

My response is a groan, my focus narrowing to the excruciating pain in my leg. As I cling to consciousness, my thoughts drift to our mission, to Ethan, to the uncertain fate of our team.

But mostly, they linger on Stitch, the unspoken promises and unfulfilled dreams that lie beyond the rubble that imprisons us.

My last thought is of my son, a young boy who will be an orphan. In this enclosed tomb, time loses meaning, and pain becomes my only reality.

THIRTY-THREE

Stitch

The darkness is absolute, a suffocating blanket that envelops me. I'm trapped, not just by the rubble, but by Jeb's unconscious form on top of me.

His weight is a protective yet imprisoning force, pinning me in place.

Thick air, stagnant and heavy with dust and smoke, coats my tongue. Pitch blackness envelops us.

Panic claws at me, a living thing in my chest. It's suffocating, like the rubble that traps us. I fight to keep my breathing steady, to push back the rising tide of fear, but breathing is nearly impossible with all the smoke and grit in the air.

"Jeb," I whisper, hoping for any sign of response. His stillness terrifies me more than the enclosing darkness.

The lack of light is disorienting, a complete absence that plays tricks on my eyes. Phantom lights flicker at the edges of my vision, remnants of hope or perhaps just my mind desperately searching for a way out.

With every ounce of strength, I try to shift Jeb's weight to free myself from this crushing embrace. The concrete and steel that entomb us are unyielding, a testament to the catastrophe that has befallen Haven.

My movements are restricted, my efforts seemingly futile against the immense weight. Tears sting my eyes, frustration and fear mingling with the dust that coats my face, but despair is a luxury I can't afford.

I have to be strong, for Jeb, for myself.

In the pitch black, my other senses sharpen: the texture of Jeb's clothing under my fingertips, the scent of sweat and blood mixing in the air, and the distant, muffled sounds of the world outside our dark prison become acutely perceptible.

I reach out, my hands exploring the confines of our prison. The rough texture of broken concrete, the cold, unyielding hardness of twisted steel. Each sensation is a stark reminder of the danger we're in and the urgency of our need to escape.

I gently probe his body for signs of life, relief flooding through me as I find a faint but steady pulse. He's alive, but for how long, I can't say. I renew my efforts, pushing against Jeb's weight, determined to get free. Each movement is exhausting, a battle against both our physical confinement and the creeping tendrils of despair.

"Come on, Jeb," I urge, my voice barely audible in the oppressive stillness. "You're not dying here." I refuse to let the darkness claim us. I refuse to give up when so much is at stake.

Slowly, painstakingly, I shift his body enough to wriggle out from beneath him. Freeing myself is only the first step; now, I must tend to Jeb. In the consuming blackness, I assess his condition as best I can, relying on touch and instinct.

My fingers brush against his leg. He stifles a groan and guilt washes over me. I should have been faster, should have seen the collapse coming.

But there's no room for regret, only action.

Jeb is alive but vulnerable, and it's up to me to protect him. The role reversal is profound—the protector is now the protected. I'm no longer just a teammate; I'm his lifeline.

The pain of my injuries pales in comparison to my concern for Jeb.

The silence is oppressive, filled with the echoes of our shallow breaths and the distant, muffled sounds of Haven's ongoing destruction. It's a constant reminder that time is running out and that with each passing moment, our chances of survival dwindle.

I shift, trying to find a better angle to move the debris. My movements are slow, hindered by the confined space and the fear of causing further collapse. Every time I shift a block of rubble, it's a calculated risk.

The darkness plays tricks on my mind. The soft sounds of shifting rubble are whispers of unseen threats. I blink rapidly, trying to dispel the illusions and focus on our situation.

Fear is a constant companion, with cold fingers wrapping around my heart.

It says we're not making it out of here.

It destroys hope.

But I ruthlessly push it back and channel it into determination.

I have to be strong for Jeb and for myself.

Fear might be paralyzing for most, but for me, it's a wake-up call, a sharp prod that spurs me into action. It's not an enemy. It's my fiercest ally, telling me to fight harder and think faster.

Fear strips away all the non-essentials, focusing my mind on what truly matters—survival.

It guides me through the darkness.

It pushes me to be braver than I ever thought possible.

It gives me incredible strength.

As I shift in the cramped space, trying to free Jeb, my fear evolves into fierce resolve.

The more I confront it, the more it sharpens my focus and hardens my resolve. I'm not just fighting against the rubble and the darkness; I'm fighting against the part of me that wants to give up.

It propels me forward. With each thought, I move a piece of debris. I gain a few inches of breathing space. Sweat mixes with the dust on my skin, a gritty film that coats my face. My muscles ache with the effort, but I can't stop.

I won't stop.

I'm scared, more scared than I've ever been, but we won't die here, not like this. We've fought too hard and come too far to let it end like this.

The more I work, the thicker the air becomes. The harder it is to take a breath. I choke back a sob, focusing on the task ahead, reminding myself to channel panic into strength. If I don't, it will drown me.

I finally make enough room to crawl beside Jeb.

In the suffocating darkness, I reach out, my fingers brushing against his still form. A large slab of debris pins him, the source of his stillness. My heart races, fear and determination warring within me.

"Jeb, please," I whisper, my voice a trembling thread in the oppressive silence. "Stay with me." But he doesn't respond, his unconscious state a stark reminder of our dire situation.

My hands fumble in the dark. The concrete is cold, unyielding, a monstrous weight against his body. I push, pull, and strain against it, but it's like trying to move a mountain.

Tears mix with the dust on my face, creating muddy tracks down my cheeks. But I can't afford to cry.

I refuse to mourn.

Not yet. There's work to be done, a life to save—his life.

I pause, my muscles screaming in protest, my lungs burning for clean air. The darkness is complete, a void that swallows hope and time alike. In this eternal night, Jeb's prone form is my only anchor, proof that I'm not alone.

I reach for him again, my hands trembling.

"Jeb, I need you to fight," I plead, though I know he can't hear me. My fingertips find his face, his skin warm but worryingly still beneath my touch.

I resume my efforts, desperation lending me strength. The debris shifts a small but encouraging movement. I redouble my efforts, pushing against the weight with every ounce of strength.

My hands are raw, my nails chipped and bleeding, but I can't stop.

I

WON'T

STOP.

"Come on, come on." It's a mantra against despair. The rubble shifts again, a small victory in this war against fate.

I'm driven by more than the instinct to survive. It's a need to protect Jeb, to repay his sacrifice. He shielded me; now, it's my turn to save him.

The sounds of my struggle are muffled, the silence around us a heavy shroud. I'm acutely aware of every grunt, every scrape of rubble, every ragged breath I take. The world beyond our tomb feels distant, a reality separate from this dark prison.

The sounds of Haven's continued destruction are distant, a world away from the immediacy of our plight. Here, in this confined space, time loses meaning. There's only the struggle, the fight to reclaim our lives from the clutches of ruin.

In the darkness, I find a resilience I never knew I had. I'm more than a member of his team; more than my skills and training.

I'm a survivor, fighting against impossible odds.

Finally, the debris gives way, moving enough to free Jeb. My relief is palpable, a physical release that courses through my exhausted body. But there's no time to rest.

No time to savor this small triumph.

Gently, I check Jeb's pulse, my fingers pressing against his neck. It's there, faint but steady, a beacon of hope in the darkness.

"Hang in there." I drag him, inch by painstaking inch, toward what I hope is safety.

Our progress is slow, hampered by the darkness and debris surrounding us. We've been through too much and fought too hard to let it end like this. I whisper words of encouragement, more to myself than to him.

"We're going to make it, Jeb. We have to."

I'm not carrying Jeb's weight; I'm carrying our dreams and unspoken promises.

I carry our future.

I have to believe we'll emerge from this nightmare, our bond stronger than ever.

I have to, because I refuse to die here.

THIRTY-FOUR

Stitch

I drag Jeb's limp form across the debris-strewn floor. Each movement is an exertion against despair, against the weight of our dire situation. There's a corner that feels marginally safer, a space where the ceiling hasn't completely caved in.

I gently settle Jeb's body. Dim light filters through the cracks in the rubble. Slowly, I begin to see around me. The diffuse light casts eerie shadows across his face. He's still breathing—barely. His face is pale. His brow furrowed in pain.

I examine him as best as I can in the dim light. His leg is badly injured, blood seeping through his torn pants. I tear a strip from my shirt, fashioning a makeshift bandage.

"Come on, Jeb," I murmur, more to myself than to him. "Stay with me." But he's unresponsive, locked in a silent battle of his own.

Once I've done all I can for Jeb, I face a terrible truth. I have to find a way out, but to do that, I must leave him. It feels like abandonment, but I have no choice. I kiss his forehead, a silent promise to return.

"I love you. I promise I'll come back." I kiss him again, this time on his lips, but there's no response.

My task is daunting.

The debris forms a labyrinth of destruction, a maze with no clear exit. I start to crawl, squeezing through narrow gaps and pushing away smaller pieces of rubble.

My hands are raw, and my body aches, but I push forward, driven by the slim hope of finding an escape.

Minutes turn into eternity as I search—each path leads to more wreckage, more impassable barriers. The air grows thinner, each breath a struggle. Panic rises within me, a tide that threatens to overwhelm my senses.

I force myself to stay calm and to think. But the truth is inescapable—we're trapped—buried alive in the ruins of Haven.

The realization hits me like a physical blow, and for a moment, I'm unable to move, paralyzed by the enormity of our predicament.

Tears well in my eyes, spilling over in silent, dusty trails. I've faced danger before, but nothing like this. This isn't a battle that can be won with skill or bravery. It's a battle against time and fate, and we're losing.

Dejected, I crawl back to Jeb's side.

I sit beside him, my back against the cold, unyielding concrete. I take his hand in mine, its warmth a stark contrast to the chill of our surroundings.

"I'm so sorry." My voice breaks. "I tried. I tried so hard."

Minutes turn to hours. The silence is oppressive, broken only by the distant, muffled sounds of Haven's death groan and our shallow breaths.

I'm lost in a whirlwind of thoughts—memories of our past, of the team, of all the things Jeb and I planned to do once this was over. I turn my thoughts to Maverick, a precious boy who managed to steal my heart.

A sob escapes me.

Maverick's already lost too much. First, his mother, and now his father.

It's too much pain. I curl my arms around myself and let the tears flow.

Grief washes over me in waves. We were supposed to make it out.

We were supposed to have a future together.

Now, those dreams seem like distant fantasies, crushed under the weight of concrete and steel.

I lean my head against Jeb's still form, my sobs muffled against his chest. In this dark, enclosed space, the world narrows to just the two of us. Our future is reduced to nothing as we face our imminent mortality.

Despair grips my heart. I'm scared, not just of dying, but of dying here, in the dark, with so much left unsaid, so much left undone.

As time slips by, unnoticed and uncaring, I hold onto Jeb and the flickering flame of my hope.

It refuses to die.

Maybe, just maybe, someone will find us.

But as the hours pass, that hope dims, flickering on the edge of extinction.

At this moment, it's not about survival. It's about coming to terms with the end, with the unfulfilled promises and unspoken words.

And so, I sit with Jeb, waiting for an end that seems both terrifying and inevitable. In this final vigil, our fate is as cruel as it is unavoidable.

Time.

It takes a long time to die, trapped in our dark prison.

Random facts flood my mind. It takes three minutes to survive without oxygen—three days without water and three weeks without food.

I figure we've got three days.

Time stretches and compresses, marked only by the rhythm of our labored breaths and the occasional shift of rubble. Hours blend into days, or maybe it's the other way around. In the darkness, such distinctions lose their meaning. The silence is all-encompassing, a void where even the faintest sound takes on a life of its own.

I drift in and out of sleep. Exhaustion and grief press down on me like the physical mass of the rubble that traps us. My thoughts are a swirling maelstrom of what-ifs and if-onlys, each one a sharp jab to my already frayed spirit.

Dust settles over us like a shroud. It coats my skin and invades my mouth. Each breath sends me into a coughing fit until my body gives up and accepts the grit I breathe in.

Jeb's still form beside me is both a comfort and a constant reminder of our dire circumstances. I check on him periodically, hoping for some sign of improvement, but he remains in a deep, unsettling stillness.

Maybe it's a blessing he's unconscious?

I press my cheek against the cool, rough concrete, trying to anchor myself to the here and now. Despair is a relentless foe, clawing at the edges of my resolve.

My throat burns with thirst, a stark reminder of our bleak situation. Here, under layers of rubble, the world has shrunk to this suffocating space of darkness and stillness.

Basic needs, once paramount, now seem like distant luxuries. Survival is stripped down to its bare essence—the sheer act of drawing breath, of clinging to each fleeting second.

I exist from one moment to the next.

But then, amidst the oppressive silence, a new sound appears. Faint, almost lost in the echoes of my ragged breaths. A soft, rhythmic buzzing. I pause, hardly daring to breathe, as I tune my senses to the noise.

Am I imagining things?

My heart dares to skip a beat.

Or is this a cruel auditory hallucination?

I hold my breath; my heart stumbles, teetering on the brink of hope and despair.

The sound comes again—clearer this time, unmistakable. A steady mechanical hum, the buzzing of a bumblebee.

No natural insect. It's too precise, too consistent. It's one of them—one of Mitzy's drones from the swarm!

This is real.

A spark of hope ignites within me.

I listen intently, every fiber of my being focused on that sound. It grows steadily, a rhythmic scrabbling that echoes in the hollow space around us. It's methodical and purposeful—the sound of something not hindered by fear or uncertainty.

And it's getting closer.

I sit up as much as the confined space allows, my senses honed in on the source of the noise. The sound conjures images of rescue teams, of people searching through the debris, of a chance at survival.

Could it be?

The thought is a fragile bubble in the darkness.

I shift slightly, wincing at the sharp pain the movement brings. "Jeb," I whisper, unsure if he can hear me. "A drone… It's here." My voice is a hoarse rasp, barely audible even to my own ears.

I extend my hand, fingers trembling, toward the sound. The drone, a harbinger of hope or doom, hovers just out of reach. "Help us," I breathe, the words a plea to this tiny emissary of the world outside.

As the drone hovers in the cramped space, I'm filled with hope. Its mechanical buzz is a steady presence, but more than that, it's a link to the outside.

It can't carry signals or speak, but its ability to record offers hope.

"Mitzy," I start, my voice a strained whisper, addressing the drone as if it were an old friend. "If you're seeing this…" I pause, swallowing against the dryness of my throat. "Jeb and I, we're alive. But Jeb's hurt badly."

The drone, its tiny lenses unblinking, seems to watch me, recording every word, every plea.

"The space we're in, it's unstable," I continue, my voice trembling with urgency. "Any shift could bring everything down. We need help, fast."

I glance at Jeb, his form still and silent beside me. "Jeb's condition is critical. He needs medical attention as soon as possible."

I reach out, my hand trembling, not touching the drone but

imploring it. "Please, Mitzy, you've got to get this to someone. Anyone. We don't have much time."

The drone, a silent witness to our plight, hovers a moment longer, as if processing my desperate message. Then, as if understanding the urgency, it turns and disappears inside a tiny crack.

Its buzzing fades into the distance.

"Go," I whisper, a prayer for its safe passage. "Find someone."

Time stretches endlessly after the drone's departure. Each second is a battle against despair, each minute a war waged with dwindling hope.

Jeb's breathing is shallow, a fragile thread binding him to life. I keep talking to him, a monologue of encouragement and fear, my voice a lifeline in the darkness.

As hours trickle by, the silence grows oppressive, heavy with the weight of waiting. My mind teeters on the edge of panic, replaying every possible scenario of rescue and tragedy.

Then, breaking through the silence, a sound. Faint at first, like the distant echo of a forgotten dream. A scratching, a scrabbling.

It grows louder, more insistent, a rhythmic clawing against the rubble that imprisons us.

My heart leaps, pounding against my ribcage.

"Jeb," I whisper, my voice cracking with hope and fear. "They're here… Help is here."

As the scrabbling grows closer, I brace myself, ready to greet our rescuers, ready to embrace the chance of life they bring.

Then, unmistakably, I hear it again—a scrabbling, clawing sound, like something burrowing through the wreckage.

The sound becomes a lifeline. My exhaustion and grief are momentarily forgotten, replaced by an acute awareness of the present.

I call out, my voice a hoarse whisper in the darkness.

"Hello? Is someone there?"

The rubble swallows the words, but the act of speaking is an affirmation of hope.

The scrabbling grows louder, more insistent. It's getting closer, carving a path through the destruction. My breath catches in anticipation, my eyes straining in the darkness for any sign of life.

A surge of overwhelming emotion flows through me.

Relief.

Joy.

Disbelief

They all wash over me in a torrent of emotions. After hours, or maybe days, of entrapment, the possibility of escape is a burst of sunlight in the unending night.

I brace myself, ready for whatever comes next, my heart pounding with fear and exhilaration.

The promise of rescue is the most beautiful thing, but then what if our rescuers are Kaufman's men?

Before I travel down that path, a beam of light slices through the darkness, blinding me.

My eyes water, but I don't look away. In that beam of light, I see the most beautiful sight.

It's one of the Rufi.

The glossy surface is marred with scratches and dents, telling a story of the harsh journey it endured to reach us. Parts of its frame are visibly crushed, the metal casing twisted and contorted in places. Despite its damaged state, the robot moves deliberately, its mechanical joints whirring softly as it navigates the rubble.

The green glow of its optical sensors, usually bright and steady, flickers intermittently, betraying signs of malfunction. Yet, even in its impaired condition, the Rufus is undeterred.

Beaten, but not broken.

"We're here!" I shout, my voice cracking. "We're here! Jeb's injured."

Its sensors lock onto me, and I feel the intelligence behind its mechanical eyes.

I reach out, touching its cool, metallic body, a tangible symbol of rescue. The Rufus responds, its movements becoming more deliberate as it clears the debris around us. Debris that was too heavy for me to lift.

The despair and fear that have been my constant companions

fade, replaced by an overwhelming sense of gratitude. I look at Jeb, wishing he could witness this moment.

As the Rufus works, I dare to believe we might make it out of here, and I'm filled with joy so intense it's almost painful.

I whisper to Jeb, my voice filled with tears and laughter. "We're going to make it!"

THIRTY-FIVE

Stitch

───────────

FROM THE MOMENT THE BEAM OF LIGHT FROM THE RUFUS PIERCES the darkness, I breathe easy for the first time in—well, since forever.

Its arrival feels like a miracle. Its metal frame bears the scars of its journey through the ruins, but it's relentless.

It never stops.

It never tires.

It never loses hope—unlike me.

I scramble toward it, my movements fueled by relief and urgency.

"I can't move him." My voice croaks like a frog, parched, scratchy, and raw.

I nod toward Jeb, lying motionless, his body battered and broken. The Rufus pauses—a momentary stillness as its sensors lock onto Jeb. With a soft symphony of mechanical precision, it activates, servos whirring to life.

It edges closer to Jeb, its form engineered for both battle and rescue. It extends a specialized appendage, engineered to have the delicacy of a surgeon yet the strength of a soldier. With the utmost care, the intelligent machine slips its arm under the collar of Jeb's body armor, ensuring a secure but gentle grip.

"Be careful."

I hold my breath, watching as it carefully adjusts its stance. Then, with incredible tenderness, it lifts Jeb's head, cradling it with the duty to protect. The robotic dog begins to move, each step calculated to avoid jostling its precious cargo.

My pulse thrums in my ears, keeping time with the Rufus's steady pace. I crawl behind them, my eyes darting from Jeb's prone form to our mechanical savior and then to the uncertain safety ahead. The Rufus, with Jeb's life quite literally in its hands, is a savior.

The destruction of Haven surrounds us, a tangible reminder of the danger we're still in. The corridors are a labyrinth of devastation, with fallen beams and shattered concrete. Each creak and groan of the unstable structure sends a jolt of fear shooting through me, a cruel reminder that safety is still far away.

Then I see it—another Rufi. This one braces a wall. Its body acting as a support to prevent another collapse.

The sight is both heartening and heart-wrenching. These machines, programmed to save human lives, sacrifice operational integrity for us.

We crawl through the narrow space created by this second Rufus bolstering the wall with its body. The air, thick with dust, makes each breath difficult. The Rufus dragging Jeb never falters, its commitment unwavering even in the face of potential self-destruction.

I can't help but feel a kinship with these machines. In their selfless actions, I see a reflection of the Guardian's mission—the willingness to risk everything for the sake of others.

It's a sobering realization that adds weight to each step I take.

Our path forward is treacherous, a maze wrought by disaster, and we move at a snail's pace.

Each step is a defiance against the odds.

The Rufus continues with unerring precision, its sensors navigating the safest path with an efficiency that belies its damaged exterior.

Behind me, the rubble shifts ominously, a stark reminder that our escape is a race against time. I glance at Jeb, his face smeared with dust, his body limp yet in the safest hands—or rather, paws?—appendages?

The journey is a blur of tension and focus. My body moves on autopilot, driven by the singular goal of getting Jeb to safety. As we inch closer to what I hope is the exit, more light filters through the gaps in the debris. It's a sign of hope, a promise that the outside world is within reach.

"We're almost there, Jeb," I whisper, once again, more to myself than to him. The thought of emerging from this nightmare, of leaving behind the ruins of Haven, is the only thing that keeps me moving.

Keeps me fighting.

It's obvious the Rufi worked together to carved out the path we travel.

It's a narrow vein through Haven's broken heart, meticulously cleared for us. The groans and creaks of the unstable structure are a constant reminder of our peril. Debris trickles from cracks in the ceiling as the wreckage shifts and settles. Each sound puts a hitch in my breath.

Each step I take is tentative.

Fearful.

Hopeful?

But not for the Rufi.

There's no emotion. No fear. It acts according to its programming.

Programming that tells it to keep us alive.

Jeb remains still, his face obscured by dust and shadows, relying entirely on our mechanical savior, but his ragged breath tells me everything I need to know.

It's not too late to save him.

We approach a precarious section where the ceiling has collapsed, forming a barrier in our path. My breath catches in my throat when I see yet another Rufus, its body wedged against a massive slab of concrete, holding it up just enough to create a narrow passage under its belly.

The Rufi dragging Jeb crouches down, scuttling through the tiny space, pulling him through. I follow, my heart pounding against my ribs as I fight claustrophobia and the fear of being buried alive.

The walls around us groan ominously, the sound of a giant stirring in its sleep. I squeeze through the gap, the weight of the building pressing down around me.

Just as we clear the section, there's a thunderous crash. I whirl around as the ceiling collapses. The Rufi that was holding it up disappears under a cloud of dust and rubble.

My heart lurches. The sacrifice is immediate and total—that Rufus gave up its existence for our safety.

Ahead, another Rufi creates a small tunnel with its body bracing against a fallen wall. The sight is both incredible and heartbreaking. The first Rufus drags Jeb through the tunnel formed by its fellow, undeterred by the loss of its counterparts.

The space narrows, rubble pressing close against my sides. I push on, hands and knees grinding against the rough ground, the weight of the confined space bearing down on me.

Every inch forward is a fight, a desperate crawl toward the promise of escape.

It's a surreal experience, moving beneath the Rufus. Its mechanical body straining against the weight of concrete and steel. As I crawl past, I can't help but reach out, my hand brushing against the cool metal.

"Thank you."

Its body vibrates with the effort of holding up the weight. This contact, brief as it is, feels like a silent communion, an acknowledgment of their sacrifice.

When we emerge from the tunnel, I take a moment to glance back. The Rufus remains motionless, its task complete. In their final acts, these machines redefine heroism—not as a human trait but as an act of pure altruism, irrespective of form or consciousness.

I take a moment to look back and give thanks.

The Rufus remains in place, its optical sensors dim but focused, a silent vigil against the chaos. In its stillness, there's a nobility that transcends its mechanical nature.

The Rufus, carrying Jeb, continues on with relentless determination. The path opens up ahead, and light beckons—a hopeful end to the nightmare called Haven.

Every muscle in my body protests, aching with the effort to push through the debris. The Rufi's battered frame whirs persistently, dragging Jeb's unconscious form. His face is hauntingly pale.

"Almost there," I whisper the words as much a reassurance for myself as for Jeb.

The light ahead intensifies, cutting through the darkness like a lifeline. It's the exit; it has to be. My heart races, a chaotic drumbeat of relief and dread.

Distant shouts pierce the silence. Hope surges within me, propelling me forward. Someone is out there.

Rescue.

Salvation.

The possibility sends a jolt through my weary limbs.

"Jeb," I call out, my voice cracking, "stay with me."

But Jeb remains motionless, his unresponsiveness a constant worry.

The shouts grow louder, more distinct, a chorus of urgency beyond our reach. We're close now, achingly close.

I crawl with renewed vigor toward the light, toward the voices, and toward a sliver of hope.

Suddenly, strong hands reach through the rubble toward Jeb. They grasp him firmly, pulling with a coordinated effort. Jeb's robotic savior releases its hold as the rescuers take over, carefully lifting him free.

A faint groan escapes his lips, the first sign of consciousness since the collapse.

Relief floods through me, overwhelming and fierce.

He's alive.

He's responding.

The rubble beneath me shifts ominously as I inch closer to the exit. Strong hands reach in.

Men grasp my arms.

As they hoist me up, a shock of clean air hits my lungs, cold and sharp. I'm lifted clear, my feet dangling, my body limp in their steady grasp.

The reality of my rescue, the transition from the darkness of Haven to the glaring light of day, leaves me reeling. Disoriented, I barely register the faces above me as they lift me free.

The moment I'm clear, a deafening roar fills my ears. It's a thunderous, terrifying crash. The ground shudders under the impact, a stark reminder of the narrow escape from what could have been my tomb.

Overwhelmed, I'm stunned and in shock. Our rescuers' grips tighten, steadying me as they double-time it away from the wreckage.

It takes a moment for my eyes to adjust and for the sounds of our rescue to replace the echo of Haven's collapse.

Max, the leader of Bravo team, is a commanding presence even in this chaos. His firm yet reassuring voice cuts through my daze, guiding the rescue.

"Are you okay? Any injuries we should know about?"

His voice is clear and focused, but my mind is elsewhere. I glance to where Jeb still lies, unmoving.

"Jeb," I rasp, my voice barely a whisper. My injuries—the cuts, gashes, deep bruising, the severe dehydration that makes my head spin—all fade into insignificance. "His leg. Crushed. Unconscious. Please. Help…"

Reduced to single words, my injuries and discomfort are secondary to my worry for Jeb.

"Booker's with him." Max directs his team with a few quick words. I watch, my heart in my throat, as they swarm over Jeb. Their movements are precise and efficient.

I sway, and my knees buckle; the adrenaline that fueled my escape gives way to exhaustion as I collapse. The pain of my wounds begins to seep through the numbness, each throb a reminder of the ordeal we've endured.

I try to focus, to recall names, but my mind is a whirlwind. Only fragments stick—Max, Alpha-One, leads with an unwavering focus; Booker, Bravo's team medic, his face a mask of efficiency as he assesses Jeb's injuries.

Jeb being loaded onto a stretcher.

Me being carried to a truck.

I blink against the harsh light, my eyes stinging from the sudden exposure. Around us, the ruins of Haven stretch out, a landscape of complete and utter destruction.

I can hardly process the sight—buildings reduced to rubble, smoke rising in lazy spirals to the sky. It's a scene from a nightmare, yet painfully real.

In the truck, Booker turns his attention to me. I want to protest, to say I'm fine, that Jeb needs his attention more than I do, but my voice fails me.

Instead, I nod, allowing Booker to examine me. His hands are efficient as he checks for injuries, his presence reassuring.

"You're severely dehydrated, and these cuts need cleaning, but you'll be okay." Booker offers a small, encouraging smile. "I'm going to start an IV."

As he tends to my wounds, my gaze drifts to Jeb.

He's still unconscious, but he's receiving the best care possible. Relief washes over me, mingled with a bone-deep weariness.

"We made it, Jeb." I reach out and grasp his hand. To my astonishment, Jeb's fingers slowly curl around mine.

It's a subtle movement, but it slams into me with the force of a tidal wave.

My heart, battered and weary, ignites with a sudden fierce joy. The simple contact, that small squeeze, is a beacon in the bleakness that's consumed me since the collapse.

I close my eyes, overwhelmed. Profound exhaustion seeps into every fiber of my being, but above that, overwhelming joy fills me.

Jeb's alive.

As I sit beside him, his hand in mine, I close my eyes and allow myself to breathe—to feel alive again.

Nothing matters but the beating of our hearts, our shared breaths, and the quiet strength of our entwined fingers.

We made it.

Against all odds, we made it together.

THIRTY-SIX

Jeb

CONSCIOUSNESS RETURNS TO ME AS A SLOW, CREEPING TIDE OF awareness. My mind emerges from the darkness, a fog lifting to reveal a world of pain and muffled sounds.

I'm semi-aware of voices, a blend of urgency and calm, near yet seemingly distant. There's a sensation of hands moving over me—professional, precise, a rhythm of assessing and treating.

Eyelids heavy as lead, I coax them open, wincing under a flood of raw daylight. The sky stretches vast and unending above me, its blues and grays melding into a hazy dome. I gulp down the air, so crisp and unlike the dank, suffocating breaths of the underground.

The act sends a jolt of pain through my body, but it's worth it for that taste of freedom.

"Jeb, can you hear me?" The voice is familiar and grounded. It's Booker, Bravo team's medic. His face hovers over mine, his expression a mix of relief and concern.

The world shifts and sways beneath me. Beneath my back, there's the unmistakable hardness of a moving vehicle's floor, vibrating with the rumble of an engine. As the vehicle lurches, my body protests, sending sharp reminders of my ordeal through every nerve.

I grit my teeth against the pain, focusing on my breaths through half-closed eyes; shadows and light play across my vision, the world outside speeding by in a blur. I try to speak, but my throat is a desert, my voice a hoarse rasp.

"Stitch?" is all I manage, my mind latching onto the one constant in the chaos.

"She's here. She's safe," Booker assures me, a hand on my shoulder, steadying.

I turn my head slightly, searching. And there she is—Stitch looking like a warrior.

Her face streaked with dirt and sweat. Rivulets of dried tears speak of incredible pain and suffering.

Her eyes reflecting a world of fatigue and relief.

Her hand reaches for me.

A wave of emotions hit me—relief, guilt, and overwhelming gratitude.

She's alive.

We're alive, against all odds.

Someone mentions an airfield, the words float to me.

A jet waits.

These words anchor me, a soft hum in the backdrop of my disoriented thoughts, grounding me to the present, but I only have eyes for the woman I love.

"You did it," I whisper, my voice scratches in my throat, barely audible.

Booker says something about my injuries, about hydration and rest, but his words fade into the background. All I can focus on is Stitch, the resilience in her eyes, the slight tremble of her lips.

She reaches out, her hand finding mine, a touch that speaks volumes. In her grasp, I find a lifeline, a connection that pulls me back from the edge of darkness.

As I lie here, processing the aftermath, a profound weariness washes over me. It's not just physical, it's soul-deep exhaustion—the kind that comes from having faced death and somehow, miraculously, having survived.

Stitch's grip tightens, her presence a silent vow of solidarity.

As I drift in and out of consciousness, tended by Booker and the others, I hold onto this feeling, this certainty. We survived Haven, but more than that, we saved each other. In the end, that's what matters. That's what will always matter.

The journey from the rubble of Haven back to HQ blurs in my mind, each moment slipping in and out of focus. Booker's at my side in the back of the truck, his voice a steady and calming influence. He administers a dose of morphine, and almost instantly, the sharp edges of reality start to soften.

Pain recedes to a dull ache, a distant thought compared to a storm of agony. The truck bounces over uneven terrain, each jolt a muted throb through my body. I float in this semi-conscious state, the world outside a hazy, indistinct dream.

Voices drift in and out, their words muffled as if underwater. I catch glimpses of the sky through half-closed eyelids, a shifting tapestry of clouds and light. Glimpses of Stitch's ethereal beauty gazing down at me.

My mind wanders, unmoored from the present. Images of Haven, of the rescue, flicker like shadows at the edge of my consciousness. They're there but not quite tangible, slipping away as I reach for them.

Time loses meaning. The journey feels eternal yet fleeting. I'm vaguely aware of the truck stopping, of being gently lifted and transferred. The sensation of flying through the air is surreal, like I'm a leaf caught in a gentle breeze.

Then there's the sensation of descending, the soft but firm support of a bed beneath me. The whir of machines fills the air, a mechanical lullaby that mingles with the distant voices of medical staff.

I drift on the edge of consciousness, the pain a distant echo and the world a soft, morphine-induced blur.

As the effects of the drug linger, reality and dreams meld. In this state, Haven feels like another lifetime, a nightmare I'm slowly awakening from.

But the pain in my leg, dulled as it is, serves as a grounding reminder of the truth.

The journey from Haven is over, but a new one, here in this hospital bed, is just beginning.

Something that will have a profound effect on my life.

I feel it.

I know it.

And I welcome it.

When I next wake, my mind is sharper and less influenced by heavy narcotics. Each throb in my heavily bandaged leg is a harsh echo of Haven. The room swims in a sea of sterile white; its brightness assaults my senses. I try to anchor myself to something tangible, but everything around me dissolves into a glaring haze.

The machines beside me beep steadily, their rhythm infiltrating the silence. It's an odd comfort, these mechanical heartbeats punctuating my thoughts. A slight shift sends a jolt of pain up my leg, contrasting starkly against the bed's softness.

The damp, earthy scent of the tunnels lingers in my memory, the grit of dust almost tangible in my nostrils. It's so vivid that I can almost taste the stale, metallic air.

Now, the sharp, clinical smell of antiseptic fills my lungs. Alone with my thoughts, they churn in my mind—a stormy sea of 'what ifs' and 'whys.'

Images of Stitch flash before me, her face in the aftermath of our escape etched with worry and exhaustion. In these moments, the smallest details imprint themselves in my mind—the way her hair clings to her face, the tremble of her hands.

I close my eyes, seeking respite in the darkness, but peace eludes me. Sleep seems a distant dream, as elusive now as it has been since our escape.

The steady beeping of the machines and the occasional flare of pain in my leg are constant reminders that our journey out of the dark is far from over.

The door creaks open, and Stitch steps into the room, her warm presence contrasting against the sterile hospital surroundings. She moves quietly, but her energy fills the space, instantly easing the tension in my chest.

Our eyes meet, and there's an entire conversation in that glance —relief, worry, a shared understanding of what we've been through.

"You're awake," Stitch whispers gently as she approaches my bed.

Her presence alone seems to ease the sterile coldness of the room. With a grace that belies the weight of recent events, she settles into the chair beside me, her fingers intertwining with mine.

Lifting my hand to her lips, she places a tender kiss on my knuckles, an act so simple yet so charged with emotion. It's a gesture that speaks volumes, transcending the need for words, conveying care, reassurance, and a deep feeling that resonates throughout my entire being.

In that soft, fleeting contact, I find comfort and a connection I hadn't realized I was craving.

"C'mere," I say, my voice warmer than I expect and slightly slurred from pain meds. I reach for her and wince when I try to sit a little straighter.

"Don't strain yourself trying to move." She walks over, a cautious smile on her face.

There's a hesitation in her step, a lingering shadow of what we've been through. When she leans in to wrap her arms around me, I breathe in her familiar scent and feel myself relaxing.

The connection feels grounding and real. She perches on the edge of the bed, and her fingers wrap tightly around mine.

"How are you feeling?" Her eyes roam my face. "I was so scared I'd lost you."

"How are *you* holding up?" I turn her question around and give her hand a gentle squeeze.

Her presence, so familiar yet so different now, fills the room with light.

"I'm okay. How are *you* feeling?" She lets out a small sigh, her thumb absently stroking the back of my hand.

"Feels like I've been run over by a truck. My leg is throbbing, but Doc Summers says I'll live." I give a half-hearted chuckle. "But seeing you helps."

"I thought we'd die under the rubble. The whole way out, all I could think of was, 'What if he doesn't make it?' I've been worried sick about you." She smiles, but there's a depth of emotion behind it that's a harsh punch in the gut.

"It'll take more than a building collapse to get rid of me." I brush my thumb across her knuckles, hoping to remove her lingering fear. "But we did make it. We made it out together, and that's all that matters. You saved me."

A weak smile flickers on her face at the praise. "I've never been so scared in my life. Watching you run into the gunfire, seeing you go down…" Her voice cracks, and she swallows hard. "Not knowing if we'd escape… It was my worst nightmare come to life."

"Hey, it's okay. We're both still here." I shift closer, pulling her into a fierce, one-armed embrace.

"I don't know how you do this every day." She clings to me for a long moment before sitting up, swiping at her eyes. "Put yourself at risk, face down dangers like that. I felt so helpless, so afraid of losing you."

I consider my words carefully. "I won't lie. It can be a dangerous job. But saving lives and protecting people make the risk worthwhile. Haven, though… That was more than a mission for me."

"More? What does that mean?"

"I'm sorry you got dragged into it like that. You should never have been on the front lines. I don't remember much after the explosions."

"I never want to do that again." Her eyes are glossy when they meet mine. "When the rubble buried us, the space was so small. I didn't know if we'd run out of air first or just be crushed."

I swear under my breath. The reality of how close I'd come to losing her hits me square in the gut. I give her hand a reassuring squeeze.

"It killed me putting you in harm's way." I tuck a strand of hair behind her ear, fingertips lingering on her cheek. "You were incredible in there. Strong, brave, resourceful. We both know I wouldn't have made it out without you. Not to mention getting all those women out? The whole mission would've been a bust without you."

She gives a small, unconvinced shrug, as if her actions had

nothing to do with saving so many lives. Stitch doesn't get it yet, but she's a hero.

"I'm sorry you had to go through that alone."

"I just did what anyone would do to protect…" she falters, glancing down.

"To protect, what?" I prod gently.

A blush creeps across her cheeks. "To protect the man I love," she finishes softly. "I feel like I can finally say that now, but I never want to be in that position again. I'm not built for that kind of fight."

My breath catches. We've danced around the words for so long but hearing them ignites something warm and hopeful inside me.

I tilt her chin up until our eyes lock again. "I love you, too. Almost losing you made me see that as clearly as ever. I'm never leaving your side again."

Her responding smile seems to light up the room.

"Tell me about what happened." I hate dredging up bad memories, but I know trauma, and Stitch needs to get this off her chest. She needs to talk about what happened.

"We were trapped for days." Stitch takes a shaky breath before continuing softly. "I tried digging us out but barely made a dent. All I could do was bind your leg and keep you warm."

I squeeze her hand, wishing I could erase the lingering pain in her eyes.

"I don't remember any of it. I'm sorry I wasn't there for you. It's all a blur of noise and pain."

"You were the only reason I didn't go crazy." She looks down, fiddling with the edge of the blanket. "I was terrified, you know. After the gunfire, the collapse… Thought we wouldn't make it. Thought I'd lose you."

"How did we get out?" I knock the side of my head.

"It was the Rufi who saved us." She shrugs as if none of it bothered her. "Well, first, one of the bumblebee drones searched the wreckage and found us. The Rufi then tunneled through and found a safe path out. One of them dragged your unconscious body behind it."

"Remind me to give those bots a gold star when I'm out of here," I say. "They're real heroes."

"They sacrificed themselves shoring up the rubble so it wouldn't collapse while we escaped. I couldn't save them…" Her voice cracks.

"You saved me. That's all that matters." I tug gently until she perches on the edge of the bed, then I fold her into my arms.

We stay locked in our embrace for a long moment, drawing comfort from each other's presence. When she finally pulls back, tears are shining in her eyes, but a soft smile curves her lips.

"I'm officially going to say it."

"Say what?"

"This hacker isn't cut out for field work," Stitch says with a shaky little laugh. "Computers don't shoot you or try to kill you. Think I'll stick to those from now on."

"I agree. Still, you were amazing down there," I tell her sincerely. "You kept it together; you helped me when I was hurt." I brush a stray curl off her cheek, profoundly grateful to be here with her.

"I surprised myself, but I had a pretty good reason to keep fighting." She rewards me with a small, brave smile.

Our eyes meet in understanding. We're both thinking of the future.

"I'm not kidding about never leaving your side."

"Jeb, I…" Her gaze holds mine, unwavering.

"I know we've got a lot to figure out," I say quickly, not wanting her to feel pressured. "But I want you to know I'm here for whatever comes next. For us."

"I think I can live with that." Her eyes soften, and she gives my hand another squeeze. A smile spreads across her face.

The conversation shifts then, to lighter things, but an undercurrent of something deeper, something real, remains.

We've been through hell together, and now, on the other side, there's a bond neither of us can deny—a bond forged in adversity and strengthened by survival.

THIRTY-SEVEN

Jeb

———

THE DAYS SINCE MY ESCAPE FROM HAVEN BLUR INTO A HAZE OF PAIN meds, doctors, and restless sleep. I drift in and out of consciousness, the steady beeps and whirs of the machines my constant companions.

In the rare moments of clarity between doses of narcotics and painful procedures to save my crushed leg, my thoughts inevitably turn to Stitch—her resilience, her bravery, and the profound bond forged between us in the fires of Haven.

I cling to our last conversation like a lifeline, replaying her words in my mind:

"However long the recovery, I'll be right by your side."

Just knowing she intends to stand by me is enough to carry me through the worst of my recovery and the darkness smothering my spirit when it becomes clear things for me are forever changed.

This morning, wakefulness comes abruptly as Doc Summers sweeps into the room, all business despite the early hour. The click of her heels and swish of her lab coat cut through the fog of pain pills clouding my mind.

"Let's take a look at your leg, shall we?" Pulling up a chair, she gently examines my splinted leg.

I try not to wince as even the lightest touch sends spikes of pain radiating outward.

"I know it's unpleasant but try to stay still." With a sympathetic glance, she pats my shoulder.

"How bad is it?" Through gritted teeth, I force out the question that's plagued my fitful, medicated dreams all week.

Her lips press into a thin line as she consults my chart and scans what must be a gruesome image on her tablet. When she meets my searching gaze again, I detect a flicker of sadness behind her usual no-nonsense demeanor.

"The damage was extensive, I'm afraid. The crush injury resulted in multiple fractures along the femur, tibia, and fibula. Severe muscle and nerve trauma as well." She indicates the network of splints and bandages swathing my leg from hip to ankle. "We've done initial surgery to stabilize and align everything, but you have a difficult road ahead of you."

My chest tightens, bracing for the worst. In my line of work, grave injuries end careers. The thought of losing my purpose as a Guardian—my entire identity wrapped up in the role I've dedicated my life to—leaves me reeling.

As if reading the anguish across my face, Doc lays a steadying hand on my forearm. Her voice softens by a fraction.

"The good news is, with extensive physical therapy, I expect you'll walk again—aided at first by crutches or a cane. You're looking at a life-long disability—stiffness, chronic pain, reduced mobility. Fieldwork or other high-stress activities… I'm sorry, but it's out of the question now."

Her final words land like hammer blows, crushing any fledgling hopes.

Not that it comes as a surprise, but I hadn't yet given up hope about being forced out of the Guardians.

I let Doc's prognosis fully sink in as I stare fixedly at a nondescript patch of tile just past her shoulder. The repetitive beeps counting my heartbeats fill the heavy silence.

"I'm so sorry." After giving me a long moment to process, she squeezes my arm in muted sympathy. "I know what being a

Guardian means to you. Losing that… Well, it's a profound loss." Her eyes glisten slightly before she quickly blinks, features schooled once more. "But it could have been far worse. Focus on your recovery—we'll discuss next steps soon."

With a bracing pat on my shoulder and a promise to return later, Doc Summers takes her leave. The chilling finality hits me square in the chest as the door clicks decisively shut behind her.

Bitter tears prick behind my eyelids, but I stubbornly blink them back. Surviving Haven to endure this crushing loss of purpose is a wicked twist of fate. Perhaps it would have been a mercy to die back in those sunless tunnels. Never before have I felt so hollowed out and adrift.

I'm moments from spiraling deep into despair when the door suddenly swings open. This time, Ethan and CJ stride in.

"Doc Summers brought us up to speed." Ethan pulls a chair to my bedside while CJ drags one in from the hall.

"How are you holding up?" CJ fixes me with his penetrating gaze.

I rake a hand through my hair, emotions choked in my throat. Instead of speaking, I laugh. It sounds more like a harsh bark.

"Honestly? Reeling. Being a Guardian is my whole goddamn life."

He and Ethan share a somber look filled with silent communication. Eventually, CJ nods, almost to himself.

"It's a hell of a loss, no question. The job becomes part of you, but the important thing is you survived. You beat unthinkable odds, and you're still here." He clasps my shoulder firmly. "That means something. This isn't the end. There are alternatives we can explore."

"What does that mean for me? If I can't do field work…?" I eye him warily, afraid to rekindle fragile wisps of hope only to have them crushed again.

CJ leans forward with his forearms braced on strong thighs. "It means we reassess and we adapt. There are always alternatives. New battles to fight."

Despite myself, I feel a reluctant curiosity stirring out of the ashes.

"Yeah, well, I'd love to hear them. Because from where I'm sitting, it feels pretty damn final."

"Your skills would be invaluable in tactical support and training. With your field experience, you'd make one hell of an instructor and mission controller." CJ scrubs a palm across his jaw, considering his next words.

When he meets my challenging stare head-on, I read only sincerity and conviction blazing behind the intensity.

"It might be time to make use of that MIT degree. Mitzy's interested. Field duty might be off the table, but your skills and tech experience are invaluable. We need a strong liaison with the Techies, someone who understands both sides of the job."

I raise a brow, skepticism etching hard lines beside my mouth, but I remain silent, allowing him to continue uninterrupted. I turn his ideas around, truly considering them. My pulse quickens at the thought of still serving alongside my Guardian brothers in some capacity.

Ethan nods emphatically. "For the most part, the Techies coming up these days need someone like you. Men who have lived it and know what does and doesn't work in the field."

"We've got more R&D and tactical gear improvements than we can handle with Mitzy's team. With your field experience, and given that you speak their language, we can develop new tech to safeguard our operators in the field. No one knows which tools function best on missions than veteran agents."

I mull this over as an undercurrent of interest begins to replace my bone-deep weariness. I can envision throwing myself into teaching the next generation, helping hone their skills so they're prepared. It's not the same thrill, but I'll still be serving alongside my Guardian brothers in some capacity.

It's better than the alternative.

"You'll find where you fit; I have no doubt," CJ delivers this last assurance with set-in-stone certainty. Between his confidence in me and the realm of possibilities laid out, I feel something long dormant unfurling within—a sense of hope.

By the time they leave, I feel lighter than I have since first waking in the hospital. My body may be broken, but my spirit remains intact.

Stitch was right—together, we'll figure out whatever comes next.

There's only one person left I need to break the difficult news to —my son. Maverick's endured more loss than any child should. I can scarcely fathom how he'll receive word of my career-ending injury and disability. Or how he'll react to Stitch entering our lives permanently.

But I have hope.

THIRTY-EIGHT

Jeb

———

THE STEADY BEEPING AND WHIRRING OF MACHINES DOMINATE THE sterile hospital room as I drift in and out of a fog of pain meds and tortured dreams.

The rescue from Haven flashes back in an endless loop behind my closed eyelids—explosions rocking the underground bunker, gunfire strafing the walls around us as we ran, the heart-stopping rumble of tons of concrete caving in.

I threw myself over Stitch before agony exploded and I was pinned by rubble. Then darkness took me, unconsciousness my only escape from the pain.

When I finally woke days later, it was to discover I was swathed in hospital bandages.

Choking guilt hit like a tidal wave—Stitch endured the long hours alone in the rubble, not knowing if we'd make it out.

They said it was days.

Days!

Days where I wasn't able to be there for her when it mattered the most.

Days where she suffered alone.

Days where she took care of me.

Yet she never stopped fighting, single-handedly pulling me to a place of safety within the rubble despite her own exhaustion. My fierce Stitch tended my leg, staved off her despair, and believed, without fail, we'd be found.

While my greatest regret is failing to protect this resilient, relentless woman, the greater truth is we survived because of her unrelenting spirit.

A sudden commotion in the hall snags my attention. Before I can react, the door bursts open, revealing my mother.

"Jebediah, sweetheart." My mom rushes to my bedside, looking ready to combust from pent-up worry.

She mutters a quick prayer of thanks before grabbing my chin and turning my head to the left and right, peering intently into my eyes.

"Mom, I'm okay," I rasp, the words scrape my dry throat.

I make a lame attempt to sit straighter, wincing as pain ricochets through my splinted leg.

"Don't try to move." Tears shine in her eyes as she fusses over my pillows. "And no, you certainly are not all right, young man. Look at you." Her voice catches on a choked sob.

Before I can respond, Dad strides in. His face splits into a grin, the weathered skin around his eyes crinkling.

"Hey, kiddo. Gave us one hell of a scare, I'll say that much." His strong hands engulf mine in a brief but firm clasp before he draws Mom gently aside to give me space. God bless his stoic marine demeanor.

Just then, a small figure darts out from behind Dad's sturdy frame. My breath catches at the sight of my son hovering with uncertainty playing across his young features. He looks so much like his late mother.

"Maverick," I rasp, emotion clogging my throat. I hold out a hand, needing his closeness to ground me and needing him to understand that I'm still me, still his dad, despite the extensive injuries. That our family remains strong.

Maverick approaches slowly, his brow furrowing as he catalogs the wires, tubes, and endless bandages swaddling my leg. My mom makes a strangled sound of sympathy, but Dad squeezes her shoulder in support.

"Give 'em a few minutes alone, Joanie." My dad murmurs in Mom's ear.

As she dabs at her eyes, my dad tugs my distraught mother, gently but insistently, pulling her toward the door.

After a quick kiss on my forehead, my mom reluctantly retreats to the hall. They pull the door half-closed behind them.

My full attention settles on my son, who lingers anxiously beside the bed. I pat the mattress in invitation and coax gently, fighting to keep my voice light.

"C'mere, buddy. Sit with your dad so we can chat. Just me and you."

After a weighted pause, Maverick climbs up and settles tentatively on the very edge of the bed facing me. His young gaze roams over the maze of bandages, hesitant to meet my eyes for more than a second at a time.

He looks far older than his five years—my fierce, brave boy.

I reach out to cup his chin, tilting his face until his eyes meet mine. My heart shatters. Lord help me, where do I even begin? Swallowing the lump in my throat, I manage a half-hearted grin.

"I know this looks pretty scary." I nod at my wrapped leg. "Do you have any questions?"

"Does it hurt?" Mav's voice comes out barely a whisper.

"Quite a lot, actually," I respond gently but honestly.

Children deserve truth in safe measure.

"Broke some bones, but I've got great doctors who will patch me up good as new, don't you worry."

Maverick processes this, eyes welling with tears. With a muted whimper, he asks, "Can you still fight bad guys?" His lower lip trembles slightly.

I steel myself, cursing inwardly. No way to shield him from harsh reality, but perhaps I can repurpose it as a teaching opportunity.

"The truth is, buddy, this busted leg means I won't be quite as fast chasing down baddies anymore." I affect a casual, good-natured tone and wink conspiratorially. "But between you and me, those villains better watch themselves 'cause your dad's got plenty of fight left in him."

My dramatic proclamation startles a watery chuckle from Maverick as I squeeze his knee affectionately. After a thoughtful pause, chewing his bottom lip, Maverick ventures, "Maybe you can make spy gadgets instead?"

I bark out a surprised laugh. My son knows me too well. I pull him gently into my arms, relishing his solid warmth. Realizing how close he came to losing me.

An orphan at the age of five.

I grit my teeth and realize my busted leg is more of a blessing than a curse. It's forcing me to focus on what matters, and nothing matters more to me than my son—for being there to raise him.

It's something my mom tried to tell me. Something I blissfully ignored, too caught up in being a *Hero*.

Now, it suddenly makes all the sense in the world. It's no longer about me. It's about being there for my son.

"You know what, champ?" I muss his hair. "That's not a half-bad idea."

And it isn't.

Over the next half hour, I field Maverick's wide-eyed questions about everything from X-rays to physical therapy. I confess my uncertainties about the future. When I assure him nothing will keep me from being his daddy—no bad guy or busted leg is that strong—his enthusiasm returns.

My heart feels lighter than it's been in ages.

As he rambles on, making plans for new backyard projects now that his "spy dad" will be home more often, fate gifts me clarity.

This may not be the path I chose, but it's the right one for me to be on. It took Haven trying to kill me to finally see the truth.

But I see it now.

I know what's important.

Our conversation shifts.

It's time that I raise the hardest topic of all.

"Hey, Mav," I gently interrupt his animated scheming. "There's something important I should tell you." I hesitantly meet his gaze. "You remember meeting my friend Stitch at the tidepools?"

"She's really nice." Maverick's eyes brighten. "I like her."

"I do, too." I allow a small smile. "She and I have gotten very close."

"How close?"

"Really close."

"Like *kissing* close?" He lowers his voice to whisper "kissing" as if it's a bad thing.

A smile fills me with joy because there will come a day when Maverick no longer thinks kissing girls is such a yucky thing.

"You could say that."

"Ewww…." His exaggerated expression of distaste almost makes me chuckle.

"Would it be okay if she and I spent more time together?" I venture slowly. "And if maybe she joined you and me sometimes doing fun things?"

My son mulls this over, brow furrowed in consideration. "Would she live at our house?" There's a quaver in his voice that gives me pause.

"Not right away," I assure him. "This would be a big change for all of us. But, Mav, you're my number one guy no matter what." I squeeze his shoulder, willing him to grasp the depths of my devotion.

"Are you gonna get married?"

"I won't lie. I'm thinking about popping the question, but I gotta know how you feel about it first."

"Can I carry the rings?"

"If you want, or you could be my best man."

"Best man?" His eyes round in surprise.

"But only if that's something you want." I chuckle at his excitement over his aspired role, but then I turn serious, taking his small hand in mine. "I would never marry Stitch if it didn't feel right for both of us."

"That makes sense." My precocious boy nods sagely. "I gotta approve any big stuff."

"You sure do. In fact…" An idea occurs to me. "Why don't you come up with some ideas for things we can do with Stitch?"

"Yes!" Maverick punches the air in triumphant excitement. But then he pauses, tilting his head thoughtfully once more. "If you marry Stitch, would that make her my mom?"

"It could." I squeeze his hand gently, infinitely grateful for this chance to pave a new path together. "If that's something you want. What do you think about that?"

Maverick considers, then offers me a brave smile that looks so much like my own. "Yeah. I think I'd like a mom."

We discuss more details, and I listen more than steer the conversation. I won't rush this.

I love Stitch, but Maverick will always come first. After several minutes of Maverick talking about things he wants to do with Stitch, he finally straightens with an air of resolution.

"I think it would be okay for Stitch to be part of things." Maverick chews his lip, looking down as he asks hesitantly, "Do you think Mom will be upset if I call Stitch 'mom' too?"

"No way, buddy." My heart clenches. I tilt his chin up gently. "Your mom loves you so much, more than anything in the world. She wants you to be happy and loved."

"But won't she feel left out if I have a new mom?" Maverick's eyes are wide and conflicted.

"You have room in your heart to love more than one person." I brush a thumb over his cheek. "Loving Stitch doesn't mean you love your real mom in heaven any less. Not even a little bit."

"Can I still keep a picture of Mom next to my bed? Will that hurt Stitch's feelings?"

"We'll always have pictures of your mom around, and I'll tell you stories about her whenever you want. It's important to remember those we've lost."

"Okay." He nods to himself. "Do you think Mom sent Stitch to help take care of me? Since she can't be here?"

"Maybe she did, bud." Tears prick my eyes. My compassionate boy never ceases to amaze me. "Your mom will always watch over you, but I think she'll be happy you have Stitch watching over you, too."

"Yeah." Maverick smiles tentatively. "Especially because Stitch makes you laugh even when you're being grumpy. Maybe she sent Stitch for both of us?"

His comment is like a kick in the gut. Children can, sometimes, be wiser than angels.

I bark out a surprised laugh and pull him in for a fierce hug, thanking heaven again for this resilient child who gives me hope and purpose when I need it most.

"Maybe she did, bud." I kiss his cheek and scruff up his hair. "Maybe she did."

THIRTY-NINE

Stitch

I PAUSE OUTSIDE JEB'S HOSPITAL ROOM, TAKING A STEADYING BREATH. He's being discharged today; our lives are forever changed by Haven's collapse and the injuries that ended his field career.

As anxious as that uncertainty makes me, it pales next to my relief at his survival.

My heart lifts, picturing those sky-blue eyes and that crooked smile.

Jeb greets me with that same grin as I enter. He eases slowly from the bed, cautious of putting weight on his healing leg. The brace is a solemn reminder of how close he came to being lost forever. But his vigor and grit shine through.

"Ready to blow this popsicle stand?" he asks with a roguish wink.

"With you? Anywhere." Cliche, maybe, but it's the simple truth after all we endured. Where Jeb goes, I follow—through hell or high water.

Goodbyes with the medical team are emotional. Especially when Dr. Summers presses discharge paperwork into Jeb's hands.

Over the next month, we settle into our new normal together. Jeb diligently tackles physical therapy while meeting with Guardian leadership about potential options for keeping him involved in their work.

I work with Mitzy and the team, tracking down another ghost in the machine. After the rescue and Rebel's revelation, we've been chasing down a new organization known only as Sentinel.

It's connected to Haven.

Specifically, Sentinel is connected to Haven through Rebel's sister, who was abducted, sold, enslaved, and forced to conceive a child for patrons wealthy enough to ignore simple things like morals and ethics.

I spend my days and nights searching, but unlike Haven, my attempts bear no fruit. I don't like that.

I like to win.

When Jeb comes home, drained and frustrated by the slow progress of mending his battered body, I sign out of work stuff on my computer and make it my mission to lift his spirits.

I create elaborate picnic dinners that we eat on the porch, where the ocean breeze carries a restorative calm. At night, we snuggle on the couch, Jeb sketching gadget prototypes with that familiar spark returning to his eyes while I continue my search for Sentinel.

We laugh—loud, often, and heartfelt. The sound of shared joy echoes through rooms too long muted by his grueling recovery.

We go on dates together and dates with Maverick. Jeb's son is precocious, a whirlwind of energy, and beautifully perfect.

My feelings for the little guy grow with each passing day.

Tonight, I have something better planned. Something Jeb desperately needs. When he comes home, I shut down work stuff and greet him with a kiss.

"Nervous about tomorrow?" I ask.

"Not really." Jeb smiles softly, taking my hand. "Looking forward to it."

"How about we go out and celebrate?"

"Out?" He smirks at me. "I was thinking we stay in…"

He gingerly lowers himself onto the couch with a grunt. He tries to hide his winces and favors his wounded leg after long days back on his feet.

"We can spend all night in bed, but let's feed you first."

Jeb chuckles, a welcome sound I'll never tire of. "I've done about as much celebrating this week as an old gimp can handle, but I won't say no to dinner if it means I don't have to cook."

We end up at his favorite bar. Jeb orders his beloved meat-laden monstrosity of a pizza while I get a veggie with extra olives. When two ice-cold IPAs hit the scarred table, Jeb gestures grandly like a lord offering a great prize.

I make a dramatic gagging sound. "Ugh, I'll stick with soda, thanks."

Our little inside joke stems from my dislike of beer, back when he first brought me here after I completed the mandatory self-defense training all new Guardian HRS hires must endure.

He's teased every time we go out since then.

We dig into cheesy slices recounting work highlights and laugh over new gossip about mutually known Guardians and Techies. It feels cozily familiar, like nothing and everything has changed all at once in the wake of Haven's disaster.

I dunk my crust in pizza sauce when loud voices and thundering footsteps make me look over my shoulder. Instantly, I break into a face-splitting grin.

"Incoming at six o'clock," I say. "Brace yourself."

Like an affectionate hurricane, Charlie team barrels through the entrance, cheering loudly and making a beeline for our table. Before we know it, Ethan, Hank, Walt, Blake, and Gabe crowd around us, slapping Jeb's back gently yet jovially in boisterous half hugs.

They summon extra chairs and flag down the harried waitress for more beer.

"Well damn, Jeb. Tomorrow, you cross the line and join the Techies. Not sure if we can hang with you if you go to the dark side." Hank drops into the seat on Jeb's right.

"Hey, there's nothing wrong with the dark side." I make my protest loud, and they all laugh.

"It's gonna be weird seeing you outta tac gear, brother." Walt slaps Jeb on the back.

Another round of pizza and pitchers make their way to the table courtesy of Walt's insistent flagging down of our harried waitress. The stories and reminiscing kick into high gear.

"Oh man, remember that time…" Blake begins, wiping tears of mirth from his eyes. "That time when Jeb MacGyvered an explosive device using nothing but soy sauce packets, pocket lint, and one of those little plastic swords from his hotel cocktail umbrella?"

Raucous laughter rings out as the men delve into the infamous tale.

I can't restrain my laughter as they fill me in. Leave it to my genius Guardian to find resourceful ways to blow things up, even when separated from his gear.

Hank slaps both palms on the table, rattling empty bottles and plates. "Well, hell, if that ain't Jeb in a nutshell! Give this boy some bubble gum and paper clips, and he'll find a way to neutralize the enemy." He elbows Jeb roughly. "We're gonna miss having your mad technical skills at our six out there, brother."

"I'd trust Jeb to dismantle a warhead blindfolded before I'd let some of those lab coat pansies touch it. No offense, Stitch." Walt nods sheepishly in my direction.

"Technically, as of tomorrow, Jeb is officially one of those lab coat pansies." I wave aside the perceived slight with an easy chuckle.

"It's true, though," Ethan agrees, suddenly serious across the table cluttered with empty bottles and shredded napkins. He locks eyes with Jeb, his expression somber. "You're Guardian to the bone, brother. Losing you cuts deep, but knowing you're still part of the team makes it an easier pill to swallow."

A chorus of grave "hear hears" sounds around the table.

"Appreciate it, guys." Jeb scrubs a palm across his mouth, his Guardian stoicism cracking. "Honestly, some days it doesn't feel real, but I'll still be backing up all your sorry asses. Just promise you Neanderthals will go easy on my gimp ass."

Ethan clears his throat and raises his glass. "I hereby dub thee Guardian alumni and brother in arms evermore. May we inflict only mild hazing on your traitorous ass when we cross paths, whether at that fancy R&D megacomplex or the juice bar across from your Pilates class."

Jeb flips him off with both hands as laughter rings out, but his grin shines brighter than I've seen in recent weeks. My cheeks ache from nonstop smiling.

This is exactly what he needs, and his teammates are absolutely perfect.

Laughter fills the rest of the night; friendly ribbing and genuine warmth overflow between this band of brothers.

The depth of sacrifice they're willing to make for each other is an invisible yet palpable force that blazes like the sun.

It hurts to see Jeb's smile tinged with melancholy while trading mission stories over pizza and beer. He's going to miss this.

As if sensing the wistful shift in mood, Ethan raises his glass. "But seriously, a toast to Jeb. Couldn't ask for a better Guardian or friend. We're damn proud you're still fighting the good fight where your strengths are needed now. To Jeb!"

Jeb scrubs a hand over his suddenly damp eyes. When he glances my way with a bittersweet smile, I offer a subtle wink and mouth, *"I love you,"* before taking a sip of soda.

Laughter rings long into the night, its echoes mingling with the subtle roar of the Northern California coastline just beyond.

By the time "One more round!" becomes too slurred for coherency, the bar's cozy warmth contrasts sharply with the cool, misty air outside. I contemplate how I'm going to haul six elite soldiers home myself, but Ethan, ever the responsible one, calls for a driver.

As the team trickles out the door, the night greets us with a gentle rain, unique to the coastline. It falls softly, a fine mist that seems to weave the ocean's briny scent into the air.

With crushing hugs for us both, Ethan pauses for a final private word with Jeb. His voice, rough with sincerity, competes with the distant call of the sea.

"You ever need anything—miss the action and crap, feel like a caged animal with those lab nerds—you call me. We'll go a few rounds at the gym, shoot at the range, whatever it takes."

Jeb, illuminated by the soft glow of the bar's neon sign, smiles slowly. "You know I'll take you up on that."

The ensuing bro-hug is a testament to their bond, solid and unyielding even in the face of change. Jeb then turns to me, his eyes simmering with love under the hazy glow of the streetlights.

"You did this." His voice is a warm rumble against the ocean's roar.

"Felt like you needed it." My words float away with the sea-scented breeze.

"I need you more." His kiss, tender and promising, is a stark contrast to the cool moisture in the air. "Now wait here; I'll grab the truck."

"No need. I don't mind the rain."

"No woman of mine is walking in the rain. Not if I have a say. I'll be just a minute."

As he heads to his truck, each step a battle against his healing leg, I patiently wait, unwilling to destroy his gallant effort. The soft glow of the streetlight casts a halo through the rain around him, and the cool droplets caress my face, mingling with the warmth of the evening's emotions.

I pull my coat tight around me when my phone vibrates. I pull it out, thinking it's Mitzy, but an encrypted number flashes before me with a message that chills me to my core:

"Steer clear of Sentinel. From one old friend to another. Or I may not be able to protect you—M"

Malfor.

His words, disguised as concern, strike a discordant note, slicing through the peaceful rain with a sinister edge.

My heart races and the rain suddenly feels colder and more ominous.

As Jeb pulls up, the truck's headlights cut through the rain. I slip the phone back into my pocket, my mind racing. The door swings open, and I slide in, the warmth of the truck a stark contrast to the chill in my bones.

"You look like you've seen a ghost." Jeb glances over, his brow creasing with concern.

I force a smile, pushing Malfor's warning to the back of my mind. "Just the rain, it's... nothing." My voice betrays a tremor I can't quite hide.

He reaches over, his hand warm and reassuring on mine. "If there's something wrong, you know you can tell me, right?"

"I know. It's just been a long night."

As we drive off into the rain, the wipers rhythmically swiping away the relentless droplets, I can't shake the feeling of unease. Malfor's warning about Sentinel lingers like a dark cloud, and I know, deep down, that this is just the beginning.

Why reach out to me now?

What is Malfor up to?

When Mitzy hired me—aka… saved me from a life in prison—I thought I left my past behind. I hesitate to tell Jeb, but when I look at him, his eyes are filled with genuine concern and trust.

The weight of my past presses down on me. Looking into Jeb's eyes, I make a decision. It's time to let someone in, to share the burden of a past I've been carrying alone.

"There's something I need to tell you," I start, my voice barely above the patter of the rain.

"What is it?" He turns to me, his expression softening.

"It's about Malfor." I feel the weight of my words.

"Who's Malfor?" His expression shifts to an attentive serious-ness, and I take a deep breath.

I take a deep breath, finding the courage to delve into memories I've long kept hidden.

"Malfor was part of an online group I belonged to. I told you about my friends." I told Jeb how their friendship saved me as a kid trapped in foster care. "He was our leader. Super smart. Reckless. Always bucking authority. He's the one who dared me to hack into the NSA."

Not knowing how much I told him before, I tell Jeb about the dare that led to the NSA hack and how Malfor's challenge was something I couldn't refuse.

"Why bring him up now?"

"I told you how I never felt like I belonged. The only friends that stayed with me were the ones I found online. That group—with Malfor—it was different. They were my family. When he issued that dare, I couldn't say no. It wasn't just about the thrill; it was about belonging, about not being the outsider for once."

"I can't imagine what that was like." He reaches over, his hand enveloping mine with warmth and reassurance.

As I speak, my words are more than just a confession; they're an unburdening of a secret I've held too closely for too long. I leave out nothing, not even the part about how Malfor wanted useless junk from the NSA.

"It was never about the information; it was about the challenge, about proving myself in a world where I thought I had to be the best."

"Why bring this up now?"

"Because he messaged me."

"When?"

"When you were getting your truck. It's been months, Jeb. Months where I haven't been in contact with anyone from that life, yet Malfor texts me out of the blue as if he's been watching the entire time. I'm scared."

"What do you want to do about his message?"

"I don't know." I press my hands together, rubbing them for warmth. Not that I'm cold. It's a nervous thing. "Obviously, I need to tell Mitzy, but Malfor knows that. He knows everything."

"What are you thinking? Is it a setup? Do you think he's involved with Sentinel?"

"I don't know, but he never does anything without a reason. Malfor is beyond brilliant, always thinking ten steps ahead. It could be as much a trap as it is a warning."

"We'll figure out something."

Relief washes over me, mingling with the rain outside. I nod, feeling a weight lift from my shoulders. With Jeb by my side, maybe, just maybe, I can confront the ghosts of my past and face the looming threat of Sentinel.

Malfor would never reach out unless there was a reason, but I don't trust him. For all I know, he's the leader of Sentinel. This might be my one warning to steer clear. Or maybe he knows about Sentinel and wants to bring it down?

The thing is, I don't trust Malfor, but I know better than to ignore a warning.

FORTY

Jeb

_____

TODAY, MY LIFE CHANGES IN SEVERAL SIGNIFICANT WAYS. STRAPPING on body armor and grabbing my weapon weeks ago was as natural as breathing. Now, my Kevlar and gear will gather dust as I trade bullets for microchips and motherboards.

Never thought I'd trade ops for a tech gig, but MIT gave me that backup skill set. If adapting means staying in the fight and protecting people while also being around to raise my son, then I'll take the limp and consider it a price worth paying.

"Nervous?" Stitch twines her fingers through mine as we stand outside the sleek glass and steel structure housing Guardian HRS's technical complex.

I glance over at her, taking in the compassion and belief shining from her eyes. No judgment, only quiet confidence that I've got this.

And damn if her faith doesn't sweep away the jittery tension knotting my shoulders.

"I know what I'm capable of. I busted my ass at MIT learning everything from basic soldering to advanced AI neural nets. No one knows resilience like someone who's rappelled out of a Blackhawk with forty pounds of gear into hot zones."

"Exactly." Stitch smiles, pride and love radiating from her face. "You've got skills most Techies would kill for."

"Let's show your nerd friends what I can do." I grin down at her with my heart swelling and fit to burst.

I can do anything with Stitch by my side.

With this brilliant, compassionate woman, I will kick ass in the cybersphere and take on the world.

"Just remember, you're one of the nerds now, too." Humor dances in Stitch's eyes as she tugs me toward the entrance. "Try not to break anything on day one."

I make my way into Guardian HRS's sprawling technical complex, gimp leg announcing my arrival with each thudding step on the polished floors. The roboticists and engineers barely glance up, elbow-deep in android guts and soldering motherboards.

There's no reception committee or hazing for the new lab grunt. I'm not sure if I'm relieved at their indifference or mourn the loss of the gritty camaraderie that awaited me in the Guardian Bullpen.

It's different. I can say that much.

I instantly spot Mitzy waiting for me in the lobby, her psychedelic pixie-cut hair sparkling from overhead lights. A delighted grin spreads across her face.

"Well, slap me sparkly. You've finally come over to the dark side."

Mitzy makes her way toward me, arms outstretched. I bend to return her enthusiastic hug, years of mission camaraderie and mutual respect immediately apparent.

"I always knew you were one of us tech freaks at heart." Mitzy playfully smacks my arm. "C'mon, let me give you the tour of all my new explosive toys…"

She links her arm through mine, chattering a mile a minute about her latest ingenious and mildly alarming projects as she guides me further inside her lair of technological wonders.

We leave Stitch behind.

When I glance back, she gives a friendly wave, two thumbs up, and mouths *Good luck!*

I shake my head in amusement, realizing this side of Guardian

HRS might take some getting used to, but at least I'm among friends.

A few hours later, after a whirlwind tour inside her domain, Mitzy finishes my tour by slapping a heavy binder into my palms.

"Here's all our protocols, standards, safety regs—ABCs of not blowing yourself or our projects sky high." She winks, then grows serious. "Take today to study up and get your feet under you. It's a lot, I know, but we're eager to see what you can bring to the table."

She shows me to my private office and leaves me to acquaint myself with—everything.

What I bring to the table are years of busting my ass in special ops, but hell, if I'll give them a reason to dismiss me as a knuckle dragger on day one.

Different from being a Guardian, this job brings its own brand of stress.

Hours blur by studying complex system schematics until my vision swims. I almost don't notice when my phone vibrates loudly against the metal table. I check the screen and feel my entire body instantly relax.

STITCH: HOW GOES DAY 1 WITH THE NERD BRIGADE? MAVERICK says don't let them give you any crap! I'm proud of you— see you tonight xoxo

DESPITE THE THROBBING BEHIND MY EYES, I BARK OUT A SURPRISED laugh. Leave it to my fierce hacker to stand in my corner and cheer me on. With renewed motivation, I flip open the safety protocols and get to work.

Before long, I head home, anticipation growing with each mile that flies by. As I pull into the driveway, Maverick is already bursting out the front door. His blue sneakers with the hot rod flames barely touch the steps in his headlong rush toward my truck.

I've barely climbed from the cab before my exuberant kindergartner shouts, "C'mon, Dad. Stitch just texted she's on the beach already. We gotta hide the goods before she gets suspicious."

Laughing, I scoop him up and squeeze tight. "Bud, we've got time, I promise."

My parents come outside, pride and encouragement shining on both their faces.

"You've got this." My father claps a bracing hand on my shoulder. "Big night."

"We're so very happy for you." My mother smiles softly, brushing an errant hair off Maverick's forehead. "Now go make that wonderful girl officially part of our family."

Tonight is no ordinary evening stroll on the beach.

When I asked what Maverick thought about making Stitch an official part of our family, my little wingman brainstormed the perfect plan.

Which led to a flurry of texts to Stitch inviting her to meet us at the beach for a moonlit picnic and stargazing.

"You got the goods?" I help Maverick with his seatbelt and ensure we don't forget the most important part of tonight.

"Got it!" He thrusts out a clamshell and opens it to reveal a diamond solitaire inside.

I steer the truck down PCH-1 until we turn down the long drive of *Insanity*, the infamous group home of the band Angel Fire. Stitch has adored this group for years, with their haunting anthems and pyrotechnic live shows. She's more than a mega fan.

She's obsessed.

Maverick practically wiggles out of his booster seat with excitement as we pass the sprawling mansion. I remind him we're surprising Stitch with a private show later, at which his grin threatens to split his face in two.

"Hey, bud, need you to keep your cool a bit longer, okay?" I remind him. "We've got a surprise for Stitch later."

"You mean when Angel Fire plays just for her?!" His words come out in a rush, eyes shining.

"Yep, but it's a secret surprise. Think you can handle waiting a little bit longer?"

"Yeah!" His grin threatens to split his face in two. "It's gonna be epic!"

"Roger that, wingman," I chuckle as the road winds higher, cresting the cliffs where the landscape falls away to the Pacific, pounding the rocks below.

I maneuver to park near a weathered platform housing the glass gondola, the only access point down to the secluded beach below the estate.

The breathtaking vista of the coastline unfurls below us. This isolated outcrop is the reason the legendary band Angel Fire christened their compound *Insanity*.

There's nothing but gnarled terrain and unrelenting ocean as far as the eye can see once the gondola descends.

Maverick spills out of the truck, his childish delight at keeping secrets making me chuckle as I grab the carefully packed picnic hamper and blanket—time to make our way down to the tidepool-dotted beach where Stitch awaits a very special sunset.

As I unload our supplies, he triple checks the small parcel containing the decorative shell holding the diamond ring nestled inside.

"Think this will make Stitch's day, bud?"

"Duh, Dad!" Maverick scoffs. "She's gonna love it almost as much as when you guys let me get a puppy."

"A puppy? Who said anything about a puppy?"

"If we're going to be a family, we need a puppy."

Leave it to this scheming kindergartner to broker deals, ensuring his beloved future pets also have a place in our family.

No doubt we'll all be eating out of his adorable, diabolical palm for years to come.

Wouldn't have it any other way.

My pulse kicks up a notch.

Maverick bounces excitedly as we load the sleek glass gondola churning down the cliff overlooking the ocean. I squeeze his shoulder gently as we descend.

Our timing is perfect.

The Pacific explodes into view, showing off indigo waves

rimmed in pearly white caps. They charge the shore beneath a violet sunset sky.

Stitch is already down there, facing the ocean. A midnight-haired siren, the steady breeze lifts her hair like ribbons of silk floating on the wind.

I'd love to know what she's thinking as she gazes at the crashing waves.

The slate gray waves froth white as they smash against the rocky formations jutting defiantly from the deep blue waters. The tang of pulverized stone and sea spray grows sharper in the air the closer we get to the beach.

We dock seamlessly onto a pristine platform at the secluded beach. As I gather our supplies, Maverick tries to run out to Stitch. I barely grab the scruff of his shirt and pull him in for final instructions.

"I know you're pumped, but we gotta play it cool."

"But *Daaad*, I can't help it." He strains against the safety bar, peering out the glass enclosure.

I ruffle his hair. "Just a few more minutes, and you can hide the ring, but stay cool for me a little bit longer, deal?"

"*Fiiine*," he sighs dramatically.

Grinning, I wrap an arm around him, butterflies swirling in anticipation. The moment the doors slide open, biting wind dances across our faces, carrying the shrieking of gulls and the steady rhythm of the charging surf.

Maverick wriggles free of my grip. He takes off, sneakers kicking up a spray of polished gravel. As my precocious wingman leaps into Stitch's arms, I make my way toward them at a slower pace.

"Stitch!" he calls out, then leaps into her arms.

"Oh, I've missed you, Mav!"

Laughing brightly, Stitch catches him in an exuberant hug and swings him around. She plants an exaggerated smooch on his cheek before setting him down, eyes dancing.

I halt several yards back, drinking her in, memorizing each graceful curve. Baggy jeans roll above high-top sneakers, and a vintage Angel Fire band tee is worn with loyal pride.

There's an effortless beauty about her.

I lay a gentle hand on Maverick's shoulder. "Hey, bud, why don't you scout some good spots for us? Check the tidepools for keepers."

With a quick conspiratorial wink, he scampers off toward the nearby rocky pools. Meanwhile, I turn to Stitch, drinking in her windswept beauty.

Her sharp eyes linger on the picnic setup, then dart my way, twinkling with dawning suspicion and delight. I aim for casual innocence, but based on her fighting a fierce grin, I fail.

I slide my palm to her waist, pulling her close and savoring her warmth. Our foreheads touch and then tilt together as I run my thumb over her jawline. The familiar play of our silent communication fills me with joy.

"So, how's my girl?"

We chat lightly about her projects and my first day. As laughter echoes from Maverick's direction, Stitch glances fondly that way. I track her gaze to where Maverick is partially hidden, clearly burying something in a rocky crevice. Stitch's eyes sparkle knowingly as they swing my way again.

Before she can comment, an exuberant kindergartner races back to tug her hand.

"C'mon, let's explore."

Laughing, she allows him to tow her off toward the tidepools.

I trail discreetly behind them, keeping my distance as Maverick bounces from pool to pool, enthusiastically but unsubtly herding her toward his hidden treasure. He tugs an amused Stitch along the glittering tidepools, his excitement barely contained. They approach a familiar niche nestled amongst weathered rocks where sunrays dance across the pool's surface.

Stitch crouches at the water's edge. "Oh wow, look at all these colorful…"

"No, over here." Maverick dashes further down the rocks, beckoning eagerly. Laughing, Stitch allows herself to be steered toward his hidden treasure.

She peers into the pool as Maverick bounces with anticipation beside her.

"Look! Look!"

"Okay, I'm looking…"

"The red shell, lift the red shell!" He points urgently.

Stitch glances at me, eyes sparking with laughter. She reaches into the glinting water and retrieves the decorative shell.

Sunlight flashes over the glossy surface. Holding her breath, she carefully pries the shell open. Inside is a diamond solitaire ring that ignites with brilliance when the sun's rays strike its myriad facets.

Stitch looks wordlessly at me, then to Maverick. I close the distance, and my pulse thunders in my ears as I sink to one knee on the uneven stones.

My injuries fade to background noise as I focus everything on the remarkable woman before me—the one who patiently helped me find purpose again.

My voice thickens with emotion. "You remind me daily that life is beautiful—and meant to be shared. We survived hell, which taught me no tomorrow is guaranteed. Almost losing you made one truth clear. However long I've got in this world, I want you beside me for all of it. I don't want to waste another minute." I squeeze her trembling hands, pulse roaring in my ears now. "Will you marry me?"

Her tearful whisper of "Yes!" sparks euphoria in my chest.

Our joyful bubble expands to include one little boy, my wing-man, and the best part of me.

Maverick drops dramatically beside me.

I wrap an arm around my son's small shoulders as he holds something out toward Stitch. It's a delicate necklace with a jeweled heart-shaped pendant. On that pendant are three tiny letters.

Mom.

"Since you're gonna marry my daddy, will you be my mommy?" His eyes shine hopeful and earnest.

My breath catches, pride and love swelling for my kindhearted boy who has embraced Stitch with his entire being from the start. I smooth his hair as Stitch draws him fiercely into her arms.

"Always and forever, my sweet boy," she answers through happy tears.

Maverick beams brighter than the blazing sunset, his little face buried in her shoulder.

My battle-scarred heart feels suddenly whole.

Maverick cheers and then scampers off to fetch celebratory snacks from our picnic hamper. As Stitch and I settle side by side on the blankets, glowing in newly claimed joy, I glance surreptitiously toward the cliff above.

Just in time, there's movement up top.

"I can't believe you planned all this. The tidepools, the ring…" Her eyes dance with exhilaration, and I can't resist brushing one last kiss over her hand.

"I've got one more surprise up my sleeve." I nod discreetly skyward, and instantly, her gaze follows.

The gondola trundles on its way back up the cliff.

Stitch gasps, hands flying to cover her mouth in sheer disbelief as I confirm what she already knows.

"No, you're teasing!" She punches my shoulder, and I chuckle, rubbing the spot. She pounces, peppering my grinning face with teary yet ecstatic kisses as the men of Angel Fire head down to the beach for a little unplugged concert magic.

"Hey now, would these rugged good looks lie? I wanted an epic way to kick off our engagement. I pulled a few strings. Your number one band wants to celebrate their superfan's epic night."

"Best-night-ever!" An ecstatic kiss punctuates each word as the gondola opens to unleash musical magic.

Stitch's very own private concert event played by her rock idols on the beach and under the stars with her new family surrounding her.

It truly is the best night ever and marks the beginning of the best part of my life.

FORTY-ONE

Stitch

THE GLOW OF MY MONITORS CASTS A SOFT LIGHT IN THE DARKENED room, a beacon in the sea of quiet that envelops my corner of Guardian headquarters.

Here, amid the soft hums and sporadic clicks, I take a moment to marvel at the path my life has taken. I'm a Techie now, a far cry from the reckless hacker I once was.

The very thought of fieldwork chills me—it's an adrenaline-fueled terror I never want to face again. But I can't deny that part of me thrives on the knowledge that I was there, in the thick of it, when Jeb needed someone most.

It's a strange twist of fate, thinking back to how Mitzy pulled me from the jaws of a prison sentence that was sure to swallow me whole.

At the time, it felt like a temporary reprieve, a stay of execution. Little did I know that Mitzy dragging me out of my prison sentence was actually me being rescued.

The Guardian's motto is to "Rescue those who can't rescue themselves," and that's just what they did. They rescued me from myself.

From the life I was bound to and freed me to live the life I was meant to live.

I had a rough start in life, bouncing from one foster home to another, always the outsider looking in, never quite fitting the mold. Belonging was a word I read in books, a feeling I could only imagine.

Now, it's my reality. I've finally found my "home."

I lean back in my chair, letting the quiet of my surroundings sink in, feeling a sense of peace I never knew in my chaotic youth. Here, in this room filled with the soft glow of technology, I have found a sanctuary.

The Guardians didn't just offer me a second chance; they offered me a place in their ranks, a purpose for my skills, and a family that sees past the broken parts.

My life, once defined by the next escape, the next hack, the next adrenaline rush, is now defined by stability, purpose, and a camaraderie that holds firmer than any firewall I've ever built.

Here, I fight for something greater than myself, and in doing so, I've discovered the true strength that comes from unity.

They say home is where the heart is, and my heart is here, with these people, in these halls, behind these screens.

The Guardians saved me in more ways than they know. They've given me a future filled with hope, a place where I belong, and a family that never gives up on one another.

For the first time, I'm not looking for a way out. I'm right where I belong, and I'm not going anywhere. This is my home, and I'll defend it with every keystroke and every breath.

Dear Reader,

I hope you enjoyed reading Jeb and Stitch's story.

As a treat, enjoy this Special Bonus Scene and catch a little more of Jeb and Stitch's story.

xoxo

Ellie Masters

GRAB THE BONUS SCENE TODAY!
elliemasters.com/RescuingStitch_BonusScene

About the Author

Ellie Masters is a USA Today Bestselling author and Amazon Top 15 Author who writes Angsty, Steamy, Heart-Stopping, Pulse-Pounding, Can't-Stop-Reading Romantic Suspense. In addition, she's a wife, military mom, doctor, and retired Colonel. She writes romantic suspense filled with all your sexy, swoon-worthy alpha men. Her writing will tug at your heartstrings and leave your heart racing.

Born in the South, raised under the Hawaiian sun, Ellie has traveled the globe while in service to her country. The love of her life, her amazing husband, is her number one fan and biggest supporter. And yes! He's read every word she's written.

She has lived all over the United States—east, west, north, south and central—but grew up under the Hawaiian sun. She's also been privileged to have lived overseas, experiencing other cultures and making lifelong friends. Now, Ellie is proud to call herself a Southern transplant, learning to say y'all and "bless her heart" with the best of them.

Ellie's favorite way to spend an evening is curled up on a couch, laptop in place, watching a fire, drinking a good wine, and bringing forth all the characters from her mind to the page and hopefully into the hearts of her readers.

FOR MORE INFORMATION
elliemasters.com

facebook.com/elliemastersromance

x.com/Ellie__Masters

instagram.com/ellie_masters

bookbub.com/authors/ellie-masters

goodreads.com/Ellie_Masters

Connect with Ellie Masters

Website:
elliemasters.com
Purchase Direct:
elliemasters.com/shopify
Amazon Author Page:
elliemasters.com/amazon
Facebook:
elliemasters.com/Facebook
Goodreads:
elliemasters.com/Goodreads
Bookbub:
elliemasters.com/Bookbub
Instagram:
elliemasters.com/Instagram

Final Thoughts

I hope you enjoyed this book as much as I enjoyed writing it. If you enjoyed reading this story, please consider leaving a review on Amazon and Goodreads, and please let other people know. A sentence is all it takes. Friend recommendations are the strongest catalyst for readers' purchase decisions! And I'd love to be able to continue bringing the characters and stories from My-Mind-to-the-Page.

Second, call or e-mail a friend and tell them about this book. If you really want them to read it, gift it to them. If you prefer digital friends, please use the "Recommend" feature of Goodreads to spread the word.

Or visit my blog https://elliemasters.com, where you can find out more about my writing process and personal life.

Come visit The EDGE: Dark Discussions where we'll have a chance to talk about my works, their creation, and maybe what the future has in store for my writing.

Facebook Reader Group: Ellz Bellz

Thank you so much for your support!

Love,

Ellie

Dedication

This book is dedicated to you, my reader. Thank you for spending a few hours of your time with me. I wouldn't be able to write without you to cheer me on. Your wonderful words, your support, and your willingness to join me on this journey is a gift beyond measure.

Whether this is the first book of mine you've read, or if you've been with me since the very beginning, thank you for believing in me as I bring these characters 'from my mind to the page and into your hearts.'

Love,
Ellie

THE END

Made in the USA
Coppell, TX
30 April 2024

31869294R10203